I0737811

THE
MADMAN ON THE
ROCKS

A FORGOTTEN GODS TALE #2

Christian Warren Freed

Copyright © 2020 by Christian Warren Freed

Excerpt from *Anguish Once Possessed* 2021 Christian Warren Freed
Cover design by BroseDesignz
Cover copyright 2021 by Warfighter Books
Author Photograph by Anicie Freed

Warfighter Books
Holly Springs, North Carolina 27540
https://www.christianfreed

Second Edition: January 2021

Library of Congress Cataloging-in-Publication Data
Name: Freed, Christian Warren, 1973- author.
Title: Dreams of Winter/ Christian Warren Freed
Description: Second Edition | Holly Springs, NC: Warfighter Books, 2021.
Identifiers: LCCN 2021930762 | ISBN 9781957326023 (hardcover) | ISBN 9780578651248 (trade paperback) ISBN: 9781735700045 (ebook) Subjects: Military Science Fiction | Fantasy | Space Opera

Printed in the United States of America

10 9 8 7 6 5 4 3 2 1

ACCLAIM FOR CHRISTIAN WARREN FREED

HAMMERS IN THE WIND: BOOK I OF THE NORTHERN CRUSADE

"I love this book. This book hooked my attention on the first page and it was hard to put down. There is darkness in this book, you know something is going to happen so you keep reading to find out what. The author writes it so good, it's like you are there experiencing what the characters are. And I love it."

"I purchased this book to read to see if it would be suitable for my daughter to read. She is advanced in reading, but some books for kids older than her can be a little to much content wise. I think this one will work out great for her and she would enjoy it as much as I did. I'm glad I came across this book and can't wait to read the rest of the series."

WHERE HAVE ALL THE ELVES GONE?

"This story is fresh and a little tongue-in-cheek, a nice fantasy change of pace with twists here and there that make you have to keep on turning the pages."

"Christian Warren Freed is a very gifted, well-spoken author and his story took me in from page 1. His descriptions of situations, momentary happenings and his vivid characters of the world within the story made my fantasy run wild. As a reader, I felt like being part of the carefully woven net of this book."

THE DRAGON HUNTERS

"Excellently written. The author is able to really capture the stress, fear, and panic of life and death situations such as combat. Greatly looking forward to the next installment in the series!"

"Mr. Freed weaves the parts of this tale together smoothly, keeping the story moving at a good pace. He uses his own military background to paint powerful battle images and then he moves on. With only a little background, he makes the reader care about the members of the band - to worry about them and want them to do the 'right thing'. He adds depth to the characters through their actions and his dialogue is very realistic."

ARMIES OF THE SILVER MAGE

"Armies of the Silver Mage was a great read...any fan of Lord of the Rings or Game of Thrones will love this book. I'm looking forward to next book."

"The book is almost an homage to the great classics like Sword of Shannara and the Lord of the Rings. The author has cleverly used his past military and combat experience to make the battle scenes more realistic."

SO, You Want to Write a Book? +
SO, You Wrote A Book. Now What? +*

* Forthcoming   + Nonfiction

For my fans. You know who you are.

Prologue
3190 A.G. (After Gods), The Deeves, planet An'kuruku.

The Bone Father stalked the Deeves until he reached the shores of Bo. His morning ritual was sullied by ill portents and bad omens. His ancient shoulders were hunched a little more than usual, his face soured. Dawn was spoiled by the portent of a falling star. The Bone Father had felt his blood chill. Such events simply did not happen. Dark clouds blackened the far horizon. A bad storm was brewing and likely to hit land soon. Experience told him these storms were hazardous and often deadly. He would do well to get back inside.

Sighing, the Bone Father used his staff to propel him away from the Deeves. The soft sand shifted beneath each sandaled step, making the going more treacherous. He was old, some said as old as the founding of the world. His skin was brittle, a coppery color reminiscent of a dying sunset. His hair, what little remained, was long and stringy. There was barely enough to cover his spotted head. His teeth were dull, ground down over the years.

He had seen too many winters with no luxury. Aged fingers curled tightly around the iron and wood of his staff. Sand tickled between his toes, his nails long and broken. His knees were knobbed. The Bone Father was tired, but he could not stop to find rest yet. Chosen by the spirits of the gods, he was forced to endure until a replacement could be found. His was an endless path, one he was both accustomed to and disappointed with.

A pair of black-winged gulls coasted overhead, squawking warning of the coming storm. The Bone Father paused to watch their flight. He sighed again.

"So much like time," he muttered. "The winds steal away our moments until we are nothing but dust."

His bone necklace clinked in the wind as if in response. As the Bone Father, he was attuned to the needs of the world. The Deeves had been his home for as long as he could remember.

His robes rustled against his skin, irritating him. The storm was approaching faster than he had guessed. He wasn't going to make it back to the relative shelter of his mud hut.

Fierce winds drove in from the Bo, rippling waves of the great ocean into a frenzy. They knocked him down. He groaned and spit out a mouthful of sand. He tried to push himself up, but pain lanced through his shoulders. Confusion twisted his face. This should not be happening. He had read the bones this morning. They whispered nothing of this. The Bone Father began to panic. Fear bled his strength as black clouds filled the sky.

"What is this?" he asked the skies, praying to the bones for answers.

There were no answers. His entire life had been dedicated to prolonging the ancient peace passed down by his forefathers. The Bone Father felt hatred on the winds, a fury seeking to undo all his life's work in the rabid howls assailing his ears. Using the last of his waning strength, he managed to rise. His knuckles were white from their grip on his staff. The Bone Father slammed the iron-capped staff on the ground three quick times. Lightning wreathed the skies around him. The ground trembled.

For a moment, the storm abated, and he was once again able to see past his arm's reach. His jaw dropped. Never had he seen the Bo so volatile. Waves crashed upon the shores of the Deeves, threatening to wash away the ancient beach and carry on into the continent. White-capped with froth and filled with flotsam, the waves stole great swaths of sand when they receded. The Bone Father felt death's icy chill deep in his soul.

A supersonic boom roared across the heavens. He cringed, strength fading with each passing moment. Concentric rings of fire burned through the atmosphere. The Bone Father recognized death and once again dropped to his knees with grim acceptance. He had failed. The end had come to An'kuruku. Doubts and wasted opportunities troubled his fragile mind. He had been the hope for the planet, and now Fate had stepped in to rob him of success. The sullied name of the Bone Father would be drowned in history.

Tears formed. He could not cry; he was a keeper of secrets. The last defender of ancient prophecy and the promise of the future.

He was a failure. The Bone Father shook his head. No. Defeatism served no purpose. His staff struck the sand harder. Ages-old mysticism pushed back against the unnatural storm. He gritted his teeth and focused his strength into the earth. Power flooded through the staff and into him.

Eldritch colors pulsed from the tip of the staff, tingling his fingertips and teasing his hair wildly. A pale yellow glow surrounded the

Bone Father. He felt renewed. Youthful vigor, long lost to the vagaries of time, expanded his conscience. He saw events before they happened. Watched the decay of lives and the sudden growth of new birth. The Bone Father became strength unabated.

He rose to his full five-foot height and thrust the staff into the sky. Circles of power penetrated the pitch black. Clouds roiled in new turmoil. Little by little, the strength of the earth beat back the unexpected hatred assaulting the Deeves. Despite the strength given to him, it was all the Bone Father could do to maintain his denial of the sudden affliction threatening An'kuruku.

Shells pelted his frail body. Fish slammed down around him. He heard whispers on the wind, dire warnings of impending doom. Still, he held his ground. The raging tempest was an abnormality needing to be purged. The Bone Father grimaced as a particularly large fish slapped his chest. The very depths of the Bo were tossed into the sky, offending the gods of earth and sea. He immediately set to stem the insanity and restore order to the Deeves.

Uttering ancient words, the Bone Father thrust up the staff again. The explosion tore holes through the storm. Endless power plunged down on his weary shoulders, desperately trying to shatter his protective shell and render him back to ashes. He resisted, though it stole much. The Bone Father felt his life skein shorten. Too many years bled back to the earth. He doubted he could survive the full fury of the storm. There was too much raw strength bearing down.

Finally, he could take no more. The Bone Father screamed, a mangled sound that inspired hope and plead ruination. Tears appeared in his flesh. His eyes, once magnificent blue, were dulled as if the slow progression of age marched too quickly. The fury abated. Blue skies seeped through the black. A single ray of light shone on his face, offering warmth and the unspoken reassurance that it was all going to be alright. The Bone Father cried. His shoulders sagged. He had won.

The clouds broke, scattered like so many empty dreams lost to time. The Bone Father collapsed. Fresh pain wracked his right arm. Horrified, he looked down at what remained of the hand holding the staff. The skin was gone, melted off until nothing but bone was left. Blood dripped on his tan robes. It pooled in the sands. The smell of burnt flesh sickened him. The earth had answered his pleas and took what it needed in return.

He felt older, more worn and used. The Bone Father knew his time was ending. Sudden urges took hold. He must find a replacement before death's long fingers took him forever. The prospect of death had never bothered him before. He knew it was the logical conclusion to all things. What is born must also die; such things were unquestionable. It simply *was*. But here, now, he felt urgency in the need to complete his task. He was in a race against an unfeeling enemy he could not avoid.

His eyes searched the Bo for any sign of the cause. The sky had returned to normal, restoring his faith in all things and the grand designs of the gods. The Deeves were safe. The Bo still chopped with angry surf, but it, too, seemed normal. Still, the Bone Father was confused. Victory was his. The earth was satisfied. Why was the Bo still angry?

Drifting across the waves he spied the glint of sharp silver bobbing with the tide. Even from a distance, he could tell it was unlike anything natural. An'kuruku was a desolate world with limited technology, far from the main interstellar trade lanes. He looked to the now passive skies and wondered what magic had come to the Deeves. The Bone Father used his good hand to tear a bandage for the wounded one, shifted his staff to the left and half dragged his battered body to the edge of the Bo.

Cool water sloshed over his feet. He lost himself in the refreshing feeling, trying to ignore the premonition nagging him. The object drifted closer. The Bone Father made out soft edges and the occasional glimpse of a window. He was reminded of a casket, memories from his childhood when his father had taken him to watch the funeral procession of the last king of Tenemenah.

The dead falling from the sky? He wished for companionship for the first time in decades. The Bone Father seldom spoke to others and hardly felt the need to. It was enough that he roamed the sparse grass and sand dunes of the Deeves to keep his people safe. He lived alone, friendless. That was what it meant to be a reader of the bones. Chosen solitude was a small sacrifice for the security of the many. The Bone Father never regretted the decisions leading him to this point.

The silver casket was closer. He traced the lines of thick cables running the three-meter length. The top was rounded, contrast to the blocky sides. Rows of sharp green and red lights blinked from banks at both ends. Perhaps it was not a casket at all. The Bone Father knew little of such things. He had never been off world, never witnessed the grandness of the promises technology offered. What he saw seemingly drifting straight for him was anathema.

Strong winds pushed the casket to shore. The Bo discarded the unnecessary. Alien items had no place in the sacred waters. The bulky frame washed onto the sand, coming to rest only a few feet away from the Bone Father. He eyed it suspiciously, half-expecting some mythic figure to emerge. He scolded himself. A lifetime of solitude had taught him many things, and fear was not one of them. He hobbled to the casket, eager and apprehensive about seeing what rested within.

Long, the casket was only a meter high, so he was easily able to peer into the small window. The Bone Father gently wiped the sand away and looked inside. His heart hammered. Resting quietly, almost deathly, was the most beautiful woman he had ever seen.

3205 A.G. (After Gods), Mefgelin Asteroid Belt.

The asteroid spun listlessly through space, colliding with smaller ones in a tempered journey through eternity. The blackness of space was an unending maw devouring everything. Sky blue lights announced the arrival of the Inquisition scout frigate entering the system. Ports slid open and ship-to-ship cannons extended, gunners plotting potential threats. The frigate was sleek, elliptical. Quad engines powered the vessel three times faster than the speed of light, forming a block in the aft — two on top and two on bottom. The engines powered down, the blue a dull reminder of the vessel's power.

Inquisition vessels were heavily armored, designed to take a beating. The only organized military belonged to the Conclave, the mighty and vast Prekhauten Guard, but that didn't dissuade heavy pirating and petty warlords from scouring the universe. The scout frigate was a light reconnaissance vessel with a crew of thirty. The bridge sat atop the main body with reinforced viewing screens that allowed a full 360 degrees of observation. A massive blue-tinged red rose was painted on the sloping decks just beneath the view ports, marking it as a warship of the Inquisition.

A small round docking pod ejected from the small hangar bay in the belly of the frigate. The small engine engaged once the pod was clear of the frigate. Pilots guided it into a straight-line trajectory, aimed for the largest asteroid rolling through space without purpose or design. Stellar cartographers accurately guessed the Mefgelin Asteroid Belt was the fragile remnants of a small moon that had been forced from orbit and destroyed by a passing comet.

Three men emerged from the dull metallic docking pod. Tiny lights affixed to their round helmets seemed insulting to the bleak nature of space. Their vacuum suits were cold grey, reminiscent of ancient armor. Using small bursts from their thrusters to compensate for the absence of gravity, they made their way towards the largest cave opening by leaping.

"Careful, we're not even sure if this structure is whole," the team leader warned.

"Copy, Lieutenant."

They finally halted in the shadow of a giant door. Granite walls were carved into the chunk of rock. Whatever the structure had been originally was lost to history texts and grey-bearded professors lecturing unimpressed students. The three Inquisitors stared up in awe. This was unlike everything they had been trained to believe.

"My gods! Look at the size of this."

Thisf nodded silent agreement. They'd been briefed on what to expect but seeing the sheer size of the door was daunting. Rumors were tossed around that this chamber was a lost haven of the gods, undiscovered for three millennia.

"Do you see any hinges or weak points?" he asked instead. They needed to stay focused. Too many memorials resulted from carelessness.

The first Inquisitor leapt closer, inspecting the door for any opening. He was disappointed. "Whoever built this had longevity in mind. We're going to have to break in."

"Fine, break out the cutters, but be careful. The Inquisitor General will have our hides if we destroy the chamber within," the Inquisitor cautioned them and dropped the massive toolkit.

Pinpoint lines of energy flared from the bulky machines. The work was difficult. The structure might have been stone once, but several lifetimes of collisions and the harsh environment of deep space had caused it to evolve into something else. The Inquisitor took a seismic reader from the kit and placed it flatly against the door, scanning for any weak spot that would make their jobs easier.

"Engineer team, this is the *LodSpear*. The Captain needs a status report."

The Inquisitor scowled. He hated being rushed and hated being micromanaged even more. Still, this mission had come directly from the office of the Inquisitor General. There was no room for error, and each moment of delay threatened failure.

He keyed his transmitter. "Roger, *LodSpear*, we are at the target. We need to cut our way in."

"Inquisitor Thisf, this is Captain Sed. Are you sure there is no other way?"

"I'm positive, sir. We need to cut." Thisf cursed silently, half expecting to be reprimanded. Inquisition discipline was second only to that of the Prekhauten Guard.

A tense pause. "Very well. Begin cutting, but do not abandon caution, Inquisitor. All of our heads are on the chopping block here."

"Copy that, *LodSpear*."

Inquisitor Thisf passed a wary look to his partners. "Don't fuck this up."

The cutters struck where Thisf identified. Blind visors automatically lowered to protect their vision while chunks of stone and an unidentified ore broke free. The procedure was delicate and stretched the limits of their air reserves, but Thisf was finally rewarded with a satisfying thud. They'd broken through.

"Easy, easy. Back off on the power and ease your cutters out. We're through," he said, trying to convey calmness he didn't feel.

Energy spikes flared and died. Thisf leaned into the cut piece and pushed. Centuries old dust clouded around him, clogging his thrusters. He kept pushing. So close to the prize, he couldn't stop now. The future of the Conclave depended on what his team accomplished today. He felt the stone grind as the square block resisted his efforts. Thisf pushed harder and was finally rewarded by the sudden clearing of the passage. The helmet light seemed tiny in the vast cavern opened before him. Thisf felt small. He gave a quick scan for any sign of danger before looking over his shoulder.

"We're in. Give me a moment to check it out," he ordered.

Thisf didn't wait for acknowledgment. Ducking to fit, he slipped into the chamber. So vast was the ceiling his light died well before reaching the top. Thisf was a seasoned Inquisitor but had never come across such a discovery. The chamber was void of decoration or design. Smooth walls stretched from the dust-hidden floor to the domed ceiling. Thisf noted the absence of, well, anything.

He delved deeper into the darkness and froze. There, in the middle of the chamber, was the largest table he had ever seen. It was easily as tall as he was. Seated around the table were seven chairs — occupied chairs. His heart began to race. There wasn't supposed to be any life here.

"What do you see?" one of the others asked as they emerged into the vast chamber.

Thisf shook his head. "I don't know."

The three Inquisitors formed a line and marched closer. Nothing moved. Whoever the figures were, they were long deceased. Their faces were mummified, hands and necks shriveled reminders of the unforgiving attitudes of time and space. Black hair fell past their backs. Their nails had continued to grow until they were curled and gnarled. Hollow eye sockets stared down at the Inquisitors in mocking silence.

"We shouldn't be here. This is a tomb."

Thisf agreed but had his orders. "We get what we came for. Look around. The artifact must be here. Check on the table, under the chairs. Search every inch of this chamber until you find it."

Thisf decided the obvious place would be the tabletop. He didn't know why these giants were here; he didn't even know why he was here, only what they were rumored to have in their possession. Speculation was a waste of time, so he refused to concern himself with such petty bothers. Thisf engaged his thrusters to reach the surface.

The tabletop glistened, miniscule refractions of his light on the surface. His blood chilled. This table was not natural; he knew it instinctively. Irrational fears sprang to life, giving credence to stories mothers told their children to frighten them into doing the right thing. Every culture had a boogeyman. Thisf had never believed until now. The seven figures seated around the hexagonal table changed his mind. They also confirmed his darkest suspicions that something terrible was coming to the universe.

Conclave officials were convinced a great conflux was set to occur soon and that the lives of every sentient being were at stake. Naturally, no one knew for sure or could say what was coming, but the office of the Cardinal Seniorus seemed apprehensive enough to fund a deep space mission to the Mefgelin Asteroid Belt based on rumor and whim. The *LodSpear* had left the Prekhauten shipyards orbiting Vau Prime with a skeleton crew and minimal supplies. Thisf had agreed this was serious; only now was he discovering just how much.

The tabletop was an amalgamation of different materials all based on human glass. But instead of being clear, the table was murky, appearing to shift colors with each blink of the eye. Thisf was hesitant to take another step. He made the mistake of looking up into the eyes of the dead and felt judged. There was no species in the known universe that fit their descriptions. Could these be gods? Somehow, that didn't seem right. The gods hadn't been seen in thousands of years, and there had yet to be any credible evidence they existed.

He caught the reflection of his team from opposite sides of the chamber. It seemed to stretch on forever. Thisf had a sudden desperate urge to leave. They shouldn't be here. The daunting stares of the seven dead provided enough encouragement. He turned to leave when he spied a rectangular shape embedded in the tabletop. Nervous emotions gave way to strength and fulfillment. He'd found what the Inquisition had sent him to find. The answer to months of searching, away from their families, away from civilization, was coming to an end. The cramped confines of the *LodSpear* now became a long-forgotten freedom.

"Over here," he called. "I think I have it!"

Thisf waited until the others joined him before kneeling over the object. He keyed the infrared scanner in his helmet to try and analyze the meter-long object buried deep in the strange table. Its alien nature daunted him, almost preventing him from running his glove over the smooth surface. A rainbow of lights danced at his touch. Sparks flared and ran down invisible lines to each of the corners. Thisf jerked back reflexively. A low, steady hum vibrated the chamber.

"This is wrong, Thisf. We shouldn't be here."

"Look! The table is opening," Thisf said, astonished and dismayed.

Harsh vibrations knocked him down. His helmet struck the table hard, but instead of a hard edge, his head seemed to sink into the table. He frowned, more scared than amazed. It took every bit of training for him not to break and run like a Novice during the initiation phase of Inquisition training. Soon, a gaping hole opened for them. The object was exposed, giving Thisf his first true glimpse. Massive in scale, it reminded him of an old chest that might be in anyone's closet. Metal handles were the only ornamentation. He tried to scan the chest, but it was made of even stranger materials than the table. Thisf decided enough time had been wasted.

"Give me a hand. I want to get back to the pod and onboard the *LodSpear*. We've done enough," he told the others.

Thisf and his team soon boarded the docking pod. The chest was surprisingly light. He guessed it couldn't have weighed more than five pounds. What in the name of the gods could possibly be within that was worth risking the lives of dozens of men and women and spending countless funds? Thisf had no desire to learn such truths. He was a simple Inquisitor. The incredible didn't matter so much as the actual.

"Engineer team to *LodSpear,* object is secure. We are returning to the ship now." Thisf had never taken so much pleasure in conveying a simple message as he did now.

The eeriness of the chamber on a broken asteroid in a forgotten part of space haunted his waking moments for reasons beyond his comprehension. He was tired. The raw emotions sparked by their discovery drained him mentally and physically.

"Very good, Inquisitor. Welcome home," came the friendly call from the bridge.

The docking pod blasted away from the asteroid.

Captain Sed watched the pod disappear in the frigate's belly and turned to give the long-awaited order to reverse course and return to Vau Prime.

"Sir! We have an unidentified contact emerging from the hyperspace lanes," the communications officer shouted.

Sed snapped around. "Show me."

The command turret spun until Sed saw the correct sector. The ship was invisible to the naked eye. Sed's combat reflexes took over. "Battle stations! All hands prepare for enemy contact."

Guns began tracking open space but were unable to pick up the new contact. Sed felt sudden tension. There was no ship in the universe capable of evading Inquisition technology. None. Fists clenched, Sed started barking commands. The crew was hard pressed to obey as fast as he could give them. It wasn't enough.

"Incoming!"

Sed frowned. "Evasive action! Get us the hells out of here. Gunnery, get me a targeting solution and return fire."

Vapor plumes trailed from the twin missiles streaking their way towards the *LodSpear's* engines. Sed's eyes widened. They were out of time. Fireballs erupted, spreading through the vessel until pressure forced the frigate to explode.

ONE

3212 A.G. (After Gods), Tenemenah, planet An'kuruku.

An'kuruku's twin suns beat down mercilessly on the sprawling city of Tenemenah, the desert planet's capital. It was barely Ninth hour and so hot most of the residents were already inside. Only those brave or foolish wandered the dusty streets. The city stretched for miles in every direction. Low buildings with domed ceilings in hues of tan and white to prevent the full fury of the twin suns from overheating the occupants comprised most of the city. An occasional tower or multileveled building broke the gentle picture, those few and far between. The only constants were the pillared squares of the Prefectures and the spiraling pillars of prayer.

Mournful wails cranked from the tops of the pillars as Ninth hour began. Citizens in white robes knelt in prayer, hands clasped together and raised skyward. Not everyone in the city shared the same religious beliefs. Plenty of foreigners from various planets in the Conclave visited the planet. Most were respectful of the local religion. Prefects and city watch patrolled the streets during prayer in the hopes of preventing unnecessary crimes. Tenemenah was a relatively peaceful city void of scandal and major corruption. The government sought to keep it that way.

Minor politicians played power games behind closed doors, brokering deals with off-world companies. Dishonest dealings took place in shadows and underground while those in power turned blind eyes or felt their pockets grow fatter. Any man or woman caught in illegal activities was instantly tried by the Prefects and either taken off to the deep desert prison facility or publicly executed. Government officials insisted An'kuruku was ruled through democracy, though a strong feeling of resentment was spreading through the people.

Conclave priests established a quadrant headquarters in the dignitary district of Tenemenah, but they didn't travel along. A host of Inquisitors and Prekhauten Guard accompanied the priests on their mission. The Inquisition watched everything with a stern gaze. Neither the Inquisitor General nor the Cardinal Seniorus were willing to take chances with another insurrection after the disaster on Crimeat two years ago.

The leaders of the known universe had been embarrassed by the actions of few and were determined not to allow a repeat. Crimeat's priest had been murdered and its Inquisitor turned traitor. Worse, the Three had been active — all of them. One alone was enough to render a world lifeless. All three were akin to universal Armageddon. No one had heard or seen any of the Three since the massive explosion that had destroyed most of the Plateau city of Reven.

Witnesses had disappeared quickly once the incident had ended. Forced retirements were given to select Guardsmen while those who had been in contact with the Three were whisked back to Vau Prime for debriefing. Presumably they remained alive, though bureaucratic red tape occluded anyone from learning the truth. Only a few managed to escape the Inquisition round up.

Mollock Bolle sat quietly inside a small tea house waiting for prayer to end. The mournful sound reminded him of dirges sung at funerals from his childhood. He had no home, no place that laid claim to his origins. Even if he did, his unique knowledge branded him a traitor to the universe, punishable by death. Mollock was a wanted man for more reasons than one.

He bore a sour expression. Too many ill dreams tormented his waking moments. A drifter, his clothes were poorly cut and his shoes falling apart. He hadn't had a haircut or bothered to shave in years — impossibly long years in which he had aged considerably. Time had always been a constant enemy, ever since he'd accidentally found that chamber buried under Reven. Mankind continued to believe in the gods despite the myth that they had destroyed themselves in a cataclysmic event on the planet Occanum three millennia before. Mollock Bolle hadn't given much credence to the Conclave propaganda until he had stumbled into the chamber and found a sleeping god.

Any other man might have died from the realization, but his lack of faith had served him well. He'd turned and run as fast and far as he could. It hadn't been enough. He was hunted and hounded across Lethendweil by shadow creatures, nightmarish guardians of the sleeping god, until fate required his path cross with Elisa in an Ugri prison cell. She had her own story to tell, and it was far worse than the decades of his flight.

Mollock rubbed his chin, taking time to rake his thin fingers through the chest-length grey beard obscuring his chin. Elisa. She remained an enigma. He hadn't seen her much since their escape from Crimeat, though he caught rumors and bits of information suggesting she had taken to the bottle and fallen on bad times. Not that he blamed her. No one deserved to be marked by the gods, especially not the way she had. The Bloody Man declared that they were chosen and in that moment of viral confusion, Elisa allowed Sorrow to convince her to take Mollock to An'kuruku and find the Paradise Tear.

Mollock smirked. Paradise Tear. Neither had an inkling of who or what that might be, only that it held the answers to the partial mystery of the fate of the gods. Sorrow had named her the Paladin, humanity's champion against the rising discontent and conflagration threatening to spread. Mollock refused to believe it, especially his own new title. Sorrow had looked past Mollock's eyes on the snow-covered steppe, deep into the limits of his very soul, and named him the Prophet. The only problem was that he'd failed to explain exactly what Mollock was supposed to prophesize.

"Religious rubbish," Mollock whispered. He blushed upon realizing he'd spoken aloud.

A few others in the tea house passed warning glares or stared incredulously at his insolence. Zealots were everywhere and always willing to sell you out to the Prefecture in exchange for meager rewards. Heretics were burned in the middle of the old gladiator arena and left to flake away in the burning suns.

Prayer ended. Mollock finished his glass of hot tea, setting the empty cup at the edge of his table. He never cared for the drink personally. It was far too sweet and unlike the bitter coffee taste he had come to love so much back on Crimeat. In fact, there wasn't much on An'kuruku he found to his liking. The air was dry and arid. The people lent the illusion of being polite with their linen dress and too-deep tans, but there was an underlying feeling of discontent in their eyes. They made him uncomfortable.

Mollock prepared to leave when a shadow fell across him. He looked up to see a thin, pale man with a shock of blond hair taking the liberty of seating himself across the table.

"Can I help you?" Mollock asked disingenuously. A tiny warning went off in his mind.

"I am sure of it," the man said in a nasally voice. He pretended to fan himself with a piece of parchment. "This is by far the hottest world I have ever been to. How about you?"

"Yes." A simple answer.

The pale man took another liberty by ordering a round of water, which he drank just as fast as the house maid could put them down. Satisfied, he leaned forward and whispered, "I know who you are."

Mollock tried to remain calm. "Plenty of people here know me. That you do is no surprise, even though I have not seen your face before today. Perhaps you would be so kind as to explain why you are interrupting my day."

The pale man smiled thinly. "Not just yet. Can you tell me where the woman is? The redhead you came here with."

Old suspicions begged him to get up and leave. Mollock was no fool. He figured this man had people outside waiting for that very thing. Perhaps it was better to stay and try to fend off the steady stream of questions. "What does she have to do with you and me?"

A pause. "She is just as important as you are. We shouldn't proceed without her."

Curiosity was Mollock's vice and damnation. He held little doubt that one day such inquisitiveness would prove his ruin. "I haven't seen her…"

"In the last three days," the pale man interrupted. He reveled in Mollock's obvious discomfort. "Come, now, you didn't really believe that either of you could blend in here? An'kuruku is a harsh place, one not kind to outsiders. You're fortunate the Prefects haven't grabbed you yet. Nasty people, from what I know."

"I think I should go now," Mollock announced, suddenly fearful for his life. "I have business elsewhere."

"Master Bolle, I did not come here to play a verbal shell game with you. You are wanted by the Inquisition, though they don't have a name. My people have been watching you since your sudden arrival here, oh, what, roughly two years ago?"

Mollock stiffened.

"Every move either of you has made has been under surveillance. The Prefects want to learn more before they arrest you, and we have a great interest in your potential," the pale man continued flatly. Inwardly, he struggled to keep the raw excitement he felt out of his voice. He'd been chosen for this task for his ability to remain calm, detached.

The tea house fell silent suddenly. A pair of crimson-robed Prefects entered. Both had thin moustaches and black goatees. Their narrow eyes scanned the crowd, searching. The pale man's eyes widened when their stern glares fell on him.

"Perhaps you are right. It is time to leave," he said hurriedly.

Mollock looked back at the Prefects in time to see one point. They started pushing through the half empty tea house. The pale man stood and tossed a small sphere towards the Prefects. Mollock opened his mouth to speak but was cut off by a crisp boom and a cloud of black smoke. He felt someone grab his arm and jerk him to his feet.

"Run," the pale man ordered.

He wanted to ask how far or fast this stranger thought his old legs would take him, but the pale man was already dragging him towards the back of the tea house. Mollock had no choice but to follow. Coughing echoed through the common room, raw and wicked. The device was obviously not fatal; Mollock doubted this man was willing to murder twenty-plus people just for the sake of abducting him.

They burst into daylight, pausing to check both directions before ducking at the crisp cackle of an ion round sizzling into the wooden doorframe. Superheated energy, ion rounds had enough power to burn through a human torso in a fraction of a second. The pale man didn't wait to give the Prefects another opportunity. He took off down the alley to the right, hoping they still had time. Mollock followed obediently, realizing that even if he stopped and somehow managed to escape, the pale man he would be charged with treason and the attempted murder of two Prefects. Fate had once again chosen for him.

They wove through Tenemenah's narrow back alleys and forgotten paths, desperately trying to avoid attention and lose their pursuit. Shouts and warning echoed through the streets as more Prefects were alerted. Mollock had no idea why they were coming for him. All thoughts of Elisa and even the mysterious appearance of the pale man fled the longer he ran. Survival was paramount, and such thoughts were mere distractions.

"This way!" the pale man shouted and pulled him roughly to the right.

Neither of the suns managed to shine here, ever. Whoever built this portion of the city had done so with the knowledge that sometimes secrecy was required. Mollock stumbled through piles of trash and the occasional dead animal. The smell gagged him. Years of life on the open path left him longing for fresh air and clear skies. He suddenly missed the grass and forests of his homeland.

They pushed through the refuse, forced to continue sideways halfway down the alley until the pale man found a small door. He knocked three times. Metallic sounds were as loud as a Prekhauten battle tank. Mollock's ears stung, but he was alive. The pale man pushed him in first before ensuring they weren't being followed.

Mollock was grabbed by a pair of hands and pulled through a pitch-black hallway. The sound of his heartbeat echoed like surf breaking on the rocks. He was covered with sweat and reeking. He heard a muffled voice coming from somewhere ahead. Finally, they emerged into a circular chamber with a low ceiling and only a single candle for light. Whoever the pale man was, he was part of a group not accustomed to being recognized. For the first time since the pale man had sat down, Mollock began to feel like he wasn't going to die.

Three others stood around a small table holding the candle. Two men and an older woman, all had seen too many summers. Shadows filled the creases in their worn faces. Their eyes were hard, still sharp despite their years. Each bore the look of patient people who knew their time was almost up. Un-fulfillment clung to them in a bitter aura.

He waited patiently for his abductors to make the first move.

"This is the one?" the woman asked. Her long grey hair hung past her waist.

The pale man nodded. "Yes. I was forced to bring him without explaining."

"What of the woman?" the man with black hair asked.

"Still unknown."

"How can we be sure the Prefects haven't taken her?" asked the other. His black echoed reflected the darkness menacingly.

The pale man didn't hesitate. "We would have heard. The Prefects are scouring the city looking for him. She should be safe for the moment."

The woman turned, studying Mollock. "But we are not. You have endangered us all by bringing this man into our fold."

"I did not intend to, Mistress Kaline, but matters progressed beyond my control too rapidly. There was little choice."

Kaline sighed, a short sound accepting his reasoning. She stepped forward and offered her hand. "I am Kaline, and it is a pleasure to make your acquaintance, Master Bolle."

Mollock accepted the proffered hand lest he offend anyone but asked, "Why am I here? I have caused no grievance with any of you."

She feigned a smile. "All will be revealed to you in time, when we feel you are prepared for the knowledge. In the meantime, what do you know of faith?"

Night fell on Tenemenah with rapid coolness. Elisa hated the oppressive heat, but the unnatural speed with which the planet cooled turned her stomach. Life on An'kuruku was unlike the hardened one she'd led on Crimeat. Water was more precious here than gold back home. These desert dwellers were shrewd and untrusting. Blending in was unthinkable, even in the foreign district. She was too old and too set in her ways to be bullied, though. The Prefects had backed off shortly after she and Mollock Bolle had arrived. Direct confrontation had led to two men in the medical wards. They contented themselves with watching from the shadows, eager for any excuse to execute the pair of outlanders.

The first thing Elisa had done after parting ways with Mollock was cut her hair. She'd frowned as the long red locks fell away. Fifty years of toil and self-imposed grief fell away with them. Elisa was a victim of her circumstances. She'd lived her life consumed with survivor's guilt and unmitigated hatred for the Bloody Man. Tears had run freely down her freckled cheeks with each cut from the scissors. Denied any hope for a normal life, Elisa struggled to cope with the flood of memories plaguing her now.

An'kuruku offered a new beginning but to the same story. She'd become a bounty hunter after Sorrow had dropped her off at the Conclave-sponsored orphanage a day's travel east of her now-forgotten village. No matter what she did, she couldn't shake the images of the Bloody Man killing and destroying. Her hatred had turned to obsession, resulting in her eventual expulsion from the orphanage at the age of sixteen. She'd made her way by stealing and scavenging. Death was ever a step behind.

She was able to take what she'd learned and became highly sought after as a bounty hunter. Elisa had taken the jobs to live, but her mind never strayed from the singular desire to hunt down the Bloody Man and tear his wicked heart out. Only when he lay dying, looking up at her blue eyes as his final breath passed his lips, would she find satisfaction. Only then.

Elisa shook her head. She still had trouble accepting the truths she bore witness to deep in the bowels of the black mountains. Could the giant being she saw really be a god? She prided herself on rationality and her unwavering disbelief in the gods. How could beings supposedly so benevolent start a war that tore the very fabric of the universe asunder and left humanity alone? No, she'd decided early on that the gods were just myths used to satisfy the craving to feel more. Death was hard to accept for most people. The thought of nothing after you close your eyes for the last time inspired fear.

The Conclave stepped in to quell that fear, assuring the populations of nearly seven hundred worlds that the gods did exist and humanity wasn't alone. Elisa had never cared, leastwise not until she'd come face to face with the sleeping figure encased in a forgotten tomb. Mollock was fervent that this was, in fact, a god. She had been disinclined to agree to that until the Bloody Man arrived.

He called her the Paladin, champion of humanity. Elisa didn't think that was fair. She was a simple person with limited purpose. The Bloody Man put more weight on her shoulders than she thought she could handle. Still, she found herself drawn into his tale, given new purpose in life. She had taken Mollock Bolle and fled to An'kuruku in search of an artifact the Bloody Man called the Paradise Tear. Crimeat had burned to a small orb as their shuttle sped through space.

Now she was no closer to finding the Paradise Tear or learning what it really was. Despair reached for her, but she was well accustomed to despair. An old friend, Elisa invited it in and twisted it to her personal gain. She strapped on her weapon belt, draping a dark brown cloak so as not to arouse suspicion, and headed for what had become her favorite drinking spot.

A few heads turned when she entered. Others dropped their eyes in the hopes of diverting her attention. She was well known in the seedier areas of Tenemenah, and people quickly came to fear her name. Elisa sat at the end of the sandstone bar, motioning the barkeep, idling debating if he was attractive or not. The diminutive man frowned upon seeing her again but reached for a dusty green bottle.

"You drink too much, *farisi*," he scolded.

She shrugged nonchalantly. Elisa was used to the name *farisi* by now, a term meaning "fair one" and neither a compliment nor an insult. The An'kurukans seldom said what they meant.

"I've earned the right to forget my pain, Ah'muf," she replied. "Why should you care as long as I pay up?"

He shrugged back, mockingly. "You are not my concern, but you add dangerous quality to my bar. The others do not like you."

She had heard it all before. "They don't concern me. Are you going to give me the bottle or not?"

Ah'muf slid it to her and offered a small glass. "Have you heard the big news today?"

Elisa frowned. She hadn't. "What news?"

The shadow of the Inquisition threatened her daily. She was certain it was only a matter of time before local Inquisitors stormed her small apartment and she was never heard from again. Staying one step ahead of a ruthless political entity with endless resources was tiring. A small part of her wanted to believe they knew nothing about her or Mollock, but hope was not a thing to leave to chance.

"Prefects raided a tea house on the far side of the city this morning right after Ninth hour prayer. They are looking for all outlanders but will not say why."

Her heart quickened a beat. All outlanders? "There are thousands of foreigners in Tenemenah, Ah'muf. What good comes from fleecing them all?"

"I am a simple bartender, *farisi*. Not the one to ask," he said in a sly tone. Ah'muf tweaked his pencil thin moustache. A dark twinkle filled his eyes.

"That's shit, and you know it. I may not know much about this world, but I see things. You are exactly the type of man to ask."

"Such language. Why do you seek to offend me?" he feigned being hurt.

"I don't want to shoot you, but I will," she said with all seriousness.

Ah'muf relented, satisfied their verbal game had gone on long enough. Leaning closer so he wasn't overheard, he said, "The Prefects are searching for a pale man with bright yellow hair. He was last seen speaking with the one you arrived with."

Mollock? She instantly worried. What trouble had that old man gotten into now? Elisa decided to press harder. "Have the Prefects called in the local Inquisitors?"

"Not that I am aware of. For now, it seems to be a local issue, but I would not guarantee that it will remain so."

"Damn. Ah'muf, who is this pale man? What do your sources say?"

Elisa felt sudden desperation spring to life. Mollock Bolle had somehow managed to survive for a very long time, roughly the same amount of time as she had spent seeking revenge, but he was not the man he once was. Time had not been kind to him. Then, there was the disillusionment of being named the Prophet. He believed what the Bloody Man had told him. He preached the word according to his limited belief structure, often in direct opposition to the word of the Conclave.

More than one riot had been put down after his slanderous tones had spread through the disaffected.

"No one knows. He arrived a few days ago but has laid low. I have heard that he comes from the inner core of worlds. Information channels have dried of late. Small informants are missing and feared dead in the arena." Ah'muf hesitated. "These are dangerous times, *farisi*."

She agreed. Thoughts of leaving Tenemenah resurfaced. The political situation was increasingly growing more uncomfortable. Prefects were gaining more power, muscling their way into the government, all under the watchful yet seemingly disinterestedly eyes of the Conclave and Inquisition. Elisa might have found it odd if not for the nightmare Lethendweil had become when a rogue Inquisitor had sided with an underground political party and incited civil war. She'd heard that the Inquisition was still heavily involved with pacifying her old planet.

So why would they let a potentially damaging situation develop and spread on An'kuruku? Elisa knew she should be disturbed but not the reason why. The Inquisition was dangerous, too powerful to confront. They would have no problem instilling their personalized sense of righteous order and ending the uprising. Yet they didn't. From what she gathered, neither the Inquisition nor the Conclave seemed remotely interested in local affairs. There was little capable of diverting the attention of the most powerful entity in the known universe from enacting its charter. The implications were staggering.

The Bloody Man.

He and his brothers must be the source of the turmoil. Immense pressure weighed her down suddenly. Memories of the battle on the Plateau haunted her. She remembered the colors most of all. White snow. Black night. Crimson blood. No stranger to human violence, Elisa prayed she never had to witness such again. The events on the Plateau were inexplicable. They were also life changing.

She and Mollock weren't going to be safe for much longer. "Ah'muf, I need to get out of Tenemenah without drawing attention."

"Ah," he said, rubbing his hands together. "That will be tricky. All of the ways are being watched."

"I wouldn't be wasting my time talking to you if I didn't think you know of a way," she pressed. The game was tired, but one she had to play if she expected to get anywhere.

He feigned thinking. "Costly, I suspect. The Prefects are everywhere, and you, ah…do not blend well with the local population. You can see my concern, *farisi*. I am but a simple man trying to feed my family. You would bring the authorities down upon me and take from my children?"

"Ah'muf, you don't have any children, and your wife left you years ago. The only thing you need to worry about the Prefects taking from you is your collection of goats," she shot back just as quickly.

"Such language! I always say you can tell much of a lady by the way her tongue spits such obscenities. What would you have me do?"

She leaned close enough to scowl at the smell of old alcohol drifting off him. Or maybe that was her? "Find me a way to get to the Wells."

He gasped, no ignorance in his tone. "Outlanders are not permitted in that sacred place. You will be burned alive just for mentioning it. I cannot help you."

"Ah'muf, please," she said.

He waved her off. "No. You and I might be friends, *farisi*, but this I will not be a part of. You risk getting both of us killed. Do not mention that place again. Every building has ears. The Prefects will know soon."

She frowned. "Ah'muf, the longer I stay in Tenemenah, the more dangerous it gets for all of us."

Elisa hesitated. Perhaps she was going about it all wrong. She'd survived the last two years by using her wit and guile. She decided she needed to find Mollock if either of them had any hope of surviving the coming storm she felt building.

Ah'muf surprised her then. "I might be able to find you a place to hide until what you fear blows over. Not all sandstorms last so long."

"That works," she answered, her mind already racing. "What more can you tell me about these outlanders the Prefects are so interested in?"

Patience was her best ally now. The Wells would have to wait for now.

TWO

3212 A.G. (After Gods), Krenz, planet Vau Prime.

The explosion blew part of the building wall across the street, knocking three men down. Crisp bolts of blue slammed into the ground around the bodies, striking one in the middle of the back. He gave a strangled cry and was still. Return fire barked from the ruined building. A pair of black-clad soldiers burst from cover to drag the survivors back to safety. Enemy fire picked up, desperate to keep the wounded from being saved.

Sweat and grime covering his face, Tolde Breed scowled. "We're getting pinned down. We need to move."

"They have snipers watching the corners. Our only option is a frontal assault," Sergeant Fies replied.

Shockwaves from another explosion pasted their uniforms to their skin.

"We don't have a choice!" Breed shouted above the din.

Fies grimaced but obeyed orders. "Jers, Beve, pour as much suppressive fire into that building as you can. Once we clear out the heretics, we'll signal for you."

"Roger, Sergeant," Jers replied, clearly uneasy with the plan.

Fies turned to his other squad leader. "Annalilly, your team is with me."

She grinned, a sight fierce and wicked. Fies had learned long ago not to tempt her aggressions, and he was damned glad to have her on his side. Annalilly had proved invaluable during the Crimeat campaign.

"My squad on me!" she barked. A half dozen heavily armed Prekhauten Guards formed two columns behind her.

Tolde was impressed, as usual, with the Guard's ruthless efficiency. A lifetime of service dedicated to the Inquisition had left him a fragment of the youth he once was. Tolde was thin but strong. He was celebrated throughout the Inquisition and Conclave as the only man to capture one of the Three.

None of that mattered now. If he didn't find a way to get his forces across the street, it was all over. He clutched his ion rifle tightly. The weapon was still alien to him, even after decades of practice. He preferred the reassuring grip of a hand-held pistol.

"Ready?" he asked Fies.

Fies regarded the man briefly. The answer was no, but that wasn't going to change anything. He nodded.

Tolde nodded back. Fies turned to Jers and dropped his hand.

"Fire!" Jers ordered.

Ion fire was so thick it looked like the street was filled with an electrical storm. The super-heated energy beams flashed and sizzled. Acrid smoke choked the air, mixed with pulverized mortar and stone.

"Now," Tolde said.

They moved, heads down and running for their lives. A handful of potshots answered back, but they were poorly aimed and hit nothing. Fies passed Tolde and crashed into the ruined wall on the opposite side of the street. The others followed quickly without further casualties.

Annalilly took over. "Stack on me! Haggle, you're point."

The slightly overweight Guard hustled to the flimsy wooden door. Two others followed. He mouthed a fast prayer before kicking the door open. Wood burst apart. He barreled in without delay and was gunned down by a pair of rounds stitching across his chest. He cried out and fell. Annalilly leapt over his body, firing as she dived to cover.

"Frag out!" Fies shouted from behind.

His guards ducked a moment before the explosion shook the building foundation. Annalilly pushed up first, firing as fast as her rifle could cycle. She was rewarded by a pair of grunts from the top of the staircase.

"First squad push up," she ground out, spitting a mouthful of blood; she'd bitten the inside of her cheek when she dropped.

"Clear down!" Fies confirmed.

Annalilly nodded and attacked.

Tolde all but collapsed against the chunk of wall. The smoke had cleared enough for him to see the full extent of the damage. He removed his helmet and ran a hand through his thinning grey hair. On the wrong side of seventy, Tolde was already past the midpoint of his life. He was tired. He couldn't remember the last time he'd conducted urban operations. This was not a game for the old or tired.

He looked up to see Haggle stumble out of the captured building, rubbing his aching chest. The young Guard's eyes were unfocused, his hair frizzed. Tolde grinned wryly. Haggle dropped his assault pack and helmet and collapsed next to Tolde.

"That hurt," he muttered.

Tolde nodded. "It will pass. Even on the lowest settings, your ion rifles pack a sting. Here, drink some water."

Haggle was too tired and sore to refuse. He removed the cap and put the bottle to his lips as the rest of the squad emerged. Annalilly and Fies came out at the same time, arguing as usual.

"You should have let me take half the squad around to the back," she frowned.

Fies rolled his eyes. "We've been over this, *sergeant*. You would have spread your element too thin and been ineffective during the breech."

Annalilly struggled to contain her rising fury. "I'm not concerned with the size of the element. What we needed was the tactical advantage. Divert their attention and punch a hole through their guts."

"And get every single trooper in your command killed!" Fies shouted back.

He almost regretted promoting her after the Crimeat campaign — almost. Annalilly unbuckled her helmet and gently set it down like a newborn infant. She'd shaved her head bald recently. Twin lightning bolts were tattooed on each side, running from temples to nape. Fies found it unattractive, but he didn't look at her like that anyway. She was the best Guardsman he had served with in a very long time. What she chose to look like was her business so long as she did her job the right way.

"It won't get everyone killed," she protested. "I can save lives, time and effort."

"How? By sacrificing some of your men?"

She frowned but stood her ground. Annalilly was determined to prove Fies wrong. All she needed was the opportunity.

"Let me try it. If I fail, then fine. I'll drop it entirely."

He groaned. "But?"

She flashed her best smile, white teeth gleaming in the haze. "I get to do things my way with my squad if I'm right."

Fies knew he was going to regret either decision. She was good but suffered from an inflated sense of confidence. The events on Crimeat, their last real combat action, were already two years past. That was plenty of time to forget valuable lessons. Annalilly had returned from that planet renewed. They'd deployed hastily, to an unknown situation, and quickly became embroiled not only in an insurrection, but the defection of an entire planet's worth of Prekhauten Guards. It was the unthinkable, a nightmare situation that tested their personal limits. Fies still mourned the loss of his long-time friend, Kastor.

Defections weren't entirely unheard of. Guard history was sprinkled, lightly, with similar incidents, but each time the Conclave had known in advance. Whoever had orchestrated the events on Crimeat had known exactly what he was doing. Fies counted himself lucky his men had come back with relatively few loses. Still, the emotional scars haunted him. Friends should not fight friends.

Annalilly had taken the incident personally and drove her squad harder than any other in the conventional Guards. She was determined not to let the past repeat itself and, if it did, to be prepared to crush her enemies with ruthless efficiency. Her shame was great, her loathing for heretics and traitors unending. Her fervor was becoming frightening, but Fies wasn't sure how best to handle it.

He finally relented, more out of professional curiosity than anything. Fies pointed a gloved finger at her. "One shot."

She slapped his shoulder hard. "Thanks, Sarge." Turning to her squad, she barked, "You have five minutes to rest. Rehydrate and rearm. We're doing it again!"

Groans and boos rumbled through the squad as they prepared to run the training exercise again. Tolde shook his head in admiration. It took years of training, patience and waiting just to be considered for acceptance into the Prekhauten Guard. These men and women were the best in the universe. He was proud to associate with them. Haggle handed him the canteen. Tolde drained the rest and replaced the cap.

He spied the lithe figure of a woman approaching. The look on her face dampened his mood considerably.

Tall and thin, Luma Kai was extremely toned. She had strength many men her age lacked, an impressive quality. Her light blonde hair was tied back in a severe bun, complimenting her pale skin. She and Tolde had worked together for since the engagement on Crimeat, but he still hadn't gotten used to the penetrating gaze of her ice blue eyes.

"Luma," he said, hoping to cut her off. "What brings you out to the training area?"

She glanced around to ensure none of the Guards were within earshot. "The Cardinal Seniorus has called the Forum. They are to discuss what must be done about the Three and this cult of Rengu. They're worried."

Tolde was skeptical. Conclave leadership had sat on the information taken from Crimeat for two years. There was no urgency from the capital of Krenz despite what the Cardinal Seniorus was insisting. Vows and what turned out to be empty promises of retribution for the embarrassment suffered by both the Conclave and the Inquisition flooded media outlets.

The Three were still at large, presumably continuing their eternal war against each other, and no one on Krenz still had the slightest understanding of what the sons of the gods were doing. Tolde feared the day the Three struck. Anarchy and chaos would bring the order of the universe to its knees.

"The Cardinals have been talking about this for too long already," he replied curtly, his distaste for the hierarchy's inactivity undisguised.

Luma kept her emotions private. "The Inquisitor General has requested an audience with us."

"The Office of Heretical Persecution?" Tolde asked.

She shook her head. "No. You and I specifically."

The last time he'd been summoned to that office, he'd found himself thrust into the middle of a conspiracy he didn't understand. Those events were still far beyond his knowledge. Tolde considered himself a simple man, one not prone to jumping at shadows or chasing whispers. Worse, how the Inquisition handled one of their own going rogue disturbed him. Inquisitor General Nye had practically blown off Tolde's concerns, making him wonder if Nye was keeping vital information concealed. Such implications would stagger the moral authority and breathe life into a thousand uprisings. Tolde kept those thoughts well hidden lest he find himself the object of his own office's interests.

The Office of Heretical Persecution had been developed to remove any threat to the sanctity of the Conclave at the discretion of the Inquisition. Heretics were tried and judged on the spot, oftentimes not even going to the main fortress for interrogation. Tolde suffered through his work without pleasure. Lately, he spent a lot of time training with the Guards, preparing for an unnamed mission yet to be defined.

"Have the Three been spotted?" he asked, doubtful there was any other reason for their summons.

Luma shrugged, her shoulders rolling under the tight grey uniform. "No one is saying. Whatever he wants, the Inquisitor General is being tight-lipped. I think we are about to get in over our heads."

"That's nothing new," he replied too quickly. He'd been in over his head for the better part of his career, ever since that fateful day decades ago when he had been dispatched to hunt down and capture Amongeratix for the first time.

"Come, we need to leave," she hurried.

He still found her difficult at best, trying most of the time. Luma Kai was not an easy woman to work with. Her no nonsense approach to her job rubbed many of her peers the wrong way, subtly ostracizing her from the inner circles. Tolde's career suffered because of it — not that being transferred to the Office of Heretical Persecution had been his idea in the first place. He harbored suspicions that he had been placed there to get him out of the way.

He figured he still had another thirty years before retirement called, though fearful that time was running much shorter than his original designs. The Inquisition was ever the secretive order, but matters had changed since the civil war on Crimeat. There was a newfound sense of ambivalence in the ranks. The higher offices denied the sudden need for action while fanning the flames of something big to come. Tolde wasn't the only dissatisfied Inquisitor. The only problem was that no one was willing to be the first to make an accusation against the Order. That path led to ruin.

Tolde harbored severe misgivings about the current Inquisitor General. Alain Nye had been a mere adjutant the first time they had met, when the previous Inquisitor General had assigned Tolde to hunt down Amongeratix. Even then, Tolde had found relatively little to admire about the man. He bore a chameleon's look. Rumors swirled under his cloak of office. Farius Graeme had been old, but not too old. His death had rocked the foundation of the Inquisition and, despite the negative findings of a formal investigation, was soon forgotten. Nye had immediately stepped in and took the oath of office.

The Order changed that day. Information was less accessible. Inquisitors were being sent on farfetched chases at the merest hint of rumor. And through it all, the Three remained hidden among the stars. Fearful of the political ramifications for dereliction of duty, Inquisition headquarters maintained the peace with iron will. Tolde suspected not even the Cardinal Seniorus was aware of the depth of Nye's plots. But again, those were things not said in the light. Not said at all if he was being cautious.

Tolde was no fool. He had nothing but a twisting feeling in his gut whispering that all was not well with the Order. He raised his guard and waited. Time would soon tell whether his fears were misplaced or not.

He took another mouthful of water before sliding it back into the carrier at his waist. A thought occurred to him, and he snorted in amusement.

"What?" Luma asked genuinely.

"I just realized that I haven't had a vacation in a very long time."

She narrowed her eyes. "Something tells me you're not going to be able to for a good while. Come, I don't feel like getting dressed down by the Inquisitor General."

Tolde excused himself from Sergeant Fies and followed Luma Kai back to the waiting air car.

Fies watched them go, his dark eyes intently studying the pair.

"What do you make of that? She's never come down here with us grunts," Annalilly said beside him.

Fies shook his head slowly. "I don't know, but I don't like it."

Lorenu Phos, Cardinal Seniorus of the most powerful organization in the universe, struggled to focus on the man addressing the Conclave forum. One hundred cardinals were arrayed in a semi-circle in four rows — the elected rulers of the massive Conclave body and the hundreds of aligned planets. Lorenu sat on a raised dais in the front. Alabaster pillars formed the outer cordon, reminding her of so many teeth. Golden symbols and letters lined the rust-colored walls. Huge marble tiles gave the floor a checkerboard appearance. Chandeliers the size of small swimming pools were spaced out across the domed ceiling.

The cardinals sat comfortably on plush crimson cushions. Forum sessions often lasted for most of the day. Attendants waited just outside the main chamber with access to the building's kitchens and offices. The Forum was used more than the actual Conclave audience building, and the designers had spared no expense. Electronic translators were built into the thin tables in front of each cardinal.

Lorenu snapped out of her daze at a mention of the Three.

"…taken us to a dangerous place. We are not strong enough to contend with them. This council has no choice but to increase the number of Prekhauten battalions and commit more Inquisitors to the field."

A gaunt man with close-cropped grey hair and watery eyes stood. Cardinal Thent looked around the chamber before addressing the group. "This body has kept a fragile peace for hundreds of years. I refuse to believe we lack the strength to do so now."

"The events on planet Crimeat suggest that our ability to control the universe has diminished greatly. We are no longer the power we once were," Porii Daam said in her gilded voice.

Cardinal Ott Gorman snorted derisively. "Nonsense. The actions of a handful of malcontents can by no means suggest that we are declining. This body remains in total control."

His double chins shook as he waggled a thick finger at her while he spoke. Porii frowned but refrained from further comment. She'd been a cardinal of the Conclave for decades and had learned the peculiarities of her peers long ago. Ott Gorman was fat and obnoxious, often drunk on his own power. Picking a fight with him in front of the entire Forum was foolish.

"Perhaps both of you are too hasty on this matter," Tinus Har suggested. Known by his peers for his golden tongue, Tinus had the ability to talk his way out of unusually tense situations. He saw no other choice now. Tinus guessed there wasn't much time before accusations and insults began to be carelessly thrown around the chamber.

Gorman's eyes narrowed threateningly. "Explain yourself, Tinus. I am in no mood for your chicanery."

Tinus smiled tightly, letting it fade quickly. "No tricks, Cardinal." He turned to the entire body. "Fellow Cardinals, we are approaching unexplored territory. How long has it been since all of the Three were active on the same planet? Certainly not in any of our lifetimes. Does that imply that we are weaker, less capable than a year before? I don't think so. Cardinal Gorman wants you all to think that we need more weapons, more Guards to defend the aligned worlds. He hasn't said as much, but it is the inevitable conclusion to that line of thought."

"How dare you accuse…," Gorman spat.

Lorenu Phos slammed the egg-shaped Osari Stone down one time. A metallic echo circled the chamber, making even the dourest cardinal take heed. "Enough, Cardinal Gorman. It is well known by all here that you are the loudest advocate for increased military strength. I will not allow you to goad those undecided into following your particular thought."

Gorman fell silent but stared knifes at the Cardinal Seniorus. Lorenu blew out a frustrated breath and turned to Tinus Har. "Cardinal Har, please get to the point. We do not have all night to sit and debate the history of each member."

His face was unreadable, but he bowed politely. "Of course. Ladies and gentlemen, the Three are the biggest threats any soul in the universe has ever faced. We do not know their intent or the full extent of their abilities. We do not even know the truth of their origin. The mythos suggests they are the sons of the gods, cast out by their father's rage. Ask yourselves what you would do in such a situation. How would you feel if you were cast down from paradise and thrown to the dark wolves of the universe?"

Some nodded their heads while others murmured to those seated beside them.

Tinus grinned and continued, "Fifty years ago Amongeratix escaped from one of our most distant prison worlds. Two years ago, he escaped from the prison on Crimeat. We spent our finest Guardsmen and Inquisitors on finding him and bringing him to justice. Tannus and the Bloody Man intervened. The Inquisition believes they are trying to make their way back to Occanum."

"You waste our time rehashing old data. Get to the point already, Tinus," Gorman snapped. The liver spots on his temple flared brightly.

"My point is that these beings can be hurt, and they know it. Our forces wounded all three before they fled to space. The advantage is ours. We have all the resources and military strength needed to successfully lock away all three. The Order of the Blood Witches has pledged their support, and I have been contacted by the Vaumagian assassins. They, too, offer assistance."

"What heresy is this?" Cardinal Arbalas accused. Slightly overweight, Arbalas was one of the more outspoken members. "Neither order is to be trusted, and you invite them into our fold?"

"The Blood Witches were contacted under the direction of me, General Strannan and the Grand Inquisitor," Lorenu interrupted. She hated having to defend herself, especially to subordinates. "Cardinal Har, please explain your reasoning for contacting the assassins. I gave no such authorization."

"Cardinal Seniorus, I did not mean to go around you, but these are desperate times. Twice now we have been bested by just one of the Three. Amongeratix is hatred in human guise. He has singularly destroyed dozens of worlds, if rumors are to be believed. I did not think we could take the chance of him slipping across the universe unnoticed. Whatever you each choose to believe, the Three must not reach Occanum."

Lorenu's thin lips tightened. "It is dangerous bringing the assassins in. We cannot control them. They could just as easily turn on us before finding the Three."

Porii Daam disagreed. "The Vaumagians are many things, Cardinal Seniorus, but they act under a code of honor."

"Honorable assassins?" Gorman scoffed. "We talk too much. This Forum is responsible for trillions of lives. It falls to us, a mere one hundred, to decide the fates of so many. I call for a vote. This council needs a stronger military force if we are to contend with the might of the Three. Fellow cardinals, we are not talking about a single planet or even those within the sectors we represent. We are talking about more than seven hundred and fifty colonized worlds. The war of the gods nearly destroyed all life in the universe. Their renegade sons stand ready to do the same again. We cannot allow that to happen. Think what you will of me, but I am only a man. Look into your hearts before you decide."

The Forum erupted in conversation. Lorenu Phos felt deflated. She slumped back in her high-backed chair with an air of defeat. She didn't necessarily oppose the expansion of military power but wanted to be sure it was used correctly and done for the proper reasons. There was no stopping the vote once a call was made by a sitting member. As Cardinal Seniorus, she wasn't allowed to influence the vote either. Her hands were tied. Lorenu Phos sat back in her chair and wondered what fate held in store for them. She never noticed to grim yet pleased look radiating from Inquisitor General Alain Nye in the back of the Forum.

"That could have gone much better, certainly more smoothly," Alain Nye said as he poured two small glasses of local brandy. He handed one to Lorenu. "I find the cardinals to be…tedious at best."

Lorenu accepted the glass with pursed lips. Her thoughts swirled around the unending arguments for more soldiers, more weapons. She looked up at Nye, noticing how grey and thin his hair had grown. There was no sign of the once-brilliant chestnut color he'd once had. Nye was old, a careless reminder of her own advancement through time.

"They represent their people. This particular bunch represents the entire universe," she finally replied.

He smiled, deep creases scarring his face. "They speak in circles. It's a wonder any action is ever begun. I do not have the temperance for such things."

"Now is not the time to rush into a war we don't understand," she countered. Lorenu winced as the harsh liquor burned down her throat. "Why do I drink this stuff?"

"I'm told it is a delicacy among the nobility. Damned nasty stuff, if you ask me, though. I prefer cold ale, but we must uphold the pretense of civility and decorum for everyone watching."

Lorenu shifted the conversation. "What would you have me do, Alain? I cannot knowingly endorse more combat forces without a relevant target."

An eyebrow arched. "The Three aren't relevant enough for you?"

She dismissed him with a wave. "Of course they are, but where are they? We haven't seen a trace of them since the explosion at the end of the battle on the Plateau. None of your Inquisitors or my spies has been able to locate a shred of evidence related to the Three."

"You're not suggesting they destroyed themselves in one moment of cosmic irony, are you?" he asked slowly, unsure where the conversation was headed.

Lorenu narrowed her eyes. "Don't be ridiculous. They are supposedly immortal. I highly doubt they are capable of killing each other after three thousand years. You haven't answered my question."

He paused. "You ask a difficult question, Lorenu. I would love to be able to tell you to give me the funding to raise a dozen divisions of Prekhauten Guards or to double the size of my existing Inquisitors, but that wouldn't be prudent. I agree we should approach this cautiously. The Three are dangerous and have made a habit of besting our best. What we can't afford to do is remain idle. Amongeratix reappeared at the end of the last century because he was searching for something. He got lazy and was captured."

"I remember the history, Alain; please get to the point. It is growing late," she tried to hurry him along.

"My point is that Amongeratix will eventually head for Occanum once he has secured whatever object he needs. We should dedicate a force to hunt him down and send a large body of forces to Occanum to finish him."

His small eyes blazed passionately. Nye struggled to maintain composure, lest Lorenu discover the depths of his hatred for the Three. He was small and painfully thin these days, but he was a fighter. Nye had survived the rumors that he'd had a hand in killing his predecessor and remodeled the Inquisition into a terrifying element that operated with brutal efficiency since the disaster on Crimeat. The only thing keeping him from solidifying his rightful place in the pantheon of heroes was the Three.

"I see where you are coming from, Alain, I truly do, but that would be a waste of resources," she told him. "We have been forced to put down a dozen rebellions in the last two years. Deep-space pirate attacks are disrupting shipping lanes to the point where the Prekhauten fleets are rendered useless. If I followed your guidance, I would expose the entirety of the universe to the depredations of chaos and ruin.

"I am responsible for the security of seven hundred and fifty worlds. I cannot and will not allow the Three to steal all our resources right when we need them the most. There must be a better way we are missing." She slumped back in the leather chair and downed the rest of her brandy.

Nye's cheeks flared bright crimson as they puffed uncontrollably. He breathed deeply, dissolving the sudden rush of anger trembling his body. "There is another way," he suggested tersely.

"Go on," she encouraged.

"I believe one of the cardinals mentioned the Blood Witches and the Vaumagians. The Inquisition is no stranger to either. I sanctioned the use of the witches from your very office once. We can do so again."

Lorenu sighed. "The Order of the Blood Witches is unreliable. The Grand Mistress sits in her abbey fortress and only deigns to contact us when *she* needs something. They care nothing for humanity on their little comet."

He had no return argument for that. The witches stayed on their comet, slowly traveling the universe while trying to read the stars for portents. And he was fairly certain the Inquisition was not in their good graces, not after the Sister assigned to help Tolde breed capture Amongeratix had been killed.

"The Vaumagians seldom fail an assignment," he offered.

"Assassins," she spat. "How can you be so willing to place your faith and hopes in the hands of an organization that hides behind gold masks? No," she continued slowly after a pause. "We must redouble our efforts and bring the Three to heel. I am no dreamer, Alain. All I want is what is right for the countless civilians on our worlds. I accept that the Three cannot be killed, but there must be a way to bring peace back to the universe. Find that way. Help me avert an unnecessary war."

"The Vaumagians have been useful before. Perhaps they…"

"They what? Can kill the Three? I think you overestimate their skills," Lorenu scoffed. She had heard enough. "I am tired, Alain. We will continue this conversation tomorrow."

"I thought you were in a rush to make a decision?" he asked sharply.

"Nothing has been done in two years; one more night isn't going to hurt."

The crispness of her retort stung, but even the Inquisitor General knew when to bite his tongue. He may control the Inquisition, but Lorenu ruled the universe. Caution was required in such delicate dealings.

He bowed curtly, clicking the heels of his highly polished black boots together sharply. "Goodnight then."

She waved him off, and he was nearly gone when a thought struck. "Alain, have we heard any information on our rogue Inquisitor? What was his name again?"

Nye slowed to a halt. His cheeks puffed. "Prowl. Ursal Prowl, and no; as of now he is still classified as missing."

Lorenu pretended to mull the issue over, though, in truth, her mind was made. "Perhaps it is time to find him and made him stand for his crimes."

"I'll have my men get on it," he told her, "in the morning."

Alain Nye left her sitting alone in her receiving parlor, an aged and tired old woman. She was tired, but she refused to be cowed by the Inquisition. Lorenu had her suspicions about the Order, certain Nye was leading them on an individual agenda contrary to the Conclave. Worse, she believed several cardinals were in league with the Inquisitor General. She finished the glass of brandy with a grimace and set the empty glass on the table. Whatever nefarious plans Alain Nye was hatching, they too could wait.

The Cardinal Seniorus rose slowly and made her way across the expansive rooms of office to her personal chambers. Most nights, she found herself sleeping in the massive Conclave Administratum complex. She dearly wished for the comforts of her own bed, but recent affairs prevented that. Fortunately, she was able to bring the comforts of home here.

Aliz yawned and sat up, pulling the plush white comforter up to her chin as Lorenu locked the door.

"You're back late," Aliz smiled. Her short gray hair gave her a mousy appeal that Lorenu adored.

Lorenu smiled back. "I'm sorry, love, but some things just can't be put off."

Aliz peeled the comforter back. "I know the feeling."

Lorenu slid into bed.

THREE

3212 A.G. (After Gods), Deep-space shipping lanes.

Deep space was hauntingly beautiful. Distant nebulas colored areas blue, red and green. The stars twinkled brighter here than in any other place in the universe. Engine trails from the massive shipping transports warped space, reminiscent of heat waves pouring off hot concrete. Planets hung like giant jewels, sparkling when the light of suns struck just right. Best of all, it was silent. None of the chatter and din of civilization penetrated these deep reaches. It was the perfect place for less-than-savory men.

Ursal Prowl stood on the deck of a rundown cruiser, hands clasped behind his back. His face was unnecessarily terse. Past humiliations had driven him *here* to the end of the universe. Any purpose he'd once had was stolen, ripped out of his chest and crushed under the Inquisition's heel. Rage swelled, but without a proper target, Ursal was forced to contain it lest he be consumed.

"Inquisitor, a Draxian supply ship has dropped out the hyper lane. It should be within range in a half an hour."

Ursal turned at the deep thunderous voice addressing him. Geres Auk was an unwilling transplant from Crimeat. The giant man was tall, heavily muscled and menacing without doing anything. Once employed by the late Baron Scura, Geres was a placed agent for the dark council of Lethendweil and Ursal Prowl.

Ursal nodded. "Very well. Call the ship to general quarters."

Geres passed a glared back over his shoulder. Running lights switched red, and a warning klaxon alerted the crew. Ursal was only slightly impressed. Even pirates needed to be proficient in close-quarter battle drills, perhaps more so than the Prekhauten navy.

"Orders?" Geres asked.

The disgraced Inquisitor sighed, reluctant to peel his gaze away from the tranquility on the other side of the viewing glass. "Target engines and life support. Boarding parties detain. Kill only if necessary. We're here to disrupt supply lines, not murder half the citizens in the universe."

The big man frowned, disappointed. He was a violent man by nature. Being forced to stay the killing blow infuriated him. "Perhaps our orders are changed. The men are pirates. A little bit of killing is expected."

"We are not having this conversation again, Geres. I have my orders from Vau Prime. No unnecessary killings. We're not murderers, despite what you and these godless bastards might believe."

"As you say, Inquisitor," Geres relented.

He stormed away. Ursal knew blood was going to be spilled, regardless of his instructions. As Geres was so fond of reminding, these men were pirates.

Shuttles hauled cargo from the crippled cruiser for the remainder of the day. The crew, the ones who survived, were shoved in escape pods and jettisoned into space. Ursal was benevolent enough to activate their homing beacons and put them on a trajectory for the nearest uninhabited moon. Pirates gunned down thirteen men and women and swore they had been forced to defend themselves against the dangerous crew attack. *Bullshit. These men killed because they could. How lawless I have become. At one time, I swore to defend the universe from scum like this.*

Ursal kept his spot, watched as the battle ended almost too quickly. Flames sprouted each time a torpedo struck, only to be extinguished by the vacuum. A handful of bodies tumbled away. They were sucked out and lifeless before they understood their fate. Ursal hoped his death came so swiftly, though he knew it wouldn't. The Inquisition was hunting him. Time was as much his enemy as those who were coming. Ursal was generally unparticular about who would eventually arrive to end his life, but his deepest desires wanted it to be Tolde Breed, the hero of the Inquisition.

Hero, he scoffed. The man was a fossil needing to be put in a museum and forgotten by all but little children seeing history for the first time. Whatever good Tolde had contributed was long in the past, certainly decades before Ursal was even born. He had tried to play nice when the Senior Inquisitor had arrived in Vaade. Tried and failed. Tolde was too entrenched in the Inquisition mindset. Too deeply rooted to idealistic principles and the need to prove himself worthy of his own legend. Tolde was a fool. History was unkind, a lesson they would both soon discover.

The battle lasted but a handful of minutes. His pirate crew was too well versed at their task and made quick work of the cruiser. Boarding parties were away moments after the first barrage of torpedoes fired. The move was risky and delicate. One mistake, and ten lives would be snuffed out. Fortunately, the pirates were seasoned professionals. Ursal continued to be amazed by the proficiency with which the pirates operated. They returned without a single casualty to their ranks.

His eyes tracked the listing movements of cargo shuttle as it disappeared under the hull. He'd seen enough. It was time to speak with the pirate leader. Ursal adjusted his battered brown jacket, a far cry from the tailored linens of the Inquisition, and stalked across the command deck. Pneumatic doors hissed open as he passed into the belly of the pirate cruiser. The long unwinding passage reminded him of being swallowed by one of the massive snakes on Prielth. He found the captain exactly where he expected, in the galley pouring a fresh glass of blood wine.

If the pirate cruiser *Shrike* was like a snake, its captain was the reason. Ursal despised the man. He and all of those like him should have been hunted down and exterminated, not allowed to thrive in deep space. Another fault of the Inquisition, he fumed.

"Ah, our disgraced Inquisitor comes to join me!" Vicente Blackheart laughed to his crew. His eyes lit up in humor.

Ursal frowned. It was an old joke. "I'm no more an Inquisitor than you a good man, Vicente."

Blackheart's face darkened. "No need for insults, Prowl."

"I merely responded in kind," he replied curtly. "What's the take?"

Blackheart shrugged. "Mostly spare parts for drive engines. We took the food and supplies, but not much else is good for us."

"Sell the parts like you always do."

"Naturally," Blackheart agreed. "But my men are getting tired of running down cargo haulers when there are fat merchant ships running out there. The major banking systems use lines not too far from here. We could do with a juicy target."

"We are not here to engage in robbery."

Sharp laughter bounced from the walls. "Of course we are; don't be daft. This is a pirate vessel, *Inquisitor*, not a ride for disaffected political refugees. If you care to debate this, I will have you tossed in the nearest airlock." He leaned forward, all mirth gone. "Try me."

Ursal studied the pirate, swallowing his distaste. Vicente Blackheart was a thin man with few assets. A long forked beard hung to his chest, the color of blackest space. A white scar ran diagonally down his face. The scar tissue was puckered and foul looking even after so long. His hair was close-cropped with only the tinniest speckles of grey poking through. His knuckles were scarred, his hands abnormally long for a man so diminutive. There was small satisfaction in knowing the feared Vicente Blackheart barely stood an inch above five feet.

Ursal decided he needed to take care of Vicente before the opposite happened, but now was not the time. A coded message from Vau Prime had come in during the battle.

"That's not why I am here."

Leaning back, Blackheart cracked his knuckles. Small, he was every bit vindictive and evil. "Well?"

Ursal smiled tightly. He was also impatient. "I have new orders. We're heading to Occanum. There is a large Prekhauten fleet about to deploy, and we are to intercept and harass."

Blackheart's eyes bulged. "We are, eh? What exactly do you think the *Shrike* can do against an entire fleet?"

"Last I heard, you were a feared pirate captain, the scourge of deep space," Ursal goaded, appealing to Blackheart's vanity. "I'm sure you can come up with something viable to ensure we survive."

"Of course. We don't go," he replied quickly. "Merchants and supply runners are one thing, but even I don't have the stones to take on an entire fleet of Prekhautens. Find yourself another ship, *Inquisitor*."

"I'm afraid it's not that easy. We all have a role to play, Vicente. Yours is to follow orders, or did you forget where your loyalties lie? You're being paid handsomely for the freedom of movement through the shipping lanes."

"You're asking me to commit suicide," Blackheart growled.

"I'm not asking anything. You have your orders, *Captain*. Make this ship ready to depart within the hour."

He waited until Ursal was at the door before asking in a threatening voice, "And if I don't?"

Ursal smiled. "Then you and the lives of every man on this ship are forfeit. Your charter will be revoked, and I will see you hung for treachery. You have one hour."

Vicente Blackheart watched Ursal disappear back down the main corridor, no doubt going to inform his masters of this latest flare-up of insubordination. He looked down at the empty cup of blood wine, frowning.

"Why don't you slip a knife between his ribs and be done with it?" Therill, his First Mate, offered.

The thought crossed his mind more frequently the longer they worked together. Blackheart only shook his head. "If we do, then we'll have that bastard Auk to deal with. He won't go down so easily."

"All men die, with the proper amount of persuasion," Therill said.

Vicente Blackheart liked his First Mate, but the man scared him half to death. He wasn't sure who to be more afraid of, a broken Inquisitor or the *Shrike's* second in command. For now, he settled on Geres Auk. Something about the man was unsettling.

"The time will come when our new friends find themselves at the end of their rope, but not now." He stewed over Ursal's ultimatum. "Secure all cargo and prepare for departure. We've overstayed our welcome."

Therill stiffened. His dark skin shimmering under the artificial lights. "Your orders, Captain?"

Blackheart sighed. "You heard the man. We're heading for Occanum."

Though I doubt we'll live to tell of it.

"You play a dangerous game," Geres Auk admonished quietly.

He despised being trapped onboard the *Shrike*. Space felt like a coffin, constricting and oppressive. Geres longed for the open steppe with a strong wind caressing his face and neck. He'd never been to space before. Geres found it all very unimpressive. Limited variety drove him past the point of boredom, left him feeling void of the necessary qualities in life. Worst of all, he wanted to kill Therill. They'd butted heads on the very first day and weren't interested in making amends.

Ursal stifled a yawn. "What other kind of game is there? We're trapped, Geres. I was sent here to distract the Conclave from finding the Three. We failed."

"Why send one ship into the middle of an entire enemy fleet? Your masters don't want us to survive, Ursal."

"No, it doesn't appear so, does it?" Ursal commented dully.

"Do you believe we have been betrayed? It was only a matter of time. We are too dangerous out here," Geres persisted.

Ursal sat stunned. The subject of betrayal hadn't occurred to him…yet. He wanted to believe his superiors on Vau Prime still needed him. The only clear thing was that the universe was changing more quickly than anticipated. Treachery was about to become the currency of the day. For a moment only, he considered abandoning these pirates, his mission and even Geres so that he might disappear and find a new life.

Ursal reluctantly admitted that nothing good had happened since he was taken out of the hangman's noose all those years ago.

"We're supposed to be dangerous. They are counting on our ability to drive as many pirate gangs into frenzy as we can. The Prekhauten navy has a finite number of vessels they can throw at us before becoming non-mission capable. We bide our time while our enemies stretch their ability to mass against us. That's always been the plan," he concluded.

"I grow weary of staying on this stinking ship," Geres ground out, disappointed with the tone of the conversation.

Ursal nodded crisply, satisfied he'd managed to quell Geres's rising anger. "Have faith, Geres. I'm not foolish enough to tackle an entire fleet without a little help."

Geres's eyes narrowed. "What do you mean?"

"I've been building a fleet of my own," Ursal smiled. "We're going to war."

Geres Auk smiled genuinely for the first time in a long time.

Matthias sat in the cockpit of his tiny one-man craft, lost in thought. Sharp eyes watched as the *Shrike* made quick work of the supply ship. Impressed, Matthias still felt nothing but disdain for the act. Questions sprang to life. The action was fast, decisive. It was over in a matter of minutes and reminded him of a very professional assault by Prekhauten Marines. He frowned. Something wasn't right, but what remained beyond him.

Very few Guards abandoned their bonds and oaths to take up a life of crime, making the scene playing out before him disturbing. Pirates were generally unorganized profiteers tending to stick to shadows and backwater systems far from the central power hub of Vau Prime. Granted, he was in deep space now, but this particular crew was leaving a string of burned-out hulls stretching halfway across the universe. The trail seemed to be aimless, no general direction prevailing. Matthias didn't like that. Everyone had motives, and these pirates struck with brutal efficiency. They were after something, but what?

A body drifted by, arms and legs hooked, a stark look of surprise forever frozen on her face. Matthias winced as the body struck the nose of his craft and bounced off into space. Other bodies drifted away, a silent graveyard forever forgotten. He almost envied the speed with which their deaths arrived. The alternative he was forced to endure pushed him beyond the fragile limits of his imagination. Matthias was a doomed man whose executioner was in no great rush to drop the axe. Days blended until anonymity threatened to consume him. Until that day came, he vowed to continue his quest to discover the truth in an increasingly deceptive world.

Much had changed since he'd battled beside Tolde Breed on Crimeat. A sergeant major at the time, Matthias had been a rising star among the Prekhauten Guards. He'd accompanied Tolde on the first mission to recapture Amongeratix after the escape from Keltoo. They'd lost most of his squad and would have been killed as well if not for the Blood Witch they'd picked up at Hawker's Gate. Matthias had nothing but foul memories of that mission, often waking in sweat and with the shakes.

The campaign on Lethendweil had proved the crescendo of a brilliant career. He'd taken his men up against fellow Guards and won, albeit at cost to the Conclave. Too many Guards were killed in the efforts to quell the rebellion and bring the rogue Inquisitor to heel. Matthias blamed himself, and, not surprisingly, so did General Strannan and the rest of the Prekhauten command.

Arresting officials arrived during morning parade ground formation and placed him in cuffs. Hundreds of Guards watched in shock as their leader was unceremoniously led off to the waiting black air car. No one spoke to him despite the unending series of questions and demands. Matthias was thrown in a cell and forgotten long enough for his hair to grow out. A thick beard in need of shaving itched his jaw. He was half-starved and nearing dehydration.

Inquisitors came for him after what he figured was a three-week stay. They escorted him down a long corridor of plain granite. Matthias immediately recognized his surroundings. He was trapped deep within the bowels of the Conclave's secret detention facility, far underground and seldom referred to. Until now, he'd believed it to be just another myth whispered back and forth. He was taken into a small square chamber with one white light hanging from a high ceiling. An examination table took up most of the middle of the chamber. Matthias spied his uniform hanging on a peg on the far wall and grinned wryly. He was doomed.

They cleaned him up and dressed him in his best parade uniform. Again, his questions were shunned. No one spoke to him, treating him like a traitor. A Phallalian surgeon came in, dressed in sterile colors and lacking personality. He inspected Matthias methodically for defects and injuries. Satisfied, he nodded to the Inquisitors and departed. They replaced him in shackles, reminding him of the last sight he'd had of Amongeratix before he and Tolde had left the Conclave prison on Prophet Isle, and marched him back down the corridor and into a massive bowed room.

Matthias looked up at the semi-circular table, all of the chairs empty save one. He'd expected a full military tribunal and court martial, not General Strannan lounging casually on the Cardinal Seniorus's chair. His scars stood out in the pure white lights. Matthias ignored the rest of the room, having no desire to see what the condemned saw before being executed. His mind raced with confusion. There was no reason for his being here. He'd performed his duties to the fullest of his ability and brought down an insurgent cell responsible for murdering scores of innocent civilians.

Davith Strannan dismissed the guards with a wave. "Sergeant Major, you should know I take no pleasure in this."

"Then why am I here, General?" he asked defiantly.

Strannan shook his head. "I may be the head of the Prekhauten Guard, but I am only one man. There are factions within the Conclave and Inquisition that saw what you did on Crimeat as total failure. This is purely political. Backstabbers and weaklings vying for power. My hands are tied."

Matthias felt cold dread spread through his body.

Strannan slid to his feet, hands clasped behind his back. "The Conclave wants me to slap you in irons and lock you away down here for the rest of your natural life. Don't ask me why. You'd think that Inquisitor pal of yours should get the blame. Huh."

He lifted his eyes. "What happened to Tolde?"

Strannan paused, careful not to convey the wrong message. "He was transferred to the Office of Heretical Persecution. The man got a damned promotion, and I'm supposed to abandon you."

A promotion? *Tolde is a Hunter now?* Matthias's head swam with unending twists and possibilities.

The general stopped a few feet away and deftly unlocked the shackles binding Matthias's wrists. They fell with a menacing clatter.

"Listen to me, son. I'm not going to keep you here for no reason, but I can't let you stay on active duty. Those damned priests would have my hide. I have a special assignment for you." His tone dropped to a faint whisper.

"Sir," Matthias said cautiously.

"I need you to deploy out past Prielth. You'll get your official orders once I can get you clear of Vau Prime. This is a close-hold operation, Matthias. You will report directly to me. No one must know of this, do you understand?"

"Yes, sir, I understand."

Strannan placed a huge hand on Matthias's shoulder. "Good. There is a tunnel leading out of here behind that desk. Take it. You'll find an air car waiting for you."

Matthias had to force himself to walk away slowly. A day later, he was in space heading for a rendezvous with pirates.

*

The *Shrike* jumped into the hyperspace lane, leaving Matthias alone with the twisted wreckage of the supply ship. He gunned the engines enough to ease into the debris field and began searching anything that might give him a clue as to the attacker's true identity. Maneuvering his craft around to the port, Matthias saw the torpedo damage and sucked in his breath. The blast pattern was similar to Prekhauten munitions, the kind used on the capital battleships. *Impossible. How could pirates get a hold of such tech?*

He mulled over Strannan's words. More than ever, he was convinced the general was keeping something back. Corruption was more noticeable than before, and Matthias feared the worst. The insurrection on Crimeat proved relatively insignificant in the scheme of the universe but showed things were not well. A rot festered in the heart of the ruling orders. Open rebellion might spread like flames.

Matthias punched in a code and waited as the ship computed the *Shrike's* destination. He looked again at the damage. These pirates were not acting alone. A series of short beeps broke his attention. Matthias set the coordinates to his own navigation and followed.

FOUR

3212 A.G. (After Gods), Grand library, planet Wexanos.

The golden sky warmed his flesh but left his heart in shadow. Pain and torment mocked him. Peace was an illusion unworthy of pursuit, though he never stopped searching.

Tannus sat upon a small hill overlooking a large lake. The air was so still, not a ripple showed on the bright water. White birds darted in and left with fish wiggling in their beaks. Lustrous green shrubs lined the lake. He found serenity here, fleeting at best but still present. Little in life kept him from the cold realities of his war against his brother.

His was a tragic tale. Once, he'd been a prince of the universe, the days filled with pride and ambition. He had roamed the planets without the slightest regard. Nothing had been taboo or anathema to the three sons of the king. Neither had all been well. Growing discord had strained family bonds until Tannus couldn't stand it any longer. He'd gone before his father and publicly questioned him. Gasps had circled the audience. He'd instantly regretted it, but the damage had been done. He and his brothers had been cast down from the halls of the gods and left to wander the universe in search of their own answers.

The war Tannus had feared came soon after his banishment. It was a long, bitter struggle. The few surviving gods had met on the world men call Occanum and done battle to the end. Tannus had wept for his father. His brothers had turned to other means, and so the war had continued.

At least that was how humanity recorded it.

Tannus smirked and snatched a handful of loose dirt. Sunlight reflected across the lake, taking him back to the happier days of childhood. He let the dirt trickle through his fingers and frowned. His thoughts turned dark again as Amongeratix's face came unbidden to his imagination. The day he'd first learned of his brother's foul obsessions started to replay itself...

Tannus strode up the alabaster steps of the Temple Ordunus with questions for the oracle. He noticed something was wrong almost at once. The temple doors stood closed. They were always open, as was the charter with the oracle. Tannus froze. He contemplated going to his father but doing so would mark him a weakling and get him laughed at. No, better to go inside and deal with this like a man.

Tannus pushed the door open slowly before peeking in. Flames flickered dangerously from several fires towards the rear of the temple. His heart quickened. There should be no flame in the oracle's presence. Tannus pushed in, hands clenched tightly in fists. Danger screamed at his senses. He fought the urge to turn and run. Nothing was right within the Ordunus.

Evil was at work. Tannus felt the presence toying with him, taunting him to come closer and peer deeply into what he feared the most. He struggled through doubt and continued. Banks of half-melted candles lined the main path, briefly lighting his way. Snakes coiled and slithered at his feet. Tannus nudged them aside.

"Brother."

His eyes narrowed at the sound of Amongeratix's voice. He kept walking, eagerly searching for his brother. Gusts of wind snuck into the temple and growled through the rows of columns in a terrible noise. Candles blew out methodically, letting the darkness reclaim lost territory. Reality shifted. Violent images of desolation and unholy fornication played in the shadows. Tannus's stomach turned. The sanctity of the Ordunus was violated beyond repair. What was his brother playing at?

"Amongeratix, come out! End this madness before father finds out," he tried to reason.

Torturous screams mixed with ecstatic moan. Confusion mocked Tannus. None of this should be possible. Reality was the one unshakable fabric in the universe. Whatever Amongeratix had done was unnatural.

"Come, brother."

The voice echoed through the pillars. Tannus quickened his pace, but the faster he walked, the longer the path stretched. Maddened, the favorite son of the king struggled to contain his rage — at least until he confronted his brother face to face. A quick glance behind showed him that all the candles and fires were extinguished. Tannus decided to run. Sweat soon covered him, dripping into his eyes, running down his spine. Cold laughter came from ahead and abruptly cut off.

The darkness faded and was replaced by unmitigated nightmare. Tannus felt his jaw go slack. A deep purple tint fouled the air. It also allowed him to see the full extent of the horror in shimmering glory. He stopped, both amazed and depressed, to take in the true value and appreciation of his brother's sudden madness. Hundreds of glossed human skulls sat on wooden stakes pounded into the dirt floor. More dangled from barbed hooks, the lower jaws torn away.

Tannus waded through the misery. He felt the victims' pain and suffering and was powerless to help. Tears choked his eyes, but he knew he couldn't stop. He briefly gave thought to the oracle. What had happened to her? Was Amongeratix capable of killing her under their father's very watch? Tannus would have answered no a day prior. He kept walking.

All thoughts shattered when the room suddenly gave way to an endless sea of brush and grass. A lone tree filled the middle of the scene, gnarled and twisted as only an ancient oak could be. The sheer impossibility of it all shocked his senses. Tannus started to feel fear. The sudden thrum of music shook him alert. He looked up and froze.

A skeletal minstrel sat perched in the crook of the tree, one leg dangling off the branch, the other drawn up in a ninety-degree angle. The skeleton wore a ruffled white blouse and black pants tucked into battered black leather boots. The wind tousled the single red feather plumed on top of the wide-brimmed hat. It was leaning back into the trunk, gently strumming a bone guitar.

The skeleton casually glanced down at Tannus, that mocking smile burning into the young blonde. It laughed suddenly and continued playing the guitar. Drops of blood fell from each stroke. Looking back at Tannus, it started to sing:

Watch your back
And fear the dark
For your brother's hatred
Will find its mark.

Tannus paused to stare at the abomination glibly warning him. He knew such things should not exist. The urge to leap into the tree and pulverize the skeletal minstrel begged to be set free, and it took all his will to keep composure. Then, the sky changed. Dark clouds poured in much faster than reality. Enormous holes tore through the black clouds. Tannus stared up into vile demonic faces leering down at him with red eyes and wicked fangs. Every desire and naked hatred was laid bare.

"You are not real," he whispered.

They laughed a terrible sound. Tannus strengthened his stance, refusing to be cowed into submission by veiled threats and petty sorcery.

"You are not real," he repeated with conviction.

The illusion faded. Darkness returned, broken only by a singular light shining down from the unseen sky. Tannus was startled to see a rope hanging down through the center of the beam. Knowing his brother waited at the end of this torment, Tannus took hold of the rope and started to climb. Fear dissolved, transformed into fury. The climb went on forever. His muscles ached. They burned.

He emerged into an entirely new scene, this one unlike any he'd been forced to experience. The devilish visions were gone, replaced with a world of such immense and forbidden pleasures Tannus nearly forgot himself. Waterfalls cascaded down the slopes of golden hills. Plush green carpeted the stretching plain. Women, mostly naked, danced and lounged near the small lake without concern. They looked up at him and beckoned. One stood, her breasts small and tight on her lithe body. She puffed her lips and curled a long-painted finger at him. She laughed at his indecision and lay back down in the soft grass.

Tannus resisted the dominating urge to join the woman. His feet were heavy, each step a labored effort. Melodious voices sang to him, beckoning him into her embrace. He squeezed his eyes shut and shook his head. They are not real, *he repeated to himself.* I am imagining this. *He fought the temptation and was rewarded by watching the nymphs slowly dissipate back to the nothing.*

Forever night settled back in around him. Another dug under his skin. Amongeratix mocked him from an unseen vantage. Tannus desperately searched the dark for his prey. He felt his brother near, frustratingly close.

"Show yourself, Amongeratix," he called.

"Here I am, brother."

The words echoed with an icy chill. Tannus spun and found nothing but the haunting laughter.

"Do you like my little tricks?" Amongeratix teased.

Tannus tensed, wary of attack. "What have you done with the oracle?"

"Patience, brother. I am only beginning."

"Show yourself!" Tannus shouted.

Amongeratix stepped from behind a darkened pillar. Madness shone in his eyes.

Tannus gasped. "What has happened to you?"

A smile, thin and disturbed. "I've been shown the truth of the universe. We've been lied to, brother."

"No games, Amongeratix. You are not well. Let me take you back to the healers. They can cure you of whatever this ailment is."

"Fool! I don't need their help. Can't you see? Everything father told us is false. We are not the supreme beings in the universe." He took a step closer.

Tannus recoiled from the overpowering wave of hatred pulsing from his brother. "What talk is this? You speak treason."

"Treason? I speak the truth! Let me show you."

Amongeratix swept his arms out and brought them together with a deafening clap. The world changed again, much worse than any imagination Tannus had been forced to witness thus far. A great battle surrounded them. Giants in ornate battle armor slashed and hewed at each other with shimmering blades and vicious looks. Tannus watched as brother slew brother. These were being he recognized. They were of his own blood, but no war of this scale had ever been fought. Another lie.

"Stop this madness before I tell father," Tannus warned.

Amongeratix stopped, fixing his brother with a deathly glare. "Ever the righteous one, eh, brother? This is our future; the one father doesn't want us to see. Look around. Do you recognize the faces? These are our people engaged in the final battle that will destroy us all and give the universe to the humans."

"No," was all Tannus could say.

Blood sprayed in vicious gouts. Bodies fell, their faces locked in death's harsh grimace. Fires raged around them, fueled by the rage and hatred of the combatants. Tannus sickened. Never had he dreamed of violence on such a scale. The air burned with the overpowering stench of evil, of pure malevolence. Still, he found he lacked the will to turn away. The body count rose.

"This can't be true," Tannus whispered.

"But it is. Every last scene I have shown you. The end is coming to us, Tannus, and nothing we do can change it in time." Amongeratix took another step closer. "It all falls down, brother. We will be crushed into dust and forgotten on the cosmic winds. This is our legacy."

The image of their father strode into view. Blood ran down the right side of his face. He bled from a dozen cuts, mortal wounds. Death stalked him. A handful of lesser men circled the king. Their weapons were dulled from overuse. Their hatred ran high. They had come to kill the king. Tannus struggled to go to his aide but discovered he couldn't move.

"Our world is ending," Amongeratix added. "Father will fall, and the reign of our people will come crashing down. History will not be kind."

"How can you know this?" Tannus forced.

"The oracle does not lie."

Tannus slowly turned his head back to his maddened brother. "What have you done with her?"

"She is gone, lost among the stars. I exiled her, brother. She will not return." He started to walk away. "Go to father if you must, but you will find no satisfaction. Our doom is written. This is our future."

"I don't believe you," Tannus ground out. Tears streaked his dirtied face.

Amongeratix leered. "There is more. You are the reason behind all of this. Your selfishness and ignorance cause our demise."

The spell broke. Tannus pointed his finger accusingly. "Lies! I am the favored son. I am chosen to succeed father. Your jealousy has twisted you."

"Has it? Do you name the oracle of Oculus false? A trickster? There is but one way for you to avoid our destruction. Join me, Tannus. Together, we can make a universe stronger than any father might imagine. I have shown you what awaits. Give in to your desires. Stop fighting your inflated sense of morality. The choice is yours."

Amongeratix held out his hands as if to embrace Tannus. His eyes remained hard, calculating every eventuality. He knew his brother would not be easily swayed. They were so unalike, Amongeratix had never felt close to him. Even now, Amongeratix knew what he had to do. The only way to stop the future was to slay his brother.

Tannus felt torn. Fresh memories replayed in his mind's eye. The candles and snakes. The naked women writhing in desire as they attempted to seduce him. The skeletal minstrel singing warnings. The apocalypse of the gods. Good and evil struggled for domination over him. Right and wrong were concepts too basic to grasp with his breaking mind.

"I will make this simple for you, Tannus. Join me or die. I will not offer you clemency a second time."

The threat echoed throughout his consciousness. Tannus screwed his eyes shut, desperate to cleanse his soul of the taint thrust upon him. He knew what he should do, but it was a far cry from what he wanted. He and Amongeratix seldom saw eye to eye, and, if not for the intermediary skills of their brother, they would have been at each other's throats long before now. Princes were expected to show decorum, not squabble like peasants in revolt, but his deepest desire was to rush forward and strike his brother down before he had the chance to spread this filth.

Slowly, he opened his eyes and fixed Amongeratix with a deadly glare. "I will not join you, abomination. You have taken and twisted reality until nothing remains but your sickening desire to do harm. Father will learn of this, and he will take action."

"Father is irrelevant! Our days race to the finish. He has led us to ruin. Only I can salvage what remains of our glory."

Tannus said, "Your words drip venom. We shall battle if we must but know that I will not stop until I have hunted you down and stripped this foulness from your soul."

"So be it."

Amongeratix charged, barreling Tannus to the ground. Fists drove relentlessly into his brother's chest and abdomen. Tannus fought back, bringing his knees up and throwing a forearm across his body to block some of the blows. Amongeratix raged harder. He struggled to pin his brother and deliver the killing blow, but Tannus was an equal fighter. Tannus managed to turn and rolled them apart. He came up with fists clenched. Blood trickled from the corner of his mouth. A dark bruise already started on his cheekbone.

"This cannot be undone, Tannus. I will never forgive you," Amongeratix snarled before he stepped back into the darkness and disappeared.

Tannus lay gasping for breath. His body ached. His mind screamed countless obscenities. He struggled to rise, the pain wracking his chest. "Amongeratix!" he bellowed, but it was too late. His brother was gone.

Knowing what he must do, Tannus picked himself off the ground and slowly wormed his way back to the palace and his father's throne.

"So long ago," Tannus mused. "My life has been defined by the insanity of another."

Three thousand years had passed since the day he'd first learned of his brother's dark secrets. Three millennia of wasted dreams, forgotten pleasures, and the unfulfilled desire to see it all end. Tannus hated Amongeratix as much as his brother hated him. They'd battled and eluded one another for so long, he no longer felt sure of the outcome. Once, when he was still young, Tannus had believed in the righteousness of his charge. He was destined to bring his brother back and fix the shattered harmony of his kind. That never happened.

Everything Amongeratix predicated had come to pass. Tannus had gone to his father, questioning the king in open forum. He and his brothers had been banished for Tannus's insolence. The war had soon followed. Millions had died for nothing but vain ambition. The final battle on Occanum had ended their rule forever.

Tannus watched a herd of black deer creep to the edge of the lake to drink. He almost admired their suspicious innocence. He forfeited innocence all those long years ago. Nothing remained of the youth who had stood up to his brother in the Oculus temple. He was hardened, less apt to show the depths of emotion he once had. Those peculiar traits were weaknesses needing to be expunged. Tannus had learned the hard way just how violent his brother could be.

Their war had carried out across the stars, ruining planet after planet. The death tolls were staggering. Entire populations were destroyed as brother tried to kill brother. The Conclave had intervened successfully when they'd created the order of the Inquisition. Tannus had formed a shaky alliance and helped imprison Amongeratix. No cage was strong enough, and the subsequent centuries were filled with a successive string of escapes.

The need for redemption fueled Tannus further. His mind replayed the horrific events from Occanum every time he closed his eyes, making his life an endless string of torments. The war had gone on far too long. At first, he had tried enlisting his other brother but had found bitter disappointment. The last brother had abandoned his true name after the battle of Occanum and insisted to be called Sorrow. He refused to aid either, choosing instead to go into seclusion until the moment was right. Tannus regretted the decision but honored Sorrow's request.

Rustling in the dry grass behind made Tannus turn slowly. He stared up into the unblinking eyes of a bull khars moose. The animal easily weighed two thousand pounds and had a spread of antlers well over ten feet. Tannus froze. He could disable the moose if needs be, but the fight would take much out of him. Better to let the animal satisfy its curiosity and be on its way than to enrage it. The moose cocked its head, trying to decide it Tannus was a threat. It snorted a deep oppressive sound that vibrated the surrounding area. Tannus remained still. Finally, it ambled off in search of a meal.

Tannus exhaled slowly, pausing to remember what he fought for. It wasn't to right the wrongs committed so long ago. It wasn't to get revenge against a brother who abandoned his faith and family to the depredations of insanity. Tannus fought to preserve the freedom of life and beauty of nature the universe offered. So much had been lost, he feared he might already be too late.

He had seen enough. Time was fleeting, especially when it took so long for him to heal. He'd been hiding on Wexanos recovering from injuries sustained fighting Amongeratix on Crimeat. More time wasted while plots thickened. It wouldn't be long now before Amongeratix was ready to make his final move and unleash the full power of his hatred. Tannus was going to need old allies if he hoped to prevail. Picking himself up, he brushed the loose grass from his clothes and turned back up the mountain path. He had an old friend he needed to see.

FIVE

3212 A.G. (After Gods), Tenemenah, planet An'kuruku.

"It is not safe," Mistress Kaline repeated more forcefully.

Mollock slumped back into the frail wooden chair in frustration. His unkempt hair kept drooping across his face, making him appear foolish. "I can judge for myself. I've been on my own for far longer than you've drawn breath."

She rounded on him, fury creasing her face. "It's a wonder you managed to live so long! This is no game, Mollock. The Prefects want all of us dead, spectacles in the arena to show the people who rules Tenemenah. Your head will grace the end of a pike if you don't do as we instruct."

"I have no interest or reason to listen to you," he replied flatly.

Kaline had ignored his previous attempts at questioning, refusing to allow even the tiniest hint of her true identity. She'd frustrated his attempts at being charming, which, admittedly, were few. Mollock was a solitary man by necessity, and the people of An'kuruku seldom trusted outlanders.

She snorted frustration. "Listen to me. We are trying to help you. An'kuruku is not a friendly place. There is more here than you know. A strange power is rumored to control the north. The government allows the Prefecture to do as it wants. Sickness inhabits our deserts. The people are in need of salvation, Mollock. Where are the spirits of the gods? Are we abandoned now at our greatest hour of need?"

He watched her suspiciously. "You ask questions no mortal should know the answer to. Be careful of this path you choose, Kaline. Once you start down it, there will be no turning aside, no friendly diversion to remind you that you have gone too far. The path will consume you until only a shell remains."

"What have you seen, Mollock Bolle?" she asked quietly. "There is torment in your eyes and sorrow lacing your words."

The others shuffled away, leaving the pair to speak alone.

"Please, Mollock, I need to know," she urged.

He tried to stay strong. "Give me a reason I should trust you."

She sighed, as if contemplating whether to tell the truth or not. "Very well. You ask for trust. I give you this. I work for an organization entrenched in every aspect of society. We represent the interests of the people, not the inflated government establishment that seeks to keep us blind to the truth. We are the strength behind a billion voices without a forum to address their concerns.

"The Conclave and its Inquisition thugs rule only through strength. Those who dissent against the status quo are rounded up and branded heretic or worse. Where is the justice the Cardinal Seniorus preaches? Where are our rights adjudicated for the good of all humanity, not the greedy fingers of a delicate few?"

"You speak of treason," Mollock whispered, eyes widened with shock.

"I speak from my heart. All we want is the right to let our voices be heard, not shunned into darkened alleys or forgotten times."

"I think I should leave now. I will take my chances with the Prefects," he said slowly.

Kaline's eyes flared with quiet rage. "Go, and you'll be dead before you leave this street. Prefects are scouring this neighborhood for you. There is no way you can last long enough to find the freedom you seek."

"The choice is mine. You speak of equality and free will, yet you threaten me with captivity for not agreeing to your principles. Truth is a double-edged sword, Kaline, not a power toy to dangle in front of men who refuse to back down."

He rose and headed for the door.

"I know who you are," she stated as his hand hovered over the door panel.

Mollock paused, dreading the words that followed.

"You didn't think it was chance that crossed our paths did you? We were searching for you, Mollock Bolle. Searching for nearly two years. I will admit that, at first, I found the stories of you embellished at best. No one has seen one of the gods in three thousand years. That you of all people could stumble upon one in the middle of the black mountains of Lethendweil was too much to believe. Until," she paused as he slowly turned, "Until one of our contacts in the Inquisition told us of two others who had been taken into custody.

"These men were secured back to Vau Prime, isolated from the rest of humanity for the sole crime of knowing what they shouldn't. Yet you escaped. Mollock, my organization knows you found one of the gods. We know you were hunted by one of the Three for the last fifty years and that you barely escaped here with your life. We know the pain and torment your unwanted knowledge has caused you, the indignant suffering from knowing too much."

Her eyes softened slightly; the faintest trace of a tear forming. "Mollock, I am here to help, not harm you."

Bitter memories mocked him suddenly. Visions of things he shouldn't have seen. Explaining to anyone, even himself on the best of days, was difficult. Was the being he found in that cave under Reven really a god? He wasn't sure he wanted to know, despite his deeply rooted feelings revolving around the matter. He'd had an ally in Elisa for a while. Granted, she was a reluctant companion born from tragedy. She knew the truth but chose to ignore it by finding her way to the bottom of a bottle each night. Mollock was alone again because of it. Alone. Struggling to comprehend all the events leading him up to this one point.

In the end, he wasn't sure who he could trust, if anyone. A solitary lifestyle wasn't for him however, and that first inkling of familiarity crept into his mind. Would it be so wrong to place trust in someone? There was but one way to find out

"How would you know what I saw when I do not know myself?" he asked, his mouth dry. "I was a simple prospector, long ago. I didn't care for the gods or the Conclave. Life was simple. I went to war when I was still young and came back a changed man. Fenrin, my best friend, and I went looking to make our fortunes in the dark places no one else dared look. How foolish we were then. Life may have been simple, but it held foul twists neither of us saw coming.

"Fenrin took ill and left me to my business. The work was hard, the profit minimal, but I enjoyed it. I enjoyed using my hands to find rather than destroy. Killing was not for me. I lost the stomach for it quickly. But the earth! I took pleasure in sifting through the ancient ground. Little did I know where it would lead me." He paused, unwanted memories toying with his mind."

Kaline sat across from him, devouring his every word as her mind raced through infinite possibilities.

"Rumor said the Plateau had one of the wealthiest deposits of gems. I should have known better. Rumors are a foolish man's dreams given birth. If such treasure truly existed, why had no one bothered to claim it before? The question only came to me long after I went to make my fortunes. Most of the Plateau is honeycombed. At least half of the tunnels haven't seen life in centuries. I took that as a good sign, ignoring the foreboding in my heart. Something didn't feel right, but I wasn't about to abandon my quest so close to the end.

He smirked. "I found the tunnel by accident, you know? A hasty wall had been constructed to conceal the entrance. I was taking a water break when I leaned back into it. The wall gave way. Once the dust settled, I was able to see a very dull light coming from the end of the tunnel. I was miles underground. There was no way a light source could exist so far down. Curious, I followed the tunnel into the chamber. It was empty but for one thing. A giant sarcophagus filled the center of the chamber."

"I gathered my courage and went to see just what I had discovered. The top was made of a glass-like material, so I was able to look down. I was shocked. Inside was one of the most serene and perfect-looking people I had ever seen! Fifteen feet tall if I'm a foot, I knew what I was seeing. This could only be one of the gods. They hadn't been destroyed at all. The Conclave spread lies and misdirection to keep us occupied. I was actually looking at a god."

Mollock paused to take the water bottle Kaline kindly offered. He failed to notice the hungry look in her eyes. "The body was the image of perfection. I reached down to wipe away dust from the glass. Then my world changed. I must have triggered some sort of silent alarm that activated the chamber's defense mechanism. Creatures of shadow dropped from the ceiling. They broke free from thousands of years of rock. I was terrified. Such monstrosities should not exist. I ran.

"My light seemed to keep them at bay, giving me enough time to flee back up the tunnel. I heard their claws scraping the stone, their breath ragged above my own. I smelled their rage down to my marrow and knew true horror for the first time. My legs burned, but I couldn't stop. The shadows would tear me apart if I did. I don't know what kept me going as I wound through the labyrinth to the surface. Perhaps it was nothing more than vain self-preservation. Regardless, I reached the blissful kiss of daylight, and the shadows did not follow."

"In my foolishness, I believed I was safe. I turned and studied them. Each time I thought I was able to make out a limb or body part, the shadows shifted, distorting my view. They roiled and hissed ever a step inside the dark warmth of the tunnel. Instincts told me to run, but my pride had been wounded. I stayed and taunted them. They came for me when the sun dropped below the rim of the mountains.

"My camp was destroyed. My pack animals were slaughtered. The shadows devoured everything of mine they could, almost as if they meant to erase me from existence. I ran again. Somehow, I made my way down to the city of Reven. Deep in the mountainside loading bays, I snuck aboard an outbound transport and escaped. Again, I did not believe the shadows could find me, and again I was wrong. Innocent people died. They were men and women I had known for years; their only crime was aiding me. I ruined so many lives with my arrogance."

He rubbed the tears from his tired eyes. "I went into those caves looking for gems. What I found distorts reality. The truth I learned should not be known."

Mistress Kaline edged closer. She needed to know more. Needed to know if he was the one they'd been waiting for. "Mollock, you do not need to suffer alone. We know what you found. We can help."

"Help what?" He snorted derisively. "My life is ruined because of my greed. I have been hunted for so long I know nothing else. What can you possibly give me to ease the pain of knowing I will never be able to return to what I once was?"

She lacked the answers he so desperately needed. Not that it mattered. Kaline, after listening to his story, was absolutely convinced Mollock Bolle was the one they'd been sent to An'kuruku to await. All she needed to do was push him in the proper direction and the future course of actions she needed to happen would begin.

"Suffering is not exclusive to you. We all have suffered, and our list of grievances grows daily. When will it be enough? When will the common man be allowed to grow, to develop to his true potential? We deserve so much more than the scraps handed down by the Conclave and its puppets. You deserve more."

"No, I don't. This life is what I deserve," he argued back.

"Your potential was stolen, Mollock. Do not deny yourself the truth in this. The gods are petty reflections of ruined greatness. Man rules the universe now, but ever are we shackled under the oppressive ignorance of the Conclave. Do you truly believe the Cardinal Seniorus sits in her lavish palace thinking of the common man's suffering? I doubt she had even heard of Crimeat until two years past."

Mollock shook his head. "She has nothing to do with me. I am trapped in perdition. There is no way out."

"Destiny is what we make of it, not the whim of a dusty god bereft of worship. Our organization seeks only to gain the ability to rule ourselves as we see fit, not to overthrow the Conclave or usurp power. Leave the power struggles and political positioning for those on Vau Prime. Is it not ironic that the ones who dictate what we should do with our lives are so far removed they have lost focus in what is good?"

"You speak treason," Mollock told her.

Kaline's cheeks flushed crimson. "I speak of liberty! The Prefects hunting you do so because their Inquisition masters drive the whip, not for any crimes you commit or offenses you make here. The universe runs on power. The Conclave has taken all of it from us, and we are forced to beg for scraps, pretending to be proud and distinguished from lesser races!"

She stopped suddenly. Her hair was slightly disheveled. "Can you tell me what harm comes from being free, truly free to make decisions for ourselves? There was a time when the Conclave was no more than one man's fancy. Let the Cardinals rule, but give us the power to choose our own destiny. That is all we seek."

"Dreams," he said as she fell silent.

Taken off guard, Kaline asked, "What?"

Mollock smiled. "I was once asked what I dreamed of. My answer was winter. I didn't know what that meant at the time, but I later learned my dreams were a sort of premonition for my future. What can you offer a man other than dreams?"

"A future."

He considered the answer. The future was a dark place inhabited by dreamers whose grasp on reality weakened with each passing day. There was no future other than the one he set for himself five decades ago. Ashes stood where possibility once held promise. Mollock was alone. He knew that and had come to accept it.

Kaline saw the doubt in his eyes. Her best arguments fell on deaf ears, despite pouring out the very depths of her soul. Internal conflicts forced themselves to be known. Mollock had the potential to become an asset to her cause, but he was also her greatest liability. He was hunted still, though he failed to realize it.

"Regrets haunt you, and you struggle to find a way clear. I can read your dejection in your eyes. The slump of your shoulders. We can make a better way, Mollock."

"I've heard these arguments before, Kaline. Words do not sway me as they once might have. You shouldn't get involved with me. Everything I touch becomes cursed."

She exhaled slowly, frustrations growing deeper. "It is not a curse to live. There are thousands just like you in need of guidance. They require strength of will to see them through the dark times the Conclave seems intent on dragging us through. You can help them. Let your voice be heard, Mollock. The time has come for you to stop hiding in caves and dark alleys. Open your heart, and let your words ride the morning winds!"

He sighed, familiar defeat holding him down. "You waste your time. This is my life now. I accept that. The gods haunt my every step. I can feel them reaching out to me from their graves. Leave me be. Find another."

Kaline frowned, her course of action already set. "That being you found in the cave was not a god, Mollock. Man only calls them that because we can think of no better name."

"What do you mean?" he asked hesitantly.

Kaline leaned close enough for him to smell her rose-scented skin and whispered in his ear. His eyes flew wide from shock.

The empty bottle rolled off the table and shattered across the wooden floor. Elisa groaned softly, her head down on the table amidst old food stains and recently spilled *valo*, a potent local alcohol brewed from the red cactus flower. Ah'muf looked up from his place behind the bar and slowly shook his head. It was a sight he was becoming more accustomed to seeing lately.

Throwing a damp hand towel over his shoulder, Ah'muf wormed through the crowd to her. "*Farisi*, you drink too much. One day it will be the death of you."

She laughed a dark and brooding sound. Ah'muf sighed. He liked the foreign woman with the flame-colored hair but she was becoming too much of a liability. Already people asked too many questions about her. His reputation was being tarnished by caring for her. Still, loyalty was a powerful tool, and Elisa had earned his not long after she'd arrived on An'kuruku when she'd stopped three would be robbers from fleecing his purse strings. Ah'muf owed her.

"Come, you need to get some sleep," he told her softly and gently hefted her to her feet. Not a large woman, Elisa was easily half-carried up the creaking stairs to the room that had become her home.

Ah'muf lay her down on an old bed that smelled stale. Dust puffed on impact. He briefly considered covering her but decided it would only make more of mess if she decided to throw up later. He left her on top of the sheets and turned back to the door.

"Stay."

He halted, hand an inch from the knob. Ah'muf looked back at her with sadness in his eyes. She was far too pale for his liking despite the exotic quality in her features. Ah'muf had once prided himself on having integrity above reproach. He wasn't foolish enough to ignore the desire in his loins for her, but he didn't wish such a thing in her present condition.

"You know I cannot, *farisi*. It is not your heart speaking," he replied quietly.

Ah'muf closed the door behind him. He could already hear her snoring.

An'kuruku's sun was already high in the sky, burning down across the deserts. Dust devils whipped up, throwing sand and loose vegetation recklessly. The hottest summer days became unbearable shortly after sunrise. Exposed flesh sizzled and blistered within minutes of exposure. Only the foolish or desperate moved during the heat. Much of Tenemenah shut down during summer days. Most, but not all. Prefects continued to patrol and administer their brand of justice, all under the watchful yet largely disinterested eyes of the Inquisition.

Waves of heat shimmering on the surface looked like a space fighter's idling engines. Elisa groaned and threw an arm up to cover her face, bright light blinding her red-streaked eyes. Her body was sore and still exhausted. Most of last night was a blank space in her memory, though she vaguely remembered offering to let Ah'muf share her bed. Elisa's face flushed with embarrassment.

Reluctantly, she rolled out of bed. The foul smell of her clothes made her wince. Elisa was growing to accept disappointment. Her life had gone miserably wrong since the Bloody Man. Raw emotion drove her actions, but she was starting to discover that even that wasn't enough. She had fallen to self-loathing. Too many nights disappeared at the bottom of a bottle. Elisa staggered over to the small stand along the far wall and looked deeply into the dirty mirror. The face looking back couldn't have been hers. Once, she had been considered a beautiful woman. Decades of anger and bitter misery left her a broken shell.

She knew there was a better life. Finding it proved problematic. It wasn't until she realized the animosity she carried for the Bloody Man had twisted her into a monster herself that Elisa decided to try and change. Unfortunately, the task was harder than the effort she put forth. One doesn't simply wake up and change after decades of following a dark road. She was trapped in a malicious spiral without an escape route.

Hopelessness crept into her consciousness. Elisa grabbed her towel and hygiene items and headed down to public baths Ah'muf kept in the basement. Perhaps a good scrubbing would ease the emotional pain. Then she had to apologize to Ah'muf. He was a good man, for a desert dweller, and deserved to be treated better. Elisa concealed most of her weapons, taking only a curved blade for protection. It was a local weapon made with cheap steel but one she favored, especially for a closed-in fight. Not that she expected to get into a brawl in the middle of the baths, but caution was a lesson not forgotten once learned the hard way.

Thankfully, most of the hallways were empty. People were either too exhausted to move or found better vocations to occupy their time. Elisa couldn't remember the last time she felt the touch of another person, tasted the longing warmth in a kiss. The need lessened with age, though a part of her regretted not having children. She often wondered if having a daughter of her own would help ease her suffering. But bringing a child into this life only subjected it to an endless series of disappointments and regrets. Better to stand alone than take another life on her mirthless journey.

Elisa felt the heat of the baths before she opened the teak door. Familiar fragrances enticed her senses, threatening to steal away her tension and leave her relaxed. She smiled through her thin lips and gently closed the door behind her. The baths were empty, thankfully. Two large pools easily able to hold fifty people filled the massive room. Alabaster columns pushed the ceiling higher than normal, finishing with a large skylight that was shaded often. Exotic plants and potted trees reminded her of the Great Barrier Jungle on Crimeat but without the insects and predatory animals trying to kill her.

The pool on the right bled steam in endless clouds while the pool on the left remained placid and cool. Sweat instantly covered her. Elisa allowed her eyes to close, relishing the feeling. Marble benches lined the far wall, well away from the effects of the steam. Cushions and plush pillows filled a small room just off the main bath, a place to relax before finding the busy day. Elisa could do without feeling like royalty. Anything was worth passing up for the luxury of immersing in the hot pool and feeling days' worth of stink and grime wash away.

She placed her towel in one of the small shelves on the near wall and stripped. Her clothes were foul and in need of washing, but that could wait. Naked, Elisa padded over to the bank of showers Ah'muf had installed. The water was cold. Gooseflesh spread across her body as tiny rivers of brown ran down the drain. She already felt slightly better when she turned the shower off and slid into the steaming bath.

Elisa hissed with the steam as the heat rushed through her. The mechanics of the pool were lost on her, not having a head for technology, but she was able to figure out that the hot bath was powered by a strange combination of the sun and a black liquid found in the deepest parts of the desert. Regardless, she could spend an entire day in the pool. Elisa tipped her head back on the checkered tile edge and closed her eyes again.

She didn't know how long passed before the quiet groan of the door opening disturbed her. Elisa tensed reflexively, her eyes opening and instantly going to the hilt of her dagger just sticking out from under her clothes. A pair of men barreled into the room, talking loudly. One barked laughter at the other's joke before setting his leering gaze on Elisa. She frowned. Fending off unwanted advances was not how she had intended to spend the rest of the day.

"My, my, look at this," the larger one sneered. The dark hair on his chest was thick enough to remind Elisa of a bear. "All alone, are you, pretty?"

"Mind your business. I was just getting out," she warned.

They splashed into the bath. "Nonsense. Join us for a spell. Been a while since we had the company of a lovely woman."

"I'm not interested," Elisa said and started to climb out.

The bigger man snarled, his mood instantly darkening. "Lucky for you, we don't care."

Only now did Elisa realize neither man was nude. They still wore shorts and sword belts. Prefects! She fought the urge to panic. The larger man saw realization dawn on her and moved to cut her off. Not that she could do much naked. Elisa needed to get to her dagger. Prefects were known to execute their own verdicts without the contrivances of a trial.

"How about you sit back down? We only want to talk," the smaller one said. His hand dangled close to the saber hilt.

Elisa studied each man, searching for any exploitable weakness. She knew there was little chance of taking both before they ran her through, but she had a weapon neither man anticipated correctly: her body. Elisa squared off on them, back to the edge of the bath. Water dripped from her breasts. The red patch of hair between her legs lay matted to her flesh, inviting. She placed her hands on her hips.

"You can talk from there, Prefect," Elisa replied tersely.

The large one grew angrier. "Don't make this more difficult than it needs to be. We know who you are. You've avoided us for as long as possible."

"Now it is time to answer for your crimes," the smaller added.

"What crimes? I am a visitor to Tenemenah, no criminal in need of your foul illusion of justice. Let me go about my business, and you two can enjoy your bath together."

The smaller one bit back a smile, his eyes drifting down to her sex. "I'd have more of a time with you in the bath, pretty."

"Enough of that," growled the other. "We came to arrest this woman on charges of sedition, not bandy temptations."

All the while, Elisa had been backing up, stopping only when she felt the reassuring limestone wall. "You'll need to do more than talk."

The large Prefect charged. Elisa kicked water up, temporarily blinding him. He rushed carelessly. Elisa sidestepped and used his momentum to slam his head down on the ledge. Blood fountained across the floor as she jumped off his back and dashed to her weapon before the second Prefect reacted.

"You'll pay for that, bitch," he told her and climbed out, saber in hand.

Elisa drew her dagger and dropped into a crouched fighting stance. "I'm not the pretty pet you think me."

Lacking the impetuousness of his peer, the second Prefect moved slower, stalking his prey. He raised his saber in a high guard and took a step forward. The larger man groaned, a shaky hand reaching up to the gash on his forehead. Blood ran down his face in sheets.

"Your friend doesn't look so good," Elisa taunted.

It worked. The smaller Prefect rushed her and swung his sword down for her neck. He aimed to cleave her to the heart. Elisa rushed at the same time, getting in under his guard. Her dagger punched deep into his ribcage. The Prefect gasped, a vicious wet sound, and staggered back. Elisa stabbed twice more. Each blow dug deeper towards his heart. She was rewarded on the fourth blow. The Prefect's eyes rolled white, and he dropped in a heap of cooling flesh.

Elisa knew it was only a matter of moments before the larger man recovered and realized what was happening. She collected the dead man's saber and turned to finish the fight. The big man looked up, his eyes glassy and unfocused. She swept down as hard as she could and struck his head from his shoulders. Exhausted, Elisa dropped the saber and sank down.

The horror of what she had just done settled in. She was no stranger to combat, but the gruesome scene played out around her was sickening. Blood tainted the waters, discolored the tiled floor. Her body trembled with a strange mixture of fatigue and giddiness. The ability to take another life so easily was intoxicating. She felt unprecedented power course through her. She also knew time was now her biggest enemy.

Elisa dressed quickly. More Prefects would be coming once these two were declared overdue. She had to hurry. Back in her room, she hurriedly packed her few belongings, strapped on her weapons and suddenly stopped. She had saved herself — for how long remained to be seen — but in doing so had placed Ah'muf in great danger. The kindness he extended her without any thought of being reciprocated had been abused by the dual killings in the baths.

Elisa now found a new dilemma confronting her. The decision was easier than she expected. She found Ah'muf behind his sandstone bar preparing to open the tavern. His eyes lit up for a moment before he noticed the blood-stained hands.

"*Farisi*, what has happened?" he asked with genuine concern.

She swallowed hard. "Ah'muf, this will not be easy for you to hear, nor is it easy for me to tell, but you must hear it."

He set the familiar hand towel down and folded his arms across his thin chest. "So like the desert spider. You wait until the precise moment to strike, and it is always lethal when you do. I dread your next words without knowing why."

"A pair of Prefects found me in the baths. They tried to arrest me," she left out the implied. Prefects killed who they arrested. "I got them first. The bodies are down there."

"What have you done?" he gasped.

"What I had to," Elisa said crisply.

Ah'muf tweaked his moustache nervously. "You cannot stay here *farisi*. Others will soon come looking."

"No, Ah'muf, it is worse. I've put you in danger as well. The Prefects will think you are hiding me and will arrest you. It's only a matter of time before they take you away to the Arena. You must leave with me."

His put his hands wide in a helpless gesture. "Leave? Now? This is all I know, *farisi*. I cannot abandon the only life I have. I am not like you."

"Ah'muf, they will come to kill you. I can't keep you safe," she said mournfully. "The Prefects will take their vengeance out on you. Please, come with me while we still have a little time."

Ah'muf was torn. "Decisions such as this are not to be made lightly. Would you ask me to throw away all I have done with my life? I am not a young man."

"Are you willing to risk it by staying? The Prefects lack mercy. I…I don't want to see you come to a foul end."

He paused. Elisa gave him no more time. She adjusted her pack and started towards the back door. "I'll not return, Ah'muf, but I wish you good fortune. Thank you for everything you have done. It has been a long time since anyone showed me genuine kindness."

She made it to the door before he called, "*Farisi,* wait. I will come with you."

SIX

3212 A.G. (After Gods), Krenz, planet Vau Prime.

The sharp click of boot heels marching down the marble corridor reminded Tolde of a time long ago when he had first made this journey. Nothing had changed physically, despite the emotional scars in his psyche. Black armored guards lined the hall leading to the Inquisitor General's quarters. Emblems and mementos of previous generals stood proudly displayed on waist-high pedestals. Tolde found it difficult to be concerned with trivial items of the past.

Inquisitor General Nye was almost a complete opposite of his predecessor, Farius Graeme. Tolde had considered Graeme a mentor and a great man. Nye lacked many of the qualities necessary to endear his order to him. Much had changed in the Inquisition since Nye came into power. Hunters were more common. Occasional arrests for heresy were expunged like cancer from the Order. Security measures were tripled, and an unhealthy air of mistrust clung to every conversation.

The Inquisition had grown dark and cold, giving Tolde cause to wonder whether it was past time to abandon his charge and find a quieter life away from the unending conspiracies of Vau Prime.

"You have much on your mind."

He glanced at Luma Kai. "One should not take a summons to the Inquisitor General's office lightly. The last time I was here was when I was sent after Amongeratix. I do not wish so traumatic a repeat."

"Times have changed, Tolde. We must do as ordered. Without discipline, the Order is nothing," Luma reminded him, practically quoting regulations.

Two years, and he still didn't fully trust Luma — or any other Hunter, for that matter. They derived too much pleasure from chasing down comrades. Power corrupted the higher echelons, and it bled down to the lowest rank. The Office of Heretical Persecution was the most paranoid of the bunch.

He paused, regretting the eager condemnation he thrust upon her. Luma Kai was not a bad woman. She put her heart into her work but did so with a deep sense of honor. Tolde wanted to think she would stand with him if events conspired against him, but he was still too unsure to give her his faith.

"This will not end well," was all he replied.

They were admitted into the antechamber without fanfare, and the door was closed behind them. No one waited, a fact Tolde found alarming. The head of the Order should never be left alone to his devices, not even in the sanctity of her personal chambers. Tolde looked down at the single blue-tinged rose in the vase on the small table in the center of the room and took a measure of hope. The rose had long been the symbolic purity of the Order, incorruptible and steadfast.

Luma swept her gaze around the chamber in amazement. She'd rarely been close enough to see the Inquisitor General, much less stand in audience. The sheer simplicity of her surroundings surprised her. Luma had expected one of most powerful men in the universe to have a larger sense of style. The table was the only decoration.

"I would offer you to make yourselves comfortable, but that is not the reason for this audience," Nye said upon entering the antechamber.

"Inquisitor General," they said in unison.

He waved them off. "Please, we can abandon formality just this once."

Tolde and Luma patiently waited.

Nye measured each silently before addressing them again. "Senior Inquisitor Breed, how long has it been since Farius Graeme first summoned you to stop the Three?"

"A very long time, sir," Tolde said.

"Indeed. You have served the Order well in the time since. I wish more men were as dedicated as you have been. Dark times edge our horizon," he paused as if forgetting himself, "but that can wait. In honor of your tireless service to the Order, I am officially promoting you to Grand Inquisitor, a promotion I believe is long overdue."

Tolde was stunned. Until now, he had been left with the suspicion that his service was an embarrassment. The events on Crimeat were still shunned from conversation in the capital.

"I…thank you, sir," he finally stammered.

"Your orders will come down by tomorrow," Nye said quickly while momentum was still his. "We know the Three were not defeated on Crimeat. Increased military presence on the planet confirms the insurrection is finished, but all traces of the Three have vanished. This presents us with difficult choices. We could squander manpower and money sending Inquisitors across the universe in a vain hunt, or we sit idly waiting for one of them to resurface, by which time it would already be too late to avoid full blown engagement.

"As of now, most of the population does not believe the Three anything more than fanciful tales to scare children or myths preached by the very old. I want to keep it that way. The Three represent dangers we are not prepared to deal with."

"Pardon, Inquisitor General, but I disagree," Tolde said before realizing it.

Nye's eyes drew down sharply. "In what way?"

"The Three are dangerous to the point they pose a liability to every sentient being under Conclave protection. Twice I have battled Amongeratix and lived. Twice I have seen men and women twisted by lies to do his foul bidding. We need to inform the population before more are subsumed."

"And be made into court jesters by our doubters? We aren't so well liked to have that choice."

"It will be worse should the truth ever escape. People will demand answers for having such horror concealed from them for so long," Tolde pressed.

Nye finally smiled. "There is more to the gods than you know, Breed. Only a very few know the depths of the truth, and it is not a fact I ever wanted. Once you are enlightened, your view on things changes. The Three must remain hidden. That is my final order. Mankind is young still, deemed incapable of the knowledge that could tear the fabric of reality asunder. I will not have my name sullied throughout history due to certain brashness that could easily be avoided. Don't rock the boat, Breed."

Tolde lowered his chin slightly, conceding the point.

"Our resources are stretched thin. The Conclave doesn't run the universe on brute force and has traditionally kept military power low. I believe, as does the Cardinal Seniorus, that war is unavoidable if steps aren't taken to mitigate it now. New intelligence confirms one of the so called dark council from Lethendweil has been spotted on Hawker's Gate running a brothel and gambling den. My sources tell me it is no more than cover for some nefarious plot."

Nye waited to see if he had hooked the Hunters. "Her name is Presha Von, and she is a known associate of Ursal Prowl."

Tolde stiffened immediately. He'd wished the disgraced Inquisitor had met a foul end, but fate conspired against him. Prowl had nearly killed him and was responsible for orchestrating the entire insurrection on Crimeat. Tolde privately suspected the man had a hand in freeing Amongeratix from the Conclave prison on Prophet Isle. He didn't need to hear the next part. If they found Von, they could find Prowl. Retribution might not be so far away as he once believed.

Nye continued. "Use caution; my instincts tell me there is more to this affair than what we have seen. Inquisitor Prowl was a dangerous opponent the first time. I fear he has only grown more powerful over the last two years."

"What are your orders for Von, sir?" Luma Kai asked evenly.

"Capture if possible. Terminate otherwise. I can't afford to have rogue enemy agents loose in the universe, not with the Three still secluded from our eyes and ears."

Tolde failed to conceal his frown. The Three ever lurked just beyond grasp, haunting shadows and dreams while lives whittled away in vain pursuit. Insanity beckoned him closer. He wanted the matter concluded but refused to retire until the threat had been neutralized for good. Amongeratix plagued his thoughts, ruining any good that might have come from Tolde's life.

"It is also possible the Three are active in that region," Tolde countered. His thoughts led him to a very dark place he dared not go. "Amongeratix has been known to attract those of lesser quality. I would like to request Prekhauten Guard support."

Nye stiffened, the request unanticipated. "To capture a single woman? I think you overestimate her ability."

"I've learned prudence when dealing with those associated with the Three. The mistakes of the past could come back," Tolde reinforced his request. "The Prekhautens add a dangerous element most people are unwilling to confront."

"General Strannan is busy developing battle plans on numerous fronts. I doubt he can spare many to support your task." Nye turned to stare out of the large bay windows, scarcely noticing the endless stream of lights from passing air cars down Redemption Boulevard. "If I recall correctly, the Guards weren't of much use on Crimeat."

"They spent most of their effort confronting heretic Guardsmen, but it was not their choosing. I was able to secure a squad in my assault on Reven. Sergeant Major Matthias was a great asset. I would like to request him again."

It was Nye's turn to frown. "Matthias was relieved of command and force retired. As senior ranking man on the ground, it was his responsibility to ensure all went well. He failed."

"He was wrongly accused. Matthias did his duty and beyond." Tolde was furious. The thought of his closest ally abandoned by the cruel indifference of political manipulations was a travesty to everything the Inquisition stood for.

"Mind your tongue," Nye snapped. "I am in no position to indulge in your desires. We are on a precipice, Grand Inquisitor. Our actions today will either avert the coming war or plunge the universe into pure chaos.

"The Inquisition has ever stood watch against the dark powers in the universe, but even now we fail," Nye continued before either could speak. "There is more going on than you know. Rumors have reached me of a self-styled prophet on An'kuruku who has supposedly seen one of the gods. He preaches against them. Others have already been silenced before they were able to cause too much damage."

Luma interrupted. "But the gods have no physical forms. They were destroyed three thousand years ago."

"There is much you do not know. Certain truths have been withheld — for the good of all humanity, of course. The gods still exist, Inquisitor Kai. They sleep, slowly recovering until they are ready to reclaim what was once theirs. We are stewards, defenders of faith the universe will be theirs once again; that much is undeniable. Until then, the burden of maintaining civility and order rests upon our shoulders."

Tolde absently rubbed his chin. The convenience of this sudden information left him with more doubts. "Why keep such information private? Countless lives stand to be enriched from the truth of the gods."

"That decision was made long before any of us," Nye answered. "Think what damage might be possible if everyone knew the gods still had physical form. Men and women would spend lifetimes trying to seek them out, for good or bad. Intent is easily turned to transgression under the best of circumstances. No, better the gods remain a myth of the past. The Conclave fills any void of faith."

"But it is a lie," Luma exhaled.

Nye threw her a sharp glare. "Truths are never forthright. Some are necessary if we are to continue as a society."

"The battle of Occanum?" Tolde asked.

"Most certainly happened," Nye said swiftly. "Archeologists have enough evidence to support Conclave doctrine. Rather than destroying themselves, the gods were able to preserve themselves in a form of suspended animation. Until recently, we have been unable to discover any. The one on Crimeat was found roughly the same time Amongeratix first escaped from Keltoo."

"Where is it now?"

Nye offered a wry grin. "Safe. Our top scientists are trying to figure out how to transport it back to Vau Prime. Every attempt thus far has been aborted. The technology levels the gods possessed remain far above the limits of our understanding."

Too many coincidences sparked Tolde's suspicion. "What of this prophet? Does he play a part?"

"He is harmless. Local Inquisitors are monitoring him closely should he step beyond the mannered constraints of acceptable heresy. He is not your concern. Go to Hawker's Gate and bring me Presha Von. She holds the answers to finding Prowl and possibly the Three. As to your previous request, I will contact Prekhauten headquarters. I'm sure I can procure some support for you. Now go; there is much we all need to do."

Tolde and Luma bowed and excused themselves, leaving Alain Nye brooding in his quiet thoughts. His narrowed eyes never left their backs, even after the doors closed. Tolde's questions came too close to uncovering truths Nye was unwilling to part with. Dangers lurked from all angles, and he was unsure who he could trust.

"You have much on your mind."

Tolde slowly broke his gaze from his half-empty glass to find Luma Kai staring intently. Her look of concern irritated him for reasons he couldn't yet place.

"We are being used, Luma. The Inquisitor General was too casual with the information he gave. I don't trust his intentions."

Luma shook her head. "He is the highest of our Order. What possible reason for deception could he have?"

"Ursal Prowl changed everything. Inquisitors investigate their peers when once we focused on heresy. Then there was the term he used, acceptable heresy. We are Hunters, Luma. When have you heard of such a thing?"

"There's nothing in our doctrine to suggest any heresy acceptable. That doesn't mean he is keeping anything from us, Tolde. His office is responsible for more than just the wants and needs of a handful of Inquisitors."

Tolde decided that nothing he was going to say was capable of arousing like suspicion in Luma, so he quickly dropped the subject lest they begin accusing each other. "At least he was able to get us a compliment of Prekhautens."

"Do you think we are going to need them? Hawker's Gate is heavily populated. I can't see Presha Von risking a full-blown firefight with so many civilians around her."

"Do not underestimate her. She was a worthy enemy on Crimeat, though one behind the scenes. She was one of the main proponents of the insurrection against the ruling council of nobles. The woman is a venomous snake."

"What have you gotten me involved in, Grand Inquisitor?" she asked, a hint of unusual laughter tugging the corners of her mouth up.

Tolde had managed to ignore his experiences on Crimeat until now. Circumstances didn't allow for many secrets between them, so he reluctantly began the tale. Luma sat wide-eyed through most of it, never once interrupting. She found much of the take too fanciful to be true despite knowing Tolde to be one of the most honest men she had ever worked with. Regardless, the tale of godlings and traitors left her feeling hollow inside. Luma Kai suddenly realized she was in over her head.

Jers nearly cried when he found out they'd been reassigned to working with Inquisitor Breed again. The recipient of numerous commendations and even a battlefield promotion, Jers was no coward. He just knew a bad thing when he saw it, and Breed was a bad thing. He passed Haggle a warning look as they boarded the frigate docked in the Prekhauten shipyards orbiting Vau Prime. The bigger Guardsman smirked and kept walking. It was a long ride to Hawker's Gate.

"Look at them, sitting there talking like its nothing," he said disapprovingly.

Haggle's eyebrow arched. "Why don't you go over and ask them to stop?"

"Shut it, Haggle. I'm in no mood for your shit," Jers warned.

Annalilly threw a slightly stale dinner roll at him. "Shut it yourself, Jers. I've had enough of your superstitious nonsense. The Guard says we deploy, we deploy. No questions asked, and I don't give a damn who we work with. Besides, this Breed is alright by me. He saved all our asses back on Crimeat."

"What about the sergeant major?"

Her eyes hardened. "Keep his name out of your mouth. Wasn't the Inquisitor's fault. Matthias got messed over because of those cardinals in the Conclave."

The anger lacing her words was enough to stall the conversation. Annalilly rubbed one of the lightning bolt tattoos and smiled. "Anyone up for a game of dice? We've been cooped up on this ship long enough for me to take your hard-earned money."

Beve looked up suddenly, his expression sullen but otherwise unreadable. "I will play," he said with a deep, rumbling voice.

"I'm out," Jers said instantly. "Beve's got the gods' own luck."

Haggle cracked his knuckles. "I'm not afraid of big old Beve."

The heavy weapons specialist shrugged. "It's your money."

Annalilly offered a sly grin and dropped the dice on the metal table.

Sergeant Fies watched his newly promoted sergeant with a mixture of interest and admonishment. He frowned on the way Annalilly continued to interact with her squad like she was still a corporal. Noncommissioned officers required greater discipline than the regular rank and file Guard. There would be a time, possibly in the near future, when she was going to have to knowingly send one or some of her Guards to their deaths. It was a cold inevitability every leader had to face. Fies doubted she was ready.

Deciding against undermining her authority, Fies left Annalilly to her games. New sergeants needed some way of bonding with their Guards, some event shared with no others. He fondly recalled his baptism by fire so many years ago as he made his way across the mess deck to where the Inquisitors sat. Not Inquisitors, he reminded himself; they were Hunters.

"Do you mind if I join you?" he asked hesitantly.

Tolde offered a half smile and nudged a chair out with his boot. "Not at all, Sergeant." He waited until Fies was settled before formally introducing him to Luma. "Luma Kai, this is Sergeant Fies of the Prekhauten Guard. He and I served together on Crimeat. There are few others I would entrust this mission with."

"A pleasure," she said, tipping her head slightly.

Fies grinned. "I fear the Inquisitor overstates my value. Plenty of good men and women would have jumped at this opportunity."

A clever lie, but one easily seen through. No one in their right mind *wanted* to go up against the Three. Especially not after the fallout from Crimeat. Luma saw Fies as more of a survivor than a recommended asset.

Tolde interrupted before either said something they might later come to regret. "We were just going over our mission brief. Your opinions are welcome."

You don't want my opinion. "Thank you, Inquisitor. My biggest concern is security. Hawker's Gate is large. It might as well be a city floating in space. There is no way our handful can secure the exits if this Von decides to flee. She's had time on the station. That makes it her territory and puts us at a substantial disadvantage."

"We have the Gate's schematics. Locking her down shouldn't prove difficult," Luma replied.

Tolde folded his arms across his chest and leaned back. "Nothing is as easy as we would like it to be. Presha Von is a dangerous enemy. Fies is right. She will have every opportunity to flee the moment she learns our frigate has docked."

"What do we do?" Luma asked, frustrated.

"I've had the captain reprogram our identification frequency. That will buy us a little time at least. Finding the gambling den may prove problematic. As you stated, Hawker's Gate is overly large."

Fies shook his head as if clearing away a random thought. "Don't we have any allies on the inside? That would make our lives much easier."

Tolde cracked a thin smile. "We do, indeed, at least according to Inquisition headquarters. I am reluctant to accept assistance without personally vetting them first."

He left the second part unsaid. Crimeat had left stains neither man was able to fully overcome. Fies had come home unexpectedly promoted and thrown into a much larger world while Tolde was left wondering the worst question possible: why? An endless stream of restless nights tormented him. Now he was heading back down a path he wished were different. Hawker's Gate. The previous administrator had been cooperative, but Tolde continued to maintain she was not what she presented. He knew next to nothing of the new administrator or the security situation. Both issues presented potentially insurmountable hurdles.

Luma seemed to read his mind. "What of the current administrator? Has he been told of our approach?"

"Assumedly, and for our sake I pray he hasn't been so foolish as to alert his security detachment," Tolde answered.

"I don't understand."

He turned to Luma. "Von will be watching for any signs or changed patterns."

"Two years is a long time to build a network," Fies added. "She'll have eyes everywhere. Our chances of catching her unaware are slim at best."

"Then we go in hard and take her out before she knows what is happening," Luma insisted. Years of field time as a Hunter left her jaded against any other approach than tackling the problem head-on.

"Our inside sources have narrowed down the location of her den, but that still won't be good enough," Tolde countered. "Sergeant, I suggest you have your men change out of their uniforms."

"Go civilian?" he asked.

Tolde nodded. "That will mitigate announcing our arrival to everyone on the station. We're walking a tight line on this one."

He considered telling Fies the truth he'd just learned about the gods, but the information was nearly too much for his own fragile mind. Testing the limits of faith was not wise days before a major operation, he concluded. Better to let Fies remain ignorant.

"I'll need to have the troops leave their rifles behind. Our tech will make us instantly recognizable," Fies said.

"Private security is everywhere," Luma told them. "It shouldn't be too hard to blend in, even with large caliber weapons. There are rumors of pirate gangs raiding shipping lanes. It's not implausible to believe Prekhauten weaponry is being used already."

Tolde didn't like the idea but found nothing to object over. "Rifles only. Leave the heavy weapons on the frigate."

Fies passed a glance over at Beve, wondering if the big man would put up a fight. Heavy weapons people were notorious for keeping their guns within reach. He contemplated leaving Beve on the ship but knew he was going to need every man he had to keep Von contained.

Tolde looked at each of his companions, leaders both and with considerable experience. His reservations dwindled the longer they planned. Tolde knew the force he'd managed to assemble was more than capable of completing the task successfully. His one concern stemmed from the uncertainty of the Three. Everything stood to fail if Amongeratix was on the station.

SEVEN

3212 A.G. (After Gods), Hawkers Gate, deep space.

Presha Von watched the busy room from her favorite place. Elevated above the main floor and concealed behind a large paned one-way window, she was able to watch the men and women intent on losing all their hard-earned money on gambling tables or at the behest of a tempting woman. Presha had learned the natural power she held over others long ago.

Born to a lower noble class, Presha had not grown up with many of the luxuries others on the council had. She'd been shunned by the privileged and impoverished alike trapped in the no man's land of the only moderately wealthy, scorn unwarranted in her eyes. Fate had seemed intent on denying her the one thing she truly desired: status. Presha had quickly learned the nobility's cutthroat manner, watching and waiting for the moment to unleash her vengeance. A pox had taken both of her parents when she was barely considered a woman. Reclaimators had swarmed in and taken everything, citing excessive debts to the kingdom.

Presha had been left penniless, homeless, an abandoned waif no one wanted, reduced to begging for scraps and constantly wondering where her next meal was coming from. For a time, she'd turned to selling her body. She'd been given a room with a bed and three hot meals daily in exchange for rendering the pleasures of the flesh. It was degrading work, work her mother would have found humiliating. Presha used it to make her stronger.

She had gone after the wealthy and powerful. Men or women, it didn't matter. Each person she slept with added to her slowly growing collection of information. Presha had methodically pursued the influential, ever with vengeance in her heart. She had wanted to tear down the established nobility and replace it with a more just, considerate ruling class. Her naivety had nearly proved her downfall.

Late one night, long after the last client had left and the house was shut down, Presha awakened to pure darkness and the harmonic whistling of a voice she could only describe as *angelic*. Presha slid from the cotton sheets and into her short satin night robe, the dark fabric was cool against her warm flesh. Opening her door, Presha poked her head into the hall. Nothing. She frowned. The source of the voice remained distant, as if the owner was protecting deep secrets. Presha thrived on secrets. Her innermost desires propelled her into the normally lit hall, now pitch black, and towards the back door.

She entered the back alley and froze. Familiar sights vanished while she watched. Buildings and streetlamps were swallowed by thick fog. Presha coughed, choking on the acidic tang in the air. Rows of thorns appeared once the fog cleared, marking a path she was sure she was meant to follow. They towered over her. She felt shrunken, insignificant against their indomitable mass. The sudden urge to flee back to her room gripped her. Presha turned to find a wall of thorns where her brothel had been a moment before. Confused, she had but one choice: to continue through the maze of thorns and find the source of the voice. Guided only by the light of a waning moon, Presha tightened her robe and pushed ahead.

"I must be dreaming," she muttered under her breath.

"You are not."

Presha's heart froze. The voice had been so close the very breath had tickled her nape. She spun but found nothing. She was still alone.

"Who said that?" she asked, confused.

"Come to me, Presha."

Planting both feet firmly in the cool dirt, Presha refused to move. "Show yourself!"

Hissing laughter echoed back, mocking her audacity. Anger swelled within her breast. Presha felt like that little girl all over again, scorned for being born low. She stormed into the maze, hungry to discover her tormentor and deliver her own special brand of justice.

Unseen things rustled in the branches, keeping pace with her. The fear of watchers made her move faster. Presha let eagerness get the best of caution. She was all but running now. The voice continued to sing, ever outside of the range of her grasp. Torches sprang to life all around. Shadows played across her face. The clouds parted, revealing a single hilltop in the distance. Ringed in ritual stones, she caught a glimpse of a tall figure in black. His left arm beckoned.

Presha ran. Crows cawed as if sensing a meal. She ducked under the oppressive flap of giant wings. The bird, unlike any she had ever seen, soared low before racing off in the opposite direction. Presha tried to get her bearings, but the hilltop was gone.

"This is impossible," she whispered. Tears choked her eyes. She felt helpless, weak.

Meters slowly passed. One hundred, two. Three hundred more she put behind before she heard the voice stop. Presha froze. Voices swirled around her. Some called her name. Others wailed in pain. Shadows moved within shadows. A single voice, the first she'd heard, changed its tune from haunting melody to hypnotic lullaby. Presha took another step before faltering. Her will waivered. Eyelids fluttered rapidly. Her heart raced.

A massive figure slowly emerged from the shadows. Nearly twice the size of a man, he towered over her lithe form. Presha's eyes glassed under his unrelenting stare. She dropped to her knees and lowered her head. No longer in control of her body or mind, Presha awaited her master.

The giant stopped a pace away and knelt. Bemusement dazzled in his jewel-like eyes. A thought sent waves of ecstasy coursing beneath her skin. Presha moaned softly through closed lips and untied her robe. The soft fabric slipped open, revealing her soft, pale breasts and dark nipples. The giant remained unimpressed.

Rising quickly, he commanded, "Come with me."

Presha obeyed. She followed the giant through the maze, uncaring of her lack of will and nakedness. Endless distance went by until her feet were sore and bleeding from a dozen small cuts. Sweat coated her body despite the coolness in the air. At last, she was led to the base of the hill and forced to climb. She faltered and fell. The giant growled under his breath and reached down for her. He set her down again once they gained the summit. Presha was brought to kneel, her robe slipping down past her shoulders.

Another figure emerged, this one scarcely taller than she was. Presha watched through dispassionate eyes. The trance of the lullaby still gripped her soul.

"Ah, good, you have arrived," the newcomer said with genuine gladness. "My overlarge friend is not one for words, so allow me. You have been brought to our attention, Presha Von. Powerful destiny can be yours if you succumb to your desires and let your soul free."

He released her from the spell with a small hand gesture. Presha gasped lungfuls of cold burning air. She looked up at the giant, impassive and motionless, and back to the man. Venom surged through her. "Who are you? Why am I here?"

She looked down at her naked body and rediscovered modesty. Presha hastily covered herself.

"All in good time," the man said. "You will have your answers, Presha, but first, indulge me. What is your darkest desire, the one so deep in the pit of your soul you don't dare utter it?"

"I have no reason to tell you." She remained indignant.

A false smile shone under his hood. "True, but you shouldn't let that stop you. I represent a very powerful faction that has chosen you to bear our mantle. The burden we wish to give you is one man has sought since the time of the gods."

He didn't wait for her to answer before continuing. "Mankind is dwindling. Our glory is already past, yet the fools of the Conclave and their Inquisition puppets wish to propagate lies upon us, thinking us fools. Vau Prime is the heart of the disease. My organization seeks to return us to glory."

"I care nothing for the glory of man," Presha argued. "I have seen what man has to offer, and it is foul at best. You are mistaken. Go find yourself another."

"Enough of this," growled the giant. "Snap her neck and do as she says."

"No, my friend. She is the one." He turned back. "Presha, think carefully what you say. I am offering you the chance to find vengeance against those who have wronged you. To help us achieve the destiny we were always meant to have. All you need do is take my hand."

He extended it with the casualness of one who already knew her answer. But Presha was one not easily swayed. She stared back at him defiantly.

"Show me your face," she demanded.

A pause. "Not yet. Take my hand, and I promise the secrets of the universe will be yours. Give in to temptation, and become the force you were always destined to be."

She still wasn't sure exactly what had made her reach out and take his hand. Years had gone by, and the answer continued to elude her. Presha Von had accepted his offer only to find a world more terrifying and gratifying than any she might have imagined. Some secrets were best left undiscovered.

"Mistress Von, you have an incoming communiqué," August, her eunuch, announced in his shrill voice.

Presha frowned, the dark memories of her enslavement troubling her again, and eyed the bronze-skinned man. Bald, August was also blind. Crude optic enhancements covered the empty sockets, whirring and contracting as the computers funneled images to his mind.

"I said I don't want to be disturbed," she ground out.

"My apologies, but he was insistent."

Presha waved him off, more angry with herself than with August. "Very well. I'll take it in my office."

August bowed and ambled off to whatever task he chose to perform. She truly despised the man. Eunuchs were useful for a great many things, companionship not one of them. August reminded her of the sympathetic weaklings who had traded morality for a few minutes of pleasure in her bed. Presha spent hours daydreaming about venting his mutilated body out of the nearest pressure lock. Not that she'd go through with it. Too many people on the station watched every little nuance, and she was in no position to be caught committing mundane murder.

The click of her polished dark blue heels echoed sharply with each step. Presha hated carpets more than she hated August. Their lushness was an unnecessary luxury in a hostile environment. The time was coming when she was going to need the harshness her natural austerity bred. Her hair, tied tightly into a thick bun, tugged constantly at her skin. The gentle pain reminded her of her purpose. Her clothes were considered fashionable. The skirt was tight at the hips, hardly dropping below her knees. Her blouse was midnight blue, the top two buttons undone casually.

Presha enjoyed simple luxuries, indulging in her own twisted passions from time to time. She kept an occasional pet close for when the desire became too strong. This was not one of those times. The sounds of the gambling floor faded as she rounded the sharp corner leading to her office.

Presha kept her office empty of decoration. She preferred the pristine condition that greeted her each day. The walls were painted white to cover the dull metal grey of the station. She'd managed to procure a space with a window, one of the true rarities on Hawker's Gate. A rectangular table made from black cedar filled the center of the room, matched by her soft leather high-backed chair. Presha calmly sat and keyed the data board on her desk.

She dreaded what awaited. Few dared summon her. Presha had spent the years of her life building a reputation as the one person not to cross. The screen flickered to life, showing her the one face she least desired to see again.

"Presha Von, how good it is to see you again," Ursal Prowl said with a false smile.

"Ursal, I see exile has not been kind to you," she snapped back. Too much bad blood ran between them still.

"We both have our assignments." Ursal bristled. "Is this line secure?"

Presha sighed, finding his concerns amateurish. "Naturally, from my end. Though I wouldn't want to speculate your part. Where are you precisely?"

"My location is none of your concern." He decided it was time to change the subject. "I've received new orders from Vau Prime. War is coming, Presha."

"Mystics and morons constantly claim so; why should now be any different? And what does Vau Prime have to do with me? I don't take orders from Conclave cowards who hide behind their robes half a galaxy away."

Veins popped on his forehead. "Mind your tongue. You aren't so far away that I can't get to you, or have you forgotten our arrangement from Crimeat?"

"You are beginning to bore me, Ursal. Why have you called?"

"The Conclave has decided to send a large fleet to Occanum," he left the reasons out. "Your area of space will be very busy soon. I'm sure more than one Inquisitor will find his way into your den. It's only a matter of time before you are discovered."

Her temper started to get the better of her. "Ursal, I have no time for random speculations. Hawker's Gate is large enough to conceal me from watchful eyes. Besides," she smiled sweetly, "I'm not the one the Inquisition is looking for. Take care of your own hide, *Inquisitor*. Let me worry about me. Do not attempt to contact me again."

She canceled the feed and leaned back, exhaling pent up frustration. Presha hated Ursal Prowl for his part in the insurrection of Lethendweil. The addiction to the oils he'd given her had taken almost a year to beat. She refused to forgive him, instead wishing for a cold death to claim him.

August's shadow falling over her over broke the dark thoughts swirling around in her head. "What now, eunuch?" she snarled.

August didn't flinch, accustomed to her mistreatment. "Mistress, it is almost time for your meeting with Administrator Felp."

Damnation. She'd nearly forgotten. Roule Felp was an important piece to her continued success on the Gate. Presha was reluctant to admit it, but she needed Felp's support in the coming months, now reduced to weeks if Ursal's warnings were accurate. She frowned. Nothing worked quite the way she wanted or needed.

"Please send a message to his office that I am en route as you speak," Presha replied calmly, concealing her inner turmoil.

"Very good, Mistress." August bowed again and disappeared to whatever hole in which he chose to spend most of his time.

Presha didn't bother watching him go. Her mind already raced ahead.

Roule Felp paced the office of the Administrator impatiently. Slightly overweight and well beyond the prime of his life, Roule was the type of man who often let life pass him by. Liver spots colored his otherwise pale skin. His hair, what little remained, was thin and wispy. Roule ate more than he should and drank in excess. Time was not his ally, and he was determined to make the most of what little he had left. Regrets plagued the senior administrator.

Foremost in his thoughts was the enigmatic Presha Von. She'd been a combination of a thorn in his side and an unfulfilled fantasy since arriving on Hawker's Gate nearly two years ago. The woman had a knack for getting what she wanted and wasn't ashamed of her methods. Roule frowned on her indiscretions. A lady should know better; he assumed she was a lady based on her demeanor and appearance. Presha was the sort who stopped at nothing once her mind was set. He dreaded their coming meeting, a meeting he had called.

"Administrator, Lady Von has arrived," Bethis, his assistant of more than six years, chimed.

Roule released a deep breath without realizing he'd been holding it. "Send her in."

"Of course, sir."

Ambling back to his desk, the one place he truly felt comfortable being in power, Roule anxiously shuffled a stack of old reports. He forced himself not to look up much as Presha glided into the office.

"Lady Von, please take a seat," he ordered mildly.

She feigned a smile and sat, knowing he was only performing for show. The true power of Hawker's Gate didn't reside with the administratum. Uncomfortable silence filled the space between them. Presha reveled in it. Roule Felp struggled not to squirm. Just being in her presence was intoxicating and revolting. She was a viper.

"I trust this won't take long, Roule. I have a business to run," she said flatly.

Thin beads of sweat dotted his forehead. "We finish when I am done. There have been serious accusations made against you, ones that I cannot overlook."

"Accusations? By whom?" Her gaze darkened suddenly. Old suspicions resurfaced. The coincidence of this conversation and Ursal Prowl's sudden communiqué earlier was too implausible.

Roule waved her off. "Not important. What is important is that several sources have come forward accusing you of running illegal activities in your establishment. Activities that are deemed immoral by the Conclave."

She smiled at his evident discomfort. "Administrator Felp, we are a long way from the Conclave. Their priests hold little sway in the deep reaches of space."

"This station is an extension of Conclave authority!" he flustered. "Don't make that mistake."

"You are the moral authority here." Presha encouraged. "How many times have you visited my establishment?"

Sudden embarrassment twisted his features. "This isn't about me, Presha. These accusations are serious. I've caught whispers. People are going to take it to the Inquisition if I don't deal with it."

She leaned back. "So deal with it. I have nothing to hide. Any Inquisitor is more than welcome to come check for themselves. Bring along a few priests and cardinals while you are at. The more the merrier."

Roule couldn't believe the sheer audacity Presha demonstrated. Any sane person would fret for their lives when faced with potential adjudication by the Inquisition. Old timers still talked about one of Felp's predecessors who had met an untimely demise after allegedly cross-dealing against the Conclave. He had no desire to meet such an end.

"Damn it, Presha, this is serious."

She let him fume a little more, enjoying the games. Presha found power in the subtle manipulations of men and the occasional woman. She'd had Roule begging the moment she boarded Hawker's Gate. He was a lonely man with limited ambitions, content to live out the remainder of his days at the ass end of the universe. Men like Roule Felp would be remembered as allowing the coming cataclysm.

"Relax, Roule. I've had people accuse me of a great many things before. What more can they possibly say about me?" she asked.

He feebly shook his head. "We are dealing with much more dangerous people than usual. I…I am almost afraid of what comes next."

"What do you suggest I do?"

"I don't know. Perhaps you could shut your house down for a week or so, at least until this blows over," he answered.

"Out of the question. I am doing nothing illegal," she insisted. "Nothing that the average citizen doesn't need from time to time. The Conclave has a tenuous hold on the true reality of the universe. We are small beings, Roule. There is so much more out there just waiting to be discovered."

Roule stiffened. "What are speaking of?"

A smile, false and warming. "Roule, aren't you tired of being told what to do by a doddering old woman millions of miles away? When was the last time you personally saw one of their vaunted Order come to perform mass or give blessings to those in need? Never. They are too worried over maintaining their seats and fighting off political newcomers to bother with the people who make them who they are. The system is corrupt, Roule. We both know it."

"The system has worked for thousands of years. We should not question."

I have you now. "That is the talk of a man who doesn't dare to dream. Tomorrow can be a rich land if you only reach out to grasp it."

"You speak of sedition," he accused thoughtfully.

"I speak of freedom," she replied. "Freedom to make our own decisions, to govern our own lives. This," she gestured to the walls, "is not life. What happened to make you want to come here?"

He chose his next words carefully, suddenly suspicious of her intentions. "It was an honor to be chosen for my position. I have the equivalent of a planetary governorship. This was my choice. You need to stop talking now, Presha. You speak of too many heresies for me to ignore. Go back to your house and promise me you won't spread these words. The damage will be uncontrollable, and this is not the time. A large Prekhauten fleet is scheduled to arrive soon. They have enough interest to arrest you."

Presha rose suddenly. "Perhaps I was wrong to be so bold as to share with you. Good afternoon, Administrator Felp. I will try to be a good girl."

He didn't allow himself to relax until the click of her heels was a distant echo.

Presha stalked out of the administratum offices with a dour expression. Events were happening quickly, and Roule had decided to throw a wrench in her plans. He was going to have to be dealt with unless she managed to swing him to her side. Having the senior man on the station in her pocket might prove useful. The new order was spreading, fanning flames of sedition and independence on a hundred worlds. The Conclave didn't have the military resources to confront all incidents at the same time. The universe would burn, and Presha Von took great pride in being one of the key instruments that allowed that to happen.

The news of a Guard fleet en route soured her plans. The Prekhautens never operated alone. A small army of Inquisitors and Conclave priests was about to descend on Hawker's Gate. Presha decided it was time to contact her order. There was still much to be done if their plans were going to succeed.

EIGHT

3212 A.G. (After Gods), Abbey of the Order of Blood Witches, Acumensiis Comet.

The Acumensiis Comet was less. Less of place since the death of Sister Abigail. Less of a home to the young women abandoned by civilization. Ruma Zzein, Grand Mistress of the Order of Blood Witches, remained self-confined to her personal chambers high atop the tallest spire of the abbey. Her mourning for Abigail was not yet finished. It was a recognized flaw but one that had no remedy. Every life was precious, a Blood Witch's more than most. Abigail's death left an irreplaceable void in the fabric of the universe.

Ruma Zzein did not weep. Her capacity for tears had dried up long ago. Horrors and nightmares had hounded her for centuries, forcing her to abandon the last vestiges of human emotion chaining her to mortality. She was immortal, or the closest living thing to it. Ruma was older than half of the suns. Empires came and passed into faded memory, yet she endured.

For the briefest time, she found her thoughts drifting back to a day long ago, a day that had changed her life and given her newfound purpose. Ruma had fled her birth planet, confident there was a better way. She had been wrong. Humanity didn't accept her specific gifts. She had been branded a witch, excommunicated from the Conclave. The turning point had come when she had stopped a group of men from raping and beating a young woman to death while local authorities stood by and watched.

Ruma had screamed in a voice that shattered eardrums, blowing brain matter through nose and mouth. The woman had clung to her in singular hope of survival. Others had not seen it so clearly. Ruma had fled with the girl. They'd hidden in caves, gathering others and waiting for passage off world. Nowhere they went was safe. Outcasts, they had been forced to take refuge on the Acumensiis Comet, condemned by the fledgling Conclave. Ruma had made a pact with the first Cardinal Seniorus. Any woman showing unique abilities was to be handed over to Ruma and her order to be trained in how to properly utilize her gifts for the betterment of humanity.

So long ago. Ruma Zzein looked up from the row of shattered globes and saw space for the first time in a year. The stars amazed her with their innocent brightness, unparalleled vitality. She'd spent most of her time in this inner sanctum, the tallest spire of the abbey. Protective shields fluctuated over the open windows that circled the chamber. Ruma Zzein was able to watch the entire splendor of space as the comet marched by on its course. The room was large and carved from dark granite, giving a gloomy feel. Golden runes marred the black floor, flaring to life whenever she touched one. Candles burned constantly from the four corners of her table. There was no chair or any other furniture. The Grand Mistress folded her legs beneath her and floated at the edge of the table. Her long diaphanous robes lightly kissed the floor, billowing slightly in the unnatural breeze.

The time for grand introspection was ended. Action was now required. Ruma had thought long and hard on the prospect of Forever Night. Mankind was still young, impossibly fragile to withstand the eventuality of what was to come. Their worship of gods hampered their ability to reason. They were blind to the demise fast approaching. They needed to help of the Blood Witches if they were to have even a slim chance of survival.

Ruma spun slowly, legs still folded, hands in her lap. Her mind was settled. The rapid pace of her nerves calmed. It was time to take her beloved order, the creation of her heart, and give it to the Conclave in the desperate hope of salvaging humanity. She made it almost to the door when a deep boom exploded in her soul. Lights and colors spread through the sanctum, throwing her back in a violent wave of raw power.

Ruma shielded her eyes from the searing light. Slivers of pain shot through her aged eyes, burning into her mind. She felt terror, true terror, for the first time in nearly four thousand years.

"Show yourself to me," she gasped.

Mocking laughter circled her sanctum. "Is that any way to talk to an old friend?"

Ruma's heart clenched. "I have no old friends. Show me your face."

"Has it been so long you no longer recognize the voice of the one who cast you out of your precious temple? Who left you to the vagaries of time? The one who made you what you are."

"Amongeratix," she hissed through clenched teeth.

An image appeared, blurred at first and slow to focus.

"What sorcery is this?" Ruma asked, knowing she wasn't about to be answered.

The image solidified, shimmering and ethereal. Amongeratix sneered down on her as if enacting old hatreds in his mind's eye. "Do not speak of those things beyond your grasp. You were ever a hack, Ruma. I don't know what my father saw in you."

"Did you come to taunt me, Amongeratix, or is there a purpose for this unwanted pleasantry? My time is precious."

"Your time is ending. It is one of the universe's cruel jokes that you continue to exist. I am come to deliver you to the abyss," he condemned.

Ruma refused to rise. "Your words are empty, *monster*. Go back to your prison and rot."

He bristled suddenly. Anger had become his closest ally. "Mind your tongue, witch. I could have killed you long ago. Consider it a mistake I let you live. Your light is waning. Do not interfere in what comes next. Disappear, and I might even forget you before the end."

"The Order of Blood Witches will not be cowed by a puppet! You think you are above the laws of life? Look closely into your own black heart, Amongeratix, and you shall find only decay and emptiness. Your time has passed. Your kind was found wanting and faded into oblivion."

"We were the rulers of the universe!" he roared. "All bowed beneath us and trembled in the anticipation of our voices. You are an aberration, Ruma Zzein. I will come to kill you if you get involved with the humans."

Ruma offered a tight-lipped smile. "I am human. I will not allow them to fall into the dread ruin that consumed your race at Occanum. You and all like you are anathema. The abyss is coming, but not for me."

Warding spells flared from key spots around the sanctum. Amongeratix's image started to fade.

"Do not cross me again or your daughter's life is forfeit," he said, the voice a mere whisper before his image disappeared entirely.

Ruma finally slumped down. Any pain she felt for the loss of Sister Abigail was drowned out by the sudden emergence of Amongeratix. He'd been incarcerated under the watchfulness of the Inquisition for so long she'd nearly made the mistake of rendering his threat minimal. His disappearance after the battle of Crimeat was disturbing, though not unusual. For him to invade her private quarters with such ease spoke terrible things. Ruma was no longer sure humanity stood a chance at all. The Three were at last returned to finish their war.

Ruma had no time to waste. She shook off the last dizzying effects of the power surge and raced to gather her sisters.

*

The Atrium was built as a welcoming hall where sisters new and old could come to share experiences and wisdom with one another. Seldom was it used during time of war or consequence. The Order of Blood Witches had drifted across the elliptical of the universe for countless years in the pursuit of knowledge and the quiet defense of a race that didn't want them. No thanks or sentiments of gratitude ever made it within the abbey walls unless expressed by a sister.

Ageless cedar beams arced the ceiling, the aroma still fresh. Thick beams of dark red oak ran the twenty meters to the buttresses. Garlands of flowers wrapped around the massive trunks in celebration of the spirit. Ten foot tall stained glass windows with scenes depicting some of the Order's most prolific achievements were spaced every five feet. Tables made to seat twenty filled the wooden floor. Light orbs hovered at intervals throughout the Atrium.

The Grand Mistress and her most trusted inner circle of advisors took seats at the head table. Only five chairs lined the far side facing the main hall. An alcove held one hundred thousand candles that never extinguished. Novices were required to replace any candle near the end of its life daily. Normally, the Atrium was reserved for merriment and fellowship. Normally, but not now.

An iron-capped stave rang against the wooden floor three quick times, bringing the assembly to silence. All heads turned and bowed as Grand Mistress Zzein drifted in. Her diaphanous robes reflected colors in rainbow patterns befitting one of such station. Silence dominated the hall, an unmatched reverence for the only woman to ever hold the position.

Ruma spared little time for reflection. She seldom did. History was not going to be kind to those like her. Already she had been forgotten, a relic from an age many believed to have never existed. Ruma Zzein was a myth. Mankind had evolved beyond her, leaving the Order ensconced on the shelves of antiquity.

Her soft eyes carried over the assembly. The sisters were her pride, the object of the depths of her heart. Nothing in the vast depth of the universe meant more than the precious few hundred gathered, waiting eagerly for what she had to announce. Only Ruma found she lacked the desire to say what needed saying. Amongeratix's intrusion into her private sanctum had been unexpected and changed all her summations of the future. Pursing her lips, she began.

"Sisters, we have come to a crossroads many of us have long feared," she told them, her deep voice booming from the walls. "Humanity has lost its course. They have squandered the gifts left them and have begun the path to Forever Night."

Gasps circled the hall, as loud as her own had been.

"I believe the time has come for us to return to the universe. To give back what has long been absent. Our time of seclusion must come to an end if any of us have a hope of surviving. The choice is not an easy one to make, nor should it be decided lightly. This sisterhood has thrived because we are isolated, away from the trials humanity imposes on itself. They have become as corrupt as the very beings they once replaced."

She scanned the audience. "I invite any who so choose to voice their opinion, for this is not solely my decision. We are all humanity's forgotten children."

"Grand Mistress, what has changed? Surely Sister Abigail's death has played some part in this design, but is it enough to jeopardize us all?"

Ruma frowned at Abigail's mention. The two had been as close as perhaps a mother and daughter. Sending her to Crimeat to support Inquisitor Breed had been no easy task. Nonetheless, Breed was an important piece in coming years. Working with him proved less a gamble than a calculated risk. Abigail's loss was regrettable and ultimately disheartening. Reverberations continued to swirl through the Order.

"Sister Abigail performed her duties as well as any of us can hope to," Ruma answered the young Sister, one of the newer arrivals. "Much of the universe is controlled by powers that have little concept of what is happening. This abbey has protected the true source of our enlightenment for millennia. Much that we do has been shrouded in secrecy. Sister Abigail showed the Conclave what we are truly capably of. We should all take heart at her sacrifice."

Another Sister rose. "She should not have been risked so casually, Grand Mistress."

Another frown. Ruma expected opposition, but not from the Mistress of Novices, Algiss Her.

"There was nothing casual in any of Abigail's actions. She sacrificed herself so that the rest might find the opportunity to defeat Amongeratix and survive. Her sacrifice should not be trivialized by personal feelings. No one here grieves Abigail more than I. She was," her voice caught, "a dear friend. I miss her dearly but will not sully her name by continuing to hide here on our little comet a million miles away from where the fate of our species is being decided."

Algiss didn't back down. "Her exposure was needless. The Conclave and Inquisition have made their choices. We should not be subject to their fallacies."

"Algiss, this is not the time for internal conflict. The Order must stand strong and undivided. Dark times approach. We are no longer safe here as we once were. Sisters, I have not told you everything. Earlier this evening, I was visited by the Shackled Man. Amongeratix appeared in my sanctum and dared threaten us all to remain neutral if we wanted to live. His audacity has overstepped any assumed authority."

Another round of gasps. The undertone changed, if slightly. Ruma detected the sudden absence of derisiveness and a push towards unity. Each Sister was vital to the Order, and she was the only one who knew their vision.

"This is unheard of," Algiss snarled to the audience. "The Order of Blood Witches has existed for three thousand years. Never has our holy temple been invaded!"

Ruma concealed a smile.

"Grand Mistress, the Three are well known to the Sisters, perhaps more so than to any in humanity. Amongeratix is indeed powerful but never has he had the strength to breach our protective wards. I speak for the novices. We stand united behind your leadership."

"Thank you, Algiss. I fear our newest recruits may have to mature more rapidly than intended."

Others rose in support of the Grand Mistress. Ruma's heart swelled. Finally, every Sister stood, hovering slightly above the freshly swept floor. The combined threat of Amongeratix and the extinction of humanity united the Order precisely when Ruma needed them whole.

"Thank you, all of you. I cannot promise victory in the coming struggle. The prophecy of Forever Night is not a kind one to know, but I pledge to devote my very last breath to each of you."

Deius Mlth, Mistress of Arms, slowly raised her hand. The murmur stopped at once. Deius had survived a battle with Amongeratix long ago and bore the scars. She knew better than most what the Three were capable of. Ruma had wasted no time in convincing the injured Mlth to become the Mistress of Arms, responsible for training cadres of Sisters to combat their most hated foe.

"Grand Mistress, I have a simple question," she said in a surprisingly melodious tone.

Ruma tilted her head. "Of course, my old friend."

"The Three are dangerous. Of that there can be no debate. Many of our kind have suffered dire wounds at their hands. I myself carry scars that will not heal, even after three centuries. Amongeratix and I have unfinished business, though that can wait. What role do we serve in preventing Forever Night?"

Ruma Zzein held her breath. Deius had asked the one question she was not prepared to answer in front of the entire Sisterhood. Choosing her words carefully, she began, "You ask for an answer that began thirty-five centuries ago, Sister. The Three started the Great War. Humanity believes otherwise, of course. How could the sons of the king of the gods be so callous as to endanger all life? Such shortsightedness is partially responsible for our troubles now. The universe burned as battles raged for centuries. I remained hidden, knowing that, should Amongeratix find me alive, he would use my gift of premonition to tilt the balance."

She offered them a grim smile. "He knew that I had already been gifted with a vision of the end. I had correctly seen the battle of Occanum, where the last vestiges of his people went to do their final battle. The dark powers had the upper hand until Tannus and Sorrow arrived. Whatever foul sorcery they used has proven more powerful than any imagined. The battle ended with their people being scattered and sent into *hibernation*. I don't offer explanation for this.

"Only the Three were unaffected. Sorrow disappeared for more than a thousand years. His mind was shattered by what he had seen and done. Amongeratix's hatred deepened, but he lacked much of his strength. He hid until such a time as he could marshal enough power to attack his brother.

"Tannus undertook the gruesome job of finishing what he and Sorrow had started. He alone took his people to every planet and encased them in capsules where they still sleep, never more than one to a planet. It took him a great many years before he found solace among his own thoughts. He is haunted by his deeds and ever seeks redemption from a father who cannot hear him." She paused to drink from her glass. The cool water soothed her vocal cords.

Ruma continued. "Humanity writes that the gods were destroyed. Now you all know the truth in this. Amongeratix knows the cold reality of this fact as well. He has longed to awaken several of his kind in efforts to reclaim the universe and take revenge against his brothers and father.

Should he awaken just one of his race, he will be able to plunge us all into irrevocable darkness.

"We have been at war for a very long time, and I fear it is all coming to an end quickly. I ask each of you to return to your quarters to meditate. The future is not written. We still have time to change the course of events and stunt the Three from achieving victory. We shall reconvene at dawn."

The Sisterhood rose as Ruma dismissed them. Only now did she sit back in the soft cushions of her chair. Unforeseen events were thrust against them, and she was suddenly blind. She waited patiently until there were just three, including herself. Deius and Algiss floated nearby, awaiting her instructions. Neither betrayed any emotion.

Ruma nodded at each. "Let us retire to my sanctum. There is much yet to discuss."

Deius spoke once all three were comfortably seated around Ruma's ancient stone table. "Ruma, I will speak plainly. We cannot hope to compete against what Amongeratix seeks to unleash. Our numbers were never many. Confronting him now will spell our doom."

Turning to Algiss, Ruma asked, "And you?"

"I'm not sure what to make of all this. The Three are not all powerful as the Conclave would have the universe believe. They can be beaten and have been by each of us in this chamber. We should not let fear govern our emotions."

"Fear?" Deius asked sharply. "It is not fear that stays my desire for vengeance. No Sister, it is prudence. This order was founded on the belief that a special few might enlighten the masses. We were never meant to be warriors."

"I founded the Order because I was exiled from my race and trying to escape the dementia Amongeratix had in mind for me," Ruma quietly reminded them. "Deius is correct, though. I never intended us to become warriors. Necessity drove us there. Loss is our binding element. We have all lost much to transcend humanity and become…more."

"That doesn't change the fact that we are not a major military threat," Deius argued. "Our efforts will be in vain if we assault any of the Three head on."

"Only if Amongeratix manages to awaken others," Algiss cautioned. "He can be beaten when acting alone. Sister Abigail showed us this truth."

Ruma held up a hand. Her transparent flesh took on the pale green color of the light orb hovering above the tabletop. "Ladies, please.

Arguments among our ranks are pointless and only serve to strengthen the enemy. Personal opinions on the Three need be set aside until the threat is reduced."

"Perhaps it is time to inform the Cardinal Seniorus of the box," Algiss suggested hesitantly.

Ruma cocked her head. "Humanity is not ready for that. The effects will be potentially as devastating as the coming war. We mention the box only if all else fails."

"All else is failing, Ruma. For Amongeratix to casually invade this most holy of chambers suggests exactly that. Our power is failing," Deius persisted.

"I will not argue the point. My ability to see into the future has lessened of late. The one certainty I can provide is that we will not survive should we choose to stand alone. We must join forces with the Conclave."

Deius frowned. "What of their witch hunters? I have no love for the Inquisition, no matter what praise you heap upon this Tolde Breed."

"I'm not suggesting we give them our trust, merely our cooperation. Each order has its merits. Together, we can accomplish what has been left unattended for so long."

Algiss lifted in the air. "I have heard enough. Ruma, I stand with you regardless of your decisions. I go now to prepare the novices. There is much to be done if they have a hope of surviving the flames."

Deius rose and followed her to the door, pausing at the entrance. "I stand with you as well, Ruma. I always have, but know I maintain severe reservations on our course. The way is unclear. Move cautiously."

Ruma Zzein watched her closest companions leave, but her thoughts were thousands of years in the past on a vastly different world. The Grand Mistress of the Order of Blood Witches struggled to keep the tears from running free as the image of her golden-haired daughter came unbidden to her. She often wondered what had become of the single most precious life in the universe, though deep in her heart she knew Amongeratix's promise of revenge went deeper than just herself.

NINE

3212 A.G. (After Gods), The Deeves, planet An'kuruku.

Crisp winds blew in from the Bo, sending chills down Mollock's spine. He had always enjoyed the purity of the ocean, but the Bo was much more. Fierce, primal, the waves slammed angrily into the abused shores. Rock formations that had stood since the world was formed were slowly being beaten down. Mollock stood just beyond the reach of the waves, marveling at how the rocks had become jagged and sharp.

Tilting his head back to catch the spray, the cool water caressing weeks' worth of beard. Mornings were his favorite time. Here, on the shores of an alien ocean, Mollock no longer felt hunted. His mind calmed. His nerves settled. Mollock Bolle finally felt like he had come home. Sadly, such was not the case. He remained hunted, if only by the local Prefecture instead of the shadow organization that had hounded him for decades.

"You should not be out in this weather," Kaline's soft voice called from behind.

Mollock frowned and sighed. The moment was lost. "The water cleanses me, Kaline. I feel pure out here."

Wrapping a light blue shawl around her shoulders, she joined him. Kaline wasn't much older than he, though life had definitely been kinder. She lacked the wrinkles and lines he had come to accept. Certain grace was evident in her movements, leading his thoughts down a path he hadn't enjoyed in a lifetime.

She wrinkled her nose. "It smells."

"The scents of life in its purest," he said with a smile. "We should all be so fortunate as to enjoy moments like this."

"I won't argue that. Our lives are about to grow more hectic." She placed a warming hand on his shoulder. "Enjoy these moments, Mollock. A crowd is already gathering. They have come for you."

He stopped. "Why me?"

Gulls squawked overhead.

"You are the Prophet, delivered to An'kuruku to dispel the myths that have bound us in submission for centuries."

Prophet. He frowned at the term. She was not the first to name him so. The Bloody Man had done the same on the frozen surface of the Plateau right before he and Elisa had escaped. Mollock knew better than to delude himself. His life was a series of wasted efforts. Nothing he did turned out the way he envisioned. He was sure Kaline's scheme was going to end the same way.

"I never asked to be a voice of the people. They should go home."

"Many have no homes, Mollock. They abandoned their lives to come here, to come to you. Are you so haughty as to deny them the only spark keeping them warm at night?" She paused. "Have you looked out the front of the castle? Have you seen the village growing daily?"

He arched an eyebrow at the mention of a castle. The stone walls and roofless rooms were anything but a castle. Moss covered most of the walls. The few bare spots showed severe structural damage. Kaline insisted her organization had found the building abandoned and in relatively good condition.

Mollock was uncomfortable here. At least in Tenemenah he had options. The natural freedom of the Deeves was the worst sort of prison. Lost in an endless sea of scrub grass and rocks, Mollock knew he was trapped. Leaving meant capture and, in all likelihood, death. He almost longed for the days of roaming across Lethendweil a few steps ahead of his pursuit.

"They shouldn't have come. Nothing I saw holds relevance, Kaline. I am a shell of a man, certainly not deserving of adoration or worship by the uninformed."

Her right cheek twitched. "Stop thinking of yourself for once. The universe does not revolve around Mollock Bolle. Or perhaps you think that little secret you discovered in the black mountains of Reven propels you to greatness? Look around. Everywhere is hardship and strife. People are afraid to leave their homes without an armed escort. Are you the one to tell them to go back to the misery that has become their lives and wallow in self pity and abject filth?"

Mollock spun on her, anger finally showing. "How dare you turn this back on me! Why doesn't anyone ask what I want? What I need? Why do I have to give until there is nothing left of me but skin and bones?"

"At last you realize what it means to be alone," she said, calmer. "Your pain is not unique, Mollock. All of us have experienced loss on a level we wished had never happened. My own sorrows far outweigh any successes. You are not alone. We are here for you, to support you during the trying times the future holds. Don't turn your back so casually. A time is coming when you will have need of as much strength as possible."

Kaline took a step closer and laid a soft hand on his shoulder. Mollock resisted the urge to flinch. Despite her smooth words and easy smile, he found the woman oddly unsettling. Something dark lurked just behind her eyes. He spent a fair amount of time wondering if she were part of the problem rather than the proposed solution. Trust was hard for him to give after spending decades constantly being hunted.

"Why?"

Kaline cocked her head. "Why what?"

"Why should I trust you? The Prefects could be in your pocket for all I know and all of this a clever ruse to get me to stick my neck out," Mollock questioned.

"We saved your life."

"I never asked you to. Give me something more than that," he insisted.

He could see the storm brewing in Kaline's eyes. Her lips pursed as she carefully debated what to say next. Mollock fought the urge to smile mockingly. He was many things, most of them nothing good, but he wasn't a pawn. A string of bad choices had left him so much less than what he might have been, what his parents had once wished for him to be. The time was fast approaching when he was going to be able to throw off the chains and live for himself.

Soon, but not yet.

Kaline threw her hands out wide. "What more can I give? What will it take to make you believe me?"

He finally smiled. "Tell me who you really are."

A pause. "Some things are best left unsaid. There is danger in too much knowledge. You of all people should know this. How many have you cursed with the secret of the caverns?"

"Enough," he slowly replied.

Kaline nodded. "This argument is pointless, Mollock. You mire yourself in baseless desires; wants and needs are inconsequential to the must. I doubt any of us would choose to be here. What matters is how we choose to live out these last few years we are given."

"My choices are being made for me. This is not living, Kaline. I am a prisoner by another name. Don't treat me otherwise."

"A prisoner? No one is keeping you here. We brought you to this place for your protection, to give you the opportunity to grow as you see fit. If these walls are a prison, then I invite you to leave."

Her unexpected admission threw him. Mollock had survived for too long on wits and guile alone. The combination left him reserving grave doubts towards any who hadn't proven themselves. Kaline just took a step closer to earning his trust.

"Why here? This is just another ocean far from the rest of civilization."

She gave him a false grin. "The Bo is revered in local culture. It is important to give the people a sense of familiarity. They will see you standing atop these cliffs and understand your relationship with the earth. Use that. It will only enhance the message we want to send."

Mollock hung his head, some of the fight blown out to the curling waves. "I will stay but know this. Should you or any of your people betray me, I will not hesitate to run a knife through your guts. I am my own master."

"I expect nothing less." She smiled warmly. "Now come, we have guests to greet."

He reluctantly held out an arm for her to take and let Kaline lead him towards the front of their run-down castle.

The Bone Father walked the crowds, ever leaning heavily on his staff. Time had not been kind. Years were spent trying to protect his people and the Deeves. Years he had happily given to his cause. A birthright few were afforded. He was worn down, inviting death to claim him.

Little pleasures kept him going. Much of life passed him by, and he cared none. The little garden behind his mud home occupied his mind, often leaving him content. Once a moon cycle, he made his rounds to nearby villages and saw to basic healing and future reading. Villagers always rejoiced when the Bone Father graced them with his presence.

That was how he first learned of the Prophet. Naturally, the Bone Father thought the hysteria nothing more than empty rhetoric and wishful thinking. No man had the ability to inspire masses without mind-influencing drugs. The Bone Father let curiosities get the better of him and followed an exodus of villagers to the shore of the Bo. He was surprised to find many of the bedraggled were from Tenemenah and other eastern cities.

Is life so bad, he wondered on the march to the shore.

The answer remained elusive despite multiple assurances from pilgrims. They came clutching wildflowers and singing old folk songs. An undeniable attitude of hope surrounded them. Hope blossomed in their eyes, and it was all he could do not to get caught up in the euphoric mindset. The Bone Father had borne witness to a great many things during his years. This was unlike anything he'd ever dreamed to see.

"Come, old father! Follow us to salvation! We will show you the true path!" they cried and begged.

The Bone Father spared a last glance back at his mud hut before taking up his walking staff. Some sights could only be dispelled firsthand. He walked many miles to reach the opposite shore, spending his time to learn what he could from the pilgrims. Most disturbing was the lack of factual information. The pilgrims traveled on rumor or whim. The Bone Father seldom found such mystery.

Now, as he circulated the crowds, he discovered an odd serenity. Food was delivered in great bushels. Fishermen took the Bo's bounty, returning the bones and entrails so that life might continue. Bakers constructed large ovens to bake enough dark bread for hundreds. Children chased one another while dogs barked. Life had returned to these cold shores. The Bone Father was amazed.

"He's coming!" voices cried, genuine passion enthralling their voices.

A young woman helped the Bone Father rise before she rushed off to the castle. He had never seen a castle, never seen a city. He took in the sights before him without saying a word. Normally, villagers rejoiced at his arrival, not at some faceless man. Again, he let his curiosity take control. He ambled off with the crowd, eager to learn the many disguised truths.

An'kuruku's sun beat down unmercifully, crisping Elisa's fair skin. Ah'muf insisted they avoid mechanized transport, despite her protests. They needed speed over secrecy. Elisa argued the Prefects wouldn't have much of a chance of catching them before they escaped into the deep desert. Ah'muf smiled and shook his head repeatedly until she finally relented. Having spent the first years of his life in the deep desert, he wasn't foolish enough to listen to an off-world *farisi*. Two days later, she continued to sulk.

"How your people manage to survive under this sun is a wonder," she complained again.

Ah'muf grinned. "The scorpion adapts to match its environment. Why should not man? The desert is not such a bad place. Give it a chance, and you might be surprised at what it has to offer."

Her nose crinkled. "I've seen enough sand, thank you."

"Ah, *farisi*, there is so much more than sand," he playfully admonished.

"Ah'muf, look at my skin! No human should be this shade of red."

"As I said," he replied, as if answering another question.

Elisa shot him an evil glare but kept her tongue. She wasn't averse to finding goodness in new situations. The deserts of An'kuruku were the harshest environment she had ever experienced, and it was past time to turn around and go home. *Home.* The world suddenly sounded alien. She didn't think she had a home any more. The tragic events that defined her life also conspired against her.

Her thoughts returned to the Bloody Man — or Sorrow, as he preferred to be called. Elisa couldn't care less what the monster wanted. His arrival in her sleepy village had been unheralded and ended in a bloodbath. Only Elisa lived to bear witness. Their meeting nearly fifty years later was not coincidence. She now believed he had marked her, for whatever foul reasons known only to him. An'kuruku felt like her destiny, and that frightened her more than she was willing to admit, even to the man who had become her closest friend.

Elisa glanced back at Ah'muf, appreciating his looks for the first time. He was thin, lightly muscled and had just a hint of a belly. She smiled softly at the thought of him sneaking sips from half-empty glasses of wine or picking through plates returning to the kitchens. Not that she blamed him. A certain measure of boredom had to accompany any man or woman choosing to stand behind a bar fifteen hours a day.

His shoulder-length hair was jet black and shiny, and he had long fingers ending in neatly manicured nails. *Those won't last long. Once we spend a few weeks hiding from the Prefects and scraping out whatever meager existence this damned desert has to offer, he'll be just as haggard as me.* His hazel eyes were deep, making his already hooked nose look longer. There was unparalleled sharpness in those eyes. Ah'muf was a man who didn't miss much.

His moustaches were thin and tailored down past the corners of his mouth. Dark spots speckled his arms and neck, reminding her of her own freckles. She frowned, finding them attractive on him and repulsive on her own body. Elisa was surprised that he had bothered to change from his normally expensive silk outfits to more conventional traveling robes. A wide-brimmed hat shaded his face from the sun no matter what direction he turned. It was far more effective than the thin material she used to cover her head.

Ah'muf shifted in his saddle uncomfortably and found her staring unabashedly at him. "Yes?'

Elisa blushed. "Nothing. I was just thinking."

Stupid. You can't come up with anything better? She was too busy scolding herself to catch the soft smile cracking his face. Embarrassed, Elisa rode in silence for a while. The last thing either of them needed was the complications a misunderstood romance offered. *Not that he's a bad catch. Any woman would be lucky to have a man so kind and caring.* She frowned again and tried to refocus on what Ah'muf assured her was a road.

*

The small oasis looked like it had been abandoned for a while. A handful of browning palm trees leaned perilously close to tipping over. What water remained was brackish and foul. Mosquitoes and water bugs hovered in thick clouds. Elisa immediately had misgivings.

"We shouldn't stay here."

Ah'muf shrugged. "Where else is there to go? We are in the middle of a desert, *farisi*. The dunes are too dangerous to travel at night. I wouldn't risk it without great need. We have enough food and water to see us through to the next oasis. The shelter provided here will be enough."

"Aren't you interested in why this oasis is in ruins?" she asked.

His swift gaze looked quickly at their surroundings. "Not really. The gods provide as they see fit. We are fortunate to have ridden so far before night falls."

The sun was finally dropping below the horizon, not soon enough as far as Elisa was concerned. She'd rather face the Ugri in the middle of the jungle again than endure too many more days of riding through the shifting sands. Reluctantly, she gave in and slumped down on a large and very warm rock as smooth as a sheet of glass. The warmth felt surprisingly good now that the temperature was dropping rapidly. Elisa groaned and pulled off a boot. A tiny river of sand trickled out.

"You would do better to leave the sand in the desert. There will be more for the next few days," Ah'muf joked as he readied a fire.

She threw her boot at him.

"Have I mentioned how much I despise sand?" she drawled.

He nodded. "Sand gets everywhere, especially where we least want it. I remember as a child my father..."

"Please, Ah'muf, no more childhood stories of wisdom. I can't take much more," she groaned. "What is there to eat?"

"Patience, *farisi*. The desert will teach you patience above all else. Man is insignificant compared to the endless oceans of sand. Think of it. So much of our lives is little more than these grains of sand."

"Ah'muf, enough!"

Elisa emptied her other boot, wishing again that she was still on Crimeat. Her homeworld had plenty of flaws, but it —

She paused. It did what? She had few friends and no family. Elisa was constantly alone, searching for more of a meaning than just the endless desire for revenge. That fateful second meeting with Sorrow had opened her eyes to how consumed she'd been. Mollock Bolle had offered a brief distraction from the insanity of the battle of Reven and their harrowing escape to An'kuruku. She caught herself about to wonder what life might have been like if she'd found the right man to settle down with.

Sensing her distress, Ah'muf bowed. "My apologies. We are a long-winded people. I sometimes forget how to speak plainly."

She waved him off, ashamed for snapping. "Don't worry about it. I'm just a little on edge again. I'm the one who should apologize."

"I realize this cannot be easy for you; nor is it for me. One shouldn't have to abandon everything on a whim and flee. The Prefecture is corrupt and the Inquisition does nothing to stop it. The problem goes far beyond my meager planet. I am not a learned man, *farisi*, but I know enough to know that An'kuruku cannot be the only planet in this whole wide universe in desperate need of change."

He fell silent, dark thoughts brooding across his face. Elisa felt compassion for him, again regretting involving him. Inquisitors and Prefects were her problem, and she had failed. Now Ah'muf suffered for her arrogance.

Elisa decided to try and mend some of the strain hovering between them. "Ah'muf, what are these wells?"

He perked back up. "The Wells are one of our most holy sites. Legends tell us all life began within the waters of the Wells. It is our duty to undertake a pilgrimage at least once in our lives to the sacred waters."

She remained confused. "Why is that our destination? We're not pilgrims. Won't our presence be considered disgraceful by the monks or priests?"

"Possibly. The monks are rumored to be accepting of our faults, even offering to cleanse our spirits so that the gods may accept us readily when we pass to the next life."

"I don't believe that," Elisa replied too quickly. "I've seen too many things to make me believe the gods are anything but evil. The Three are nothing but merciless killers. I refuse to believe in a race that kills for sport or pleasure."

His eyes widened. "You have met one of the Three?"

Damnation! I never did know when to shut up. "I have, and he murdered everyone in my village when I was just a girl."

Silence separated them. The sun sank lower until on the barest sliver hung above the sands. Elisa sighed heavily. Resentment and anger was so deeply ingrained into who she had become that she couldn't escape. Confessing the horrors of her childhood experience to Ah'muf had been a mistake. He was a faithful man who still viewed the gods and their sons innocently. She wanted to apologize but didn't know how.

"I do not know what to say, *farisi*. To have met one of the Three!" Child-like amazement laced his words. If he heard the disdain in her voice, he chose to ignore it. "What was he like? Was he as tall as legends say?"

She smiled softly, sorrow reflecting off her blue eyes. "Ah'muf, the Three are not what you have been taught to believe. I stood there and watched as all three battled in the snow. It was terrible. Mollock and I were lucky to have escaped."

Elisa lacked the heart to tell him she had been shown an actual sleeping god. Such knowledge would ruin his moral foundations and possibly cast her in a negative light. Right now, she needed as many allies as she could get.

Ah'muf seemed undisturbed. "Legends say they are trapped in an endless war. You are fortunate. Few have ever lived to write of their experiences."

"Can we change the subject? I don't feel like reliving old nightmares tonight," she said. "Sleeping in this foul place is going to be nightmare enough."

He grinned sheepishly. "Of course, how foolish of me. We should rest. The ride to the Wells is not easy, and we will have need of strength to make it alive. I will see to the horses once the fire is going."

"I can do the fire and get dinner started," she said.

Ah'muf feigned indifference. They'd been around each other long enough for him to recognize the strength in her nature. Fighting her was pointless. He also noticed she didn't volunteer to do the harder work by taking care of the horses. Ah'muf smiled and bowed, leaving her beside the brackish pool.

The pair ate in silence. Nothing needed to be said. Elisa was hungry, but the taste of travel rations left much to be desired. The biscuits were just old enough to be hard on the outside. Dried meat from an animal she couldn't identify was tough to chew and only went down with a mouthful of water. A handful of nuts and dates, a fruit she still hadn't acquired a taste for, left her famished. The only highlight was a small green apple she'd brought from Tenemenah.

Night was much cooler than she'd anticipated. For all she knew, deserts were supposed to be hot, not near freezing when the sun went down. She frowned. Truthfully, it was nowhere near freezing but the transition from 120 degrees to 70 made it feel that way. Sand wolves howled in the unseen distance. Bats and other night creatures drifted close to the oasis out of curiosity. Elisa unrolled her sleeping bag and tried to ignore the creepy-crawlies moving around.

"Ah'muf?"

"Yes, *farisi*."

She smiled. "They were just as tall as the legends say."

TEN

3212 A.G. (After Gods) Frigate *Indomitable*, deep space en route to Hawkers Gate.

Tolde unsteadily picked himself up off the floor to the accompaniment of warning klaxons. Blood trickled from the small cut on his forehead. Books and other personal affects were scattered around his cabin. The *Indomitable* shuddered again, this time more violently. Tolde scowled. *That was a weapon impact*. Tolde lurched to the partially opened door and hit the intercom.

"Captain Falchi, what happened?"

"Weapons hit! We're losing power." Falchi's voice was cracked, distorted.

Tolde recognized the unmistakable urgency in the captain's voice and headed for the bridge. Crewmen scrambled down the darkened corridors. Emergency teams geared up while defense teams drew weapons from the arms lockers. A thin cloud of smoke clung to the ceiling. Yellow lights darkened the ship's interior. Running lights sprang to life along the floor.

The look on the crewmen's faces were the same: shock. Impossible as it seemed, the *Indomitable* had been knocked out of hyperspace and disabled. Tolde couldn't think of any weapon in the Prekhauten inventory capable of pulling a ship back into real space.

"Tolde!" Luma shouted from behind.

He kept moving. "Get to the bridge. We're under attack."

Luma slammed into the hull as the ship rocked from another hit. More warning sirens went off. Frowning, she started to run.

The bridge was in complete chaos. Medics worked on two downed crewers. A handful of fires burned deep within ruined consoles. One of the small view screens was a mess of broken steel and cables. Tolde found Falchi standing, not sitting, in the middle of it all and directing the reaction.

"Inquisitor," he said calmly after Tolde and Luma finally made their way over to his position. "I wish I had answers for you, but I'll be damned if I do."

"Is there anything you can tell us?" Luma asked hastily.

He nodded. "We were running nominally when the engines suddenly died. Engineering thinks it was from a concentrated magnetic pulse, but I don't see how. Magnetic weapons are tricky enough in normal space. Firing one accurately on a ship traveling through hyperspace is nearly impossible. Regardless, our engines are offline, and we are under attack from at least two positions."

Tolde scowled. "What is being targeted?"

"Weapons and life support."

Falchi gingerly touched the large burn spot on his left cheek. The skin was raw and blistered. He refused medical attention until the last man was treated and the *Indomitable* out of harm's way. His gaze centered on the sole working view screen, desperately trying to find his attackers. Empty space stared back. A twisted, blackened piece of the outer hull drifted past. Falchi clenched his fist.

"Captain, I have two heat signatures!" the weapons officer shouted.

Falchi rushed to the station. "Show me."

He studied the computer intensely, trying to find a way out of their situation. "They have us flanked. Do we have any weapons?"

"Torpedoes are offline. Heavy cannons are as well. I might be able to bring up reactive anti-ship missiles but not much else."

Falchi clasped the younger officer's shoulder. "Do what you can. I'll take anti-ship missiles."

"Yes, Captain."

"Incoming torpedo! Port side at one thousand meters."

Falchi looked at his weapons station and sighed. Everything was still offline. He limped back to his command chair and shouted into the intercom, "Brace for impact!"

Tolde scrambled to find a place to anchor down, all the while praying he wasn't blown into space. The prospect of a cold death frightened him. He began counting slowly, marking the seconds until the torpedo slammed into the hull. A nervous glance showed Luma Kai gritting her teeth from behind the captain's chair.

The *Indomitable* lurched under the impact as the torpedo slashed through the hull and into the engine room. Plasma and cooling liquids vented into space, accompanied by a handful of the crew. The frigate lurched to a slow stop. They were dead in space and without support. Tolde was just as helpless. Not a naval man, he'd spent his career hunting down heretics on the ground. He would only be in Falchi's way here.

Falchi took the impact harshly and scowled. The enemy was attacking with specific action in mind. Logically, only two options remained. They could either continue attacking until the *Indomitable* was pulverized to little bits of scrap metal or board her. Falchi knew what was coming.

"Inquisitor Breed, I believe I have need of your Guardsmen," he said sternly.

Tolde nodded. His face was ashen; the imposed fear of being vented along with the engine room crewers nearly rendered him incapable of action. Still, he forced himself to key his communicator.

"Sergeant Fies."

A short delay. "Inquisitor, what in the hells is going on? We're getting beaten up down here."

Tolde frowned. "Do you have any casualties?"

"Negative; nothing serious, at least. A few broken bones and cuts and bruises, but we are fully mission capable."

Tolde edged closer to Falchi. A pall of black smoke hung around them. Falchi stood like a man whose grim realization forced his hand, because that's what he was. The enemy must have known the *Indomitable* was an Inquisition charter frigate. They knew exactly where to strike and how hard. Falchi was an old hand and had seen his share of naval engagements. This ambush was almost textbook if not for the fact they had been *pulled* back into regular space.

Worse, he knew he didn't have the combat power available to properly defend his ship. That aching truth gnawed down through the sharply pressed uniform and his tough skin. There was the very real possibility that he might lose his beloved *Indomitable* without much of a fight. Worry passed quickly through his features before Falchi calmed himself and faced Tolde.

"Inquisitor, may I?" he asked.

Tolde read the intent in his eyes and handed the communicator over.

The captain cut in. "Sergeant, this is the Captain. I need your Guards to gear up. We've been attacked, and I'm fully expecting boarders within the next hour or less."

If Fies was concerned, his voice didn't betray it. "Roger that, sir. I'll have my squad combat ready in ten. Where do you want us to position ourselves?"

He winced as a fresh wave of pain lanced his burned cheek. Falchi much preferred to see his opponent; at least he'd have some clue as to who attacked and what to expect in the coming critical moments. Blind, his reactions were severely limited. The *Indomitable* was an aging frigate. He needed as many advantages as he could get, advantages that weren't available.

"Move down to deck five. There is an access hatch twenty meters stern of the engine room. My guess is that's where they're going to hit us."

Fies had the same question as Tolde. "Any idea what we can expect?"

"Unfortunately, no." He abruptly stopped himself from finishing his thought process.

His mind raced through every possible variable and option, none of which left him with much confidence. Reluctantly, he turned back to Tolde. "I've been trying to figure out who could have taken us out so easily. My answers aren't…acceptable." He continued quickly before Tolde made him stop and before he lost the nerve to speak his mind. "Pirates are known to operate in this part of space. It is not unheard of for them to attack Prekhauten ships, but the technology is far too advanced for pirates."

"Your second theory?" Tolde asked slowly. He dreaded what came next, for it closely matched his own thoughts.

Falchi swallowed hard. "We've been attacked by a rogue Prekhauten battle group."

Most of the bridge crew stopped what they were doing and stared with undisguised shock. The possibility of traitors was so far from their minds it numbed them into inaction. Tolde felt his heart sink. The Inquisitor General and Prekhauten command had decided to keep the heresy on Crimeat under wraps. Tolde had been shuffled off to the Office of Heretical Persecution under the pretense of a promotion. Fies and his platoon had been given menial assignments and shunned from the main pool of Guardsmen. The reinforcement elements weren't even told about the involvement of rogue Guards under the command of Ursal Prowl.

Prowl had managed to escape before Tolde was able to apprehend him. The very real possibility that it was Prowl in command of whoever had attacked them sickened Tolde. It also failed to explain the weapons technology used. The denounced Inquisitor could only get advanced weapons like that if he had powerful friends in either the Conclave or the Inquisition.

Deciding it best to keep these dark thoughts to himself, Tolde let Falchi continue.

"I never thought the day would come when I would *ever* think of accusing my fellow Guards, but I just can't come up with a better option. Pirates are scum with low-grade tech. Them, I can handle. Not this."

Tolde chose his next question thoughtfully. He wanted to come out and tell Falchi everything, for it might mean the difference between life and death, but he needed the man to come to his own conclusions. Especially in front of Luma. She was the only wild card from his point of view. They'd worked together for the last two years, but she hadn't done much to convince Tolde she was a true partner rather than an Inquisition watchdog.

"What leads you to believe they are Prekhauten?"

Falchi reached for the blisters on his face again. "The attack was too coordinated. Pirates don't normally work together. Still, I can't say for sure, at least not until we see where they try to board us. Standard Guard tactics are to board as close to the engines as possible and disable the enemy ship before the defenders have the chance to react. Works like a charm. They come at us aft, we'll have our answer."

"I pray you're wrong."

"So do I, Inquisitor. So do I." Turning back to weapons, he asked, "Do we have anti-ship capability yet?"

"Any moment now, captain. Most of the wiring is shot, and targeting is offline."

Falchi grinned. "Then we do it the old-fashioned way."

"Manually?" the weapons officer asked incredulously.

"Damned straight," Falchi said. His confidence slowly passed among the crew. "With a little luck, we just might take out some of their boarding pods."

Tolde admired the man. The Prekhauten Guard were fortunate to have men like him in service, but the *Indomitable* was going to need more than just blind luck to see it through the end of this engagement.

"Enemy cruisers approaching at flank speed! I mark three cruisers and a command frigate," helm called.

That's a lot of boarders. There's no way we can win this. Falchi squared on the view screen. He was able to make out the grey-black ships coming in for the kill.

"Boarding pods away!"

Falchi swallowed. "How many?"

"Seventeen, Captain. Current trajectory has them heading for the engine room," the helms-man said in anticipation of the obvious question.

Falchi merely nodded. No words needed saying. This was the one time he wished he was wrong. He clicked the communicator open. "Sergeant Fies, boarders are coming your way. You have about five minutes before they dock. And Sergeant, there is more incoming that you will be able to stop. I've already rerouted as many defense teams to your deck as I can spare. Good luck."

The admission was just as good as committing his crew to their deaths. Time dropped into a slow crawl. Falchi was helpless to do anything except watch the instruments of his destruction ponderously move closer. That feeling of helplessness was as close to overwhelming as Falchi cared to admit. Space looked blacker, more ominous in light of his situation.

Tolde watched the older man for weakness. The stress was enough to break a less capable man. Falchi stood on his command bridge and left no doubts as to who was in charge. The Inquisitor admired him for that. Still, the hint of despair clouding Falchi's eyes was telling enough.

"I should go down with Fies," he announced, more for Luma Kai than for Falchi.

The embattled captain failed to see any purpose for an Inquisitor going into the fight unless he meant to inspire the Guards. Even then, Breed was only going to be in the way, doing more harm than good. Falchi took Fies as a man with little tolerance for the unnecessary. He decided it best for Fies and the *Indomitable* to keep Tolde away from the thick of the fight.

"I could use your assistance directing our defense, to be honest, Inquisitor," he said quickly. "I have a feeling this is going to get messy, and we need to have a reserve ready to deploy in the event the enemy boards in multiple positions. Standard boarding operations won't work until my counterpart realizes what we already suspect."

Tolde reluctantly agreed, despite his better judgment. Most of his career had been spent on the line or conducting his own investigations with only his discretion as a moral compass. Those brief stints in which he'd been forced to sit behind a desk or anchored to the Inquisition headquarters on Vau Prime had been unbearably constricting.

"Very well. Your orders?" he asked.

Falchi had barely opened his mouth when the weapons officer shouted, "Anti-ship missiles are back online!"

The captain grinned savagely. "Target the boarding pods and fire at will."

"Aye, Captain."

The message was quickly passed to gunners throughout the four firing batteries. Twenty-four missile crews tediously tried to plot firing solutions without suffering illusions of making kills. Naval gunnery relied too much on computers and not enough on the old ways. Not that it was going to stop the crews from doing their best to kill as many boarding pods as possible before they were under safe firing range.

The *Indomitable* lurched from the kinetic force of the first outgoing broadside attack. The bridge crew watched as the one-ton missiles streaked painfully slowly away from the ship. Falchi wasn't expecting many favorable results, so he was greatly surprised when two explosions rippled the incoming assault. *Two down, fifteen to go*. The crew cheered as the weapons officer tried to relay their success back to the gun crews.

Tolde watched the battle unfold. He still didn't see a way for this engagement to end well. Dull grey boarding pods lumbered closer, as unable to maneuver around the incoming missiles as the gun batteries were to target them. Another salvo launched, this time with negative effects. Try as he might, Tolde couldn't take his mind away from the prospect of suffocating in deep space. The thought nagged him, forcing him to think through likely and unlikely scenarios.

"Captain Falchi, what would the enemy need to do to completely cripple us?" he asked suddenly, much louder than intended.

Falchi shrugged, almost annoyed with being distracted from the battle. "Fire an electronic pulse. Our systems would be fried, and they would be able to sit back and wait until our air ran out. Not that it would take long. We've been venting oxygen at a slow rate from the first torpedo hit. Automatic stabilizers are keeping the damage minimal, but if an electronic pulse hit us, we'd be dead in less than an hour."

"I think we should consider the very real possibility that the enemy may do just that. They already have magnetic weapons; an electronic pulse is much easier to find on the black market."

"Damnation, you're right," Falchi admitted through clenched teeth. He'd been so absorbed with the naval action, he had neglected the obvious. "Weapons, do we still have the disrupter?"

"Negative, sir. The enemy took it out on the first blow."

Prekhauten warships came with standard pulse disrupters to prevent the scenario Falchi had described to Tolde. Nine times out of ten, a ship could take massive damage and still beat off an electronic pulse so long as the disrupter was functional. Without it... Captain and

Inquisitor shared skeptical looks while wisely keeping their comments to themselves. This was not the time for the crew to see doubt in their senior leadership.

Three rapid explosions tore through the incoming boarding pods. Flames sprung to life and were quickly extinguished in the vacuum as men and metal tumbled off into the darkest parts of space. Falchi stared wide-eyed at the scene, knowing the *Indomitable* was not responsible.

"Helm, who in the hells fired those shots?" he barked.

"Unknown attack craft just entered real space. It is engaging the boarding pods."

Falchi flashed a look of relief. "Get me an open line with that commander. I want to know whether to consider him hostile or buy him a drink."

"Aye, sir."

It was much too early to be safe from immediate danger, forcing Falchi to remind his crew their celebrations were premature. He keyed Tolde's communicator again. "Sergeant Fies, we're still a long way from home, but the odds are turning in your favor. Looks like very few of the boarding pods will make it to our hull. Stand by for further updates."

The smile in Fies's voice was unmistakable. "Roger that, sir."

Falchi nodded once and switched channels. "Engine room, get us back to full power before our enemies can react to this new development. I don't want to be a lame duck for them."

Another pair of pods was blown apart, leaving only ten. Falchi figured each pod held ten combat-ready men. The odds still worked out against him. At best, he had forty security personnel, not including Fies men. Defenders held two distinct advantages. Their enemy clearly wanted the vessel intact, meaning they weren't willing to risk destroying it. That limited the amount of firepower they could unleash. Second, and most importantly, enemy boarding parties would be forced into a tight funnel until a suitable landing area was established and secured. All Fies had to do, nominally, was take up a good defensive position and unleash every bit of firepower he had at his disposal. Falchi had seen it done when he was younger and still prone to getting excited over such things. He'd also seen it fail miserably. *Which is exactly what might happen if the troops stuffed into those boarding pods are Prekhautens.*

"Sir, I have the captain of the attack craft online," helm reported.

"This is Captain Falchi of the Prekhauten Guard frigate *Indomitable*, whom do I have the honor of speaking with?"

A stiff cackle of static filled the air momentarily. "Captain Falchi, my name is Matthias. I'd like to be able to explain more, but you'll appreciate the need for discretion for the moment."

"Of course. We have three identified enemy ships. I'll have my helm transfer their coordinates to you."

"Unnecessary, I already have firing solutions plotted. Please tell your gunners to stand down while I finish off these boarding pods. I'd hate to be blown away accidentally."

Falchi passed a nervous glance to Tolde, who merely nodded. The relaxed look on his face was enough to convince Falchi to go along with it. "Helm, inform mister Matthias that we are grateful for his assistance and will comply. Good hunting."

He turned back to Tolde. "Well, what do you think?"

"He's a good man. I trust him implicitly," he replied without hesitation. *I just don't understand how he came to be* here *at this particular time.*

Falchi nodded. "Good enough for me. Operations, clear a landing bay. I wish to speak with Matthias once he boards."

"Aye, sir."

"Is it safe to talk here?" Matthias asked as he and Tolde finished shaking hands.

Tolde, Luma and Falchi were waiting in the landing bay when he arrived. Tolde's heart warmed upon seeing his old friend again. Naturally suspicious, Luma Kai stood with arms folded across her chest, silently judging. She wasn't the sort to give in to the superstitious belief of coincidence, and that made Matthias a potentially dangerous man — especially considering his curt dismissal from the Prekhauten ranks. Luma didn't care how many pirates or heretics he'd just killed. She didn't trust him.

The landing bay had been cleared and secured by Fies and his platoon. Tolde gave him a crisp nod. "Safe enough. What are you doing out here?"

"That's a long story, and I doubt we have time enough for it, but here's the short. I've been tracking this group for about a month now. Would it surprise you to hear your old friend from Crimeat is in charge over there?"

Tolde froze. "Prowl?"

"The same. He turned up about half a year ago, running mostly with pirates and smuggler scum. The interesting thing is he's gathering his own fleet."

"A pirate fleet?" Falchi said incredulously. "That's unheard of."

Matthias eyed him with disdain. "In most cases, I'd agree, but I've seen enough to convince me otherwise. Captain, the universe is changing."

"You're suggesting the Prekhauten navy isn't enough to keep these brigands subdued?"

He flashed a toothy grin. "I'm suggesting the navy is being told to look in other directions while *this* is happening."

Tolde eased into the conversation, eager to keep the two from coming to blows. Level heads were required if the *Indomitable* was going to make it to Hawker's Gate in one piece. "Perhaps you should start by easing the good captain's concerns. It can't be coincidence that has you following this specific ship."

"No, it wasn't. General Strannan assigned me to monitor the deep space shipping lanes due to increased pirate attacks. Normally, Guard command wouldn't get deeply involved. The main shipping companies have proved more than capable of handling their own defense. Strannan figured — correctly, I might add — that these pirates are being coordinated by a former Guard or Inquisitor."

"Ursal Prowl," Tolde concluded.

Falchi offered a blank look. He, like most naval captains, had been left in the dark over the Crimeat affair.

"Captain, Ursal Prowl is proof that your suspicions about traitors are credible. He was an Inquisitor until two years ago."

"Now he's just a fugitive," Matthias added darkly.

Luma whispered, "A heretic."

"A man I intend to bring to justice. He has much to answer for," Tolde growled. The lines under his eyes deepened with anger.

The Inquisitor General never came out and said it, but Tolde's actions on Crimeat were widely viewed as a failure. He had allowed all the Three to escape, nearly destroying a major industrial complex in the process, and failed to capture or kill the man responsible for inciting an insurrection and leading the entire planetary detachment of Prekhauten Guards against the Conclave.

By all rights, Tolde should have died on Crimeat. Amongeratix had certainly been set to complete the task begun five decades earlier on the Conclave prison world of Keltoo when Tolde had first been assigned with bringing him back to captivity. Good men had died, though not as many as in the tunnels of the Plateau. Nightmares refused to let Tolde sleep in peace. So many bodies ripped apart like sheets of paper. Never had he witnessed such awful carnage. The blood. The body parts. The massive level of destruction that was only averted because Amongeratix had been after a bigger prize.

Tolde's thoughts drifted to Sister Abigail, the Blood Witch. She had sacrificed herself so that the remainder of Matthias's Guards could escape. Trust between the Inquisition and the Sisters had always been an obstacle for Tolde. Those walls had crashed down the moment she'd died in his arms and collapsed into dust. Her death and the untold number of military and civilians in Reven demanded vengeance. Ursal Prowl was the target of that need.

Once, when youthful arrogance had still ruled, Tolde had thought he was above such base desire. Revenge was a thing committed only by the weak and petty. Crimeat had showed him the error in his thoughts. Revenge drove him on when his peers silently decided he should have retired by now. Dark venom pumped through his veins. His time spent in the Office of Heretical Persecution was not wholly wasted. Countless hours had been spent digging through personnel files and old records surrounding both the Three and Prowl. Tolde believed in fate and knew that he and Ursal would meet again. And when they did…

Falchi swallowed uncomfortably. He was a space captain, unused to the political intrigue the Inquisition introduced. "Perhaps we need to reconvene in my quarters. This is not a con-versation to be had in the open."

"I thought you said this bay was secure?" Matthias suddenly doubted.

Falchi bristled. "Secure enough, but I wasn't expecting such…distressing knowledge. Everything I've seen today tells me we are heading for dark times, and I'll not be responsible for loose lips escaping my ship."

"Your stateroom will be perfect, Captain," Luma interrupted.

Tolde listened to the exchange with interest, hoping to gain new insight on his partner. Luma, however, kept her life private. She had shared her considerably limited service record but stopped there. Tolde caught himself frowning. Luma Kai had been approached by Inquisition recruiters at a young age. She she'd barely been out of her teens when the recruiters had arrived at her home and practically told her parents they were taking her. The reasoning had never found its way into the records hall, building Tolde's suspicions that she was not what she seemed. The Inquisition was keen on acquiring *gifted* people for unorthodox tasks.

Most of her career was blacked out, marking her a special operator. Luma bore the scars of missions she preferred to forget, enlightening him on occasion. She was a very closed woman but had a gifted tongue when the need to talk arose. He'd seen her talk her way out of several tense situations in which lesser Inquisitors would have broken. That earned his respect, but not his trust. Luma would only get his trust when she proved where her loyalties rested.

Tolde followed the group down the corridor to Falchi's stateroom. His thoughts strayed to dinner. He had a feeling it was going to be a long night.

ELEVEN

3212 A.G. (After Gods), Krenz, planet Vau Prime.

Sunset shaded the rows of ancient willow trees a mild shade of red, offsetting the natural yellow leaves. Winds blew just hard enough to tousle the drooping branches, making them wave at the flow of traffic up and down Redemption Boulevard. Summer was coming soon, bringing a miserable combination of heat and humidity, but for now the weather was as close to perfect as it could get.

The massive eternal pillars of light pulsed brightness back into space in a simulacrum of the sun. Meant to inspire hope, the lights could be seen from the edges of the planetary system. They served as guides for incoming freighters and beacons to pilgrims of the promise of better days. Decorative parks surrounded the massive columns stretching into the heavens. Flowers and trees were constantly in bloom, making it one of Vau Prime's most romantic destinations.

Cardinal Seniorus Lorenu Phos enjoyed sitting beneath the freshly blossomed cherry trees, listening to the bees dart between flowers and the tender kiss of wind in her hair. The parks offered a calming effect, releasing her from the increasing worries of office and church. Her first few years as the head of the most prominent organization in the universe had been mildly uneventful. Lorenu wasn't foolish enough to think the Conclave was the most powerful entity among the seven hundred-plus worlds, but those other organizations chose to remain hidden.

Lately, she'd been forced to abandon her nightly stroll through the parks, often working so late she ended up sleeping in her offices. Religious demands were increasing, and the Conclave was feeling the strain. Cardinals were being pulled in too many directions. Many had been accused of heresy and placed on trial. The problems on Crimeat were responsible for fueling a million tiny fires throughout the universe. Inquisition and Guard forces were stretched thin already and getting thinner with each new world or issue to deal with. She couldn't see a way out no matter how hard she thought.

Lorenu yawned and set down the latest batch of reports. Three more rebellions, all fortunately on minor worlds, had been put down with the assistance of Prekhauten battalions. She understood people being dissatisfied with the rule of government. Such opinions were a natural right. What she couldn't fathom was how news from Crimeat had spread so quickly, and with enough strength to create havoc. Normal dissent was fueled into an incoherent rage directed against the three ruling classes.

She wanted to get away.

"Cardinal Seniorus, Cardinals Gorman and Har are here," Aliz announced with a slight bow.

Lorenu smiled at her, though not for the message. The thin aide had a mousy look, with close cropped brown hair and a deceptively thin body. She was the one person in the universe Lorenu felt comfortable telling everything.

She waved with a dismissive gesture and sighed. "Thank you, Aliz. Have them come in."

Lorenu wanted nothing less than to be bothered with the complaints of two over-pampered cardinals of the Forum. Both men were petty, caring only for their own issues rather than the good of all. Unfortunately, Lorenu was powerless to have them removed from office. She smiled at the thought of both being accused of heresy and led off in chains to a forgotten prison world at the edge of the universe. A fanciful thought and wholly unrealistic.

Ott Gorman entered first, his great bulk filling most of the wide doorframe. She watched with mild disgust as his two chins bounced with each step. The liver spots on his bald head made him look like a diseased jungle cat. Lorenu frowned. Tinus Har was the exact opposite. He had neatly kept dark hair and equally black eyes that seldom missed anything. Lorenu thought the man bore a foul demeanor, reminding her of black market dealers in Vau Prime's underworld.

"Cardinal Seniorus, thank you for seeing us on such short notice," Gorman started while helping himself to one of the luxurious chairs at her desk.

Lorenu frowned but held her tongue. The chairs were an imported luxury from her homeworld. They were the one constant of an easier life.

"It seems I have little choice these days. Gentlemen, please make yourselves comfortable," she replied.

Tinus scowled briefly and sat. "These are troubled times."

"Indeed. I've just finished going over the latest reports from General Strannan. The news is not good."

Gorman shifted uncomfortably. "The Conclave is —"

"Useless to the masses, I'm afraid," she cut him off. "We rule Vau Prime and watch the rest of the universe suffer."

"Perhaps the people lack faith," Tinus suggested. "The gods only fail us when we fail them. There is a severe crisis of faith, Cardinal Seniorus."

Crisis of faith? Are you fucking kidding me? "Faith is not the issue. Somehow, word of the insurrection on Crimeat has spread. Heretics are spreading lies against the Conclave using Crimeat as their rallying cry. We are almost powerless to stop them all."

"We need more troops," Tinus said quickly. "General Strannan is a capable commander, but the Prekhautens were never meant to be an army. Private militias and amateur armies are springing up on dozens of worlds."

"Unauthorized military entities are as much a hazard to us as heretics," Lorenu scolded. Her eyes narrowed sharply.

Tinus spread his hands. "But, as you say, we are powerless to stop them. We could send the reserve battalions in to forcibly disarm these upstart armies or issue commissions."

Gorman coughed unexpectedly. "Commissions? Impossible. We'd only be adding to the problems."

"Problems that we can all agree are only getting worse."

"Gentlemen, calm yourselves!" Lorenu interjected. "The decision to add untrained military forces is not going to be made between the three of us tonight. We have more pressing issues. Have either of you heard rumors of this cult of Rengu?"

"Unfortunately, yes," Tinus said. "There are flame banners being raised in dozens of capitals. The Inquisition is increasingly busy and frustrated."

Lorenu nodded absently. "I've got the librarians trying to dig up anything they can on this Rengu, but thus far they've been unsuccessful."

"It is not entirely unheard of," Gorman said. "Many of the lesser gods are still relatively unknown."

She briefly contemplated telling them the truth: that the gods weren't dead at all. The Conclave was responsible for the security and continued spiritual growth of the population, but only a select few knew the deepest truths. Not even the Forum, the one hundred cardinals designated to make the most important decisions of church and state, was read in on the truth. Tinus and Gorman would have to wait, if they were ever included.

"You suggest Rengu is a god?" she asked.

He shrugged. "It is not impossible. We all know that names have changed since the Conclave was first established. We certainly aren't privileged to all the god's secrets. Perhaps Rengu is a reinvented deity."

"Perhaps. For the moment, the cultists are content to worship peacefully, staking claim to despondent worlds where faith is the weakest." Lorenu stated.

"Faith is strained everywhere. It's only a matter of time before the cultists turn to open acts of violence against us," Tinus said. "All the more reason to accept these militias into service. Pay them a stipend, offer bonuses, and let us be done with the whole sordid affair."

"Conclave coffers don't run so deep," Lorenu said dismissively. "Forget the militias for the moment; I want to focus on this cult. Part of me agrees with you, Tinus. Violence is only a matter of time. Religious zealotry is more dangerous than many of us give credence. One thing concerns me, though. Every world Rengu has sprung up on is far out the way. It simply doesn't pose a significant threat to warrant total military action."

Gorman cleared his throat uncomfortably. "Lorenu, we ignored the rumors of unrest on Crimeat for years, and it continues to haunt us. Do you think it wise to make the same mistake again so readily?"

Lorenu opened and shut her mouth quickly. Crimeat had been a mistake. The entire campaign never should have happened. She could have taken the weaker way out by blaming the negligence of her predecessors, but Lorenu had been raised honorably. The Cardinal Seniorus had accepted full responsibility and begged forgiveness from the families and governments the Conclave's inaction had ruined. The stain was an immovable black mark on her office.

Hindsight being what it is, Lorenu focused on the future instead of dwelling on the past. That road led to a foul place she was loath to ever return to. Reluctantly, she was forced to agree with Gorman.

"What is your proposed solution? Send the Guard in force and crush all who stand accused of heresy? I don't know how you honestly feel, but I think we throw that word around a little too much."

Tinus cocked his head, black locks flapping against the side of his face. "What word, Cardinal Seniorus?"

"Heresy. Name someone a heretic, and you remove the moral inhibitors that keep us civilized. Panic ensues, practically causing more harm than good," Lorenu admitted. She secretly contended that the Inquisition held too much power.

Tinus flashed a predatory grin. "The Inquisition is more than capable of handling heretics, Lorenu. That's what they were created for. I say we let Nye loose. Let his people dig out this cult quickly."

She was no fool. The only way a cult could have sprung up on a dozen worlds simultaneously was through advanced organization and planning. Investigations were required before she was willing, or able, to send in a wave of black-cloaked Inquisitors. The shock value alone would drive the cult so far underground the Conclave would never root it out. Lorenu understood she was locked in a treacherous position. Hardliners in the Conclave and Inquisition routinely called for her to step down or act at once. Other, more empathetic cardinals demanded she continue doing as she always had. Either way offered damnation or salvation in equal parts.

"Cardinal Gorman, take the matter of the militias to the Forum for a vote." *Before Strannan makes the decision without us.* "I will not, however, commit the entirety of our resources to hunting down this cult of Rengu until we have concrete evidence of who the leaders are, how deep their resources are, and where their command and control is located."

"That might take years," Tinus cautioned.

Lorenu offered a hard glare. "So be it. I don't want another war unless I know we can cut the head off our enemy and end their rebellion. I am not saying no, gentlemen, just not yet. The day is coming when Rengu will meet his demise, but I can't act until I have more concrete information to go on. Now, if you will excuse me. It is already late, and I still have much to do before I can retire. Good night."

Gorman and Tinus rose and bowed, leaving Lorenu alone once more. She sighed as the door clicked shut. Her gaze briefly focused on the golden wood paneling of her office. The brilliant colors complimented the dull white marble floor. Right now, it was merely distracting. Trouble within the Conclave was worsening, if tonight's meeting was any indication, meaning that keeping control was going to prove challenging. She prayed the advance teams of Inquisitors was able to come up with something fast. The alternative was not promising.

Cardinal Tinus Har finished recounting his conversation with the Cardinal Seniorus and sat back down. His normally tanned face was reddened and blustered. He was a man of few words, but the indignity of Lorenu's unwillingness to act was insulting.

Alain Nye stroked his chin, delighting in the feel of stubble prickling his fingertips. He'd listened intently, clinging on most of it from the comforts of his worn chair in his private office. The Inquisitor General was a calculated man, neither prone to rash decisions nor too cautious to prove ineffective. His gaze drifted across each of the ten people in the room, mentally calculating the strengths and weaknesses of each. Trust was too precious a thing to be thrown around carelessly.

Pursing his lips, Nye calmly replied. "The Cardinal Seniorus is under much stress these days. Failures on Crimeat rest heavily on her shoulders. Failures, I might add, not entirely hers. One of my own turned rogue and caused a lot of trouble that I believe we can all agree is still rippling through our organizations."

He paused to count the head nods and quiet grunts of acceptance. Not as many as he'd hoped, but enough for what he intended. "My friends, we are coming to a crossroads. The Conclave has lost power. There can be no denial of that fact. The decline began nearly fifty years ago when Amongeratix first escaped from Keltoo. We have been unsuccessful in permanently recapturing him or any of the others. It has been two year since Crimeat. The Three are turning the universe to chaos, and the Conclave sits immobile in its own fear.

"I don't need to tell any of you what this means. War. Plain and simple, we will soon find ourselves in a war the likes of which hasn't been seen since the gods destroyed themselves at Occanum." He sneered at the lie. Gods, indeed. Their bodies were scattered across the universe in the vain hope of never letting another war of such magnitude happen again. *Unfortunately for them, I want a war. All it will take is a little push, and the universe will burn.*

"War is not the necessary conclusion. Surely there is another way to wrest control from the Conclave?" Colonel Mobus Kale growled.

Nye briefly considered the career Guard. He had close-cropped blonde hair and an angry look. Lean and undeniably aggressive, Mobus maintained an unhealthy level of rage ever since he'd lost his right arm three years ago. He wore the prosthetic because he had to, hating the equipment every moment it was attached to the ruined stump of his arm. It gave him purpose, fueled his need to act. Nye knew it was only a matter of time before Mobus became a liability to what he was trying to achieve.

The Inquisitor General exhaled sharply through his nostrils. "It is already done. Pieces are already en route to starting points. All it takes now is the catalyst."

"Unfortunately, the Cardinal Seniorus will not acquiesce. She is a stubborn woman." Tinus Har reminded harshly.

"Lorenu Phos is a strong woman, but her mind is filled with a combination of regret and doubt. Controlling her isn't an option," Cardinal Arbalas added. She had always been jealous of Lorenu's election by the Forum. In her mind, it should be her sitting in the office, not some nobody from a backwater world.

Nye held up a hand for silence. Every person in the room recognized and feared the power he could bring against them. All except for Mobus Kale. The Prekhauten was sterner than Strannan had ever dreamed, and Nye reluctantly admitted he was more than a little afraid of the man. Nye rummaged over what he remembered from the Guard's personnel jacket.

Nye closed his eyes for a moment, lost in the depths of the colonel's emotions, but it wasn't just hatred. No, Mobus had something darker festering in his soul. It made him dangerous and worse. Aspirations to power were potentially damaging, especially in a man who craved it so badly he was willing to do anything. Nye began plotting ways to eliminate Mobus.

"This conversation needs to start at the beginning. The current Cardinal Seniorus is a threat. Can we all agree that she needs to be removed before the war begins?"

More nods.

"Let's be done with the bitch tonight. Time is wasting," Mobus concurred.

His zeal gave him a feral look, making the others shrink away.

Nye smiled tightly. "Not so fast, Colonel. We have no grounds for removing her this early. Doing so only exposes us but will serve to solidify resistance. She will be dealt with in due time."

Mobus disagreed but said no more. He folded his arms across his chest and leaned back in the rickety chair. His pride was wounded by the quality of the room Nye had chosen for this meeting. The luxury of Krenz was far away under the reasoning that it wouldn't do to be caught in their own offices. Alain Nye had taken them to a forgotten part of the city where city guards often refused to venture.

The dark environment lent a nefarious attitude to their meetings. Nye found it oddly comforting. They'd been meeting in secret for almost five years and hadn't so much as seen a Guard civil patrol. Of course, a few well-placed bribes and an occasional missing persons report helped maintain the illusion of secrecy. Only Nye knew that each scrap of conversation was recorded and analyzed by a very small circle of men and women he trusted completely.

Most the building Nye had chosen was crumbling. Some of the roof was collapsed. Walls were caved in. Void of running water and electricity, the building housed vagrants and rodents. Trash piled higher than the front bank of windows. Nye had taken the sole room in the basement, had what was left of the dilapidated furniture brought in, and filled benches with candles. He much preferred the comforts of his office, but these were delicate matters the rest of the Conclave and Inquisition weren't ready to learn just yet.

He idly scratched behind his right ear and listened to the continued debate. Nye often found it hard to concentrate when so many opinions were being tossed carelessly about. One or two of those assembled were more boisterous than the rest, marking them as liabilities. Nye silently watched those men and women, his mind already drifting to the most convenient way of disposing them once they'd outlived their usefulness.

Nye's thoughts focused as Mobus resumed his argument.

Binary communications beeped and whirled through the internal communicator, but the listener never opened his augmented eyes. He sat patiently in the deepest shadows without moving, hardly breathing. His golden mask was a featureless, sophisticated combination of technology and biology concealing his face and locking his identity in permanent secrecy. Removing the mask meant death. He didn't care. Mission parameters required total anonymity. His clothes were made from genetic carbonate, clinging to his body and shifting with each minute movement. Cybernetic implants in his brain and central nervous system enhanced thought capacity and reaction time, making him not quite human.

Names were forbidden, considered a human characteristic that only served to define one's identity, not liberate it. He was one of a thousand who dressed and looked the same. They came from all walks of life, the unwanted and the destitute. Those who survived the trials were born again and given new life. He was one. He was a Vaumagian assassin, one of the deadliest killers in the known universe. And he was in the employ of the Inquisitor General.

The assassin sifted through the steady stream of data coming from the clandestine council meeting, processing vocal strains and breathing patterns for signs of treachery. Alain Nye had approached the shadow order years ago when he was still just the aide to the Inquisitor General. They'd had a mutually beneficial partnership since. Nye took control of the Inquisition and turned their heads in the opposite direction when the Vaumagians were contracted.

It was Nye who had sent the assassins to Crimeat two years ago to meet with Ursal Prowl and the upstart Baron Scura. Assassins had swept in and murdered a healthy part of the twelve ruling nobles in a single night. Nye cared little for their internal politics. The violence was meant to shift the balance of power and incite a war. He had used the young noble's emotions and ambition against him, turning Scura into a puppet that took the blame for fomenting a rebellion not only against the ruling body of Lethendweil, but the Conclave itself. Scura's death was officially ruled a suicide. Nye knew better. The man had been another loose end easy enough to remove.

The working relationship between the Vaumagians and the Inquisitor General continued to evolve beneficially for both parties. One day, Nye would try to betray the golden-masked killers. It was an inevitable conclusion to their affairs. The assassins were prepared to take necessary action when that time came. Until then, they would continue to monitor all of Nye's dealings exactly as he contracted.

The assassin's head jerk back suddenly and cocked slightly. He replayed the piece of code to ensure what he'd heard was correct. Standing slowly, the diminutive man edged along the shadows and looked out the second story window. Six men in Prekhauten Special Unit combat gear were slinking their way up the street in bounding movements. Their destination was painfully clear. Nye had been betrayed by one of his own. Calculating the threat potential as he moved, the assassin computed the best angle of attack. Six men presented a healthy threat but not an insur-mountable one. The Vaumagian order was among the best trained warriors, far surpassing the advanced combat tactics of the Guard.

He waited until the squad leader, obvious due to his position in the assault and the small set of communication antennas attached to the back of his grey helmet, crouched a meter from the door. The assassin leapt out the window the same instant the Guards stacked and kicked in the front door. Wood splintered apart as the boot drove through. Four of the Guards were already inside clearing the immediate area before the assassin hit the ground. Drawing a wicked, curved blade of black steel, the assassin landed less than a foot away from the squad leader. He sliced the man's throat in one fluid motion, ropes of dark blood splashing through the humid night. The man died with a strangled gasp.

Enhanced reflexes propelled the assassin into a tight ball and onto the next Guard's back before the first body hit the ground. The curved blade whistled as he plunged it into the Guard's exposed neck, severing the spine. Chaos erupted in the tight foyer. Built-in infrared sensors failed to register the assassin as he threw the first flash bang. He closed his eyes a moment before the brilliant flash all but blinded the Guards.

"Contact!"

Red laser beams sliced across the chamber, wildly searching for a target. A lesser man might have grinned at the ease of the kill, but the assassin had willingly abandoned his emotions the day he was chosen to have the golden mask surgically attached to his face. He was a soulless killer intent on protecting a client. The deaths were clinical, emotionless. The remaining Guards never truly had a chance.

They died without firing a round.

TWELVE

3212 A.G. (After Gods), deep desert, planet An'kuruku.

Elisa awoke to loud clicking coming from the night. She yawned, half-stretching as she rolled over and tried to find sleep again. The crunching continued to get louder. A tickle in the back of her mind warned Elisa to get up, quickly. She fumbled for her side arm and sword. Weapons ready, she searched the darkness for…she didn't know what. The desert remained anathema to her despite living in Tenemenah for two years. She wasn't used to the creatures, heat or unbearable cold. There was no way she could ever have been prepared for what she saw lumbering out of the darkness.

The scorpion was ridiculously large. Massive claws oozed neurotoxin resin designed to incapacitate the prey while the scorpion fed. Elisa was mortified when she noticed the insect's head was nearly as large as her body. She fired a quick pair of rounds. Black ichors oozed from the wounds, but the scorpion wasn't even slowed.

"Ah'muf! Get up!" she shouted and fired again.

The horses reared back, struggling to break free from their tethers. The scorpion retched a nightmarish squeal, and Ah'muf didn't move. Elisa struggled to fight down the surge of rising panic. Thoughts of her friend dead already threatened to paralyze her before her mind calmed enough to react. She emptied her clip into the monster and dashed back towards the oasis. Her priority was to get the scorpion away from Ah'muf and the horses. If any of them died, she would follow quickly.

"Ha!" she bellowed and ran.

The scorpion lumbered after, slamming its stinger into the sand where she'd just been. Acid melted the sand, pungent smells choking the air. Enraged, the scorpion charged after Elisa. The left claw swung, shattering a dying palm tree in an explosion of slivers and browned leaves. Unable to rationalize, the scorpion wasn't used to prey that put up so much of a fight.

Elisa reloaded on the run. She was able, luckily, to find her exploding tip rounds and load six out of seven before the scorpion managed to sweep her legs out from under her. Jagged rocks tore her shirt, slicing the fabric and flesh beneath. Wincing, Elisa struggled to roll free. Giant legs stabbed. Elisa cried out as the claw punched into her calf. She emptied her pistol into the scorpion's exposed head. The mass of explosive tips detonated deep within the brain cavity, instantly killing the scorpion.

The giant insect shuddered, tail thrashing wildly. Sand and saw grass whipped through the air in every direction as Elisa dragged herself out to safety. Or so she hoped. The scorpion collapsed slowly. Its great bulk slammed down on leg joints with great crunching sounds. Gaseous clouds escaped the wounds. She choked. Blackness swirled around the edges of her vision. Her entire leg had gone numb by the time she managed to get free. The scorpion's corpse crashed in a great cloud of dust and sand less than a meter from Elisa.

Elisa's thoughts took her back two years, to the Great Barrier Jungle on her homeworld. She'd been attacked by one of the larger predators and only narrowly survived. Her horse had been mortally wounded, though, and she'd wept as she was forced to end its suffering. This time was the opposite. Poison coursed through her veins, rapidly moving to her hips and down her other leg.

She struggled to cry out, to let Ah'muf know of her dilemma. Nothing but a strangled gasp slipped past her lips. Elisa raised and arm, desperately waving for…she didn't know what. She started to choke, her upper body shaking violently. Froth spilled down her chin. Elisa looked up and saw the shadow-darkened figures of four men standing beside her. She started to laugh uncontrollably as the hallucinations bent down.

"Where am I?" she asked groggily.

"You are a very foolish woman," a thickly accented voice scolded. "The deserts are no place for outlanders who lack a camel's sense. By all rights, you should be dead."

Elisa found she couldn't move. Cold dread twisted her face. Fears of permanent paralysis refused to be spoken. Her companion noticed her worried look and placed a reassuring hand on her shoulder.

"We were forced to restrain you while the poison bled out."

"Bled out?" she asked, growing more concerned.

His face came into focus, slightly. He had a hawkish nose and tanned skin so dark it was almost black. Pale amber eyes stared down from under thick eyebrows. His cheek bones were angular, giving his face a boxy look. Small ears were tucked against the sides of his head, the tips hidden beneath a light tan head wrap.

Elisa shook her head, sharp needles of pain making her instantly regret doing so. She was able to notice his light robes and the curved saber tied to his hip once the pain lessened. Her exposure to the deep desert tribes was severely limited, but she recognized the garb for what it was. He seemed to approve, nodding once.

"I am Tanzeil. You are a guest in my village, for the moment," he said.

"Until you decide whether I'm a threat," she added sharply.

Tanzeil gave her the thinnest smile. "Trust is to be earned, never given. Even an outlander should recognize that much."

Elisa understood, though she disliked being strapped down. The last time she'd trusted anyone had resulted in violence and bloodshed. More painful memories mocked her thoughts. Try as she might, Elisa couldn't remember a time when life had been kind. And it was all because of the damned Bloody Man. Fresh anger coursed through her. She wanted revenge, needed release. Too many wrongs continued to pile up, and she felt helpless under the weight of it.

"I can here with a…friend," she said, changing the subject before her emotions spiraled out of control.

Tanzeil nodded again. "Yes, the city dweller. He recovers now, though he may yet be in grave danger. The poison of the giant scorpion can kill a fully grown man in mere minutes."

"By that reckoning I should be dead as well," Elisa protested.

He shrugged. "The gods seldom give us reasons for their actions."

She stopped listening as he continued to drone. Elisa suddenly became intent on wiggling her toes. The movement was simple, natural from birth, but was one of the most rewarding feelings she had had in a very long time. Joy broke a wide smile. She wasn't paralyzed!

Tanzeil suddenly noticed her inattention. "I apologize. It is rare that we have visitors to whom I can explain many of the hidden dangers in the desert. My people elected me for obvious reasons." He paused. "I have talked enough. Now is your turn. Convince me why I should let you and your friend free."

She licked her lips and cleared her throat. Much of her tale was too incredible for her to believe; making others without any ties believe would be no easy feat. Elisa struggled with where to begin. So much had happened, she often found her grasp on reality slipping away. *How do I tell a stranger that the gods have found special purpose for me, sending me to An'kuruku to find something called the Paradise Tear?* She lacked the answer.

Do I begin by telling him how my life was destined to become one hellish misery after another? How the Bloody Man murdered my village and smiled at me like a loving grandparent? Or do I tell him how Mollock Bolle and I were duped into helping a false war take shape so renegades could seize control of Lethendweil? No, he won't believe any of it, because it didn't happen here. My best bet is to explain what happened in Tenemenah that led me here. Wherever in the blessed hells here is.

"Can I have water first?" she asked.

Tanzeil flushed. "Of course, how rude of me."

She gulped down the lukewarm water before he had the chance to admonish her foolishness. Thirst sated, Elisa looked up into his amber eyes and asked, "What do you know of the Paradise Tear?"

Tanzeil recoiled and touched his thumb and index finger to his lips with a mumbled prayer. "Do not speak of such sacred things!"

She grimaced. It was going to be even harder than she thought to win her and Ah'muf's freedom.

She wasn't sure how long she'd been alone. Long enough for the harsh midday heat to bleed off the tent and get cool again, she supposed. A tray of fresh fruits and (of course) dates was brought in along with a pitcher of water. Elisa failed to accept the desert world delicacy, avoiding them when possible. She wasn't tied down anymore but knew better than to try to leave her canvas prison. Tanzeil came across as a highly competent leader, no doubt an equal warrior as well. Elisa wasn't in the mood to have her head chopped off under the misconception of trying to escape. Not that she had a clue as to where she was right now. For all she knew, Tanzeil had taken her back to Tenemenah.

No, that's just paranoia. It's too hot to be in the city. He's taken us to his camp, probably deeper into the desert. Elisa wasn't the sort to give in to irrational fears. She decided to use her time wisely. A long trip around the tent tested the limits or her legs with disappointing results. Bandages on her wounds concealed the atrophy she felt. *The scorpion was deadlier than I imagined.* Frowning, she sat down and rummaged through the fruits, pointedly ignoring the dates.

Sea spray covered Mollock's face and outstretched arms. He titled his head back, enjoying the cool, salty feeling embracing him. The Bo, he'd come to find out, was a magical place. Raw energy flowed into him every time he touched the waters. He felt powerful, more than at any other time in his haggard life. Mollock realized this was what he'd been missing all those long years on the run from the gods. He silently thanked the Bloody Man for putting Elisa in his life. Without her, he never would have found this place of wonder or a sense of purpose.

The lie of the gods had weighed heavily on him from the moment he'd first discovered the sleeping deity beneath Reven. Mankind was taught to believe that the gods were gone, shadowy fragments of the power they once were, and incapable of giving aid when it was needed. Mollock's discovery proved Conclave doctrine wrong. The gods were still alive; they merely slept. He decided that the Three were locked in a brutal struggle to either free the gods or keep them imprisoned.

Mankind had a right to know the truth. He was the voice that promised deliverance from the ignorance of eternity. Three thousand years of lies needed to be dissolved, washed away like the morning tides. Here, on the shores of the Bo, Mollock finally understood his calling. The great mysteries that had twisted and ruined his life now made sense, laid bare for him to see. He no longer fought against Kaline, though he still maintained a healthy level of mistrust in her. Politics and religion were a deadly combination designed to enslave humanity to the will of the Conclave. Mankind deserved freedom. Mollock Bolle wanted to give that freedom.

His beard, mottled grey and black and hanging down past his chin, was wet enough to cling to his neck. The scratchy feeling annoyed Mollock, but it was a minor torment compared to the pain of sudden enlightenment. A message rested in his heart. It was a song that needed to be sung. Only when the rest of the universe knew the truth would Mollock find his long-awaited rest.

"A storm is coming," Kaline said suddenly, appearing behind him.

Dressed in a long crimson gown that concealed her from neck to ankle, Kaline reminded Mollock of death. Blood was an ill omen. Her dress left much to the imagination, neither flashy nor well tailored. She had the potential to be an attractive woman but chose to keep those qualities hidden. The better part of life was already well past her, but Mollock found his desire growing. It had been too long since he'd last lain with a woman.

"There is always a storm coming," he replied softly, the words barely audible above the roar of crashing waves. "Whether this one or the next, it makes no difference. The desert needs the rain."

"Deserts are deserts for a reason, Mollock," she admonished. "You would do well to remember we are not gods."

He smirked. "Are the gods even gods? Kaline, we've lived a lie; that much I will concede to you. I've seen the Three. Witnessed their undying hatred towards each other. It was the most terrifying experience."

"The Three are surrounded by such lore. Their myth is nearly as great as that of the gods. It makes sense that they would be equally violent."

"Violent? They can bring the universe to its knees. If we had but a fraction of their power…" He let the thought trail off. Mollock was many things, but a dreamer was not one of them.

Fleeting images of Tannus and Amongeratix battling in the falling snow haunted him still. The Three were much more than myths. They were the legacy of hate-induced rage that nearly consumed the universe. A practical man, Mollock had refused to believe at first. Even his discovery of the sleeping god had seemed too unreal. He'd tried explaining to his best friend, Fenrin, once, but the words wouldn't come. Centuries of philosophical indoctrination weren't going to be changed after a ten-minute conversation.

Fenrin. The man had been a good friend, the best in Mollock's long life. He regretted getting Fenrin involved, but they had both been considerably younger and somewhat more innocent. None of which made a damned bit of difference when the shadow guardians had chased Mollock away. He'd fled, leaving Fenrin locked within the presumed safety of his ignorance. Mollock had returned once, years later, and found the home dilapidated and abandoned. Part of the roof had collapsed. The look told Mollock his friend hadn't lived there in a long, long time.

Friends were more of a liability than a necessity. Mollock had never learned whether Fenrin had survived his encounter with the shadow guardians or not. He also stayed as far away from civilization as possible, going into villages and towns only to buy much needed supplies during his exile. He hadn't had another friend since Fenrin, though a few like Elisa and Kaline came close.

He shook the memories off. "The Three are more dangerous than you suppose. Don't be so naïve as to think otherwise. Your best chance is to avoid their attention."

Kaline picked up on the quiet terror in his last sentence. *What dark secrets torment you in the middle of the night? Who are you really, Mollock Bolle?* "Mollock, the Three can't harm you anymore. The old life is finished. An'kuruku offers you a new beginning with infinite possibilities. Step out of your shadow and become the man you were always meant to be."

"If only you knew the truth," he muttered. "The Bloody Man spared my life, mine and Elisa's. He didn't have to. He *wanted* to. Do you understand? The bastard looked me in my eyes and named me the Prophet. Of what, he refused to say. I've been marked, and there is no escape. My life is already defined, and nothing you or I want is going to change that."

Kaline felt unexpected sorrow. Even Mollock had to know she was merely using him to achieve her goals. Truthfully, those goals belonged to an organization that was so spread out and entrenched in society the Inquisition would never be able to excise it fully. Emotional attachment was a trap Kaline seldom fell into, but the tragedy of Mollock Bolle practically demanded it.

Her own life was disturbingly similar. Born into a wealthy family, Kaline had been indoctrinated into her current belief structure and knew nothing else. In many ways, she was as much a slave to her condition as Mollock to his. Life seldom asked opinions. The biggest difference between them was that she embraced her path. Nothing was ever what it seemed, a simple fact Kaline had learned at an early age.

Unlike Mollock, she'd grown up on Vau Prime, under the corrupt noses of the Conclave and their Inquisition watchdogs. Many of the senior clergy were unwitting benefactors to her cause. Kaline had quickly learned to delight in their fumbling ignorance. The mere thought of using one of the clergy against the Conclave delighted her more than it probably should have. The great game, as she'd come to call it, was far older than her thirty-seven years, but there were few to equal her skill.

She'd first learned of Mollock Bolle shortly before the dramatic events on Crimeat. He fascinated her. The case of Mollock Bolle reminded her of one of the great romantic tragedies written by the classic playwrights Ghidus and Flovian. Abandoned by all, an outcast doomed to roam the universe in search of a meaning already in front of his face should he choose to see it, Mollock embodied unenviable sadness. Kaline almost made the mistake of sympathizing with him. Almost.

The game was still in its early stages, and she needed to push him further before his time was done.

"Life is a joke, Mollock. There is no cosmic design, no ulterior motive from long forgotten gods. We are the masters here. It is time for mankind to break free from the constricting bonds of the Conclave and rise to our true potential. Throw off the shackles and be *you!*"

He shook his head, dejected at the rehashing of a now familiar argument. Kaline was quite persuasive, but she failed to see his point of view. The arrogance of youth, he supposed. Young people seldom listened to what should be sage advice and wisdom from their elders.

The lines around his eyes deepened when he winced. "Kaline, I don't care to have this empty philosophical discussion again. We've learned all we can from each other. I need you to realize that I can't move past the place the Three left me."

He turned and started to walk back to the castle.

"What if you could?" she asked suddenly.

He paused. Not that the idea didn't intrigue him, he just couldn't find a way out. The cycle was unending and equally vicious. "Unless you can show me, I'm not interested. My life is controlled by strings."

Kaline eased beside him. Her loose-fitting gown drifted easily across the weather-beaten rocks, reminding Mollock of spilled blood. "Our discussions are anything but empty. Faith should not be looked down upon. All our lives, we are told what to worship or how. When do we get the chance to think for ourselves? Never, if the Conclave stays in power. We will never be free, Mollock, and that is the sad truth of life."

"What's the alternative? The Conclave does its best to protect us. Don't confuse my sense of respect for apathy. I lost faith in the priests the night I learned that the gods aren't dead. But you simply cannot expect to replace an entity as large as the Conclave. That's sedition!"

"As opposed to what we are doing now?" she asked mockingly. "Look around you, Mollock. This is the future. Those old fools in the Conclave are as outdated as our youths. Call me a heretic, call me worse. I don't care! All I want is the chance to make choices for myself and my *friends*. Where is the crime?"

She grinned at his stricken reaction. Clearly she'd made the impression she'd been trying to since their meeting in the back alleys of Tenemenah. His shoulders slumped. His eyes clouded with fond or painful reminiscence, she couldn't be sure of which. Kaline decided to press her advantage while she could.

"We all need friends, Mollock, and I would very much like to be able to put this behind us and become friends. Your voice is what draws these people here. Have you looked at the Deeves lately? An entire village is thriving just beyond our walls. We are the first strike in the coming revolution."

"Heresy," he half-heartedly whispered.

"Does it matter what it's called? Look around. The people are tired of their daily dose of Conclave stigma. What proof have the cardinals given anyone that the gods serve our best interests? What assurance that we are loved and cared for? The answer is plainer than even you care to acknowledge. No one in the Conclave gives a damn about the general population. They are greedy, power hungry abominations too intent on maintaining control to stand up for what is just. Don't continue to be a tool of an outdated regime, Mollock." Kaline softened her tone. "We have all been deceived by a most ingenious lie. The Conclave keeps secrets tucked away in hidden caverns meant for only them. Truth is enigmatic, an open-ended question we struggle to come to terms with. You know this, else you wouldn't be here."

Mollock recognized the truth in her words, though he remained loathe to let them into his heart. Decades of frustration and fear had left him a burnt husk. Fractured images of what life might have been like teased his thoughts and dreams like jilted lovers come the dawn. Unreachable happiness was his constant torment. Mollock agonized over lost time and his perpetual inability to become more than a haunted man.

Sorrow changed his path in life, somewhat. Dark, winding passages previously inescapable now seemed less. The Bloody Man's confidence in him astounded Mollock. Two years later, he still felt nothing like a prophet — at least, that is, until Mistress Kaline and her people had found him in the dead ends of Tenemenah. People like Kaline were sharks, predators with toothy grins and devious intent. Still, he took odd comfort in her tone, the softness in her eyes when he caught her gazing longingly at him. Mollock wasn't so naïve as to think she found him desirable or even remotely attractive, but something in the way she looked upon him bolstered his confidence and warmed his aching heart.

It had been so long since he knew love.

"Come with me, Mollock. Walk to the front of the keep and look down into the crowds of downtrodden and despairing. These people need salvation in any form. They come to hear your words, to hear you preach against the fallacies and careful lies only you have seen through. Don't deny so many the privilege of truth."

Time to become the Prophet and spread the truth of the gods. Mollock Bolle sighed and nodded.

"I will come, though I am no hero or great orator" he said. "I can't promise strength or conviction in my words."

Kaline took his offered arm. "Let us see together. Give them your heart and see how things change."

That's just it. My heart is as cold as a glacier.

Kaline had assured him that there were well over a thousand people massed at the crumbling base of their castle. Humility prevented him from believing that so many disaffected had come solely for seeing him rave against the falsehood spread by the Conclave. Most of those assembled had never seen a priest, much less been indoctrinated into their specific thought culture.

Mollock stood on the edge of a balcony, heart pounding. Soft green lichen coated half of the aged stone railing. Cold winds slashed in from the Bo, gradually wearing the dull grey stone down. The smell of human waste and offal pulsed up from the crowd. He felt sickened. The squalid conditions invited plague or worse. One question continued to play havoc with his already fragile mind: why have you come? He doubted the answer was ever going to present itself.

Lost amongst the seemingly endless throng of peasants and hopeful pilgrims stood the Bone Father. He dressed in his finest cape of bones today, so special was the occasion. Doubt stained his lips. The Bone Father knew Mollock Bolle for what he was: an imposter. No one spoke for the gods. Evidence of such audacity replayed over and over in his mind. The first attempt by this so called Prophet ended dismally. Mollock Bolle barely spoke a handful of sentences before fleeing from his aggrandized stage. Since then, the Bone Father remained convinced the man was a fraud, a charlatan bent on conning these people into some nefarious purpose.

Wise beyond imagining, the Bone Father recognized the potential to sway these people back to the proper fold. A thousand bones jangled when he walked, woven into an impressive, if not ghastly, cloak that showed his stature and strength. His was a power sent down from the skies from time immemorial. Nothing on An'kuruku held as much prestige as the Bone Father. Latest in an endless line, he protected mankind's sensibilities and faith. In many ways, he was no different from the Prophet. They both spoke against the false truths of the Conclave, insisting on liberty from the porous shell of what a select group of men and women *thought* the old gods were.

Only he had no angle. The Bone Father knew glory and had borne witness to a miracle very few ever would. Times were changing. A great conflagration was coming from the darkest corners of the universe. He saw it every time he cast the bones. War. Soon, all of mankind was going to be forced to take a stand, to decide for themselves whether the

Conclave was what they truly needed. He had no answers, no sage pearls of wisdom to assuage their fears or guilt. No, the Bone Father was just a man. He had no answers for any but himself. Others needed to search the depths of their hearts for more.

He watched, amazed, as Mollock raised his tired hands and an unprecedented hush fell over the crowd. Anticipation choked them. Many had seen his first aborted attempt and still clung to the desperate need for him to speak clear and true. The Bone Father couldn't grasp why. Was life so bad that these people, *his* people, had nothing left?

Mollock stared down on the crowd and felt his stomach clench. Hands shook. Only now did he realize he'd never spoken to so many. He closed his eyes, recalling a moment when Kaline insisted that the delivery was all part of the show. What choice did he have but to engage as a great showman?

"What is truth? Is it the mundane acceptance of ageless words spoken and recited day after day by men or women in positions of authority? Are we supposed to patiently accept what those who wear the red robes of priesthood so dutifully spew at us in an unending stream of rhetoric?" Mollock paused to shake his head. His vision swam. His palms were clammy, his heart pounding. He closed his eyes for a moment and let his mind run free.

"I say to you all the answer is resoundingly NO! Truth cannot be found in the pages of an ancient text or cast from the lips of some decrepit old man who has secluded himself from the very people he swore an oath to protect! Truth is not a toy to be cast around the hearth so carelessly we lose our faith and conviction. Truth is not a whim that can be discarded because it doesn't fit into our ideals or desires. Truth, my friends, is the one constant that is ever hidden from us. It lurks behind the turn of every corner, every page. Truth is the cosmic joke none of us understand. Truth…is a lie."

The expected wave of murmurs and dissent never came, leaving Mollock swaying under the strength of what he'd just said. Truth was certainly all those things, but it was more subjective than anything. Malleable, truth could be shaped to suit any purpose.

Mollock let loose a slow, deep breath and continued.

"Our emotional security is shattered under the guise of false moral authority and wretched politics. The Conclave has unrightfully usurped the truth, the message of individuality that each of us must find for ourselves. The priests hear your confessions. They take your guilt and offer penance for supposed moral crimes. What they don't give is hope. They let you wallow in grief while they get richer. Do not think for an instant that the Conclave leaders on Vau Prime bother with the things that concern us. You will never see a cardinal among you, getting his robes dirty in the filth we are forced to endure, all to protect a false truth."

"Who among you has voted to put a priest or cardinal into power? Who has taken it as a personal crusade to endure the political ramifications of the Inquisition lapdogs while their masters sit on a secluded island in the great sea of stars? Not I. We come from all walks of life. We are the experience, the very soul of the cosmos. And we are voiceless!"

This is it. After today I won't be able to go back to being just Mollock.

"Friends, let me tell you of the terrible truth I learned long ago. Let me tell you a tale the Conclave would see me dead for telling. Let me tell you of sleeping gods."

THIRTEEN

3212 A.G. (After Gods), Hawker's Gate, deep space.

Designed to serve as a liaison port between deep space worlds, Hawker's Gate was over two hundred years old and considered a bankrolled failure. Pirates and less-than-desirables roamed the once pristine white corridors intended for diplomats and rising politicians. The Conclave abandoned the project after a decade of running in the red. Profits from storage and usage continued to dwindle well into the Gate's second century. Reputation had much to do with the decided lack of official usage. No one of stature wanted to be associated with an abysmal social disaster.

That being said, Hawker's Gate wasn't entirely without backers. Banking officials and independent entrepreneurs poured a small wealth of finances into the half-empty station, turning it into one of the more successful separate endeavors in modern times. The Gate, as deep spacers named it, transformed an all but abandoned metal monstrosity into a manmade paradise, a home away.

Upon seeing how successful the Gate was becoming, the Conclave swooped in, citing universal jurisdiction. A small office was established after intense negotiations, which had no choice but to end in the Conclave's favor (a Prekhauten Guard war frigate was very handy when you couldn't be sure of things going your way). A platoon of Guards was deployed on station, along with a steadily rotating cadre of low level Inquisitors still trying to make names for themselves.

The Conclave was clearly disfavored amongst the rank and file who made the Gate their home or port of call. The garrison, small as it was, remained a ghost of what it was meant to be, a fact the less than desirables took full advantage of. Thousands of credits worth of unmarked goods and, occasionally, unaccounted for weapons shipments were destined for illegal organizations operating beyond the Conclave's jurisdiction.

The local administrator was established with the intent of mediating between the factions who financed the Gate and their Conclave warders. It was so much more. The past few administrators, all chosen by banking guilds, established a healthy record of being corruptible. Current politics demanded a certain flair for turning the head in the opposite direction as underhanded deals were carried out. What the Conclave didn't know, couldn't possibly fathom, was that the administratum was deep in the pockets of the anti-religious revolution sweeping across the outer star systems.

Unchecked, a healthy subculture soon developed in the lower decks. Men and women seeking to turn a quick profit arrived under the guise of refugees, turning an area the size of a small city into a hive of drugs, crime and prostitution, all things the Conclave stood against. With only a handful of priests and a single Inquisitor, the Conclave was forced to sit back and watch helplessly as the beast they allowed to live flourished and took on a life of its own.

Secrets were a rarity. Anyone who had anything at all to say had best do it before docking else word would be spread before that person had a chance to deboard. So it was as the wounded and severely battered *Indomitable* pulled into dock. Thick black spots marked her hull where enemy rounds had struck. Fresh plating inexpertly attached in haste turned the once proud ship of the line into a ragged patchwork barely able to maintain drive on her own.

Tolde Breed stood, hands clasped behind his back and dressed in his sharpest uniform, on the bridge beside the haggard Captain Falchi. Both men were stretched to their capacity and in desperate need of proper recovery, much like the *Indomitable*. Both understood Fate was indifferent to their individual needs. The polished rose, red petals tinged with blue, stood out against the flat gray tunic and black pants of the Inquisition uniform.

His eyes were streaked through with red from a decided lack of sleep. His left arm twitched every so often, sending ripples up his immaculately pressed blouse. Gray hair, the last vestiges of brown naught but a fleeting dream, sat disheveled atop his head. There was the slightest hint of sag in his shoulders, one Tolde would never admit to. Proud and intelligent, he was also practical. He knew better than to show any sign of weakness in front of subordinates lest he lose all credibility. Still, he longed for a long soak and an undisturbed night on clean sheets.

"Captain, Hawker's Gate flight command requests control," the helmsman announced.

Falchi nodded. "Very well. The Gate has the con. Sit back, gentlemen. Your work is done for now," Falchi replied.

The differences between captain and Inquisitor were painfully obvious. Falchi had abandoned his battle fatigues in favor of the formal naval attire. Immaculate white as pure as a fresh snowfall stood out starkly against the dull tones of the Inquisition. Neat rows of multicolored ribbons decorated his left breast. Random medals hung below, marked by the brilliant red sash cutting down from his left shoulder to right hip. Regardless of differences, Tolde stood impressed. Amassing so many awards and recognitions for service was no easy feat.

Falchi turned towards Tolde, eyes lighting on Luma Kai standing slightly behind. "I imagine the easiest part of our journey is ending."

"Undoubtedly. Ursal Prowl is clearly working with more assets than the Inquisition is aware of. We've crossed the threshold into a dangerous new game." Tolde frowned suddenly, painful memories mocking him.

Falchi barely shrugged. He'd been through worse during his tenure as a battle captain. Chances were he'd already seen whatever Ursal was bringing to the table, seen and defeated. "Rebels always seem organized in the beginning. Every engagement leaves the defeated commander thinking his opponent has learned some new tactic capable of sending an entire fleet into defeat. Truth is we often forget the simple tactics that we all began with. Time, Inquisitor. Time gives us the wisdom we need to see through the night tides."

"Time might be the one commodity in short supply," Tolde countered. "Pirates are historically singular entities with little regard for each other, much less the average citizen. For so many to be working in concert bodes ill for all."

Falchi remained unconvinced. "Our attack was coordinated by a man with a personal grievance, Tolde. Any man with that much hate in his heart can achieve a great many things before he's stopped. Ursal Prowl will be no different."

"I pray you're right but know better than to trust such whimsical ideations. I suggest you keep your crew to the ship as much as possible until Inquisitor Kai and I can declare the station secure. My previous experiences here left me with less than favorable memories."

"That much I'll give you. Hawker's Gate is filled with every sort of riff raff and unwanted imaginable." Falchi grinned. "It gives a certain flavor space crews tend to enjoy, but I can manage my crew well enough. What is your plan?"

Tolde paused. His initial plans had collapsed the moment Ursal attacked the *Indomitable*. Cold realization from the back of his mind warned him of worse to come. He looked back over a shoulder to Luma, who merely shrugged. She clearly deferred to Tolde in this matter — a fact not lost on him, nor did it sit well. It felt like he was being tested.

"Normally, I prefer the direct approach. Unfortunately, that is impossible. No doubt Ursal has contacts on station and they are well prepared for anything we can offer. I'm not counting on much support from the local Guard or Inquisitor." *Especially not after my experiences on Crimeat.*

"You're going to need all of the support you can get. My crew are spacers, not grunts. I can provide a few security personnel but nothing you can use to turn the tide in your favor. And all my guns will be out of commission. I have no problem taking risks, but I'm not about to stand before Strannan and explain why I opened fire on the universe's largest space station."

"Sergeant Fies and his men are more than eager to deboard," Luma interjected.

"Guardsmen? They'll stick out the moment their boots touch the deck," Falchi snorted. "You'll need better than that."

"Our potential enemies already know this is a ship of war, Captain Falchi. I somehow doubt they'll be caught off guard when they see a platoon of Guards disembark. We need to strike while we still have a semblance of advantage," she insisted. The lightest touch of crimson flushed her cheeks.

"You can't go storming into the Gate thinking to root out trouble like it's some peasant village on a backwater world," Falchi cautioned. "People here are suspicious enough about us already. They don't need any more encouragement to turn against the Conclave."

She frowned. "Popularity is not our mandate. We have orders to capture or kill a known fugitive for crimes ag—"

"Spare me the political message, Inquisitor Kai," Falchi stopped her with a hand. "Like I said, no one here is going to be interested. The Conclave has its mark stamped on the hull but has no real presence. They came in with strong-arm politics and turned a quarter of a million people against them. Not very smart, if you ask me. I am not your enemy here, Miss Kai. Don't treat me as such."

"My apologies, Captain, I…overstepped my bounds," she replied quickly before any of the bridge crew could talk. "Perhaps the pirate attack has left me more frazzled than I supposed."

"Perhaps," Falchi agreed slowly.

Tolde's mind swirled with endless possibilities and conclusions as to what had just happened. None of them seemed appropriate or well intended. Tensions continued to rise, sparked by the catalyst of the pirate attack. A familiar feeling crept back into his thoughts, dark and brooding.

The similarities between now and the events on Crimeat were constantly growing, leading him to the only available conclusion: Ursal Prowl had help from someone placed high enough in the Inquisition to avoid notice until he decided the timing was right for victory. That, more than anything, disturbed Tolde deeply.

The Inquisition was no stranger to corruption. Too many documented cases soured the archives, tarnishing part of the gleam of what the Inquisition was *meant* to be. Distracted, the senior leadership chose to hunt ghosts and whispers rather than fact-based heresy. More and more from their own ranks were under investigation for various purported crimes and misconduct. The Office of Heretical Persecution devoted intense amounts of manpower to hunting down the slightest hint of rebellion against the Conclave. Too much, as far as Tolde was concerned.

"What is your opinion?" Falchi asked him suddenly.

Tolde blinked twice, clearing the distant look from his eyes. "We are too concerned with what might happen rather than what is happening. Our enemies are smart and highly organized. No sane pirate captain would dare go head to head against a Guard warship. So why did they? My guess is that Ursal Prowl has been busier than we know. It is very possible he has a fleet of corsairs ready to wreak havoc on the navy."

"An armada? I'd say that should be impossible. Men like that don't tend to collect in one place or fly the same colors," Falchi disagreed.

"Times are more delicate than even two years ago. Even you must admit that our ability to properly do our jobs has diminished."

Not the words my crew needs to hear. Such simple phrases can be more damning than a broadside of torpedoes. "This conversation would be better suited to my wardroom. Space crews are a superstitious lot. It won't sit well to jinx us before the Gate clamps us in."

Realization slapped Tolde across the face. He immediately felt foolish for making such a mistake. Crews were no different from the Guard infantry. They needed to have full faith and confidence in their leadership. The alternatives were less than attractive.

The three left docking operations to the First Officer and departed the bridge. Much remained to be said, much that none wanted to speak of.

Hawker's Gate was close enough it blocked even the distant sun. Flat gray sheeting with streaks of various colors randomly painted filled the view ports of the *Indomitable*. Guards flocked to the side to catch their first glimpse of the famed station. Few, if any, had ventured this far from the Conclave's center of control. The Gate offered temptations delicious enough to condemn a man's soul.

"Look at you all!" smirked Annalilly. "You look like teenage boys catching their first glimpse of a naked woman."

"Like you'd know," Jers fired back.

She barked a laugh. "I've seen plenty of naked women, and there ain't none I like better than my own self. But you'll not be the one to find that out, Jers."

Laughter circled the mess deck. Jers scowled, knowing better than to get into a verbal sparring match with his squad leader.

"Nothing wrong with a naked woman or two," Beve, big brutish Beve, said out of the blue. "Suits me just fine."

He shrugged his massive shoulders and ambled back to his unfinished meal. The others could only stare as the most dangerous person in the squad sat down and started to eat. Even Annalilly was amazed with his one-line wit.

"Ain't that something," she whispered.

Haggle shook his head, extra skin hanging under his chin wiggling in a deceptive show of weakness. Easily thirty pounds overweight, Haggle was the beneficiary of the suddenly relaxed height and weight standards. He'd been in the Guard for almost a decade, counting the near seven years of waiting to be accepted into the vaunted ranks, and his weight had plagued him the entire time. Finally, someone in command had decided that being overweight didn't mean you couldn't fight or be a good Guard. The running joke was that no one was too fat to die for the cause.

Never particularly liked by his peers, he'd gotten his name from his uncanny ability to barter over everything and to turn a bad situation good. Haggle earned his friends through loyalty and an unflinching devotion to taking care of them. Annalilly wanted to throw him into a team leader position, but Sergeant Fies said no. The big man wasn't quite ready to tackle a leadership position.

"I didn't know Beve even cared for women," Haggle said.

The heavy weapons specialist fixed him with a menacing glare and continued to eat.

"Careful, now, Haggle. I don't think he takes too kindly to your insinuations," Annalilly warned playfully.

He shrugged it off and asked, "Have you been to the Gate before?"

She nodded. "I was born in the next system over. Everyone in the quadrant has been here, or at least they should have been. Hawker's Gate is one of the great manmade wonders in the universe. Rivals that of the old gods, or so I heard."

She glanced out the viewport, guessing it was going to be at least another hour before the *Indomitable* was properly docked. Painful memories threatened to drop her in a less than welcome nostalgic mood. The past was a thing she didn't want or need to remember. Too many bad things had happened in her life to have any semblance of happiness on the Gate. Reaching into a special pocket she'd had sewn on the inside of her blouse, Annalilly pulled out a tiny bag of dice. "If you can keep it in your pants long enough, who's up for a game?"

"Shouldn't we be prepping for the mission?" Jers asked.

"Hush your tongue, Jers. We've done nothing but prep since we left that damned ambush. What's left to do?" she scolded.

"Lock and load," Beve added between bites of a dark gravy covered meat that left a horrible and lasting aftertaste.

She nodded. "Exactly!"

"Sarge isn't going to like that," a new voice chimed.

Eyes leveled on the boy, silently forcing him to keep quiet. Annalilly jumped off the end of the silver table she'd acquired as a perch and stalked towards him. Visible fear rippled just under his skin. His bleach blonde hair and tanned complexion set him apart from the rest, making the twin lines of odd tattoos running down the length of his arms all the more unnecessary.

"Guardsman Kedric, did you say something?" she snarled, leaning menacingly forward. The torrid look in her eyes made him swallow.

Kedric started shaking his head. "No, Sergeant, er…I mean yes, Sergeant."

"Make up your mind boy. Is it yes or no?"

Haggle forced himself to turn away before his laughter became uncontrollable. Others followed. Mission time was close, and no one was willing to risk Annalilly's ire right before they got tossed into the fire.

"Sergeant, I…"

"You what? Thought your few months of training and time on the waiting list entitled you to question your commanding officer?" she asked.

Kedric snapped his jaws shut and straightened his back, ready to take whatever lashing his squad leader had in mind. Annalilly drew to her full five-foot three height and placed her hands on her hips. The twin lightning bolt tattoos on her scalp rippled as she clenched her jaw.

"That's enough, *Sergeant*."

She turned slowly, shaking her head as Fies entered the mess. The first thing she noticed was his lack of standard uniform. No kit, no weapons, at least none visible, and no uniform.

"Sergeant Fies," she acknowledged.

He gave a curt nod and pointed at Kedric. "Who's this?"

"Guardsman First Class Kedric, Sergeant."

"Well, Guardsman First Class Kedric, the next time I hear you questioning one of the noncoms I will take a personal interest in seeing you drummed out of the Guard. There is no time or tolerance for insubordination. Do I make myself perfectly clear?"

Kedric could barely nod, even as Fies leaned down to place his mouth next to the young Guard's ear. "For the record, I don't like it. Now carry on."

He tried to say yes, sergeant, but the words got stuck in his throat. Haggle reached in to drag him away before Kedric found himself in actual trouble. Unable to contain it any longer, laughter spread through the mess deck in booming gales.

"I didn't mean nothing by it," Annalilly cut Fies off.

Fies frowned. "Doesn't matter. The boy was right. This isn't the time for throwing dice. We need to get our heads in the game. Accidents happen otherwise."

She bit the end of her tongue. Hands snapped behind her back in the eternal display of proper military respect, Annalilly dug her nails into her palms to bleed off some of her building rage.

Fies kept his voice intentionally low. "I'm not going to dress down my best squad leader in front of her men, but I need you to be on top of your game for this one."

She rocked back. "When have you known me not to be?"

"This time is different. Breed's given us new orders. No kit. I'm taking your squad in with me on a recon op."

"Undercover?" she asked. "That's a job for local security, not Guards."

He certainly agreed but asking the locals to get involved in what was essentially an Inquisition grudge match wasn't the smartest idea. They'd already survived one civil war. Fies had no desire to get embroiled in another. People tended to act *different* when they were fighting for personal ideations.

"You and I both know the situation here isn't that good. Chances are this Von is already so entrenched in the administrator's pockets we're going to have to fight just to get into the command offices." Fies frowned. "This is one fight I'm not looking forward to. Neither is Breed. We go in wearing civilian clothes, sidearms only. Ensure none, and I mean *none*, of your people draw unless they are fired on first. Understand?"

"Not really my style," she replied. "I've been through the worst this place has to offer, and I'm not about to let an identified threat roll up on me without taking action."

Fies rubbed his hand over his face. "Annalilly, we can't afford it. The Gate is about as openly anti-Conclave as you can get without declaring independence. We don't have enough firepower to pull our asses out if the other side incites a full-blown riot."

Annalilly flashed a toothy grin, amazing him again with how white her teeth were. "I know, Sarge. I was just messing with you. The boys will be ready in ten, though Beve's not going to like leaving his babies behind."

"A man that big should enjoy pummeling an opponent into submission, don't you think?" he asked.

"We've both seen him do it," she confirmed.

He'd seen enough. Annalilly often played down her skills at precisely the wrong moment, a fact Fies found infuriating. The polished recruiter image of the Prekhauten Guard was meant to lure fresh faces with unlimited ideals into service. That image died the moment those faces exited the last transport to basic training. Yelling and screaming aside, the real Guard was just as mean and dirty as the worst the universe had to throw back at them. Fies idly wondered if Kedric still suffered from self-induced delusions. The coming trials would certainly wipe them away.

"Good. Have your squad assemble at the boarding sleeve in one hour." Fies turned to leave.

"That's it?"

He paused. *What more needs to be said?*

She took a few steps closer, ensuring her squad was well out of hearing distance. "I've been thinking about our…arrangement."

He swallowed but managed to maintain composure, barely.

"Maybe we should take it a step further," she suggested demurely.

Fies swooned. They'd spent more nights than he could remember coupled in a naked, sweaty mass of flesh and pleasure. Neither was inclined to ask for a relationship. Death was a Guardsman's constant companion, the one entity no one outran or outlasted. Not even the gods. Part of the initial agreement was that neither tried to force something greater than just a sexual fling, as incredible as it was, on the other. Caught off guard, Fies wasn't sure how to take her.

"Now isn't the time, Annalilly. We're about to go into..."

She cut him off. "Gods damn it! Don't you think I know that? Every time we suit up and head out that door with a loaded weapon is another chance for big, bad death to come stalking. And every time we come back you and I find a way to be alone in secret. That's no way to live a life, Fies!"

He gawked.

She blushed. "I'm not saying kids or anything radical like that, but more than just a quick fuck in the back of the supply room would be nice."

Fies couldn't keep the grin from splitting his face. "Annalilly, are you going soft on me? I don't believe what I'm hearing. You want a relationship. After all we've done and been through? I can handle that."

"With conditions."

Naturally. Show me a woman without conditions, and I'll have a corpse on my hands. "Name them."

She reached out and grabbed his crotch. "This doesn't go soft."

He gulped. *"You have an hour, Sergeant."*

Presha Von shifted the light green shawl over her shoulders and continued to watch the black and white monitors showing the familiar face of Tolde Breed and his Guards deboard the *Indomitable*. Her eyes narrowed to hard slits, wrinkles pulling her cheeks up. Recent communications with her sources on Vau Prime had alerted her to his impending arrival, but seeing the Inquisitor again raised her hackles. Mission success depended on her ability to charm and guile the local authorities into complacency. Having a pair of die-hard Inquisitors — from the Office of Heretical Persecution, no less — trampling through her carefully wrought designs was the absolute worst thing that could have happened.

Fingers tapped the glass desk so hard a nail broke. Presha fumed, venting silent curses and pledges. She blamed the current situation on Ursal Prowl's continued display of incompetence. The disgraced Inquisitor had bungled everything she, and others, strove to accomplish on Crimeat, leaving much of the continent of Lethendweil a war-torn mess. Good people were washed away under the tide of violence and mayhem. The dirt claimed more than even she cared to admit, and for what?

Anger threatened to cloud her judgment. Presha exhaled deeply and switched camera views to accommodate Tolde and his poorly disguised band of Guardsmen as they entered the customs area. Fools. Did they truly think they could outwit a devotee of Rengu? She shook her head, momentarily daydreaming all manner of horrors she intended to inflict upon them. They would beg for death before she was anywhere close to consigning them to the grave.

Presha idly traced the circular symbol affixed to her inner blouse. The small black dot in the center of a blood red circle was the adopted symbol of the cult of Rengu. Fanatics, some claimed, but devoted worshipers of one of the most notorious old gods. Rengu was the god of chaos and despair. His will was what, purportedly, had forced the war between the gods that eventually led to their destruction. Those foolish enough to think the gods were truly gone would fall to bloody knees and madness when the chaos god returned.

Presha had been indoctrinated as a young girl, rising quickly through the ranks as she discovered the carnal pleasures Rengu offered. She learned from her elders and found inventive ways to remove them from her way. Destiny beckoned, a dark star at the end of the universe, leading her to Crimeat and an ill-fated attempt at awakening Rengu.

Amongeratix was the key. His anger and hatred, unsurpassed in the brief history of humanity, were the only things capable of freeing Rengu from the chains of his eternal prison. They'd come close, even going so far as to deliver a false message to the Shackled Man while he festered in the Conclave prison on Prophet Isle. One hundred sacrificed bodies were burned once the ritual was completed. That brief spark was enough to open a neural pathway to the sleeping Rengu, allowing him to free Amongeratix but no more. The failure stung her. She'd come so close to finally seeing her life matter.

The comm panel chimed.

"What?" she snapped, crueler than intended, but it got the point across. She was in no mood for petty problems.

"Mistress, Administrator Felp is trying to contact you."

A cold smirk won free. *That fat bastard isn't worth his weight in water. It will do him some good to sweat under the glare of the Inquisition for a while.* "Let him stew. The official Inquisition representative has arrived and is his problem, not mine."

"There is a chance he could give up certain information," her assistant hesitantly told her.

True, but again, that wasn't her concern. Her mind was already racing towards the possible effects of Tolde Breed ripping through her affairs. "Inform the Administrator that I am unavailable and expect to be so for the time being. Oh, and do not disturb me again, or I'll have your body vented out of the nearest airlock."

With attention drawn to the battered Prekhauten Guard frigate, no one bothered with the small, one-man craft maneuvering into port on the far side of the station. Matthias was far too seasoned to think the sudden interest in the *Indomitable* was anything more than sheer nostalgia and the curiosity of being trapped on a floating tin can at the back end of the universe. Spies were undoubtedly tracking his every move and reporting back to their masters.

Matthias double-checked his sidearm and extra charge packs before buttoning his faded brown leather jacket. The look was alien at best. He missed the familiar feel and sense of authority a Guard uniform gave. Officially, he wasn't on the rolls any longer — a discarded piece of equipment better left forgotten and reprimanded over an inexcusable event. Shame continued to wound him, despite the knowledge that he'd done nothing wrong and wasn't being punished. General Strannan believed in Matthias's current mission enough to offer immediate reinstatement upon successful completion.

Running a gloved hand through his unusually thick hair, Matthias forced a grin. He hadn't had so much hair in more than forty years. Such simple luxury briefly reminded him of a simpler time, when he was still a young sergeant with everything to prove and nothing to lose. Sad reflection aside, those days were long past. He was getting old, slow. His mind continued to strengthen, developing tactics and scenarios to the maximum desired effect, but his body was breaking down. Not even the longevity drugs administered by the Phallalian Surgeons did much for a steady diet of wounds and combat injuries.

A smart man knew when it was time to hang up his rifle and move on. Matthias was considered extremely intelligent, but he was equally and, perhaps detrimentally, morally obligated to continue his service to the Guard. He was the last one from the original mission to recapture Amongeratix with a young Tolde Breed, a dinosaur awaiting extinction at the end of his last sunset. Matthias harbored no illusions that this would be his last mission. He felt it more than anything. Time had become as stern an enemy as the Three ever were.

Sighing, he punched the button opening the outer airlock hatch and was immediately met by a young, twenty-something kid in a local uniform.

"Welcome to Hawker's Gate, sir. If you will follow me, I can take you to customs and ensure your stay here is enjoyable."

Matthias rolled his eyes. Of all the luck.

FOURTEEN

3212 A.G. (After Gods), deep space shipping lanes.

Rough hands snatched him from his simple bunk. He groaned and twisted, sleep still rendering him impotent. Ursal heard raised voices, felt the blows as punches and kicks slammed home. A rib snapped. Blood trickled from a split lip. Certain voices rose above the clamor, voices he fully expected to turn treasonous. His hands were tied at the wrists. Standing, they shoved him out of his room and down the cold, dimly lit corridor. The spine of the ship was considered haunted by the older crewmen. Ghosts stalked the long hallway, wailing in the quiet hours. Ursal Prowl didn't believe in ghosts, but he was perfectly interested in making some once he and Geres Auk managed to get free. Assuming Geres was already a prisoner. *Never trust a pirate.*

The cell they unceremoniously dumped him in was small, barely large enough to store ammunition much less a grown man. His eyes watered. A lesser man might call it tears. Ursal was made of sterner material. He spat a mouthful of blood and saliva and peered at his attackers through swollen eyes. He marked their faces, recalled names. Each would suffer for the injustices committed against him.

"Don't look so damned tough now, do you, boy?"

Vicente Blackheart stalked into view, his crew parting respectfully. The galivant pirate captain looked down on the bound Inquisitor with menace.

"It took enough of you to do it. Make it a clean fight and see what happens."

Blackheart barked a deep laugh. "That doesn't give me much incentive to fight fair, now, does it, Mister Prowl?"

Ursal spit again, ropes of bloody saliva drooling down his chin. "I knew I couldn't trust you, Blackheart. Pirates are too predictable."

He shrugged. "Didn't stop you from getting caught. I have to level with you; I never cared for your arrogance. You and that gods damned Auk. He's one I'd like to vent into space and watch choke."

Ursal had known this was coming; it was a sad inevitability when dealing with treacherous men. It had just come too soon. Too much was left to be done yet. The rebellion was in its infant stage, barely a larvae and incapable of even remotely defending itself. He frowned as he calculated the sheer weight of resistance stacked against him.

"Why now?" he finally asked. His throat hurt. Bruises were forming where hands clamped too tightly around his neck.

Vicente tossed another careless shrug, emphasizing his nonchalance. "Now's as good as later. You see, Prowl, this is where we differ. I am a man of impulse. Oh, I tried long ago to control it, to find some measure of patience, but the truth of the matter is that I rather enjoy doing what I do. There are too many men in positions of power who lack the stones to make their move. History forgets such men. I don't intend to be forgotten. One day, my name will go down as a tyrant great enough to rival the gods themselves!"

Idiot, Ursal mused. *Men like you are* always *ground under the heel of those of us patient enough to find the proper time. No one will remember Vicente Blackheart. No one at all.* Parts of the pirate's predictions were true enough. There were far too many men and women in control that were stuck in their own lethargy. The universe demanded change. Silent screams echoed across the solar winds, driven by the unquenchable need to discover a better life. Ursal Prowl was a small part in affecting that change, but an integral part if the rebellion was to succeed. Blackheart was a puppet whose strings had become too long. Time was coming when those strings would be cut.

He started to laugh, a broken, twisted sound. "Now who's arrogant? You're nothing the universe hasn't seen before. It's not too late, though. You still have time, a little to be sure, to release me and save your miserable hide."

"I can't see you in a position to make promises," Vicente growled as he leaned closer. "You're all used up, Prowl. Keep running your mouth, and I'll have you gutted like the spineless swine you are."

"You really don't understand, do you? This, you and your miserable little ship, all of it is expendable. Do you think my masters on Vau Prime would send me into a den of thieves without backup? We've been tracked the whole trip, ever since leaving Drespai."

Darkness clouded his face. "Maybe so, but you're forgetting the most important piece to your little puzzle."

Ursal raised his chin, wincing from the pain. "What's that?"

"You don't have a way of communicating with them. You're on your own, betrayer!" Blackheart and his men broke out in laughter. "Slam this rat in his cage, lads. We've got business to be about."

Ursal watched silently as the light shrank and the heavy iron door rang shut. The clicking of the lock echoed for a very long time. Trapped, he had nothing to keep his mind off the pain. Blackheart's men had savaged him in a short time. He felt broken bones and bled from obvious places. The real pain would come after he awoke, if they let him live that long. Ursal's ploy about being reinforced was a bluff. He and Geres were alone. His Inquisition allies certainly knew his precise location thanks to the tracking devices surgeons implanted in both, but, unless Ursal wasn't being told everything, help wouldn't arrive until long after he was dead.

Ursal Prowl sat back and closed his eyes.

"The big bastard killed two men, Cap'n."

Blackheart looked down at the unconscious Geres Auk. A hint of admiration passed across the pirate's face, quickly disappearing before any of his men noticed. Any slight change could be perceived as weakness, and the crew already had their blood up. It wouldn't take much to incite a mutiny, and Blackheart was currently in a bad position to try and stop one. Crew was normally banned from carrying weapons while on board. The arms master kept all power weapons and sabers (as old fashioned and obsolete as they were, some pirates maintained a healthy affection for them) under lock and was answerable only to Blackheart. That wasn't to suggest the arms master wasn't capable of a moment of weakness.

He could use a man of Auk's caliber. The brute was cunning and stronger than ten men. Whatever bond of loyalty the man shared with Ursal was breakable; all bonds came with a price, some hefty, others less. Blackheart had little doubt that he could find what motivated Auk, and when he did.... *Now, now, Vicente. Don't start counting results before you make the plans. He's a beast of a man that could crush you like a can. Breaking him will be a task, make no mistake. This needs to be cool and deliberate. Otherwise, I'll just have a crew of corpses to keep me company.*

"I trust he's still alive?" Blackheart asked slowly. The answer was obviously yes. He watched the man's chest rise and fall with shallow breaths.

"Aye, he lives, though I'd like to run him through. He's a savage bastard, that one," growled one of the crew.

If only we were all that way. "Keep him alive for now. He may be more useful than the other one."

The crew bristled. Two of their own were dead, murdered at the hands of an uncontrollable beast. It had taken repeated blows to the head and neck with thick steel pipes and wrenches to finally get Auk unconscious. Gashes and gouges where flesh had been ripped out scarred his head. His nose was broken and a shoulder blade fractured, but Auk had only fought harder before a blow to the temple had dropped him for good. Only the First Mate had been wise enough to step in before the crew managed to kill him.

None of the crew moved.

"Was I unclear?" Blackheart snarled.

"No, Cap'n, it's just that he's dangerous. Man like that needs to be crippled, hobbled if nothing else."

There's an interesting notion, though I doubt his usefulness will be the same. Not to mention the massive level of hatred that would fester like a wound in his soul if we did that. "I want him alive. A man like this can fetch a good price on the slave markets. He'd make a good pit fighter and could earn us a lot more than a corpse. Anyone have a problem with that?"

No one answered. Blackheart took it as a good sign that the crew was still amiable to maintaining order and good discipline. The *Shrike* was still in good fighting shape despite the unexpected attack from an unmarked ship. A score of his best had been slaughtered in their boarding pods, never having a chance to fight for their lives. It was an inglorious death, but one Blackheart could empathize with. Hard men made hard choices, and any little victory to even the odds was acceptable.

Therill pushed through the crowd. The First Mate was an angry man with cold, calculating eyes and a knack for murder. Few were unwise enough to cross him, especially unarmed. He'd delivered the final blow on Auk and still felt the numbness in his arm from the impact.

"That's enough, you dogs! Back to your posts, or I'll flog the skin from your hides," he barked.

The crew dissolved, leaving captain and first mate alone with their prisoner. Therill waited until he was satisfied they were alone.

"That could have gone either way," he cautioned.

Blackheart waved his concerns off. The puckered scars on his face rippled with each subtle movement. "They're loyal, Therill. Don't give them a reason to turn on us."

"Keeping him alive is dangerous, Captain," Therill insisted. "The crew may be right. He took out Pas and Rack without breaking a sweat. If he gets loose…"

"The bars are electrified, correct?"

"Aye."

Blackheart nodded. "That should be enough to keep him complacent, at least until you and I have a chance to sway his loyalties."

Therill whistled softly in disbelief. "You don't really believe a man like that is going to switch sides easily, do you?"

"I wouldn't trust him if he did."

The First Mate remained unconvinced. "This is a bad idea, Captain. He's already killed two of our crew and is not the sort of man to take this act lightly. I suggest we place additional guards and chain him to the deck."

Blackheart was forced to admit Therill had a legitimate argument. Geres Auk was a danger no one could risk letting loose. There was no way to accurately determine how much damage he *might* cause; how many more lives would be wasted in an act of raw ambition. Something dark and malevolent brooded just behind Auk's perpetual glare. Even the strongest man was forced to turn away lest he became the object of such unending levels of malice.

But all wasn't hopeless. Vicente Blackheart had managed to do some checking before they'd left the docks at Drespai. Men like Prowl came with baggage, and, no matter how hard or well they tried to conceal those shadowy tidbits they didn't want the rest of the universe to know, they always forgot to check every access point. It took meticulous searching, but Blackheart was finally able to piece together enough of Prowl's past to set his betrayal in motion. He imagined the Inquisition would pay handsomely, not to mention a healthy pardon for crimes committed against the Conclave, for turning over one of the most wanted traitors in the universe.

Geres Auk was another matter. The man was generally reclusive, choosing when to speak to achieve the maximum desired effect. He was a stone-cold killer, the type of man who was happier on a battlefield wading through rivers of blood than chained behind a dying sun like Prowl. Perhaps that's why he abandoned his last employer, Baron Scura, so easily. The scent of doom carried on the winds, making it easy to spot weakness. Death was an indiscriminate familiar, a boon companion ever chasing across the echoes of time. Men like Auk turned around and chased Death back.

Most of the records from the rebellion on Crimeat had been purged in the zealous fires of a vengeful Inquisition. The humiliation suffered from one of their own going rogue continued to ripple through the under-communities. Naturally, Conclave and Inquisition officials refused to comment on the matter, labeling it an internal affair. No one was fooled. Rumors of corruption in the clergy and their watchdogs were the talk around the dinner table. They were fueled by subversive agents of this new rebellion taking root in the lower star systems. Blackheart cared little for causes and crusaders so long as he stood to make a profit, and the way he saw it, Ursal Prowl offered a major payday.

He shifted his gaze up from the prone Auk to Therill. Blackheart hadn't gotten this far by being a trusting man. In fact, it was quite the opposite. He'd murdered and removed everyone who stood in his way, right up to the last captain of the *Shrike*. Therill had played an integral part of that mutiny, helping to cull those crewers who didn't see eye to eye with their new leader. Pirates were scum; Prowl was right about that. Not a man on the Shrike was generally worth his weight in piss, much less gold. But Blackheart would drive them all to the cusp of demise at the edge of a sharp blade if he thought he stood a chance of stealing from Death. Predators were commonplace in his business, but it took a man of exceptional violence to achieve a real name.

Vicente Blackheart intended to be the most feared name in the deep space shipping lanes, seeking one day to be reviled on Vau Prime itself.

"Auk is a murderer, same as you or I, Therill. Don't let his haughty attitude fool you. He can become a valuable ally. There wouldn't be a captain alive that'd dare to challenge me with him behind me."

Naked ambition flared through his words, enough to make Therill flinch. The possibility of being replaced was ever at the back of his thoughts, though he somehow always doubted Blackheart would truly betray him. Practically all the blood was on his hands, and that made Therill a potential problem.

"I say we either kill him or dump him in an escape pod and be done with it. Remember the people you are dealing with. Some are still hostile over your mutiny. They wouldn't be averse to having another if it worked out in their favor," Therill cautioned.

"Where did you learn such big words?" Blackheart smirked. "I know damned well what this motley bunch is capable of, and I'll vent the first one that so much as passes a nasty thought."

"Perhaps I can smooth their suspicions if you tell me what you're planning."

Clever bastard. I tell you, and that makes you indispensible, right? Fine, I'll need you until Auk decides to see things my way. "Simple; I intend to sell our fallen Inquisitor and turn Mr. Auk to our cause."

"Even if you do, we'll be a bigger target for the Conclave. You don't have the support necessary to succeed," Therill warned in a drawn-out voice. His mind was already racing through the impending possibilities.

None were good.

"That's where you're wrong."

Feigning unconsciousness, Geres Auk laid on the cold deck plating with his eyes closed, listening to every word. Their audacity insulted him. Once a counselor of lords, Geres remained as imposing of a threat as he had been. The shamed loss on Crimeat failed to tarnish his lust for the inevitable schism that would shatter the Conclave and free the universe. It took an incredible amount of will not to shatter his bonds and tear out Blackheart's throat.

Resigned to his temporary fate, he studied the pitch in their voices, the way the debate turned. *Amateurs*. Blackheart was a smalltime crook with ambitions much too large for his own good. Geres had never considered himself a masterful tactician, but he knew the easy way out when he heard it. There was a rift forming among the crew, widening so long as he and Ursal lived. All advantages rested comfortably in his grasp. The chains weighing him down wouldn't hold.

All it took was a thought and the will to earn his freedom.

Sunset over Krenz was a beautiful occasion. Vermillion skies slowly darkened accompanied by a cacophony of bird calls and awakening insects. Blooming flowers gave off strong scents, and the trees shined in golden hues. Sunset was the beginning of the time for rest and more. An entirely different function rose in conjunction with the setting sun. The pillars of light flared hotly, inviting all to come and bear witness to the crowned glory of the universe. False gods were said to reside within the ancient city. They cowered in the day, withering under the watchfulness of the clergy. False gods cringed in the shadows while gathering strength, a strength needed to one day usurp human will and plunge the universe into chaos.

Cardinal Seniorus Lorenu Phos watched the daily transformation from the wide-paneled viewing windows of her outer office. The panoramic scene offered the full glory of the capital city's vista. Spires and cathedrals towered into the sky in a mortal attempt at reaching the gods. Soft plumes of white clouds drifted carelessly past on winds threatening to drown the world in unprecedented change. She suppressed a shiver. Not even summer's full heat offered warmth for the problems of office.

She felt her grip slipping. The universe was moving away from the indomitable will and protection once offered by the Conclave. Priests and cardinals weren't as welcome in the less civilized places as they once were. People looked back with open disdain at men and women, many of whom had come from their own ranks, who chose to answer a higher purpose and serve their peers.

Differences in opinion divided the Forum. She dreaded to think what it was doing to the main body of clergy. Mankind wasn't as strong as it assumed. Weakness, malleable and manipulative, clung to the tired shoulders of so many downtrodden. Rising waves of crime and poverty were at previously unheard of levels. And through it all, Lorenu was all but powerless to do anything. The political machine had grown too strong, too out of control, to be halted by the whims of a single woman.

Lorenu softly clasped her hands behind her back and struggled to repress the overwhelming sensation of failure gripping her. She knew it was foolish pride more than actual failure. Some crisis or another always seemed to grip the Conclave, but this time it felt…different, real. Times continued to change without first consulting her, much as her own Forum tended to do. Doubts assailed her from every corner. They rendered her immobile, disconnected.

She lost track of how long she watched the sunset — long enough for the vermillion to turn black. Her door chimed and hissed open. Lorenu closed her eyes, dreading the inevitable conversation Alain Nye had come to engage.

"Cardinal Seniorus, I apologize for scheduling this meeting so late, but my offices are slightly busier than usual."

"Alain, thank you for coming," she replied without turning.

He bristled with the familiarity of her greeting but knew it was to be expected. Technically, they were equals and expected to be on a familiar, first-name basis. Nye forced himself to remain calm. The seriousness of his requested meeting went much beyond first names and a sip of tea whilst two colleagues reminisced over old times long forgotten.

"May I sit?" he asked.

"Of course. Make yourself comfortable." She shuffled around to the opposite side of the small glass top table and cushiony tan leather chairs.

"I've never really cared for these chairs. My back has given me trouble for years now. These don't offer me nearly as much support as I prefer," he told her casually.

She smiled tightly. "They remind me of home. I find that we often give up too many of the comforts from where we came from."

"Where do you come from? I don't believe I've ever asked."

Lorenu leaned down and poured water from the crystal carafe, offering a glass to her counterpart. He accepted because etiquette demanded it.

"No, you haven't. We seldom find the time sit down and be civil. The demands of office are sometimes too taxing."

"Making it more important that we each have confidants to remind us of simpler times," he added quietly.

His thoughts drifted back to the path taken to get to the Inquisitor General's office. Born into a life of privilege, Alain Nye was a man used to getting what he wanted. It was only a matter of time before his mind turned towards the Inquisition and the inevitable dreams of power inherent to the role. A small fortune secured his position within the august organization. The rest was up to him. He'd weaseled and forced his way up the ranks, not stopping until his eyes settled on the aid to Farius Graeme, the previous Inquisitor General.

It had taken years longer than anticipated before he was finally able to remove the former aide and duck into the position, but a fake family emergency and then a deep-space transit accident had opened all the doors he needed. Graeme had taken him into his confidence, and Nye had continued to plot. Popular conspiracy theorists claimed he was responsible for Graeme's murder. They could all rot. Not that he was innocent in any regard, but the truth would go to the grave with him.

Lorenu smiled, genuinely now. "I was born in a small farming community on the low continent. Nothing like Krenz. I don't remember having an air car or much in the way of amenities, but we made it all right. Life was hard, but it was good. My parents were communal farmers. They never had much. Many times, it was a struggle just to put food on the table for my siblings and me. I never complained, though. Life was what we made of it, and I am a better person because of it."

She stopped, suddenly realizing just how much she'd divulged. "I'm sorry. I don't normally go in depth with my past. I suppose it's been a long time."

"Perfectly all right. It feels good to speak of the past from time to time. As you say, we must remember where we come from if there is hope of success," he replied.

"Indeed. What do you have your mind this evening, Alain?"

She decided the best way to reclaim the advantage was by deliberately changing the subject and getting to the heart of the matter. Alain Nye was crafty enough to realize what was happening and adjust his tactics. He was also by no means what she considered a close confidant.

His eyes narrowed ever so slightly before returning to normal. If Lorenu noticed, she wisely kept it to herself. "As you know, times are…strained. The Inquisition is stretched to capacity from one end of the universe to the other. Not to mention the overuse of the limited Prekhauten battalions and fleets. Admiral Fhi is prepared to deploy at dawn, by the way."

"Good. Increased pirate attacks on our shipping lanes. The recent assault on the *Indomitable* was most distressing."

"Times have changed, Lorenu. Not even the Inquisition standard is what it once was," he said quickly, almost too quickly for it to be genuine. "Which brings me to why I am here. Things are changing rapidly, and I think I can safely speak for all of us by saying we are struggling to figure out why. Power has been reduced for all three branches. Worse, the people are disaffected with us. They no longer respect the value of the Conclave or Inquisition.

"You are viewed as a stagnant figurehead atop a dying fire, whereas I oversee a ruthless band of lackeys and murderers who jump at shadows."

Lorenu took a slow drink. "Pleasing everyone is impossible, Alain. The common good must be maintained if there is to be balance across the universe. We have the populations of over seven hundred worlds to worry about."

"Precisely the problem! The worlds furthest from Vau Prime are slowly breaking away. Faith is disintegrating, and not one damned person has asked why." Alain jumped at the chance to give her this one last chance to decide which side she stood on.

She struggled to keep from bristling. "Faith is the one thing they all have in common. Are we to abandon our foundations and principles on the whim of rumors and popular trends? You're made of sterner stuff, Alain. These storms come in like a midsummer hurricane, blowing out just as quickly before any remember their initial worry. Our two offices are the pinnacle of virtue. Without us, the old ways would fade, and anarchy would reign."

"The old ways are already fading." *And I'm doing my damnedest to speed the process.* "It is entirely possible the truth about the gods has been leaked."

"By whom?" she snapped. "The amount of people who know the truth is very small. All trusted men and women. What you speak is of heresy within the one place we thought impregnable."

He held up his hands to stay her building rage. "I'm not insinuating the whys or hows. Lorenu, we can sit here all night bickering back and forth, but that doesn't change the fact that there is a war coming."

"War?"

The word came out deflated. The one promise she had made to herself was the vow to keep the sanctity of the Conclave intact until the torch was passed to her successor. If what Nye said was true, she had failed.

"I see it in every report. Davith and I sat down last week and discussed the possible outcomes. War is all but inevitable now. This cult of Rengu is gaining popularity, and we have been unable to discover any of the perpetrators. I can't kill what I can't find. None of us can. Without a direction, our military might is useless, to a degree."

Her upper lip quivered ever so slightly. Nye pushed further. "I've already run a hundred leads down, and they all came to dead ends. The cult is highly organized and efficient at evading our authority, physical and moral. We may have superior firepower and professional uniformed assets, but they have the will of an increasing amount of the people, and that, Cardinal Seniorus, is the crux of the problem."

"Every administration has had its unique set of problems and driving circumstances. This one is no different, yet I refuse to believe that the bulk population of seven hundred worlds has suddenly lost their faith. The gods are the foundation of this office. Without them we are…"

"Nothing," Nye finished.

Lorenu suddenly felt deflated, as if he'd just gut punched her. She recalled being shocked when she'd first learned the gods hadn't been destroyed, learned that they still drew breath, silent in the crystal tombs, waiting for the time when they could return and reclaim dominance to the universe. She dreaded that day. Dreaded what would happen to the countless trillions when they suddenly learned the truths they were told were, in fact, lies. Her moral conscience screamed to break the three thousand year cycle, but the lie was too entrenched. Civilizations had sprung up around it, nurtured by the thought that humanity was alone to govern itself according to the whims of the Conclave. Should the gods suddenly reawaken...

"I'm not arguing with you, Lorenu. Faith is everything. It is also the one constant factor across the board that is failing. The cult of Rengu is successfully subsuming all we have done, all our predecessors have done to install a stable and peaceful democracy."

She shook her head. Denial burned her eyes. "How? How have we let this happen? Your Inquisitors are supposed to be rooting out heresy while the priests give comfort. Rengu should never have been able to develop."

He held out his hands in a helpless gesture. "That doesn't matter now. The cult is alive and growing. We are powerless to halt it. This is not easy for me to say, or even think, for that matter. Perhaps we are wrong."

"In what way?"

He frowned. "We've clung to the belief that the gods were infallible, going so far as to ensure the general population believes they no longer exist. What happens if we are wrong? What if people discover the truth that the gods are very real and waiting to be reawakened so that they may take control of the universe again? The lie has never sat well with me. I'll be the first to admit that."

"It is a lie born of necessity. Anarchy and total chaos would reign if that many people suddenly learned their lives were lies. Crime would surge. Our orders would be hard pressed to maintain any semblance of the law. We would crumble," Lorenu said sharply.

The very thought that she was the main protagonist in the universe's most complex lie galled her. She knew the truth, the complex reasoning behind what she and the others were forced to propagate. Once, it had bothered her, but those days were long gone. Lorenu embraced the lie with trepidation. What little comfort the night offered was stolen by her need to justify her actions. So many people depended on her, she was nearly overwhelmed daily. And now this.

"We must double our efforts, Inquisitor General. I want the head of this cult struck from the body. Take the head, and the rest will wither away," she suddenly said with more force than he'd thought she possessed.

He cautioned, "Until a new head is formed."

"Don't debate the pettiness of politics. I want this victory. We need to show the people that we are still in control. That their best interests are still close to our hearts. Without the people, we will fold." Her gaze stiffened. "I will not be the one who goes down in history for letting the universe dissolve into oblivion."

Inquisitor General Alain Nye finished his water and sighed. *Very well, Lorenu Phos. You have made your declarations. The sides are chosen.*

FIFTEEN

3212 A.G. (After Gods), deep desert, planet An'kuruku.

Elisa was still having trouble moving her limbs. Stiffness in the joints combined with an unnatural swelling from the giant scorpion's poison. Most of the pain had subsided, leaving her with the haunted memories of her near-death experience. She considered herself an accomplished warrior, but nothing in her life had prepared her for the fury of being attacked by a five-ton insect. Every day, she hated the desert planet just a little more.

Her wounds looked better, if a nasty combination of purple and black bruises leaking a foul-colored puss was better. Elisa was thankful Tanzeil and his tribe had arrived when they did. The other result was less than favorable. She lacked the desire to be digested in a bug's belly. Much had happened since her brash decision to abandon the relative civility of Tenemenah. Rightfully, neither she nor Ah'muf should be alive. The bar owner and now her friend was a long way removed from his time in the deep deserts. City life had spoiled him much more than he would ever admit.

Images, warm memories of Ah'muf, entertained her in those moments she felt most vulnerable. Right now, she found the thoughts unwelcome, practically invasive. Elisa needed a clear head if she was going to get them both through this crisis. Tanzeil welcomed them with open arms and a charming smile, but it was all too false for her liking. The man was hiding something potentially dark.

Considering the direction her life had taken, Elisa didn't find it too remarkable that she instantly saw the bad in people. Others might label her a defeatist, but she knew better. No one who had been forced to witness every single thing she knew murdered before her eyes would find joy in the sunset, smell the beauty of freshly bloomed roses. No one had the right to judge her for her discriminations.

Tanzeil. The dark-skinned man with the warm features managed to say all the right things at precisely the right moments. He sickened her in that regard. Back on Crimeat, he would have been treated as a petty con man, a charlatan with ill intent. A dark stain echoed in his words, tainting his proclaimed innocence with venom just as deadly as the scorpion's. Elisa would do well to stand clear, lest she fall under his sway. As it stood now, she fully expected him to turn on them when the moment best suited his needs.

A hot wind blew across the endless sea of dunes. The hot kiss was as unwelcome as a prior lover. Not that she had much experience in that regard, though her eye was suddenly focused on Ah'muf. His genuine warmth and kindness softened the rough edges she'd grown accustomed to. The familiar hardness kept her warm on cold nights, the fires burned hotly from the depths of her heart as she searched tirelessly to avenge past grievances. The Bloody Man had returned to her long after his crime, offering assistance and a new purpose to the hatred her life had devolved into. Elisa had accepted his task on the surface, but nothing he said or did would ever remove the miasma of guilt clinging to her soul.

Her face darkened under the soft cloth wrapped around her head for protection from the unforgiving desert sun. It darkened further at the forced kindness in Tanziel's smooth voice.

"Ah, it does me good to see you up and moving," he told her. "Scorpions have a vicious sting. The weakest perish quickly."

"Life has other uses for me, Tanzeil. I somehow doubt it's going to allow me to perish as quickly as you're suggesting."

If he was offended by her slight insult, he refused to show it. "I do not suggest anything of the sort. Sometimes what we want to say is obscured by translation, is it not? I will be the first to admit my tongue does not always mirror what my mind wishes to explain. It is a curse, I think."

She stopped listening. Long-windedness was a plague among many of An'kuruku's population. Their inability to get to the point was infuriating, but she managed to maintain her poise, mostly. Elisa took a slow draw from her canteen. The water was warm but still cooler than the rising oppression of the sun.

"Tanzeil, I've spent the last two years on this planet listening to men not speak their minds. While I respect the customs and culture here, I also must ask that you do not shy away from my directness."

That should shut the smug bastard up. I'm still not well enough to handle him in a fight. I need to get off this rock. Every day I can feel my sanity slipping. I need to get out of this desert. I need to find the Paradise Tear and the first transport back to civilization. Let Sorrow do his own bloody work from here on.

"I profess I lack the experience you have. These sands are all that I own. I would be lost in a different environment. People look at my home and see only desolation, a ruined waste of land and resources. They do not understand," he told her.

"What should they understand?"

He smiled, yellowed teeth gleaming. "That there is more life in these particles of sand than in all of Tenemenah. Life began out here, Elisa. Did you know that? The first guy'ang lizard pushed up through the hard, sun-baked crust and began a journey that would follow millions of years of evolution, culminating in what we see each other as today."

Your entire society stems from lizards? No wonder you're all fucked in the head. "You can't ignore the gods, Tanzeil. They had a part in your evolution."

Silence for a moment. "The gods hold no sway out here. This is my land, my time. The gods are rusted relics best forgotten in humanity's museums for those still curious enough to be fooled by antiquity. Any strength the gods had is lost. We are free to make our own destiny."

Elisa reluctantly admitted he had a point, if skewed. The gods were more relevant than his limited experience allowed him to believe. She didn't doubt the desert tribes were strong, or that they found truth in their convictions. She merely knew they were wrong. Mollock Bolle had shown her the error in her own thinking, the concealed truth hidden behind three thousand years of Conclave falsehood. Seeing the sleeping god on Crimeat had been overpowering, raw. A gaping hole in her conscience ached to be filled by something that made sense.

Her thoughts strayed to An'kuruku. Where did their god sleep? Was it buried beneath these sands, lost forever to the vagaries of mankind's inability to properly remember the past?

"Destiny is overrated, Tanzeil."

"You don't believe?"

She paused before shaking her head slowly; strands of greasy, red hair licking the sides of her face and neck. "I believe that we are what we are. There is no cosmic force guiding our actions. We make decisions based on reason and emotion. Nothing more."

"Those are the words of a blasphemer," he warned. "We are blessed to be alive, no matter what happened to these unnecessary gods. Be careful what you theorize. Even this deep in the desert, the wrong people have means of discovering the black stains in our hearts. I would not see ill befall you."

His last sentence was drawn out, leaving unanswered questions. Elisa felt her heartbeat shudder. He was plotting against her and Ah'muf. The tavern owner! She'd almost forgotten about him while Tanzeil attempted to charm his way into her thoughts. The chance that he might able be dead was very real.

"Forgive me, Tanzeil, but I must go check on my companion. He took the worst of the scorpion's attack."

The barest tilt of his head. "Of course, how careless of me. We will continue this conversation when you are both better rested. Until this evening."

Tanzeil excused himself, turning his camel away while ensuring he rode at an angle where he was able to watch her every move. She was going to fetch a good price. Slavers paid top coin for off-world prizes. Tanzeil broke into a great smile and began whistling a favorite childhood song. They were still a few hours from where his tribe had concealed their ground skimmers. The massive craft ran on a combination of steam and solar power. Word had already been passed ahead. The men and women guarding his tribe's most precious resources should already be preparing the vehicles.

The Wells were less than two full days away after that. Two more days, and he was going to be a rich man.

Elisa slid from the worn cloth saddle. Frayed edges threatened to tear under her light weight. The desert tribe may be proud, but they were financially poor. No amount of faith or internal belief contributed much to sustaining such a large group of people. Need of food and supplies, replacement items and basic necessities threatened to drive the tribe into abject poverty.

Not that any of that was her immediate concern. Elisa was almost too focused on Ah'muf. The whimsical, tanned man had placed something deep inside her. A strange combination of emotions conflicted within. Elisa was always the type of woman that knew what she wanted and was focused on achieving her goals. Few obstacles were large enough to keep her from the end once her mind was set.

The camel continued to plod along, herd instincts taking over. Elisa wasn't sorry to watch it go. She'd never been so sore after only a day's ride. Slightly bowlegged, she hobbled up the three rickety steps to the back of the medical wagon. The healer on duty nervously looked away upon seeing her brazenly enter the wagon. Such things were not approved of amongst the tribe. Elisa didn't care. Her friend was hurt, and she harbored a gnawing suspicion worse was coming.

Ah'muf opened his dark, hazel eyes and tried to smile. The pain was still too much, and he collapsed back into waves of unfiltered pain.

"*Farisi*, forgive me for not getting up," he joked through clenched teeth. Sweat beaded his forehead, and his normally dark skin was bleached white.

She smiled for him. "You need to rest. This heat is unbearable."

"The heat should be our friend. It takes away our weaknesses and remakes us into stronger, better versions of ourselves."

Elisa shook her head. "Doesn't anyone speak their mind on this miserable planet?"

"The challenge lies in deciphering," Ah'muf said gently.

She laid a hand on his forehead, gently wiping the sweat away. His skin burned to the touch. He was sick. The poison was spreading.

"What happened?" he managed to ask.

She still found the affair unbelievable. Nothing on Crimeat could have prepared her for such an event. "We were attacked by a desert scorpion."

He choked suddenly, eyes going wide. "And we lived? You are indeed a formidable woman!"

"Unfortunately, I wasn't up to the task. The scorpion nearly killed me and would have if Tanzeil and his tribe hadn't come along when they did."

Ah'muf's eyes hardened. "I know this name. Tanzeil. *Farisi*, we are in trouble."

"I figured as much, but neither of us is in much shape to do anything about it," she replied quietly after ensuring they were alone. "He claims to be taking us to the Wells. Whether he tells the truth or not remains to be seen, but I don't take him on face value. The man reminds me of a snake."

"He is much worse than a snake. His bite is the desert adder's, poisonous and deadly. Any offer of comfort or aid comes at a price."

"What can you tell me about him, Ah'muf? I need to be able to come up with a way out of this situation."

It was his turn to shake his head. "There is no way out. Tanzeil has made his fortunes in the trading of human flesh. He is a slaver. If he is taking us to the Wells, it is with ill intent."

Elisa cast a glance towards Tanzeil, now a distant blur in the shimmering desert. "He claims we should be there within the next two days."

"Then we have only two days to figure out how to escape."

His courage, limited and wounded as it was, inspired her despite the gnawing feeling that she was, at last, trapped. Captivity was no stranger. The Ugri had found her in the Great Barrier Jungle during her hunt for Mollock Bolle. She'd been treated fairly and even fed, but she doubted the desert slave traders would be so kind. The memory left a sour taste. She'd been duped into hunting down the one man who had discovered the truth of the gods by the dark council, though she suspected they were much more than what the lords of Lethendweil saw on the surface. People like that were akin to a virus. So long as one lived, others would succumb to their temptations.

Elisa refocused on Ah'muf. His eyes were struggling to remain open. Most of his strength was gone. Enough to leave her with doubts about his health. The poison should have been nullified by now. Tanzeil's healers were either incompetent or ordered to keep him weak in an attempt at controlling her. She found the idea repulsive, not to mention cowardly. Women on An'kuruku were treated like second class citizens, ignored and forgotten unless needed. Elisa despised that cultural aspect but wasn't averse to using it to her advantage. Men here tended to think past her abilities, forgetting she came from a violent world and was more capable of wreaking havoc than any of them.

Escaping alone wouldn't prove too difficult, but it would mean leaving her only trusted friend behind to whatever depredations Tanzeil could conjure in revenge. Ah'muf was a definite liability to her survival. He was also a dear friend she feared she was starting to have feelings for. The alien thoughts warmed her after the suns dropped and left the sands bone-chillingly cold, and they terrified her at the same time. She didn't know love, having abandoned the concept after that fateful day Sorrow had appeared.

Leaning close so only he could hear, she whispered, "Don't worry, Ah'muf. I'll figure out a way to get us out of here."

I just don't know how.

Tenemenah was restless. A fire was ready to break out, carrying the seeds of burnt destruction across the countless and crowded streets. Thousands of innocent souls would perish beneath the crushing heat of flames, leaving nothing but charred husks where flesh and bone had once stood. Tenemenah would die. The bones of the city would be picked clean by vultures and sandstorms. Time would pass, and memories would fade. The horrors of that single night would ease with time, slowly turning into legend, myth. All it would take is a single spark.

Prefect Lezorsu Pine looked down with a father's pride at the small army he'd ordered mobilized. Truthfully, they amounted to little more than an overzealous militia reinforced by a company of Prefects. Most were peasants seeking to reaffirm their faith in the eyes of the local government. Lezorsu doubted many had experience with weapons, much less formal military discipline. *Still*, he mused, *they'll make good fodder*. Enough to soften the insurgents properly before he unleashed his Prefects.

"Prefect, the militia is assembled," Sub Prefect Jut announced.

One eye missing, Jut's face was a mass of puckered scar tissue. He refused to shave off his twenty-year-old beard, though. Rough patches marred the otherwise perfect, black hair. He was Lezorsu's second in command, a hard man as comfortable killing a man as training one.

"How many?"

"Close to two thousand," Jut replied.

Lezorsu nodded absently, his mind already racing to the possibilities awaiting him in the Deeves. "What are the insurgents' latest strength estimates?"

Jut paused briefly. "More than double."

"Does that concern you, Jut?" Lezorsu asked mirthlessly.

"Yes."

"Good. A commander who underestimates his opponents often fails to live long enough to realize his mistakes. We will do well to remember most of the people standing so eager to meet death are simple farmers, not the hardened warriors we might otherwise expect to put down a rebellion with."

Lezorsu's raspy voice was thin, nasal. A childhood pox had partially crippled his larynx, leaving him to be mocked by the other children. His voice held a haunting effect, and he'd exploited it throughout his career in the Prefecture. His was the will of subtle dominance. Lezorsu twisted and manipulated others through fear and threat of ultimately failing their gods. Bullies, he learned quickly, fell away the moment he stood up to them. The pencil-thin Prefect enjoyed his reputation. The citizens of Tenemenah named him Doomspell, the reincarnation of death itself.

"All we have with us are peasants, Lord," Jut pressed. "I need more fighters if I am to have a chance at stopping the rebellion."

Lezorsu rounded on the bigger man, who recoiled a step before catching himself. "Peasants have the ability to change the world if they weren't so mired in their thought processes. Look at the thousands assembled in the Deeves."

Jut frowned. "I don't understand. What makes them different from the ones we have in our employ? Peasants are peasants."

Lezorsu grinned, sparkling white teeth poking through his thin lips. "Our peasants are inspired by the natural fear we instill in them. How many do you think would stand and fight if the threat of reprisal wasn't behind them with sharp blades? Not many, I assure you. It has always fallen to the handful of truly powerful to push those less ambitious to whatever ends necessary.

"Our peasants come out of respect for the law and a healthy dose of fear. The rabble assembled on the shores of the Bo are the complete opposite. They go because they are disaffected with current society's social structures. They complain that our rule is too stern, too strict. They whine and dicker like people who think they are entitled to better without having to work for it, to earn it. They are a stain on all we have tried to accomplish, and I will not suffer them any longer."

Jut shifted his weight to his right leg and clasped his hands behind his back. "They are traitors, heretics by any other name. You almost sound as if you admire them."

"In a manner of speaking. Any man willing to stand up for what his beliefs deserves a modicum of respect. That doesn't change the fact that they have turned their backs on the Prefecture and possibly the very Conclave. I cannot, will not stand for such blatant heresy. The rebellion must be crushed. Every last man, woman and child needs to die namelessly to ensure another rebellion never occurs."

Not even Jut's lust for battle was prepared to accept what his superior had just admitted. "You're speaking of the total annihilation of a large portion of the population. How can there not be another rebellion? We will become the most hated entity in a dozen star systems. I'm not prepared to murder four thousand civilians."

Lezorsu edged closer, wicked intent blazing in his pale eyes. "Then I will find another who can. One of the luxuries of being in command is that I know who I can trust to accomplish any task. Do I need to make an enemy out of you, Jut?"

Lips pursed, Jut endured a private struggle between morality and loyalty. He'd never once considered acting contrarily to the will of the Prefecture, of Lezorsu Pine. Ever the loyal servant, Jut had done things he wasn't particularly proud of but things that had needed doing. His strength stemmed from blind loyalty and the natural ability to read a battlefield. Instincts told him good from bad. Others looked to him as a beacon of reliability, an immovable rock against rising tides of dissent.

It was with grave difficulty that he managed his next words. "Murder goes against all that I stand for, all the Prefecture means. We have been chartered by the Guild Leaders and by the people of Tenemenah to uphold the law. Justice is our watchword, no matter if others are opposed. My conscience won't allow me to cut down unarmed children in the name of frivolous desires."

Lezorsu struggled to contain the storm erupting in his soul. Here stood his second in command, a man only slightly less powerful than himself, threatening to let his mind overrule his sense of duty. Appalling! "You would be wise to rethink your answer, *friend*. I don't give second chances."

A slow exhale. "My mind is decided, my conscience clear. I will not lead the militia against the rebellion."

"Those are…regrettable words," Lezorsu seethed. "Very well. I strip you of all rank, title and authority under the code of Prefecture. You are hereby disgraced, shamed into exile. I give you one full turn of the sun before I set the dogs after you."

To his credit, Jut stood his ground. "You know where I will go."

"I pray you do."

Jut stood glaring at his former commander and one-time friend. Only it had never been true friendship. Lezorsu was an idealistic opportunist who used everyone who got in his way.

"Get out of my sight, Disgraced," Lezorsu growled, turning his back on Jut for the final time.

It was a calculated move. Jut was every bit considered one of the best armsmen in Tenemenah. He could easily strike Lezorsu down and end it all right now, but the man named Doomspell knew what he was doing. Honor ranked highly among the Prefecture — a fact not lost on either. If Jut struck Lezorsu down, he'd be branded a traitor and hunted to the ends of An'kuruku. No. Escape was the only viable option. The bigger Prefect decided to bide his time and wait for the right moment to revenge.

"This will not be the last you see of me," he warned and stormed out, leaving Lezorsu grinning.

Althas Pey swept in shortly after. His cloak rustled across the dull marble floor, limiting any effects of grandeur Althas might have desired. Shallow cheeks gave him a shadowy look. His eyes, dark brown, were deep-set, piercing. He bore the look of a hawk. Predatory, sharp, Althas Pey was a man hunting down more. More power. More wealth. He wanted it all, to include Lezorsu's position.

"That was anti-climactic," he criticized. "I rather expected Jut to put up more of a fight. Of course, not even he would be foolish enough to assault the vaunted Doomspell in his own chambers."

Lezorsu scowled. "I've never liked that name, Althas. It gives people the wrong im-pression."

"But a true one. You are doom, Lezorsu. Make no mistake. The people know you are the viper hiding in the sack of grain."

"Are you done?"

Althas shrugged, walking over to the round onyx table to snatch a green apple. "For now. We have a campaign to plan, after all."

Lezorsu questioned his decision to remove Jut. This pompous ass needed to be flogged publicly for his interminable combination of arrogance and ignorance. He was suddenly reminded that the gods must love stupidity. Too many people suffered from it to be mere coincidence.

"Yes, that. Jut informed me we are not where we need to be to successfully execute this campaign. Is that true?"

"True enough. Most of the people we have are amateurs. I wouldn't trust many with an open blade, much less expect them to know which way to point a rifle." Althas bit deep. Juice spattered from the corners of his mouth.

"Not good enough. You're telling me we have two thousand corpses waiting to be slaughtered," he countered.

"War is an ugly affair. These apples are very sour. Are you sure you bought them ripe?" Althas asked.

"What of the rumors of this prophet?" he asked sharply. Undisguised hostility dripped from his words.

"He's nothing. The true power hides in his shadows, using him as a puppet to incite the population of the Deeves. Most of the province has already abandoned the Bone Father in favor of this new prophet."

"Ancient mystics and petty charlatans. Their time is ending. We don't need their corrupted version of sorcery or their obsolete belief in the gods."

"You're suggesting the gods are corrupt? That's high, even from you."

Lezorsu's face darkened. "No gods motivate my decisions or actions. I am my own man, Althas. No one else's. What I do is answerable only to those who employ me. Speaking of which, has there been any word on my request for support from the Inquisition?"

"Surprisingly, no. The rose bearers don't seem inclined to rush into another domestic political dispute. I fear they are still licking their wounds from that abominable affair two years ago."

"So we do this alone."

He was almost relieved. Intervention from the Conclave or Inquisition would only serve to stifle his drive. His militia might be unorganized, but it was better armed and guided by *his* fervor. The indignation of this Prophet, this usurper, offered to solidify the rest of the people fully behind the Prefecture. After that, it wouldn't take much to oust the Conclave and its ineffective priests. A man should know better than to tread where he is unwanted. Especially in the deserts of An'kuruku.

"Jut was confident the militia will not be sufficient to stand up to the rabble on the shores of the Bo," he commented idly.

Another shrug. Althas spit out the second bite of apple and tossed both pieces to the table. "Jut knew what he was doing, whether you agreed or not. There are close to five thousand peasants gathered to listen to the Prophet. Most are unarmed and close to starving, but that doesn't mean we should discount the sheer weight of numbers. Worst case scenario, we lose seven thousand peasants and start over."

Althas said that last part almost too easily for Lezorsu, even though being relieved of so many hungry mouths might prove a blessing. A reduced population would be equally beneficial and problematic. More would seek to rebel, if not openly. The Prefects stood on a delicately balanced blade. A fall in either direction might prove deadly.

Lezorsu pursed his lips briefly. "I want the militia marching within the week. Every moment we delay weakens our position. We cannot be allowed to appear to give these heretics an open lead without reprisal. Althas Pey, I want you to lead them."

"I can do that easily enough," Althas nodded slowly. "I'm assuming you want maximum casualties?"

On both sides would be nice. "As many as you can create. Kill them all, and I'll give a hundred gold pieces to every militiaman who survives."

Althas finally found a reason to grin. He snatched another apple and quickly stuffed it into a pocket before turning to leave. "You really should throw these out and get new ones. It's unbecoming for the mighty Doomspell to be passing out sour fruit to his guests."

He almost made it to the door before looking back at Lezorsu one final time. "Oh, and I suppose you want me to take care of Jut as well.

No worries. I'll do that one for the pleasure. Always was a pain in my ass."

Lezorsu watched him leave, teeth grinding.

SIXTEEN

3212 A.G. (After Gods), Hawker's Gate, deep space.

Nothing on the deep space station could be considered elegant. People came this far out for a variety of reasons, most of them from sheer desperation. It took a stern person to live in a fabricated environment for years on end without breathing fresh air, listening to the wind rustle through the grass or standing in the brilliance of a sun. Long lines of administrators did their best to replicate a comfortable, habitable environment, but they all admitted it wasn't enough. The light colored walls and ceilings attempted mirth, but it was a failed endeavor. No matter how hard they tried, the Conclave officials continued to find disparity between planet dwellers and spacers.

Matthias strolled down one of the main corridors, looking every bit the interested tourist. Partially, he was. Neither he nor Tolde had been here in more than a decade, if not more. Much of what he'd seen thus far was vaguely familiar, but the current administrator had been busy with some much-needed renovations. Matthias was instantly suspicious of the massive level of changes being undertaken. It almost felt like the station was preparing for war. Almost. His eyes narrowed reflexively, forcing him to stop and adjust his disposition before he ran in to someone in Von's employ.

Presha Von. The name dripped through his thoughts like a slow working poison. What was it about the woman that inspired so many to go against the will of the Conclave? He'd never actually seen her, despite their proximity on the Plateau two years ago. The truth of her involvement hadn't been learned until well after those events, and even then Matthias was left with grave doubts. Too little of her was known. Much of that was speculation or worse. He'd like nothing better than to wrap his hands around her slender neck and...

He shrugged, suddenly aware of the curious stares from a crew of deck workers. Getting noticed was the last thing he needed if he had a chance at completing his mission. A mission whose parameters he still wasn't sure of. General Strannan had been as vague as possible, leaving Matthias with the growing sensation of dread. He couldn't say why, but his gut warned of a coming war. A large war. If it came to that, the Prekhauten Guard would be sorely pressed to maintain order and discipline across the hundreds of inhabited planets.

The implications of a universe-wide conflict staggered him. Death and destruction would rage on a scale larger than anything in humanity's short history — perhaps only rivaled by the final war of the gods. *Is this to be our death knell? Were we nothing more than a whim in the cosmic scheme?* Matthias didn't enjoy the prospect. Too much pain and misery accompanied everyday lives. What point was there in purposefully making more?

He nodded at the workers, hoping to avoid further scrutiny, and continued down the corridor with measured stride. *War*. The word shook his spine, trembling the foundations of all that he was. No stranger to violence, Matthias had been involved in well over a hundred engagements, and those were only the ones he remembered. The grey ghost of death was a constant companion that kept him occupied during those long nights when he questioned why he still lived. Maybe that was why he never took to alcohol. He knew too many comrades who lost themselves at the bottom of a bottle. Those once valiant warriors too often wound up face down in the gutter. When death finally did catch up, Matthias had no intention of meeting it any other way but face to face.

The corridor opened suddenly while he was lost in rumination. Matthias first noticed the raised voices and the typical noises associated with large crowds of people. A market area. Strannan insisted a reliable contact was somewhere onboard, a man or woman with enough actionable intel to successfully guide Tolde and his Guards into taking Presha Von down. The only problem was that Matthias didn't have a clue where to begin. He slowed briefly, trying to wrap his head around the sights before him.

Hawker's Gate was a conglomeration of a hundred different civilizations. People of every color and creed intermingled in the name of galactic harmony while trying to turn a profit. No one did anything for free, not even the Phallalian Surgeons. Matthias had been given a substantial credit account to accomplish his mission. A lesser man might be tempted to take it and disappear; the sum was large enough to last a handful of lifetimes. For himself, Matthias couldn't comprehend what could possibly be so expensive.

Wide eyed, he soaked in the many banks of neon signs and holographic projections. Anything imaginable was available for purchase. Slavery was officially outlawed by Cardinal decree but was more evident the further away from Vau Prime you traveled. Mines still needed unwilling workers. Heavy industry still needed men and women to build what the big three orders needed. Matthias wondered when the last time was that an official Conclave delegation bothered touring the distant star systems. Certainly not in his lifetime. It felt almost as if the Conclave had abandoned Hawker's Gate, marking it an acceptable loss and moving on. No wonder the seeds of dissent were so blatantly evident.

"Come over here, handsome. I can give you what you're looking for," an ebony skinned woman crooned from the far wall. She had closely cropped hair the color of midnight and wore very little.

Matthias didn't bother slowing. He'd seen more than his share of bottom-dwelling whores trying to charm their way into his pocketbook. Once, towards the beginning of his career, he had been a willing participant. Exquisite women were a weakness he chose to keep hidden from his Prekhauten commanders. Had they known of his proclivity for the opposite sex, he would never have advanced to the rank of command sergeant major. Now, he was older and, supposedly, wiser. The need to test his manhood was gone, a faded stain on his conscience.

She persisted. "Come on, soldier boy. I know you want this."

Matthias froze. Soldier boy? Naturally, he knew there was only a very slim chance he would be able to conceal the professional mannerisms and movements of a lifelong soldier, but he couldn't believe he was being called out by a prostitute. He turned, wheeling on the woman, and prayed she was only guessing.

"What did you call me?" he asked aggressively.

She flashed a toothy grin, making her more beautiful than before. "You think me crazy? I know a uniformed man when I see one, whether he chooses to wear one or not."

Matthias held up a hand. "You're wrong this time. I'm not soldier."

Which was technically true. He'd been officially retired from active duty for the mishap on Crimeat and removed from the payroll. Any work since was covert and under the watchful and private eye of Strannan's personal staff. Outside of that, only Tolde Breed and Luma Kai knew the truth. He wished Luma had been absent when he and Tolde had met again. The Office of Heretical Persecution was notorious for arresting anyone with the slightest difference of opinion from Inquisition doctrine.

"Don't try to fool me. You walk like one of them. I know my men in uniform, and you, my tall, handsome stranger, are definitely one. Come back to my quarters, and I'll show you how much I appreciate your service."

"This is a waste of time," he snarled and started away.

She closed impossibly fast and wrapped an iron grip around his wrist. Leaning to his ear she said, "Strannan said you'd be coming soon. I'd like to test that theory in more ways than one."

Strannan. That single name chilled his blood. Unless there was a serious breach of security, she must be his contact. Still, the need for secrecy remained paramount. Any man who let his guard down so casually was a detriment to any future success. He needed to move carefully. His free hand drifted to the concealed knife tucked inside his belt while he turned to face her.

"Get your hands off me, and we can talk."

"Not here. Too many ears are waiting for the right piece of information to send back to their masters. Follow me."

He remained still.

Sensing his hesitancy, she smiled again. "What's the matter? Scared of little old me? I thought you people were built of tougher material."

Hand never leaving the knife, Matthias followed her down a dark, twisting passage carved from the main corridor. He reluctantly admitted that none of the watchers in the administration even knew this was here. Too much money made it easier for some to disappear one day and reappear as a new gambling den or worse. Matthias decided to go over his mission while trying to figure out what to do with the strange woman leading him to where?

"Sit, soldier boy. We have much to discuss."

He sat nervously.

"You seem to know too much about me, but I wasn't briefed on you."

Another smile. "What would you have me say? I'm just a poor woman trying to make my way in the universe. Business is business, after all."

"Bullshit. Start with your name."

She stiffened, visibly angered. "Very well. I am called Gedrick Silk."

"Not very feminine."

"Because I'm not."

Gedrick stepped back and held her arms out to her sides. Matthias leaned back, hand drawing the blade a fraction from the scabbard. Whatever sorcery Gedrick was about to unleash needed to be countered quickly if Matthias had any chance of surviving this. The woman blurred, a mask of frozen, shapeless images bland of personal identification. Shadows coalesced around her and dissipated in the blink of an eye, leaving Matthias stunned with confusion.

Where the dark-skinned woman had stood was now a thin — almost too thin — man with bone white skin tinged in blue. Matthias thought he looked dead. Veins were painfully visible, lending him a sickly air.

Gedrick enjoyed Matthias's foul look. "Better?"

"What are you?"

"A Jhedge."

Matthias shook his head. "I've never heard of them."

"No, I don't expect you would have. There are very few of us left. Most of our species was hunted down during the age of your gods. Others were placed in servitude, mostly willingly, to the Blood Witches. A good life, but not one worthy of reclaiming any lost honor. Those of us still alive make a living doing odd jobs, spying mostly for whoever can afford it. That's how Strannan found me. I've been an ace in the pocket to the Guard for a very long time."

Jhedge. The concept of such a race bothered Matthias deeply. No one should be able to change appearances at will, especially not sexes. It was all…unnatural.

"How can you change like that?" was all he could ask.

Gedrick shrugged. "Our molecular composition has elements that make us unstable, according to the Conclave's official condemnation. We are shape changers, but with limits. I can only change my appearance, not my species. Humanity it seems remains our cruel joke."

"You make it sound as if you're still hunted."

Gedrick blinked. "Aren't we all?"

There was no counterargument. Matthias considered all he'd just been told. None of it made any sense. Humanity was the predominant species in the universe, but there were hundreds of less evolved species out there. Many that hadn't been discovered yet. The Jhedge must be one of those barely known — making it that much harder for him to give the shape changer his trust.

"I can see the confusion in your eyes, Guardsman. You worry about trust. My kind may be able to shift appearances, but loyalties aren't affected. I am a faithful servant to General Strannan," Gedrick said after noticing Matthias's hesitation.

"Until a better offer comes along," he countered.

Another shrug. "We are all creatures of fate. We can stand here questioning each other's motives, or we can get down to the matter at hand. Strannan believes a war is coming, and Hawker's Gate will be a focal point. He needs to know where the loyalties of Administrator Felp lie and whether or not he can trust the very small garrison stationed here. Correct?"

Like it or not, Matthias was forced to concede that Gedrick was, indeed, his contact. "Correct."

"Good. I dislike games. Too much time is wasted in trying to decipher the whys and why nots. I have one question for you: what do you need from me?"

Where do I even begin?

"Am I the only one who feels like a fucking idiot dressed like this?" Jers grumbled in disgust from the pasty green shirt and sky blue pants he'd been issued.

Annalilly snickered. "You've never looked lovelier."

"Easy for you to say. At least you have a dress."

She snarled, giving him her most menacing glare. Dresses were not among her favorite clothing, and they all knew it. She knew she looked ridiculous in the bright floral dress.

"But it doesn't match your tattoos," Haggle laughed.

She spun on the portly Guard. "One more remark, and I'll have you scrubbing out the shitters with your tongue."

Haggle's smile continued to dazzle in his dark blue eyes.

"I think you look like an old fashioned court jester," Beve said quietly.

All eyes turned to the heavy weapons specialist who, as it happened, didn't look half bad at all. A black tank top and tan pants gave him the rugged look of a dock worker or laborer.

Annalilly frowned. "Enough of this. Let's go and leave the rank on the *Indomitable*. These damned clothes are going to give us away on their own, we don't need to help them any."

They marched down the length of dull grey docking sleeve as only trained professional Guardsmen could do, making Annalilly curse more. They weren't going to make it past the greased up customs office without being spotted. What was the Inquisitor thinking?

"This isn't going to work," she told Fies quietly once she caught up to him.

Fies puffed out a mouthful of air. "Sergeant, if I had to tell you every detail of the Inquisitor's plan, you'd want to smash your head into the hull."

"Who says I don't want to now? We're Guards, Fies, not sightseeing tourists going ooh and ahh at the dumbest shit."

Fies shook his head. It was an old argument, one the two had been having since she was a fresh-faced Guardsman First Class. Nothing changed in the Guard, a fact he liked and appreciated. People died when leadership decided to change tactics or plans in the middle of an operation. Both knew Breed was one of the most capable, confident leaders in the field and that they were lucky to have him over anyone else. He was also one of the most experienced. Fies only hoped none of the Three were on the Gate. The damage would be astounding, even by Guard standards.

"Have you stopped to think that maybe we're the diversion?" he asked.

She pulled up, slapping the back of her right hand on his chest. "What? I'm wearing this dress to attract attention?"

"I never promised you a firefight."

If she was mad before, Annalilly was close to furious now. "I… am… not…a…decoy."

"You are today. We don't make the orders, Sergeant. I get mine from the Inquisitor and the Captain. You get yours from me. Now buck up. We're professionals. Leave all the griping and whining on the ship. We've got a job to do, and I need you focused and watching my back. This is hostile territory, Annalilly. I've got a bad feeling that we're going to need Beve's cannons before too long."

"I'll do my job, the boys too. Don't worry about that. I just want to know why the Guard felt the need to put us in this choice of clothing."

He laughed. "It wasn't the Guard. These clothes were donated by some of the crew. You should be thanking them, not cursing command."

"Thanking them? For this? You're a sick man, Fies."

"Haggle was right. Those tattoos don't go with your dress."

"Not another word."

Clearing customs was relatively painless. They got a few stares but were written off by almost everyone on duty as a poorly dressed mercenary crew. Deep space was filled with unsavory sorts trying to make a living in the trade of violence. It was another area the Conclave chose to ignore for the betterment of the greater universe. Another handful passing through Hawker's Gate wasn't enough to warrant much attention, although Annalilly's exotic tattoos combined with the very feminine dress drew far too many stares to leave her anything but calm. She kept her fists clenched the entire time, much to the amusement of her squad. None were foolish enough to say so, though.

She did stand out, much to Fies's chagrin. The operations order had said they would be conducting urban operations. No one had mentioned civilian clothes. If command knew, they kept it to themselves until the very last possible minute. Fies was used to that. Missions, especially the more dangerous ones, tended to go more smoothly when the rank and file didn't have excessive time to think about what could go right or wrong. A soldier with time to think was almost as dangerous as one with a loaded weapon.

"That was painless," Haggle smiled as they entered the first market area.

Annalilly clenched her fist tighter. "Speak for yourself. Heads up! I want everyone on the lookout for a clothing merchant. I intend to get out of this shit."

"She doesn't have the body for it," one of them whispered from behind.

Even Annalilly knew better than to fall for that.

Fies grabbed her forearm and dragged her along. "Stop fraternizing with the lower enlisted, Sergeant. Besides, would it kill you to act like a lady just once?"

He tried to duck away but was too slow. Annalilly's fist caught him in the jaw with a loud smack. Fies dropped, body limp. The rest of the squad managed to subdue her before she was able to leap on him and continue the assault. Guardsman Kedric stood in obvious horror, every bit of this unconscionable. Beve slapped him on the back and barked a deep laugh. The younger Kedric nearly buckled from the force of the blow.

"Relax, young blood. This happens all of the time."

Kedric blinked. "Why?"

"Ain't it obvious?" Jers asked. "They're in love."

Love? *How could anyone find love in this mess*? Kedric decided that, if this was love, he didn't want it. Nothing so violent could be healthy. He watched while Beve hauled the dazed Fies to his feet.

"That...hurt."

Annalilly shrugged off Haggle and Jers. "I am a noncommissioned officer in the Prekhauten Guard. I expect to be treated as such, nothing else."

"And if you say it any louder we might as well go back to the *Indomitable* now and tell the Inquisitor we got busted."

"Fine by me. *I hate this dress!*"

He watched the motley assortment amble awkwardly through the market with a limited amount of amusement. They were clearly amateurs at blending in, no matter what else they might be. His sources were correct. The Prekhauten Guard was attempting, rather clumsily, to infiltrate Hawker's Gate. He wasn't a privileged man, but even Okolo Mung recognized the signs of something big about to happen. A Mastieq, Mung possessed enhanced senses, including the mild ability to *see* into the future. What he saw told him Hawker's Gate was about to change drastically.

Okolo Mung found the woman with the twin tattoos on her scalp interesting. He pegged her as the most dangerous of the group. *And it isn't just her dislike for the dress.* She had a killer's instincts and had no doubt been called upon to use them time and again. Okolo decided that, when it came time, she was his first target. The big man was next. A man of that size made a formidable opponent. Okolo looked forward to the test of strength. Unfortunately, that would have to wait. His primary task was to watch these intruders and report back to Presha Von. She would decide when she wanted to unleash his particular talents.

"What do you think about this?"

Fies gave her a sideways glance. "It makes you look like a dockworker. Can't you pick something more feminine? We're supposed to be undercover."

She snarled but placed the clothing back, content with seeing Fies flinch in anticipation of being struck again. "You know we're being watched, right?"

He nodded. "Since we left customs. Big guy, almost as big as Beve."

"Bald, blue eyes and tanned. Good muscles. He's a fighter."

Fies frowned. "That's enough, sergeant."

"What?" she asked playfully. "I'm supposed to pay attention to these things. Besides, he's bald."

"Maybe he likes butch women."

Annalilly grinned fiercely. "Jealous?"

He shook his head. "I have more important things to worry about than your raging hormones. Pick something already. We're not getting anything positive accomplished."

"Sure we are. I'm learning quite a bit about you."

"Perfect," he said and rolled his eyes. "If you don't hurry up and pick something, I'll have you parading around looking like one of the damned prostitutes. We've got a job to do, Sergeant. Stay focused."

"I'll get you for this."

Fies shrugged again and whispered into his earpiece. "Beve, keep eyes on the big man that kind of looks like you. We might need to give him something to think about."

"Roger."

"Are you ready for a fight?" Fies asked Annalilly.

She threw him a look suggesting he couldn't be serious. "When have you ever known me not to be ready? Do you think it's going to come to that now?"

"I don't. This guy looks like a pro. He'll want to tag us for as long as possible to report back to his masters. We'll take him when he decides he's seen enough."

That didn't sit well with her. "We're giving him the control. Not good. And if he was that professional, we wouldn't have spotted him so easily."

"I'm sure he's saying the same thing about us."

"Great. I think I need a vacation."

"Sergeant Annalilly, haven't you learned yet? This is a vacation."

Kedric and Haggle happened to walk by just then. The older Guard nudged Kedric to keep moving and close his mouth. He waited until they were out of earshot before addressing the many questions the young Kedric had.

"We don't operate like most other units. We've been through things together that most of the Guard has only read about. I assume they told you we took part in the action on Crimeat?"

Kedric nodded. Truthfully, he was still in awe of being selected to work with such proven and decorated veterans.

"It wasn't like they told you in training. What we did was much worse. A Guard should never have to kill a fellow Guard. Never."

"But you did," Kedric added.

"You're damned right we did. The ones we went up against had turned their backs on the Conclave and were preparing to make war on their planet. We stopped them cold, but it was regrettable. Only a few enjoyed the killing. We didn't. This squad fought its own demons that day, and we came out changed." Haggle paused, painful memories taunting from the recesses of his mind.

Kedric felt adrenalin building. The thought of engaging a well-trained, equally matched opponent in combat thrilled him. He was nearly thirty and hadn't had to pull his weapon in action yet. The need drove him. The desire consumed him, but it was a quiet desire he couldn't convey to anyone else. They'd laugh, or worse.

"Did you lose anyone?" he asked suddenly, breaking the eerie silence between them.

Haggle gave him a deadpan look. "Aye. We lost people. Kastor was one of our best."

His mind went back to Kastor's last stand. The blood stains were vivid every time Haggle closed his eyes. The old man deserved better than what he got. Brood Hammerling, one of the nastiest Guards ever to wear the uniform and a confirmed traitor, had taken pleasure in killing Kastor. It was a crime that never should have happened. Prekhauten Guards were supposed to be above petty grievances and typical standards. Their demeanor was of the highest quality, their professionalism and loyalty above reproach. They were meant to be a model for the universe, a shining emblem for the less fortunate to emulate.

"This is a nasty business," Haggle said softly.

Kastor you old bastard. Why aren't you here now? We need you.

Kedric shuffled uneasily. The thought of having to fight a man or woman he called friend was sickening. He almost wished he'd never applied for the Guard — almost. There was an undeniable pride associated with the stern grey uniform. It meant something. He was bigger than himself, stronger as a team. He desperately wanted to believe the situation here wasn't about to devolve to the point where he'd be expected to point an ion rifle at a fellow Guard in anger.

"Do you think it will happen again?" he asked.

Haggle didn't bother to look at him. The question was valid, but Kedric should have known better than to ask it. Some things needed to not be said. "It damned well better not. I pray for the universe if it does, Kedric."

They kept walking. Each lost in his own thoughts. Both had much to think on.

Jers yawned. He hated being assigned to reconnaissance duty. None of the talents he had acquired over the years applied in this situation. There shouldn't be any fighting, no shooting. He was expected to sit back and talk to people. Why? They had a pair of Inquisitors to do that. The Prekhauten Guard's name had been tarnished back on Crimeat, casting a shadow he personally hadn't been able to outrun. Certain elements of shame mocked him for reasons he still didn't comprehend.

He suffered from an abundance of pride, a quality he kept hidden from the rest of the squad. They labeled him a complainer, the first one to pitch a fit when things didn't go his way. That was fine. He wanted them to think that. People tended to underestimate him that way. Jers was one of the first to jump into the fight. One of the first to start firing and always dependable when the storm was at its darkest.

Ever practical, Jers recognized there wasn't a single standout characteristic that made him special. He'd been born into a farming community. Beaten and abused for most of his formative years, Jers had learned how to fight, to defend himself when no one else would. He had been twelve when he'd finally stood up to his abusive father. That night had changed everything. Jers had broken three of his father's ribs and his nose and had fractured the lower jaw before his mother pulled him away. He'd packed a small bag and left home before dawn, never looking back.

"You're going to give us away," Beve growled absently. He picked up a curved blade with runes engraved along the hilt. "I like this. Good steel. I wonder if Sergeant Fies will let me keep it."

Jers blinked. "What do you need a knife for?"

"Knives make me happy."

Jers paused, unsure whether he wanted to continue this line of conversation. Instead, he asked, "What do you think we are really doing here, Beve?"

"Shopping. Can't say that I like doing it. Life is much simpler back in the barracks. You don't need to cook, pay bills, even think for yourself. I like that too."

"Did your parents love you?"

Beve broke into a grin that spread across his entire face. "Very much. My brothers and I call home as much as possible. We are a close family."

"Brothers? How many more are there?"

Beve silently counted off the names. "Six brothers, a sister and my parents. Not really that big a family, but we manage."

"I fear for the universe if they are all like you."

Beve chuckled and went to ask the merchant how much he really wanted for the knife. The price stamp was just a starting point. The more you haggled, the more respect you earned. At least that's how Beve saw things. Of course, if it came down to it, he was much, much larger than the slender merchant with painted nails.

"All Prekhauten teams are away," Captain Falchi said, kicking back in the soft cushions of his leather chair in the command conference room. He interlaced his fingers behind his head and breathed out slowly.

"This is a dangerous gambit," Luma Kai said quickly, the thought of placing highly specialized combat troops in the middle of a major population center with nothing more than a few sidearms and their natural ferocity didn't sit well with her.

Tolde Breed walked to the viewport and stared blankly into the forever of space. "A calculated risk, Luma. We need information."

"But sending in Guards? They stick out!"

He grimaced. "Would we blend any better? Our training is just as specialized, if not more so. Show me an Inquisitor who can hide undercover successfully."

She conceded, knowing there was no legitimate way either of them would have been able to pull off this mission. Luma stewed over the helplessness of being kept inactive. The pirate ambush a few days ago had awoken a battle rage that had slumbered too long. Now she thirsted for action, the chance to gun down a heretic in the name of righteous persecution.

"You two bicker like an old married couple," Falchi said nonchalantly.

They took his meaning and fell silent. With all the Prekhauten elements on board Hawker's Gate, the Inquisitors still had much to do. Complicating matters was their inability to determine if Administrator Felp was loyal to the Conclave or to…other factions. That doubt gnawed at Tolde as much as sitting still did at Luma.

"A side effect of working closely together, Captain, as I'm sure you've been fortunate enough to experience." Tolde stifled the urge to yawn. There was no reason for him to be tired.

"Indeed. It keeps things interesting, to be sure, and me on my toes. I don't like to be caught napping."

Tolde empathized. They'd been caught in a trap like novices. Justice demanded retribution, and Tolde vowed to deliver. His wrath would come down the hardest on the cell of heretics operating on the Gate.

Luma rubbed her eyes. They burned. Unlike Tolde, she hadn't slept much over the last day and a half. Too many variables and last-minute details needed to be worked out. As always, the prospect of matters going horribly wrong once contact with the enemy was established haunted their decisions. Every commander on every battlefield doubted some aspect of his decision to send people into harm's way.

"So we wait. What's our next move? I don't imagine a target as crafty as Presha Von is just going to sit still while our Guards roam her backyard," Luma said.

Tolde finally turned, hands clasped leisurely behind his back. "Naturally not. There'd be no reason for a heavy military presence if she wasn't considered a major threat. I've pulled her personnel doc and spent hours examining every aspect of her psyche. She is a very complicated woman."

"Wait, you've never met her?"

He shook his head. "No. Our paths didn't cross on Crimeat. Actionable intel says that she was one of the main people behind the uprising and insurrection among the council of lords of Lethendweil. She and Ursal Prowl ran a shadow council behind everyone's backs."

"Any association with this cult of Rengu?" Captain Falchi asked.

"Unknown, but I'd be willing to say yes based on her known associations. Rengu has become prevalent on too many worlds to discount their strength. They've even found purchase on Crimeat, or so I've heard."

Luma ran the tip of her tongue over her bottom lip. "We could execute her on our Office's mandate. The Inquisition takes priority in these matters."

"Kill her now, and we lose any potential information. No, Presha Von is more valuable to us, and the Conclave, alive."

She eyed Tolde sharply before shrugging. The Office of Heretical Persecution was unique amongst the Inquisition in that Inquisitors had the ability to make judgment calls of life or death in the field. Luma very much wanted to run Presha Von through with a dull, rusted blade. Or vent her into space at the very least. The thought brought a smile to her face.

"What are you smiling about?" Falchi asked, surprise evident in his tone.

"Nothing. A private moment of recollection is all. Tolde, this is going to prove to be a most difficult task if you intend on capturing her."

He agreed. "I see no other viable option. She has information we cannot afford to lose. She must be captured alive."

"I'm sure your Guard detachment is up to the task, Grand Inquisitor," Falchi added. He might have been a naval man, but they were all Prekhauten Guard. That bond of brotherhood could never be broken, no matter where they chose to fight.

"Gods willing, we'll be done with this mess in the next few days. I have a suspicion that there is a war coming," Tolde said.

He stopped short of explaining his feelings. Too much was speculation to be taken seriously. As of now, the universe was at peace, save for the dozens of petty squabbles and interplanetary disputes that constantly popped up. Tolde's instincts warned of a terrible confluence fast approaching. He couldn't say why, but he knew Presha Von had an important part left to play — one that might involve the fate of millions.

Tolde prayed they had arrived in time. But in time for what?

SEVENTEEN

3212 A.G. (After Gods), Conclave routing station, planet Prielth.

Stars. An endless, empty sea of stars that taunted him every day. Captain Alren hated space duty. He was a land warrior, born and bred to fight with both feet on the ground, not marching down deck plating in artificial gravity. He still wasn't sure who he had pissed off in his brief career to get him assigned to the *Modius*, a Conclave subspace routing platform. The *Modius* processed millions of communications daily. There was no threat but boredom.

Alren sighed, disappointment permanently etched upon his brow. Reflecting on his career was pointless. There wasn't anything new that he might discover. Alren had been down that path a hundred times since getting posted to the small, thirty-man station orbiting the salvage world of Prielth. There was no logical answer. He'd been on the fast track for promotion, a company command all his own.

Alren didn't have any combat experience. Then again, practically none of the current Guard did. He'd helped put down the occasional rebellion or localized dispute that turned to open arms and the use of force. None of those were a substitute for what Sergeant Major Matthias and his men had encountered on Crimeat. Pangs of jealousy tormented him. Alren desperately wanted to be in on the action, but his name wasn't even considered when reinforcements were dispatched. Left behind, he began to question his motivations and those of his superiors. He filed a formal protest at being passed over for such a large, prominent mission.

Coming from a noble family, Alren deserved to be at the sharp end of the sword. He needed to lead troops in combat, needed those badges and ribbons to run up the ladder through the ranks. Instead, he was left with nothing. Stripped of honor and glory, Alren sulked while hundreds of his peers took part in the pacification of planet Crimeat.

That was not the end. Word of his discontent went up that ladder he'd never found. Unofficially reprimanded, Alren was sent to Prielth and given a token promotion. His charge was an aging routing station with a fully civilian crew. The slap in his face was more damning than any he'd once thought possible. Career effectively finished, there was little choice but to accept his assignment and try to figure out what came next.

Some of the older Guards talked about war on the horizon. Alren considered such talk rubbish, the result of too many years of boredom and inactivity. He dismissed their speculations. It only took a few months in the Guard to learn that most of the senior noncoms enjoyed sitting around to theorize. Alren wanted action, not the limiting conversations that defined all too many careers.

He wanted more. He firmly believed he was destined for greatness, worthy of the remembrance of history itself.

"Shit," he muttered under his breath. The orange and brown orb of Prielth was rotating into view, breaking the monotony of space. Another day was beginning. Another day with a million more communications he neither cared about nor was interested in. Alren truly hated his life.

"Ah, Captain Alren? We have something you need to see."

He turned, reluctantly, to the smiling face of communications tech one Sarai Tel. Normally, her smile was the most pleasing part of his day. The nervous tick in the corners of her eyes stole even that from him.

"What is it, Tel? I'm not particularly in the mood for —"

She quickly interrupted, used to his taciturn state. "We've picked up a large group of signals heading our way."

He paused. "What sort of signals?"

"Unidentified. Dill thinks they are ships."

Ships? That doesn't make sense. He'd have been apprised of any incoming fleet. Alren felt his pulse quicken. Logically, he knew it was likely nothing. The *Modius* wasn't exactly a priority on the Prekhauten command channels. Still, there was the slight — too slight for his liking — chance that the incoming fleet might be something.

"Take me to the bridge. I want to know what's heading towards us," Alren ordered, forgetting she was a civilian contractor. "Have Dill raise Vau Prime. I don't want to be caught with my trousers around my ankles."

"Are you expecting anything?" Sarai asked nervously.

"I don't know."

Alren entered the normally placid bridge, amazed to find a bustle of activity and conversation. He'd never seen the tiny room so active. Alren knew it was more than likely just a routine patrol and nothing to get excited over. But he wanted to be excited. He wanted these civilians to come alive with the thrill of dealing with a Prekhauten battle fleet en route to who knows where. He wanted but refused to get his hopes up.

Too many times disappointment had reared its ugly head to spit in his face.

Not this time, you bastard.

"Dill, what have you got?"

The older man shook his head, long grey beard brushing against his chest. "There seems to be some sort of jamming keeping us from getting a lock on their ID." He punched a few keys. "This doesn't make sense."

"Could it be spatial interference?" Alren asked, concern sparking.

"No. Whoever it is, they're jamming us."

The Guard wouldn't do that. "Dill, put me through to the nearest Guard garrison."

"I can't, Captain. All frequencies are being jammed. We can't receive, send or trace whoever is coming. We are effectively blind."

That concern grew. Alren struggled to fight down his rising panic. No matter what happened next, he was an officer in the Prekhauten Guard. "Tel, get our defense grid online. I want guns ready in sixty seconds."

Nothing the *Modius* had would be enough to even dent a warship's shield plating. Alren hoped the incoming ships were friendly. The other option was…

"Contact!"

Alren found himself leaning closer to the viewport, desperately trying to catch the first glimpse of the unidentified ships. His heart beat faster; his mind raced through scenarios and impossibilities. None of this should be happening.

"Identify!"

Silence. He picked out the small blue-green sparks of ships reentering real space. A lot of sparks. There was no way his antiquated defense grid could repel even a fraction of the heavy metal pushing towards them.

"They're broadcasting Prekhauten codes," Sarai said, confused.

Guard? "Impossible. Give me visual."

Two dozen long hulls filled the monitor. Sleek and gunmetal grey, they were predators, but Alren didn't recognize the markings. Whoever they were, they were not Guard.

"Open a channel. I want to talk to whoever is command."

Gill's fingers thumped across the keyboard. He sat back, exasperated, and shook his head again.

Sarai all but cried out, "They're firing!"

Alren jerked his head up. Dozens of tiny light pinpricks streaked across space. Far too many. He stopped counting at fifty. *There's no way we can stop so many.* Alren closed his eyes. This wasn't supposed to happen.

What was left of the *Modius* would orbit Prielth for months before finally burning up in the atmosphere, adding to the unending piles of scrap metal and trash.

"Where is Ursal Prowl?"

Vicente Blackheart sat back in his chair, hands behind his head. He smiled, a terrible sight. "Mister Prowl has overstayed his welcome. I'm calling the shots now."

The image of Inquisitor General Nye flickered, shadowing his frown. "That's not acceptable."

"I don't really give a shit what you find acceptable, Inquisitor General. Yeah, I know who you are. One of the most powerful men in the universe, and I have you by the balls. If you want to talk, you deal with me."

Nye bristled visibly. "Very well. I trust you have something useful to report."

Blackheart grinned again, the gold caps on his teeth sparkling. "Naturally. The routing station has been destroyed. All hands lost. Communications are down throughout the entire sector."

"Your success is…unexpected. Are you sure you were undetected?"

"I wasn't there. I dispatched a squadron of friends. They ensured me your little secret is safe. No transmissions were intercepted."

Nye scowled. "What do you mean you weren't there? I want to speak to Prowl."

"I already told you, he's unavailable."

"Listen to me, pirate scum. There are plans in motion far greater than anything you might imagine. Do not cross me."

Blackheart barked laughter. "Or what? Don't make threats you can't follow through on. It would be a shame if I had to inform the Conclave of your subversive activities. This conversation is boring me. Contact me when you have another task." He terminated the transmission and spun his chair around like a child.

Nye wouldn't be able to let him alone for long. He'd proven to be a liability, far too dangerous to operate freely. Sooner or later, Nye would be coming for him.

"You're playing a dangerous game, Captain," First Mate Therill cautioned.

"All games worth playing are dangerous."

Therill shook his head slightly. "The Inquisitor General will not take your insubordination lightly."

"I should hope not," Blackheart replied. "We've come too far to back out. And we have an advantage."

"How can you possibly find any advantage in all of this?"

"Nye doesn't know the how united the clans are or that I'm the acting head now. We can tear down their infrastructure and replace it with our rules, our justice."

Therill eyed his captain suspiciously. He'd witnessed too many men fall from lofty dreams of power. He doubted Blackheart would be any different. There was always another waiting in the shadows with a knife in hand. All it took was that single moment of distraction to collapse dreams to dust. Blackheart had earned his loyalty, but the word lacked meaning in their world. Men were butchered for less.

"You dream too big. The Conclave won't fade quietly. Their hounds would be unleashed and see us destroyed to the last man. Is the chance worth the risk?"

Blackheart's gaze thinned. "If I didn't know better, I'd say you were having doubts about our partnership."

"You are my captain."

Precisely my point, you fool. Blackheart knew too well how mutinies began. Not too long ago, he'd done the same to his captain. It was almost a rite of passage. Blackheart knew there was a dagger waiting with his name etched on it. At least he should if Therill was worth the price he'd paid to get him aboard the *Shrike*.

"You think I'm taking this too far?" he asked suddenly.

Therill tried to find the right words. "Your decisions affect us all. I am First Mate. It is my responsibility to ensure the crew's safety."

"I know your responsibility. Tell me what I asked."

"You take too many chances with our lives. The crew will not stand for it if you lead us down the wrong path."

"Life is about chances, Therill. We can't achieve greatness without them."

"Do not dream so big. Some men weren't made for immortality, Captain. The crew is comfortable with what we have."

Blackheart lowered his arms and crossed them over his chest. "Go back to the bridge. Make ready for Drespai. There is work to be done."

"Aye, Captain."

Blackheart watched him go, unmoving. *I think perhaps there is a dagger waiting for you, Mister Therill. After all, this is a kill or be killed universe.*

Strannan paced angrily across the antechamber. His face was twisted. Unchecked rage threatened to break free. There were days when he hated his job.

"Will you stop pacing already? What's done is done. There's no going back from this."

Strannan cast a stern gaze on Nye. "The destruction of the *Modius* presents a serious blow to our efforts at countering these rising cult incidents."

"Are you listening to yourself? Cultists couldn't possibly have done this. They are only slightly organized and have no creditable naval capacity." Nye said. "Whoever did this wanted us to think it was this cult of Rengu."

"Who do you propose did it?" Strannan asked sharply. "We are the dominant naval power in the universe."

Nye paused, mulling over his next comment. He had to admit it sounded implausible, even to him. "Pirates," he said finally. "We already have evidence they are more organized, stronger than previously documented. The attack on the *Indomitable* can attest to that."

"Unorganized rabble. The clans have never been a significant threat, and you know it."

"They've also never had a disgraced Inquisitor providing them with critical information. You're forgetting Ursal Prowl. He's the key to all of this."

Strannan resumed pacing, unable to grasp how one man was able of manipulating so many. He paused, casting a wary glance at Nye. Too many coincidences were becoming evident as the mystery progressed. If he were a suspicious man, which by rights he should be, he'd think Nye had a hand in all of this.

"Your pet has slipped his leash too many times," Strannan carefully accused.

Nye stifled a disinterested yawn. "Pet? He's a wanted fugitive who will meet the end of a short drop when he's finally caught. You're not suggesting I'm allowing him to carry on?"

"Don't be absurd. My frustrations are getting the better of me," Strannan replied quickly so as not to arouse suspicions. Nye's dramatic answer was enough.

"We are losing focus on the main issue. There is a major threat, a military threat, to challenge us. So long as the pirate clans are active and mobile, we will keep losing face with the general population. Support will follow approval, and soon enough we'll be forced to intervene in hundreds of civil wars and rebellions. Neither your Guard nor my Inquisitors are strong enough to engage on so many different fronts."

Strannan nodded. The puckered scar flesh around his eyes twisted. "Agreed. We lack a proper target, one that will break the pirate clans into useless scrap. Without a viable, well-known target, we will only be squandering our resources."

"Drespai."

"What?" Strannan asked, taken from his thoughts.

"Drespai is their main shipyard," Nye said. "As well as a recruiting station. Their strength comes from the thousands who flock to Drespai in the hopes of finding fortune and fame at the expense of others."

"Drespai is a myth. There is no known world with that name."

Nye flashed a very political smile. "Not officially, no, but it does exist, and I know where to find it."

You smug bastard. What game are you really playing at? "Do I have to try and guess, or are you going to tell me?"

Nye nestled deeper into the soft cushion of his chair, enjoying this. Davith Strannan was a man who needed to be taken down some from time to time. The Inquisitor General wanted to build a healthy air of suspicion in as many top-ranking officials as possible. Little did Strannan know, but several key personnel in the Guard had already been subverted — not to mention enough senior cardinals to bring the Conclave and Lorenu Phos to their knees. All he needed was the proper distraction.

Vicente Blackheart's ignorance might just be enough.

"Drespai is, indeed, a myth. A legend pirate captains have used to keep us from discovering it. Ask a hundred men, and each will give you a different location. There is no actual Drespai. It is a figment of our imaginations, designed to spark fear and awe in a lawless band of brigands. They want the romanticism those more…susceptible are willing to give."

Strannan frowned. "That suggests they are being given illicit support. Against Conclave directives."

"You don't think an entity as large as they have become gets that way solely from being self sufficient?"

He paused. "If Drespai is just a name, how can you have a precise location? By your very definition there isn't one."

"That's where you're wrong. There is a very real supply and support hub being used as we speak. An abandoned orbital platform, a former mining shipyard I believe, in orbit over the planet Spindle."

"Spindle? That's on one of the major trade routes!" *No wonder they've been so successful raiding the shipping lanes lately.* "How long has the Inquisition been sitting on this information?"

"Not very long. We learned the truth from a captured frigate in the De Loy System about a month ago. I didn't want to bring it to your or Lorenu's attention until I was able to confirm."

Strannan began pacing again. Spindle. Finally, a hard target. Battle plans started formulating. His desire for revenge, for action bordering frenzy. Should Nye's sources prove correct, Strannan stood to go down in history as the man who single-handedly brought the most significant threat to the Conclave since the days of Foundation to its knees. He'd be able to wipe out the pesky pirate clans — or at least enough of them so that they would take decades, perhaps centuries, to become a valid threat again.

Numbers, troop strengths all ran through his head. He knew exactly how many ships he had to spare, who he wanted to command the fleet, how much force it would require to completely obliterate the orbital platform. All it took was the go-ahead from their combined offices — and the Cardinal Seniorus, of course.

"If what you say is true and they are massing near Spindle, I can have a fleet deployed within a week. Providing Lorenu consents," he said slowly.

"A week? It was my understanding that your fleets were spread thin across the universe. Remember, we can't discount the cult of Rengu," Nye cautioned. It wouldn't do to let the General get too far ahead of himself.

True, the majority of Prekhauten naval power was dispersed widely, much too widely for his liking, in efforts to contain and eradicate the rising numbers of cultists. If he looked too closely, he might be distressed. Threats were nothing new. The Conclave had been defending itself from would-be usurpers and heretics since inception. To date, none had succeeded.

There were more than enough ground divisions for combat purposes. Unfortunately, the main threat now was a problem for the navy. Compounding problems was the surprising lack of troop transports. Too many ships were in dry docks going through overhauls and refits. He had the combat power but not the capability to get it where it needed to go. Strannan exhaled sharply, running a hand through his hair.

"I have the reserve fleet sitting in orbit at our moon base. Thirty of the newest frigates, cruisers and battle carriers. Give me a week, and I'll have them loaded out and ready for combat."

"There is still the matter of getting the Cardinal Seniorus to concede."

"Will Lorenu go along with this?" he asked. "She normally doesn't get in the way." She just takes too long.

Lorenu Phos was famous for her cautious approach to less than favorable situations. How many times had they gotten a late start on a vital operation because of her inability to make the proper decision? Even then, it wouldn't be so bad. Strannan was the type of man who made a tactical decision quickly, based on current information, and stuck with it until events forced him to adjust. Lorenu was the opposite. She wanted to know as much as possible to make an informed decision, time be damned.

Nye offered a shrug. "I don't see why not. She's under twice as much pressure as we are. Rumor has it the Forum is growing increasingly agitated at her inaction concerning this Rengu nonsense. She needs a victory, and this should give her the proper boost to quiet the cardinals."

Strannan's mind was already well beyond Lorenu Phos. Her approval was but a bump in his path.

"We need to see her now."

"Patience, Davith. We have time. My sources tell me there is a massive pirate fleet en route to Drespai. It wouldn't do to take the orbital out with so many ships still in transit. We can see Lorenu in the morning."

"I agree. I want to crush these pirate scum as harshly as possible. As you said, we need to make a statement."

Nye concealed his smile. The satisfaction of knowing Strannan had taken the bait was enough for now. *No, my friend. Convincing Lorenu Phos isn't going to be a problem at all.* He almost chuckled. This was proving too easy.

Prekhauten Guard Orbital Shipyards, planet Vau Prime.

Admiral Fhi glanced in the mirror one final time before leaving his quarters aboard the flagship *Righteous Fury*. A man of impeccable character, Fhi had spent the last forty years in the fleet. Often underestimated because of his height, or rather lack of, he'd decided the best, quickest way through the ranks was by maintaining unmatched quality in demeanor and appearance. His uniform was crisp and fresh daily. A dozen rows of ribbons and a handful of medals adorned his left breast. Rank pips stretched across each shoulder. The flat grey uniforms of the rank and file were a thing of his past. Flag officers wore royal blue, yellow stripes running down the outside of the legs. His shoes were brilliant black and polished to the point he could see his smile reflecting back.

Fhi enjoyed looking his best; vanity was a wicked temptress. His hair was closely cropped, all of the color long faded to grey. He kept a thick goatee, painstakingly dyed black daily, and the thinnest of moustaches. The dark hair offset his pale green eyes and shallow cheeks. His jawbones protruded enough to make his face angular, a trait he hated. Lightly muscled, Fhi was in better physical condition than many of his junior officers — a fact he exploited to make his Guards better, stronger. He was a man who wanted the very best, needed to have the most respected fleet in the Guard.

Smoothing a minor wrinkle from his jacket, Fhi sighed and headed towards the bridge. It was time to conduct one final inspection before General Strannan arrived. Not the sort to become intimidated by rank, Fhi enjoyed the feeling of a superior commending him on the quality of his vessel. Having Strannan aboard to send him off was an honor he intended to milk through his crew.

One thing soured his mood. He'd learned that the auxiliary fleet was being mobilized to combat the gathering pirate clans on the planet Spindle. Fhi understood the reality of the situation well enough to know Rear Admiral Khe-Zhehan was going to be in for one hell of a battle. She had thirty combat vessels crewed by relatively untested Guards. A more experienced commander was needed to quell the pirate threat the way Strannan intended. Fhi should be going, not Khe-Zhehan.

He recognized there was undeniable honor in his current assignment, but there was yet to be a definitive target. Cultist cells were popping up across the universe, but certainly nothing worthy of dispatching the main fleet. And to Hawker's Gate? How much further from the action could he be sent? He might have found it insulting if he wasn't already committed.

"Admiral on the bridge!"

Crewers snapped to attention, the Captain rendering a crisp salute.

Fhi halted to return the honors. "Captain Tygg, are we prepared for General Strannan's arrival?"

Alten Tygg nodded. "Yes, Admiral. His shuttle is en route as we speak."

If Fhi was the epitome of professionalism, Tygg was a close second. Captain of the flagship, Tygg pushed his crew hard, not to impress the Admiral, but for his own gratification. One day, he hoped to wear those same pips and have an entire fleet at his disposal. For now, though, he gladly accepted second in command to the awesome amount of firepower.

"How long before he arrives?"

"Less than five minutes, sir. We should move down to the docking bays."

Fhi passed a look around the bridge, catching every detail. Immaculate. He didn't feel the need to compliment Tygg on the caliber of the bridge crew. It was expected. Fhi wasn't the sort to casually pass around watered down compliments. He praised the extraordinary, reprimanded the deplorable and left the rest to individual interpretation. Men and women under his command had learned long ago not to expect praise simply for doing their jobs. Too many in the Guard expected it. Fhi thought it made weaker soldiers.

He nodded again and followed Tygg back down the corridor. "I don't expect this visit to take too long, Alten."

"I've been given his itinerary. He's mostly interested in combat readiness and a brief lunch with you."

"Hopefully there will be more details concerning our mission," Fhi commented. "I don't appreciate being left in the dark, especially when it concerns my fleet."

"I'm sure General Strannan has important information. Perhaps we are being reassigned to combat the pirates."

Fhi arched an eyebrow. "At the last moment? I highly doubt that. No, Admiral Khe-Zhehan will suffice. She is quite capable."

They went the rest of the way in silence. Fhi wasn't given to prolonged conversations when he had nothing but speculation and personal rumor to base his opinion on. Strannan boarded less than a minute later and followed Fhi and Tygg back to the bridge where he offered a few words of encouragement and well wishes on the upcoming mission. Of course, he told them he wished he was going with them, a comment that was well received if not entirely true.

The rest of the inspection went quickly, much more quickly than even Fhi expected. Strannan had a rushed air about him, as if he had a wealth of information threatening to break free. Fhi was salivating with anticipation. Orderlies served a modest lunch of roasted fish, baby potatoes and coffee before leaving the three officers alone in Fhi's wardroom.

"I don't envy you," Strannan began. "Nothing about this task is going to be easy, despite what you may think."

"Honestly, General, I don't know what to think," Fhi answered sharply.

Davith Strannan considered telling him everything. He was grooming Fhi to take his place when retirement finally beckoned. But no, no one in this fleet needed to know exactly what was happening. Not yet, at any rate.

"There are rising threats that require immediate military action. Officially, you are being sent to hunt down and stop the Three. We have reason to believe a major force of enemy elements is massing in the systems surrounding Hawker's Gate. That's the official story. You'll appreciate the operational security of the situation, of course."

Fhi did, even though it infuriated him. He *needed* to know, to satisfy the myriad questions and scenarios floating in his head.

"You'll want to know about Khe-Zhehan, I assume?" Strannan asked, taking a bite of fish. "This is very good. Almost as good as a fine restaurant in Krenz."

"Our chefs will be delighted to hear your praise, General," Tygg smiled.

"Will she be enough to end the pirate threat?" Fhi asked, uncharacteristically forward.

"I have every reason to believe the auxiliary fleet will be more than a match for whatever has gathered above planet Spindle. Fhi, make no mistake, yours is our primary focus. The future of the Guard, the Conclave and Inquisition depends on how decisive your actions will be."

Tygg struggled to swallow the mouthful of potatoes. Cold dread tickled his skin. He wasn't sure why, but he had a sudden feeling this mission was about more than just the Three. Visions of violent demise began taunting him.

EIGHTEEN

3212 A.G. (After Gods), The Great Library, planet Wexanos.

Tannus stretched to his full height, relishing the crisp evening air. The confines of his deep-space flier sometimes proved too much, especially during those weeks-long transits between systems. He enjoyed the fresh air, the sights and smells of life. Too much of his life had been a tragedy filled with death and sour undertones. He envied humanity the gift of death. Their lives held more meaning, a sense of urgency he had only felt once.

He tried and failed to imagine what it must feel like knowing that every moment lived was one less. One step closer to the end. Did they despair? Were they mired by the inescapable conclusion that their time was much too short? Tannus wished he had answers. The precious gift of life meant something to humanity, unlike his own race. He'd seen thousands of lifetimes come and go without so much as a ripple in the fabric of the universe. Life had grown mundane. An unending struggle to maintain sanity. Tannus had lost his desires. The sound of waves crashing against the shore, the humbling feeling of deep space, none of that aroused even the slightest spark. He felt dead inside.

Whatever faith he'd once placed in humanity was shaken. The greed and avarice he'd been shown on planet Crimeat had rocked the foundations of what he'd once believed unshakable. Humanity was no different from his own kind. No matter how many times he'd seen the scenario play out, there was always another madman lurking in the shadows ready to steal the throne and plunge his kind into tyranny.

The cold, sad reality of this made his heart weep. Three thousand years spent tolling after the remnants of his species, despairing the decline of civilization and vacuum left in the universe, and he realized he had nothing to show for it. Perhaps it would have been better if he had let Amongeratix kill him all those centuries ago when he'd stumbled upon the dark ritual in the temple of Oculus.

Still, there was some good left in the universe, if difficult to spot. Father Dye had given him hope right when he'd thought it lost. The older priest had stood up to tyranny in the face of grave adversity, nearly losing his life in the process. Together, they'd crossed half a continent to stop Amongeratix. Tannus wondered, briefly, what had happened to the old man. He was a good soul, one of few. If anything happened to him…

The sudden thought made Tannus stop. He had no memory of leaving Crimeat. No recollection of what had happened once all three brothers had battled atop the plateau in the middle of the snowstorm. It had been a titanic struggle, one destined to become legend in the histories of humanity. Few in their short past had witness the Three battle. Even fewer had survived such engagements. Tannus preferred to stay away, to let the children of his race find their own destiny, their own paths through life. That his personal war with his brothers had become public frustrated him to no end.

Sorrow had tried to stop him and Amongeratix from killing each other. Tried and failed. Strong magic had nearly destroyed them all. Tannus had blacked out during the explosion, awakening in a green land under pale blue skies. Naked, his wounds were healed. He felt rejuvenated as he lay basking under the brilliant sun. When he arose, he didn't recognize his surroundings. He was lost on an alien planet without attire or memory.

He hadn't known how much time had passed, still didn't. How many days or weeks had been lost as he wandered aimlessly without recollection of who he was or why? Trees and rivers had passed beneath his great strides. Herd animals had barely paused from grazing to mark his passing. Birds had squawked as they raced overhead or perched high up in the pines to study this gigantic stranger.

Tannus had felt pure. He had no anger, no aggression. The tranquility of this planet had left his soul cleansed. But from what? He couldn't figure it out. How could anything be so bad when life thrived? Surrounded by plush green fields and crystalline bodies of water, Tannus had been reminded of a newborn child, looking on the world in wonder and awe. The purity of life was so simple, he'd walked tirelessly with a smile engraved upon his once weary face.

Finally, he'd come upon a sleek, onyx black flier parked atop a large knoll. The seat, the controls, the sheer size of the interior suggested it had been designed specifically for him. Confused, Tannus found a set of clothes; light fabric pants and a green, sleeveless tunic. They fit perfectly. Again, he was utterly confused. Who had left all of this here? Why? Answers weren't available, and he pushed his doubts aside once he slid into the pilot's chair. His fingers danced across the control panels, flawlessly hitting the right keys.

The flier hummed to life. He didn't question, instead trusting instincts that pulled him in a direction he didn't remember for reasons he had long forgotten. A screen suddenly turned on. Tannus peered closer, suddenly eager to learn the one word blinking in neon green. Wexanos. He didn't know what Wexanos was or who, but knew that he was supposed to go there. Regretfully, he left his private paradise behind and traveled halfway across the stars in search of the place beckoning him.

His quest led him to Mannus Prime and the great library of Wexanos. Once the single greatest cultural center in humanity's dwindling experience, the library was nearly as large his father's palace. Tannus continued to be amazed by how much had been saved or rescued just from three centuries. Better, there were no guards, no watchers against any potential threats. The wealth of knowledge was truly intended for the betterment of an entire species, not suborned for the whims of a select few.

Tannus stalked towards a set of enameled doors rimmed with black metal. The light brown, almost red color of the wood contrasted with the black and grey paving stones lining the path he took. Statues of poets and scholars, history makers and kings lined the causeway, intermingled with immaculately groomed shrubs. He was amazed at the details of each sculpture, subtle hints reminding him of better times, better worlds. The doors cracked open when he was still a few meters away, and he stopped.

Two men in yellow robes appeared and bowed deeply. Tannus replied with a simple nod.

"Lord, you have returned so soon," the taller man said.

Confused, Tannus asked, "Why am I here? Who are you?"

"Ahh. This is the grand library of Wexanos, a treasure almost forgotten by both of our kinds. I am Fistel, chief librarian and custodian of the eternal light of truth."

"You clearly have been expecting me, but that doesn't help. I have no memory of this place, wondrous as it is. Tell me, Fistel, why was I compelled to come to Wexanos?"

The librarians passed cautious looks. "Perhaps we should go inside. There is a storm coming, and it wouldn't do to have you getting wet. Come, please."

Tannus accepted, gracious for the warmth of the invitation. He passed through the doors without having to duck and entered the glory of Wexanos. The doors closed without a sound.

Days later, Tannus sat looking out a twenty foot tall stained glass window. The images enshrined with painstaking quality showed him battling his brothers on a distant world and a forgotten battlefield. His memory had returned as it had, he'd found out, numerous times before. One of the great mysteries of Wexanos was its caretakers and their eternal charge to assist him when he needed it.

His loneliness had helped create this revered temple of knowledge, partially as a testament to his once-proud species and partially as a recovery vehicle when he battled his brothers. Too many times over the centuries he had returned to Wexanos to have his memory restored. The librarians were ever eager to please, often leaving him to his rumination.

Tannus studied the glass images of Sorrow and Amongeratix, following the curve of their jaws, the lines of their faces. The battle was different with each window, but the scene remained the same. Only Tannus and Amongeratix were engaged in mortal combat. Sorrow always seemed to be lurking just beyond, waiting for the right moment to stop them from killing each other. Why?

They were all sons of the king, each blessed and cursed with peculiar gifts befitting their station in life. Each embodied a distinctly different human emotion. He'd forgotten any reasoning for their actions or desires, the meanings lost in the myriad of burned out stars spanning the universe. Much of his culture had been utterly destroyed during the Great War. A tragedy, to be sure, but one he suspected might be better for all life. If he and his brothers were any indication of the truth of their race, humanity was better off alone. Tannus closed his eyes, mind wandering the darkened paths of thought. He and his brothers were the key to humanity's future and that of the whole universe.

Amongeratix was the harbinger of anger, rage unchecked. Never had Tannus witnessed such hatred. At times, he felt helpless. They were the privileged few, heirs to their father's throne. Amongeratix had no logical reason to act so aggressively, but then logic seldom played into the laws of life. Slightly larger than Tannus and Sorrow, Amongeratix fueled his anger with dark arts and forbidden magics. The concept was anathema to their kind. Magic and sorcery held no place in humanity's new universe.

Some way, somehow, Amongeratix had learned how to channel the darkness — Tannus suspected through his torturous manipulations of the oracle. Tens of thousands had died as a result. Whole planets were reduced to lifeless rocks. Tannus tried to stop him, to reason in the cause of life. Amongeratix was too far gone, lost in madness and certainty that his was the right path. All life would bend a knee or be lost.

Tannus was nothing like Amongeratix. He sought redemption, but whether for himself or something greater he didn't quite know. His actions were partly to blame for the vastly divergent courses their lives had taken. If he hadn't questioned his father, if he had simply accepted what was, they wouldn't have been cast out to fend for themselves. Tannus had spent centuries trying to amend what he'd broken, to fix the growing rift between the three of them. In the end, he'd failed miserably.

One brother lost himself in the depths of hatred and despair. The other fled to the unknown parts of space, eager for the solitude he required. Tannus only wanted his life to make sense. To be more than what he was. His father had cast him out for daring to question his will. That singular event drove the destinies of countless millions. Oh, how little he had known then. Could his father have predicted the unending theme of hatred and violence that resulted from his burst of anger?

Rather than stifle in internal lament, Tannus turned his thoughts to Sorrow, the one brother whose real name was lost, stricken from any history. Whoever, whatever he once was, Sorrow chose to be something else. Once, in the beginning, Tannus had tried to convince him to join him and bring Amongeratix back. There was still love between them. Only later would Tannus realize that love was no more than dying embers left untended. How naïve they'd been to think things could simply return to normal.

Sorrow. Sorrow was the very soul of regret. His soft eyes were often stained with tears. The capacity for violence was within, for he was certainly capable of extremely violent behavior. Tannus had tracked down a hundred scenes of slaughter, investigating what he suspected was the work of his often forgotten brother. None of the scenes made any sense. Sorrow was intent on a path of nonviolence. The slaughter of innocents left Tannus wondering whether the two had sided against him. But no. Any time Sorrow showed up, he acted as peacemaker.

Too many games were being played. Tannus found it hard to keep up. He focused on his blood-covered brother, the images in glass frighteningly lifelike.

"Where have you gone this time, brother of mine?"

Tannus scratched his jaw. His mind was torn in two. Amongeratix was highly predictable. He craved power, a return to glory and the ultimate destruction of what remained of their kind. Three thousand years had been spent desperately trying to return to the hallowed place where it should have ended. Amongeratix would be trying to make his way back to Occanum to complete the task once started.

It was Sorrow who gave Tannus trouble. Ever unpredictable, he hadn't been able to figure his brother out. Confounding things was the fact that Sorrow seemed eternally covered in fresh blood. Many great mysteries filled the universe, and this was surely one of them.

"Lord, we have refreshments prepared for you."

Tannus paused, glancing at the hooded librarian. Time was the one factor that meant almost nothing to him. A luxury of presumed immortality. *How long have I been standing here? The sun was barely risen when I stepped before these images.* He looked outside. Darkness coalesced around the edges of Wexanos.

Built on the gently sloping peninsula with hundred-foot cliffs, pale blue waves crashing against the ancient stone, the library was a feat of beauty. Smooth lines looked almost curved rather than the bulky, traditional designs on hundreds of worlds. Towers crowned with open observation decks stretched up to the heavens in tribute to humanity's endless desire to learn the secrets of space. Endless halls filled with every known book and manuscript represented the efforts of a few hundred librarians.

Roaring fireplaces kept visitors warm on cold nights. Antique chairs and tables were scattered across the massive structure. Tannus always felt comfortable here, nestled amidst the greatest wealth of knowledge ever known. If times were different, he might have spent several lifetimes perusing the tomes. Unfortunately, time was not a luxury he possessed any longer. He couldn't tell for certain, but every recent action felt like he was being pulled towards a conclusion.

He smiled down on the diminutive librarian. A woman, he guessed. Barely five feet tall. He doubted the title of lord truly applied anymore; those days weren't any more than myth. Still, it felt good to be recognized for what he had once been.

"Thank you, librarian."

She bowed curtly. "Please, follow me."

The grand dining hall fell silent as Tannus entered. Those assembled rose in respect, hands clasped together at the waist. He was both humbled and awed. These men and women viewed him as a deity, treating him with the reverence befitting a god. He greatly desired to tell them not to, to ignore their need to believe in a higher power. That he was just a man, unworthy of worship or divinity. Doing so would shatter the foundations of belief. Tannus vowed not to be responsible for the destruction of yet another civilization.

"Please, remain seated," he said warmly.

Fistel approached, one of the few who seldom wore the hood of his robe. "Lord Tannus, I trust you are finding your stay useful?"

"Of course, Fistel. Wexanos reminds me of more pleasant times. Would that I never had to leave."

The chief librarian paused, silently questioning Tannus's motives. "You give us much credence."

"The future of humanity is in good hands if you continue to cultivate new generations willing to put the past ahead of themselves. I fear, however, that I will not be staying long."

"You have found the information you seek?"

A nod. "I believe so. The future is fluid, preventing me from knowing. Still, I cannot afford to sit here any longer. Already I have been gone for two years."

Heaping plates of boiled blue shell crabs were brought before him. He smiled despite himself. The crabs were a local delicacy and a personal favorite. Bowls of roasted potatoes and other vegetables, all grown in the massive gardens to the rear of the library, and loaves of freshly baked dark breads finished his meal. The aromas took him back to simpler times when he hadn't felt pressed. Pitchers of pale ale and water were set before him, the librarians bowing respectfully before going back into the kitchens.

"Always a feast, Fistel. I am continually impressed," he said between mouthfuls.

The hard shells of the crab legs cracked loudly before surrendering their succulent meat. His fingers were quickly coated with grime and residue, and he loved it. This meal almost made him forget the trials of his brothers. Almost. He smiled suddenly, realizing Fistel must have anticipated his imminent departure.

"We try our best to please."

I'm sure you do. "Do you know what truly amazes me?"

"With all your vast experience I find it incredible to believe any of our meager efforts here can impress or amaze you, Lord. This is a grand place but filled with simple people. We are not warriors, nor great adventurers. Our quest is the preservation of knowledge. You honor us with each visit."

Tannus nodded curtly. More would do to suffer from such humility. "Yours is the most important work in the universe. Without the knowledge of the past, we are lost. I would not see humanity fall the way my own race did. I digress. What amazes me is that never has a shot been fired or sword drawn in anger here. We are both children of violence. To have none here is one of the most impressive feats I have ever witnessed. I only pray we can keep it that way."

The awkward silence between them deepened. Fistel hadn't been expecting the sudden admission. He suddenly feared the future.

"I must leave tonight. There is one I need to speak with before I act," Tannus followed up after noticing Fistel's dismay. "But not until I have had my fill of these wondrous crabs. One day, I shall retire here and become a simple fisherman."

The notion sounded foolish leaving his lips. He'd been at war for so long, a lifetime of peace was unfathomable. Another envy for his librarian friends. They knew no war nor strife. Each day lived was a blessing, a chance to learn and grow. If only his life were so simple.

Fistel cleared his throat, taken off guard. "I will have your effects taken to your flier along with food and drink for your journey."

"Thank you, Fistel. You have been a true friend these long years."

The head librarian blushed, wondering what he had done to gain such confidence from one of the lords of the universe.

Abbey of the Order of Blood Witches, Acumensiis Comet.

Ruma Zzein felt old, much older than the four millennia already behind her. Fatigue slumped her shoulders, bowed her back. She walked with a cane now, when she summoned the drive to leave her sanctum. Perpetual tears clogged her eyes. More than anything, she felt like a failure. Amongeratix had finally returned to find her. She'd thought, prayed she had escaped his depravity, but fate was not so kind. All she had built here on the comet was now at risk. Now, more than ever, Ruma Zzein was convinced Forever Night was approaching. The end of the universe was coming.

"Grand Mistress, there is a flier requesting permission to dock."

Ruma reluctantly took her gaze from the mass of stars and multi-colored nebulas. Her encounter with Amongeratix here, in this most sacred of chambers, had left her shaken and barely able to focus on what needed doing. But there were still some things that couldn't be shirked. No one had requested to enter the abbey in centuries. Her heart quickened. Could it be? Had Amongeratix come to finish what he'd started?

"A flier?"

The novice nodded. "Yes, Grand Mistress. It is not a make or model we have in our database. Mistress Her wishes to bring the defense grid online."

A flier. Now, after all this time. Amongeratix's earlier intrusion was meant as a threat, leaving her uncertain. *Would he dare request to land when he could so easily return through his foul sorceries and kill me at will? No. It must be another. But who?*

"Does this flier have any weapon systems?" she asked sharply. Her mind surged through an infinite amount of possibilities.

"None that have been activated, Grand Mistress."

Ruma tapped a slender finger to her lips, face drawn in thought.

"Inform Mistress Her that weapons will not be necessary. Have my honor guard formed and awaiting me at the landing pad. They must be prepared to act should this turn ill for us."

"At once, Grand Mistress."

The novice left Ruma Zzein with too many questions. Not to mention a quickened heartbeat. Time was now her opponent. She wouldn't classify it as an enemy, at least not yet. There was still time to salvage the future from Forever Night. Ruma almost allowed the briefest flicker of hope to come alive. Almost. She smoothed the fabric of her gossamer robes and hurried to meet this most unexpected visitor.

Twenty Sisters stood behind her in two columns. Each held her unique powers ready should the guest prove dangerous. Ruma hoped they would be enough to stop one of the Three. The alternative left a foul pain in the pit of her stomach. Deius Mlth, Mistress of Arms, stood just behind her. The dour look on her face said it all. She'd argued for the use of their weapons systems along with Algiss Her and had lost. None of this felt right, and she had no qualms about making her opinions known. Still, she trusted Ruma Zzein — at least until such a time as she proved her trust wasn't deserved.

The Grand Mistress looked over her guards one final time, catching as many of their eyes as possible, before nodding to Deius. The hatch on the boarding sleeve hissed open. A hulking shadow fell over the Blood Witches. Ruma forced herself not to rock back in shock. She looked up at the massive figure standing before her. Amongeratix! Her mind screamed to attack. Her every desire wanted to lash out, to strike him down with all her rage and fury.

Deius's hissed breath broke her trance-like state. Ruma checked her power and looked closer at the giant standing with his hands patiently at his sides. Warm recognition suddenly filled her.

"My lord," she said reverently.

Tannus bowed in return. His eyes never left the image of her face, that perfect quality that had often inspired him to works of greatness before the Fall. Even his advanced intellect found trouble reconciling the woman standing in shocked admiration before him. The Oracle! By all reason, she should have been dead. He had come to the abbey looking for answers but now found only more questions.

"Oracle, by all that is holy. I never thought…" he began.

Deius Mlth shot her a questioning look. Oracle?

Ruma waved off her concerns. "Lord Tannus, you honor us greatly with your presence. Mistress Mlth, you may have the honor guard stand down and return to their meditations. I will be quite all right."

"But Grand Mistress," Deius protested.

Ruma smiled gently. "I will be fine, Deius. We are…old friends."

Reluctantly, the Mistress of Arms obeyed, leaving Ruma and Tannus alone. The pair could only stare for long moments, so impossible was their meeting. She had once trusted the whims of the cosmos to guide her, to ensure that the very best possible outcome was given every chance for survival. There was no way she could ever have predicted this. Once she discovered her tongue, she suggested they retire to her sanctum, the hallway being no place for a proper meeting.

Tannus stared out into the vastness of the universe, marveling at the view Ruma must surely take for granted. "Most impressive, Oracle. I had almost forgotten that there is an inherent glory among the stars. So far has my kind fallen. It does my heart good to see you again, though I would have the circumstances changed. Had I known that the fabled Grand Mistress of the Blood Witches was you, I would have come sooner."

"My lord, we have all lost much. The universe is a lesser place," she replied, standing just over his shoulder.

He nodded absently. "Indeed, but there is still hope. Humanity is young yet. They have much to learn, and I cannot help them. Nor should you."

She paused. Did he know the comet was en route to Vau Prime and a meeting with the leaders of the Conclave and Inquisition?

Telepathy was never prominent among his species, leaving no reason to believe he suspected as much from her.

"Your arrival is most unexpected," she tried changing the subject.

Tannus turned slowly. "Much has happened, Oracle. I fear there is an age of strife coming to us all. Oracle, I need to know what happened between you and my brother those many lifetimes ago."

NINETEEN

3212 A.G. (After Gods), the Wells, planet An'kuruku.

Blood drenched the floors, running down the slant into the streets in unimaginable waves. The smell of iron tainted the air. Pain and abject misery clung to the city in a pall unlike any felt in recent history. The end of the world had come at last. Bodies were everywhere, scattered where death carelessly threw them. It was unconscionable, but a scene that had played itself out time and again throughout the universe's long history. Now it was happening again.

She strode through the carnage, carefully avoiding the blood when at all possible. How many of these people never saw the end? Failed to notice the confluence of dark powers screaming down at them through the ether? Humanity was young still, incapable of understanding the sheer amount of hatred seething among the stars, waiting for the chance to exact revenge on the upstart species.

Pain coursed through her in waves. Each face she looked down on stared back with the all too familiar questioning gaze. It was a scene she'd witnessed a hundred times, a thousand. And no matter how many times she saw it, it failed to make sense. Who deserved this?

Finally, when she could stand no more, she stopped. A pair of bodies lay twisted and broken at her feet. Wordless power made her drop down. She didn't know why. It didn't matter. She felt compelled to stare into these last pairs of eyes to witness their grief. She vowed to remember them. To sing their praises when all memory faded. She paused. Recognition, clouded, flashed. She knew them!

Kneeling, she gently straightened the wreckage their flesh had become and struggled to bite back the tears. Dark blood stained the woman's bright, red hair, covering one broken cheek. Lithe, almost painfully thin, she was a fighter. Her hands were calloused and thick. No dainty courtesan. Dozens of wounds riddled her body. She had died well, much more than could be said for her male counterpart. He had the dark skin of a native. A massive hole emptied his chest cavity. Viscera and innards spilled in a gooey puddle. He'd clearly sacrificed himself to save her. But why?

Death was indiscriminate, seldom caring about personal feeling or emotion. She wanted to cry, but it would only serve to insult their memories. Instead, she reached down to close their eyes. Her fingertips had barely touched the woman's flesh when her eyes opened and a bloodied hand weakly grabbed her wrist.

"Save me."

She awoke with an awful scream, pupils dilated, sweat caking her golden hair to her face. A dream. She hated dreams. Too often they were misinterpreted by the weak of mind. Greed demanded each read the dream according to his or her most intimate desires. She put no stock in dreams, but this had been too real. The faces. The carnage.

Sliding from the clean sheets, she went to the washbasin and splashed the cool water on her face. Much about the dream didn't make sense. It had been too hot, reminiscent of the deep desert. Most of the bodies were dressed like the priests and monks of the Wells. Another large group was dressed in the style of deep desert nomads, raiders and murderers. The last two bodies didn't fit in. A pale woman, clearly from another world, and a city dweller.

She resisted the urge to go to the deck and look down on the Wells. Her dream had happened here, but there hadn't been a single act of violence in this holy place since, well, since her arrival. She'd have heard the sound of battle. The screams of carnage. No stranger to violence, she abhorred the idea of people being slaughtered in the name of self-righteousness and vanity.

No clear answer presented itself, leaving her lost in confusion. Answers could be just as problematic, she scolded. The risk of this dream coming true was too great for her to sit back and ignore it. Frowning, she decided to get dressed and visit the priests. Perhaps they had the answers she needed — or, at least, could point her in the right direction to solve this mystery. It might be the only way for her to clear her mind and regain the peace she had struggled so hard and long to find.

Visions of broken faces mocked her every step. She knew then she was in for a very long day.

Sea spray caressed his face and hands, easing the torment perpetually administered by the sun. His liver spots were darker, the wrinkles and lines deeper, shaded. His eyes felt pinched, even when he had them closed to enjoy the ocean's kiss. Most of his life was well behind him now, a lamentable fact but one he had learned to cope with. The Bone Father found little pleasure these days. Much of his time was spent lost in thought, contemplating those things he knew better than to ask.

Change had come to the Deeves, brought by the crimson robe wearers of the cult of Rengu. He knew the name. An old name from times best left unremembered. The more he listened to Mollock Bolle preach, the more he was convinced action was necessary. He was not a man of violence. The thought sickened him without end. Premonitions gnawed at his subconscious. Every time Mollock opened his mouth, a foul rant polluted the minds and ears of those who were once the Bone Father's charges.

Mollock had turned the Bone Father's people against him. The Deeves were no longer the comforting mixture of tranquility and solitude he'd once appreciated, loved. All he'd spent a lifetime trying to achieve was crashing down around him, and he was next to powerless to stop it. Unless he found a way to silence Mollock Bolle forever. The idea warmed him on chill nights. He knew murder was wrong, but he struggled to make it justifiable. Rengu was justification enough. Should the death god be released, for surely that was the intent of the cult, all life would wither and fade. The Bone Father vowed to prevent that from happening in so much as he had the power to do so.

Mollock Bolle had to die.

His biggest concern, surprisingly, came down to who he could trust. Men and women he'd once named friend now scarcely took the time to glance in his direction. No one here held his counsel, asked for his advice. He was a non-entity, and that left him empty on numerous levels. Misery demanded tribute, tried to force his knees to bend and accept the unacceptable. The Bone Father refused to succumb. His was the will of the Deeves, yet only the Bo now listened. He feared his hands must get bloody if the good of the people was to be done properly. But how would they receive him, this murderer of the Prophet of the gods?

Another wave crashed against the rocks, the spray coating him, stealing his thoughts while leaving him cold, shaking.

"Bone Father, you should come back to the village. You'll catch your death out here on these shores," a gentle voice called.

He turned. "I find the sound of the waves comforting, Marta'les. We are all too caught up in what is happening to take time for those little things that define us."

The raven-haired woman pursed her lips, carefully considering what she was going to say. His comment had sparked an almost forgotten memory in her. She'd been a child when she'd nearly drowned that day he had pulled her to safety from the angry Bo. A life was no easy thing to pass aside, but Marta'les couldn't help but find sedition against the Prophet in his words.

"The Prophet is about to begin the noon sermon," she said quietly, as if in doubt. "If you would only listen to his words and accept them into your heart, you would not be so troubled. Please, come with me."

It was all he could do to keep his disdain hidden. *Have you become so blinded by the anger in his voice, the helpless feeling he has bestowed upon you all? Where is the child I pulled free from the waters of the Bo?* "I am an old man. There is little I can still take comfort in. You go and listen to the Prophet. I will remain here with the Bo."

She found it odd, her heart fluttering dangerously. "But Bone Father, what will you do out here in the midst of such vast emptiness?"

"Listen to the Bo. She has never disappointed me," he smiled.

"It's just water. What is there to learn?"

He sighed. Much of his wealth of knowledge, his intimate relationship with the land, was lost, consumed by the growing cult of Rengu. With no successor, the Bone Father feared all that he was and knew was quickly coming to its twilight. The end, he worried, was not going to be kind.

"You should go back, Marta'les." He turned his back on her, content with the dis-appointment that his words fell on deaf ears.

The people of the Deeves were lost. And it was all Mollock Bolle's fault. A gentle hand clasped his forearm sternly.

"Bone Father, leave this place. It is not safe for you here. You will end up like the others."

The grip relaxed, and he listened to her quiet footfalls on the weather worn rocks. He wanted to call out, to find the answers he so desperately needed. *Others?* Her words dripped malice, hidden warnings that disturbed him more deeply than he cared to admit. Instincts screamed at him, begging him to heed her warnings and flee back his home. The universe was a terrible place with fresh dangers being imported to his tiny corner of the Deeves.

Finally, he turned back, but she was gone. A great commotion broke out on the far side of the ruined keep. The madman on the rocks had come back to preach. The Bone Father gave the gentle waters of the Bo one final glance before moving on. The moment was lost. He sighed heavily, untold pressure weighing down his soul. He decided to head back and listen to what Mollock Bolle had to say. Perhaps his words would fuel the rage the Bone Father needed to carry out his desire.

Night was always darkest after the sun finally dropped below the horizon. The Bone Father sniffed the wind, fetid with the rot of human waste. Occasionally, he caught a whiff of saltwater, and it brought a small grin to his weary face. He sat in his tent, reading by candlelight. No one came to seek his advice anymore. No one was interested in his outdated belief system and the promise of a brighter day. The Deeves was losing its soul one misguided person at a time.

He looked up suddenly. The harsh sound of the tent flap being thrown open startling him. His heart beat a little faster as his gaze settled on the figure taking a seat opposite of him without being invited. *Is this my executioner? Come to make good on Marta'les's predictions?*

"So you are the famous Bone Father. I expected more." The voice, a woman's, sounded flat and highly unimpressed.

He bristled at the insult. "Show me your face."

She slowly reached up and removed the heavy hood of her cloak. The Bone Father choked back a gasp.

"I know you."

She offered a thin smile. "You only know my face. You have no idea who I truly am. But please, my mother insisted on manners. My name is Kaline."

He pointed an accusatory finger. "You are the witch behind these lies and blasphemies."

Kaline chuckled softly. "Strong accusations from a decrepit old man too blind to see that his time and faith are coming to an end."

"We are all prisoners of our own choosing."

"Indeed. You failed to choose. The future has come, old man, and there is no place for you in it."

"Your pawn offers lies to my people. How could I ignore their suffering and fade away?" he asked.

"Pawn?" She paused. "Perhaps I underestimated you, Bone Father. Mollock Bolle is a broken man. He has seen things no living man ever should. It makes him unique, a man of consequence, relevant to the future I am trying to create."

"A world dedicated to this death god cult. That is not a world I would choose to live in."

"Mind your words. I can make them come true."

It was his turn to smile. "I expected better than simple threats, Kaline. If you had come to kill me, I expect you would already have done so. Why have you really come?"

She pretended to smooth out a few wrinkles in her lap. "These are…difficult times for us all. I don't profess to know which way the wind will turn, though I hope it will be in my favor. What I do know is that you are a very real threat to what I am trying to accomplish on this backwater world. I don't want you dead. That will come soon enough. But I do need you gone from here. There is an aura about you, and I don't like it. I've taken your people. There is nothing for you here."

"You mislead my people, seducing them into mental slavery or worse. How can I abandon them now when they need me the most?"

"Your passions are admirable if misplaced. I could crush you right now, and no one would ever know. If I thought I could use you, I would introduce you to Lord Rengu and let you see how wrong you are."

He shook his head, his long decades wearing on the motion. "All lies. What did it take for you to first succumb to the death god?"

She bristled suddenly. Anger flashed hotly in her cheeks. "I suffer you only because you are obsolete. Do not tempt my vengeance."

"How fitting, don't you think?"

Kaline stood, fists clenched in rage. "You have until the dawn to leave the Deeves. I don't care where you go or what you become, but you will not be welcome here again. If my people find you, they will kill you without question. Go to Tenemenah and become a street performer, for all I care. The only thing I care about is never, never seeing your worn face again." Kaline stormed back to the tent flap. "Until the dawn, old man."

He slumped back in his chair after she'd gone, lost deep in thought. The Bone Father knew her threats were true. All his wild imaginations were coming crashing down. He only had a few hours to figure out how to kill Mollock Bolle and change the winds back in his favor.

She stalked through the ruins, focused and intent. Those she passed shrunk away lest they incur the growing wrath in her eyes. Others less fortunate had disappeared after displeasing her. Kaline enjoyed the feeling of fear she inspired in her followers. It gave her strength, lent her will to dominate all life. What more were people than stepping stones marking her path to eternal glory?

Of course, she hadn't started that way. Kaline came from humble beginnings. The daughter of a farmer, she'd quickly learned that her life wasn't enough for her. Nothing her family did was enough. She wanted more. Deserved more. She went to temples, asking priests for guidance.

The Conclave, she felt, was hiding something — something that could potentially change the universe. She wanted to know what.

She'd followed her quest for knowledge to the stars, hungry for any scrap of the great puzzle. Her life had changed for good when she'd stumbled upon the legend of the Three and was able to cross-reference different histories. They confirmed her darkest suspicions. The Conclave, for all its supposed righteousness and almighty attitudes, was just another corrupt entity. Unfortunately, it was the controlling organization for over seven hundred colonized worlds. Bringing it to its knees was certainly daunting, if not impossible.

Kaline had used her knowledge to gain followers and build a base. Her influence grew rapidly but was without focus, guidance. She'd lacked the unifying spark that would take her organization to the next level and, hopefully, bring the Conclave down. Many obstacles blocked her path. The Inquisition. The Prekhauten Guard. Too many men and women in positions of power had refused to abandon their continued wealth. She was almost lost in the myriad of corrupt priests and politicians. Then, she'd discovered Rengu, and all had fallen into place.

Through Rengu, she'd managed to build a cult-like following. The disaffected rose from the gutters of a hundred worlds, pledging support and more to her cause. Her movement gained momentum. Several lower level priests and even a few Inquisitors changed allegiance, lending tactical support and precious insight into the most powerful organizations in the universe. Kaline wanted more.

She had come to An'kuruku with the hope of meeting Mollock Bolle, a man who had survived the anger of the gods for most of his adult life. Convinced he was the key, Kaline had turned his name in to the local Prefecture, forcing Mollock into her waiting arms. Diabolical, yes, but necessary to persuade Mollock to become the face of the disaffected. His words now echoed in the minds of hundreds, and that was just here in the Deeves. Soon, Kaline would take her following back to the stars and continue her rampage all the way to Vau Prime and the very heart of corruption.

No fool, Kaline understood the quest remained in a perilous position. This Bone Father threatened to undo all she'd tried to accomplish here. Letting him go was a calculated risk, but she couldn't afford to have him killed. The people of the Deeves were easily swayed and could just as easily go back to his outdated beliefs upon learning of his murder.

Lost in thought, all swirling round too much to make her comfortable, Kaline came to Mollock's chambers and knocked. She entered without waiting for his reply. Too much needed to be said to wait for modern conveniences. Mollock, to his credit, didn't bother looking up. He already knew.

"What if I told you that there are greater mysteries than you have assumed?" she asked quickly.

Her voice was rushed, as if time had become a dire foe.

He shrugged. Much of his life had been spent running from mystery, not charging towards it. Mollock wished he could go back and change that fateful day when he'd discovered the sleeping god deep in the catacombs of Reven. He wished he had never been so curious or greedy. But, alas, it was not to be. His actions were done, his fate sealed. The gods and their agents would stop at nothing to remove him for good.

"I would say your words are falling on the wrong man. I have seen too much, Kaline. I am not the man you want me to be."

She pursed her lips. "Shut up, Mollock. I didn't come to bandy words. You think you know the truth of things, but the only truth is you are blind to what is truly going on. I have kept much from you, on purpose, of course. There are certain items that only a select few need to know. For protection's sake."

"Kaline, I am tired."

"I need to tell you everything, Mollock. You need to know the truth of what I am trying to accomplish and the truth about Rengu."

He finally turned to look at her. The tiniest tremor of horror flickered in his eyes.

The deep desert, planet An'kuruku.

Elisa awoke to intense pain. She curled up in a ball, clutching her stomach while fighting back the tears. Another sharp blow took her in the ribs. She cried out before being stifled with an old rag in her mouth. Rough hands pinned her to the ground. Her arms were peeled back and bound behind her. She felt the warm trickle of blood drooling down the side of her face.

"Careful. We do not want our most prized possession damaged."

Elisa struggled, but her captors were too strong. Through her haze, she failed to recognize Tanzeil's voice. Her vision swam, patterns and shapes colliding violently every time she moved.

"Is she hurt?"

"Nothing a little make-up won't fix," one of the men laughed.

Elisa heard a thin whistle followed by a wet smack. The severed head rolled past her feet, coming to rest a few feet away. Empty eyes stared up in muted shock.

Tanzeil stepped closer, allowing her to see who had done this. "I am not a man to be trifled with, Elisa."

She mumbled something. He frowned and had her gag lowered.

"Why have you done this?" she demanded weakly.

Calloused hands spread wide; he smiled and said, "I am a businessman at heart. Do not take this personally. You will fetch me a goodly sum at the Wells. You see, I am upholding my end of the bargain. I am seeing you, safely, to the Wells. Of course, what happens to you after that is not my concern."

She struggled, uselessly. "You bastard. I should have known better than to trust desert scum."

He feigned hurt. "I have done everything honorably, offworlder. Did you think that you could just come into the deep desert and have your way? There are rules here. You're not the first offworlder to behave so impudently. I do not expect you to accept your fate. Slavery is no easy thing to get used to, or so I have heard. I'm sure you will be taken by a wealthy merchant. Your fair skin will see to that."

"I'm going to kill you," Elisa growled.

Tanzeil grinned sheepishly. "I doubt that. You're going to make me a very rich man, Elisa. I thank you for that."

"What of my friend?"

"The city dweller? Bah! He's not worth his weight in water. If he's fortunate, he will be taken to the mines and forced into hard labor. I doubt he will last long under the grueling sun." Tanzeil's arrogance bled through his words. "Gag her."

The sun was starting to rise. Streaks of pale colors shredding through the dark. Tanzeil's tribe broke into action. Massive tarps were pulled back from the desert floor. Sand and dust forming clouds so fine they choked. Elisa stood immobile, watching as those around her uncovered large vehicles she had never seen before. Twenty meters long and flat but for a foot-high rim and what looked like a control deck, the vehicles were clearly intended for flight. Men and women began loading each with supplies. *That explains how they can move so quickly across the deserts.*

Ah'muf was brought beside her. His skin had taken an unhealthy glow. He was sick, still poisoned from the scorpion attack at the oasis.

Without proper medical treatment, he was going to die. Elisa knew this and was powerless to prevent it. Her heart ached. A wall broke then, one that had been in place since the day the Bloody Man killed her family and destroyed her village. Reluctantly, she admitted that she loved Ah'muf.

It was a relationship doomed to fail. Named the Paladin, Elisa wasn't long for An'kuruku. Whatever fate the Bloody Man had thrust upon her back on Crimeat, she felt it all coming to a head. One way or another, she was done with this world. Only she still hadn't found the Paradise Tear, nor did she have even the faintest idea who or what it was. Another riddle. She hated riddles.

Elisa gave Ah'muf the best reassuring look she could manage given the circumstances. He winced in his attempt at smiling. She noticed his fingers trembled slightly, like a drunk who hadn't touch alcohol in days. He was worse off than she had previously guessed. His pain translated to her. Again, nothing seemed in her favor.

She tried to find some way out of this predicament, but no options presented themselves. Like it or not, she was trapped and bound for the slave pens. Elisa despised the thought but waiting to be bought might be her best option. Unfortunately, Ah'muf wasn't going to live that long. Tanzeil was being overly unrealistic. Her friend, her love was closer to death than to the Wells. She briefly contemplated putting him out of his misery herself. A mercy killing. He deserved that one act of kindness she was still capable of delivering. The truth was that she didn't think she had it in her.

Elisa struggled against the rising tide of depression threatening to consume her. Bound and gagged, she couldn't see a way out. Once again, she'd waited too long to act despite knowing what was coming. Ah'muf's warnings had fallen on deaf ears. But instead of dropping into second guessing herself and the torment that came with it, Elisa pushed through her despair. A singular thought kept her going. *Ah'muf.*

A pair of guards half-shoved, half-dragged her onto one of the massive skiffs and forced her down atop a stack of supply crates. She glared up silently, marking their faces. They would be among the first to die if she could only get free. Elisa struggled against her bonds, but the toughened leather was as good as steel.

Tanzeil was the last to board. With a gesture, his fleet of five skiffs lurched up from the desert floor, hovering a few feet above the ground, and pushed forward. They weren't exceptionally fast but saved the horses and camels from undue stress or worse. The desert tribes had learned the need for efficiency early during their self-imposed exile from the cities. What they couldn't find or barter for, they stole with ruthless abandon. Elisa had no doubt Tanzeil had come by these skiffs with a price in blood.

As if sensing her eyes glaring hotly on his back, he turned and gave her his most charming smile. "You did not think we were going to ride all the way to the Wells, did you? It is a five-day journey by camel. Now, we will be there by nightfall. Be thankful. A slower journey would mean the death of your friend."

And give me the chance to stick a knife in your belly. Elisa blinked but remained surprisingly calm. Tanzeil was no fool. He knew she was a threat and, despite the tribe of trusted fighters at his disposal, stood a very good chance at killing him long before they reached the Wells. Only fools took unnecessary chances.

She was fed and allowed to relieve herself near dusk. The aching in her bowels and bladder nearly prevented her from being able to stand. Dehydration was setting in as well, leaving her weak, delirious. Elisa wasn't prepared for the level of negligence Tanzeil was exposing her to. She assumed it was an attempt to break her, to stymie her will and leave her body in a dilapidated state. That way, she wouldn't put up a fight when he sold her off to the slave pens. At least it made sense to her.

The alternative was considerably worse. Tanzeil was cunning, smooth and diabolical. He despised city dwellers and their off-world commercialization. An'kuruku was a sacred place, sullied by the filth of adventure seekers and fortune hunters. He wished for a day when the deserts once again belonged to his people. He wanted nothing more than to drive the offworlders back to their starships and off his world. He wanted. Tanzeil looked at Elisa with disgust. She was everything wrong with his precious desert.

He contemplated sticking a knife in her and dumping her corpse in the dunes, but he'd never actually killed anyone before. Not to say that plenty of others hadn't died by his command, but he considered himself an educated man, refined and upstanding. It wouldn't do to have blood on his hands. Tanzeil relied on others to do the dirty work. He was a prince, after all.

The skiffs raced over the sand sea, breaking dune peaks in prickling sprays. The heat lessened slightly as the sun began to set but still hovered over one hundred degrees. It was a dry heat, the kind that made you sweat but not uncomfortable. Tanzeil loved the heat. His bronze skin darkened. The heat baked his skin deliciously. It was both blessing and bane. One day, when his dreams became reality, it would be time to abandon the desert and return to the cities. On that day, he would become the tyrant.

Night fell slowly, casually covering the land in darkness. Elisa continued to watch Tanzeil for a time, eager to spot any hint of exploitable weakness. The man was a rock, immobile and daunting. She noticed the dangerous glint in his eyes but couldn't find an acceptable reason for it. That worried her.

Eventually, she drifted off to sleep, awakening to the sounds of civilization and the first kiss of the desert sun. Dawn had arrived, and so had they. The Wells sprawled out before her. Her heart crashed. Any hope of escaping Tanzeil had died the moment the skiffs passed the outer ring of run-down huts and shops. They had arrived.

TWENTY

3212 A.G. (After Gods), Hawker's Gate, deep space.

The stars were ambivalent, caring nothing for the trials of humanity. The birth and death of countless suns continued without so much as a backward glance at the sharp decline threatening the universe. The stars were also unforgiving. They swallowed dreams, stole hope and left lifeless husks, shells of what had once been men, drifting across the cosmos until a gravity well sucked them down to oblivion. How many times had Tolde Breed dreamed of such a death?

He shivered, suddenly aware of how thin the hull of the *Indomitable* was compared to the Gate. It wouldn't take much, he knew. One little puncture, and all he was would be sucked into the great vacuum of space. The notion was absurd, or so he told himself as he stared out into the unending ocean of blackness. He stood a better chance of being shot dead in the night than being vented into space.

This wasn't the first crippling fear he'd had to battle. Much of his life was spent loathing the dark, a childhood fear gone horribly wild. It had taken most of his adult life to beat that fear. And it wasn't until his first battle with Amongeratix that he was forced to confront it.

The last seventy years hadn't been kind. He was just past middle age but already felt as beaten and abused as a man twice that. Death mocked him, laughing at his decisions and inability to see past the single unifying factor in all of humanity. His muscles ached. His hair was thinning rapidly. Soon enough, he despaired, baldness would settle in. Lines and wrinkles creased his face mercilessly. Tolde Breed was tired. More than once, he thought about abandoning the Inquisition and finding a nice, quiet planet to spend the rest of his years. But every time he did, visions of the Three returned to haunt him. They were the real reason he continued to serve.

He would lay down his crest when they were no longer a threat.

"It is almost time, Tolde."

He gave Luma Kai a brief nod, barely moving his head. So it was. Opting to leave his cape behind, he and Luma headed to the docking sleeve and their meeting with Administrator Felp. The man had much to answer for, and Tolde suspected he was in league with Presha Von. The slightest piece of evidence would be proof enough to arrest the man and order martial law on Hawker's Gate. He couldn't help but think back to his first visit to the Gate, during his first hunt for Amongeratix. The administrator then had been a smooth talker. She'd convinced him that he was looking in the wrong direction, that she had nothing to do with what he would later discover was a greater conspiracy.

What a fool he'd been. Young and inexperienced, it had been his first real assignment, and he'd let eagerness blind him to what was going on around him. Tolde vowed never to let that happen again. As an agent of the Office of Heretical Persecution, he had every authority to execute Administrator Felp summarily. Tolde hoped it wouldn't come to that. There had to be some people still loyal to the Conclave. There had to be.

"Your mind isn't focused," Luma said.

"There is a great deal happening that we are not aware of, Luma. I admit that I feel somewhat lost."

"Perhaps you should stay aboard the *Indomitable*."

He smiled despite better judgment. "I'm fine. We have a job to do here, and it's going to take all of us to see it through."

"Distractions can compromise the mission, Tolde. They are the one thing we can't afford. Not here. Not now."

He stiffened. "How do you wish to handle the administrator?"

His message was clear. Drop it. Luma caught on and let her concerns settle, for the moment. "We must assume he has been compromised by Presha Von. All intelligence suggests he is a weak man prone to giving in to his vices. I say we play on that and get him to talk."

"Agreed. If he is part of her plan, it will most likely be as a pawn."

It had taken him the better part of a year to discover how diabolical Presha Von truly was. Much of what had transpired on Crimeat was, in part, her doing. Too many questions remained open-ended for Tolde to feel comfortable, though. Her relationship with Ursal Prowl kept him off guard. His inability to identify who was in charge kept him from acting decisively and ending the entire affair. He very much desired to confront this woman. Then he'd be free to act.

"Are you listening to me?"

He paused, recalling nothing of what Luma had just said. "I'm sorry, my mind drifted slightly."

She forced a sigh. "You're making me uncomfortable, Tolde. We are on the brink of war, and you're too focused on this woman."

"She is the key."

He winced, knowing it was a weak defense at best. Reluctant to admit, Tolde recognized his obsession was becoming a liability. He needed to step back, reanalyze his position and all concerned facets. Perhaps then he might find the missing pieces he so desperately needed.

"Tolde, we know next to nothing about Von. She's a major player, sure, but we can't confirm anything beyond that."

Luma frowned, tired of the same old argument. The Inquisition had scoured the record halls of Lethendweil tirelessly after the insurrection but found absolutely nothing about Presha Von. She had become a ghost. All traces of her past had been removed from public knowledge. They hadn't even found a birth record. For all intents and purposes, she didn't exist. That only convinced Tolde of her importance on a larger scale.

"I know this is hard for you to grasp, but what I learned on Crimeat all suggests she is perhaps worse than Ursal Prowl. I suspect she might even be more highly placed in the conspiracy revolving around the Three than he. Our conversation with Administrator Felp will help me identify the depth of her involvement."

She frowned at his usage of the word *me*.

"You said war."

"What?"

He stopped, hand a breath away from the access panel connecting Hawker's Gate to the *Indomitable*. "You said we were on the brink of war. What did you mean?"

"Nothing that has happened makes sense, Tolde. There are too many moving pieces. We have never seen this much subversive activity against the Conclave. Increased pirate attacks on the shipping lanes. A wave of cults all surrounding this Rengu deity. Minor revolts on a dozen different worlds. And now all the Three are in play. If what you suppose is correct, this all began on Crimeat, but for what purpose? War is the only logical conclusion."

Tolde closed his eyes briefly. His worst fears were being realized, and he felt he had no one to turn to. That nagging suspicion had been lurking since his first attempt at recapturing Amongeratix, now more than fifty years ago. Luma's concerns closely matched his own. He was glad she voiced them. It gave him an oddly comforting reassurance that he was not alone after all.

"I fear that we may already be too late to stop a war. What you say is all true, but there is more. Ursal Prowl is not the first Inquisitor to betray his oaths. Dozens of cases have been reported to the Inquisitor General's office, but those reports never made it to the Conclave."

"Are you suggesting Nye is covering it up?" she asked hesitantly.

"I don't know what to think. The only certainty is that a rift is forming in the lower ranks. Who knows how far up it goes?"

Luma repressed the sickening feeling growing in her stomach. The implications that the head of the Inquisition was involved in some conspiracy shook the foundations of every principle she believed in. The potential for a universe-wide civil war threatened. She suddenly felt very small, despite trying to rationalize her fears. She refused to give in to the temptations of simplistic thought.

Hitting the button, Tolde rushed through the hatch and into the customs office. Agents on duty recognized them and waved them through. Tolde and Luma wore their official uniforms, striking black disturbed only by the vibrant red and blue rose, the symbol of their office. Not even a fool would stand in the way of an Inquisitor on the hunt and, judging from the stern looks etched in their faces, the Inquisitors were hunting.

Bethis practically jumped up when the Inquisitors entered the administratum offices without knocking.

"We are here to see the Administrator."

He looked up at Tolde, the hint of fear speckling his eyes. "Of course, Inquisitor. He is expecting you."

Luma scowled. The diminutive man showed too much apprehension to be expecting a routine meeting.

"If you will follow me," Bethis squeaked.

Roule Felp looked up from a stack of morning reports. His face paled. Beads of sweat formed in his hairline as he recognized Tolde Breed, the famous Inquisitor who had hunted down Amongeratix twice and lived.

"Administrator," Tolde acknowledged with a curt nod.

"Inquisitors, please have a seat."

Tolde settled into the stiff-backed chair. "Let us avoid unnecessary pleasantry. We are here to apprehend Presha Von and all her compatriots. I believe you know exactly where she can be found. Your help would be appreciated."

"Lady Von runs one of the classier gambling establishments on the Gate. She is a woman of good standing," Felp replied.

"She is a traitor to the Conclave and a threat."

Luma leaned forward. "Administrator, we are here for her. Your cooperation is appreciated but not necessary. We can still hunt her down with you sitting in one of your own prison cells."

Felp swallowed. "That won't be necessary, Inquisitor. My staff and I are at your disposal. I merely ask that you use discretion in your actions. Explaining her arrest is going to be touchy with many of the more influential merchants and factors."

"How is it possible she has become so integrated in less than two years?" Luma pressed, unsatisfied with his answer.

Felp offered a thin smile. "As you know, much that transpires on this station is not entirely sanctioned by the Conclave proclamations. Officially we are a tax paying member of Conclave rule, but even the Cardinal Seniorus tends to look the other way. No one makes any more waves than necessary. It is not hard to imagine a woman of Lady Von's stature taking full advantage of this."

"You sound as if you admire her."

His cheeks flushed. "She is an exceptional woman, but I know next to nothing of her life before arriving at the Gate."

Tolde finally unclenched his jaw. "Would it surprise you to learn she was responsible for an insurrection that was nearly successful as well as the deaths of hundreds?"

"I don't question what people do before they come here, Inquisitor. We all have our ghosts."

"Indeed. Where can we find her?"

A pause. "She owns the Arboretum on deck P 12. Most times, you can find her there. Will you require support from my guards?"

"No, thank you. We have our own security." He failed to mention they were already in place in various strategic locations across the space station.

Tolde harbored no doubts that the security of Hawker's Gate was compromised. Subversive elements had infiltrated so deeply he was having trouble believing Felp's proclaimed innocence. Prepared for the worst-case scenario, Tolde was ready to make the call and put the entire station on lockdown.

"A guide perhaps? The Gate is quite large and difficult to navigate, even for those of us who have been here a while," Felp insisted. He didn't like the idea of Inquisitors running loose on his watch. Fear of Presha Von kept him in line. He knew he'd already crossed her, but there was little real choice. Self-preservation demanded he act in a manner befitting an appointed Conclave representative.

Tolde was about to reply when he felt Luma grip his forearm. She leaned forward and smiled, disarming and predatory at the same time. "Administrator Felp, we would be pleased to accept your offer. With luck, we will hunt Von down and have her in custody before too many of your daily operations are hindered."

"I would prefer you acted more discreetly than that, Inquisitor. This station runs on commerce. Shutting down even a single sector will greatly impact our ability to fulfill every order."

"Naturally, but you would do well to remember that this is a Conclave station and we are acting on behalf of the Cardinal Seniorus."

Meaning they had priority. Felp slumped back in his chair. There was no foreseeable way around the Inquisitors' will. He feared he'd already signed his death warrant. Presha Von would be ruthless when she discovered his betrayal. Sadly, there was no other way. He instructed Bethis to guide the Inquisitors to the Arboretum and waited until the outer office door hissed closed before thumping his head down on his desk in defeat. It was all unraveling.

Presha Von clicked the transmitter off and settled back in her chair. She'd heard enough. Suspicions and fears seemed warranted after all.

"August, we will be expecting guests soon. Get me Mung."

"Problems, Mistress?"

"That fat bastard Felp just sold us out to the Inquisition. I want his head."

"We are not prepared to act yet. Removing the Administrator now will only complicate things."

She appreciated his concern and forethought but knew there was little choice. The Conclave turned a blind eye to what happened here, at least until now. Not only had two Inquisitors and a cruiser full of poorly disguised Prekhauten Guards been dispatched, but the Inquisitors were part of the Office of Heretical Persecution, by far the most zealous organization in the Inquisition. Making matters worse, she recognized the name of Tolde Breed.

Presha flashed back to two years ago. Their paths had never crossed, but she knew all too well how relentless Tolde had been. His actions had almost singlehandedly ruined her plans for Crimeat and more. Her distaste for the Inquisition rose daily. First, that bumbling control freak Ursal Prowl had betrayed her trust and tried to get her killed. That was bad enough. It had taken most of the last two years, but she'd finally managed to overcome her addiction to the oils that had practically enslaved her to Prowl's desires.

A free woman, Presha turned her thoughts towards revenge. The cult of Rengu offered her the best chance for redemption. She didn't buy in to the ridiculous notion that the gods were coming back, nor did she really put much faith in the cult's ability to reshape the political model currently ruling the universe. What she did believe was that Alain Nye's vision was more beneficial to them all. It was time for the people of the Conclave to understand what a true dictatorship was.

"We don't have much of a choice. Felp showed his hand. I don't care if he felt he had to cooperate with the Inquisition." *I expected more from him. Not much more, but at least enough to delay them for a few more days.*

August clicked his tongue. "Mistress, even the hardiest soul would buckle under pressure from two Inquisitors. He did assign Bethis to escort them."

"Bethis is barely better than a simpleton. He's just as likely to lead them straight to us," she snarled. "Have Mung sent here immediately."

"At once, Mistress."

Presha picked up her glass of dark blue wine and returned to the main gambling floor. The time had come to secure Hawker's Gate and make it hers.

Okolo Mung frowned when his communicator started to beep. Setting down his hastily emptied mug of ale, he yawned and reluctantly answered.

"What?"

"Okolo Mung, you are required to report in," August announced matter-of-factly.

A dozen replies went through his mind. None of them would get him paid, however. "Why? Tell your owner I am busy."

"Mistress Von has received updated information. Your mission has changed." He paused. "Perhaps a true Masticq would have already seen this."

Okolo bristled at the insult. He wanted nothing more than to wrap his hands around the eunuch's miserable neck and squeeze until his head popped off. His sand-colored skin darkened with rising anger. Visions warned him of an eventual betrayal, but they failed to suggest when. Okolo idly wondered if Presha's change in plans meant an early demise.

He glanced up, noting how the bald woman with the strange tattoos and the brutish man accompanying her continued to bicker over a meal. They weren't going anywhere and were in no condition to act. Not that Prekhautens needed much preparation time. But these two were only armed with poorly concealed hand weapons. No real threat to a Mastieq.

"Tell Von I will be there shortly."

Fies sucked in a forkful of noodles. Only his eyes shifted towards the target Annalilly identified. There was nothing special about him. Plain clothes, plain appearance. Yet he walked with the enhanced stiffness Fies associated with men in uniform.

"We should take him out now." Annalilly said from across the table.

"He hasn't done anything."

"Why wait?" Annalilly asked sharply.

Fies pointed a scolding finger. "Orders, Sergeant. We are not to make contact unless directly engaged. I'm not going to be the one to get on Tolde's bad side."

She paused to consider his warning. Every instinct warned this man was dangerous, and he was stalking them. That made him a very real threat.

"Screw orders. Our position is compromised now, Fies, and you know it. Are you willing to let him kill one or two of us before the Inquisitors say we can act? I thought we were given the ability to read the situation and act accordingly."

"Keep your voice down, or we're going to find out."

Annalilly fumed. "At least put a trace on him."

"Based on a hunch? Finish your food." He took another bite and jerked slightly when his beacon went off. Pulling the small object from his jacket pocket, Fies carefully read the message. "Sandy's going to have to wait. Breed is moving on Von. We need to collect your squad and meet him on deck P 12 ASAP."

About damned time. "What size enemy force are we expecting?"

"Unknown. Hells, they can't even confirm if she is there," he replied.

She frowned. "Will station security help us, or will we have to fight our way through them?"

"Go with plan b. I don't think anyone on this station is as friendly to the Conclave as the Cardinal Seniorus would like to believe."

"We should go back to the *Indomitable* and gear up," she suggested.

"Too late for that. They need us now."

Annalilly scowled openly and finished her drink. "I should have taken leave."

"Come on."

They failed to notice the increased foot traffic suddenly moving through the market areas.

Roule Felp sat behind his desk, helpless. He felt the walls closing in, constricting what had once been a dream of grand design. All that had ended with his betrayal of Presha Von. It was only a matter of time before she returned and repaid the favor. He briefly contemplated fleeing but knew better. There was no place in the universe far enough away from her reach. Nor would he be able to depart the Gate without notice. Too many had already gone over to her side, abandoning the principles he tried to cultivate.

He cringed when he heard the front doors hiss open. Roule wasn't expecting anyone, and Bethis wouldn't be returning anytime soon if he knew the Inquisitor's instinct for the hunt. Reaching into the top drawer, he pulled out a small handgun.

"I knew she couldn't wait," he said as Okolo Mung stalked into the office.

Okolo merely shrugged. "It's nothing personal."

Roule noticed Okolo's hands were empty and, mistakenly, thought he had a chance. He drew his gun and aimed with shaky hands.

"That's not wise," Okolo cautioned. He took a step closer.

"Stay away or I'll shoot."

"When's the last time you shot anyone, Administrator?"

Roule waved the gun. "Stop trying to distract me."

"Trying? No. I don't want to get shot is all," Okolo's smile was a weak attempt at making himself look harmless.

His stocky body, bunched with muscles, was poised to explode into action.

"How did she know so quickly?"

Okolo paused, taken off guard slightly. He cocked his head, studying the trembling Felp. "How does she know anything? There are some things it's best not to question. Wouldn't you agree?"

"You could let me go," Roule suggested weakly. Even he was forced to admit the plea sounded pathetic.

"I'm afraid I can't."

Roule struggled to find a solution that didn't end with him dead. He couldn't. Roule fired twice. Okolo easily sidestepped the sizzling hot rounds of energy. The wall behind him caught fire where the rounds struck. He looked over his shoulder. A thin stream of smoke rising from his jacket.

"You're making this more difficult than it needs to be," Okolo warned.

"Stay back! I'm not afraid to shoot you!" Roule screamed.

"I believe you. But are you ready to kill an unarmed man?"

Roule paused, at a loss for words.

Okolo eased another step closer. "You have one unfortunate thing going against you, Administrator. Mistress Von wants you dead in one piece. This is going to hurt, I'm afraid."

He rushed, catching Felp's gun hand and breaking it at the wrist. Roule screamed in raw agony. His weapon clattered across the floor. Okolo placed both hands on either side of Roule's head and closed his eyes. Waves of unseen pressure poured from his skin, swirling around the helpless Felp. Roule screamed one final time before the pressure penetrated his skin, finding his heart. Okolo exhaled sharply and used his power to burst the life-giving muscle.

Blood trickled from his eyes, nose and ears. Roule's eyes rolled lifelessly back into his head as Okolo let the body drop. He spied a single drop of blood on his shirt and scowled. Ruined. Presha Von owed him a new shirt. Whistling, he turned and made his way back towards the bazaar.

The sleek black flier roared towards Hawker's Gate undetected. Tannus found the anonymity comforting, especially given the information he'd learned from meeting with Ruma Zzein. Three millennia had passed since he had helped rescue her from his brother. Three thousand years, and he had had no idea that she was still alive, nor that she was the vaunted Grand Mistress of the Blood Witch order. *How much more have I missed during my self-imposed exile?* The prospects were haunting.

He had once prided himself on his ability to stay ahead of Amongeratix, to stay in control of the situation. Recent events suggested just how wrong he had been. Time and again he'd been foiled by his brother's cunning. How? Amongeratix had spent most of the last five decades locked away in Conclave prisons. That implied he was getting help, from the very people Tannus was sworn to defend. Why? He shook his head. Too many questions.

Tannus was always a step behind, frustratingly so. Making matters worse was the invasion of the abbey on the Acumensiis Comet. Amongeratix had never had such power, and it frightened Tannus. How deep had he delved to obtain those secrets no living soul should possess? And who was helping him? Man was easily corrupted. That much was undeniable. The thought that there were humans ready and willing to help Amongeratix achieve his goal of the final destruction of the last vestiges of the gods was horrifying.

There was a time when Tannus had had armies at his command, eager men and women who willingly fought against the horrific promise Amongeratix offered for the future. Now, he was fortunate if a handful followed. Perhaps humanity was outgrowing their belief in the gods. The notion frightened him. This was not the time for a changing of ages-old principles. He needed allies but didn't know where to turn.

Tannus rolled his left shoulder, an old ache throbbing deep in the muscle. He never did like space travel, especially the deep-space runs. There was too much time alone with his thoughts — thoughts that proved much darker in recent years. He closed his eyes and thought of what Ruma Zzein told him before he left.

"You must go to Hawker's Gate. The help you need is there."

"That's it? Can you not see deeper? Who should I seek?" he asked, desperate to learn any scrap of information that might help him succeed.

Ruma shook her head, her diaphanous robes shifting slightly in a dazzling display of light colors. "Much is clouded, but I feel the events about to happen on that station will help shape the course of things to come. Should our enemy succeed, we stand to fall into darkness forever."

Tannus opened his eyes. The cold black of space stared back at him, silently judging him. A warning alarm chimed. He was coming into Hawker's Gate. The time for reflection and the endless questions and problems posed from solitude had passed. He exhaled one last frustrating breath and began pre-docking procedures. The space station loomed in the distance, barely a speck amidst the stars.

TWENTY-ONE

3212 A.G. (After Gods), Krenz, planet Vau Prime.

Barnalus yawned and stretched. The day was nearly finished, and he was looking forward to going home. Maintaining the massive sewer complex under Krenz was a never-ending chore, and, despite having done it for the better part of the last ten years, he went home exhausted every night. Best not to mention to horrid stench he brought with him to his wife and kids. He smirked, knowing the scolding he was going to get when he stepped through the door would be just for show.

Packing his bag, Barnalus headed home. It was the last day of the week, and that meant Falela had made her best roast. The promise of slow-roasted meat with a variety of vegetables and fresh dark bread watered his mouth. What's more, he'd made a little extra this month and was able to buy a bottle of classy wine to take home. Falela would like that, and he was seldom able to spoil her the way she deserved. Besides, he figured she needed to get the alcohol cravings out of her system before the baby was due.

The thought of her belly rounding soon with their first child filled Barnalus with more pride than he'd ever imagined having. He bragged to his friends, who had long since stopped listening. Waving goodnight to the door guard, Barnalus headed down to the transit stop and waited the usual five minutes before the air train arrived. An hour later and he'd be home, after a quick stop at the nearest wine shop. Barnalus took the first seat he came to and leaned back, comfortable with the twice-a-day ride.

He briefly heard a loud boom followed by the sound of whipping energy and screams before the air train detonated.

The sun was setting by the time Aerena made it to the nearest marketplace. She'd failed to get enough items on her last trip a few days ago and was now forced to scramble to get home on time and have dinner prepared for her children. She rushed through the shelves, grabbing this and passing on that. She'd forgotten her list at work and was trying to remember exactly what she needed, all the while knowing she was going to end up buying more than what was necessary and not everything on the list. It was the curse of the successful woman. Finally, she was done and hurried to the checkout lines.

"Aerena, how are you today?"

She looked up at the sound of the friendly voice greeting her. "Exhausted. How have you been, Thel?"

The older, decidedly plumper Thel smiled warmly. "Well enough. Our grandchildren are visiting from Prielth."

"That's wonderful. How long has it been since you've last seen them?"

She never found out. The suicide bomber standing two places in front of her detonated without a word. Shrapnel and flames ripped through the market and out into the streets and neighboring buildings. Secondary explosions echoed down the roads leading up to the market. Columns of black smoke billowed into the sky even as debris and body parts rained back down.

The explosion destroyed three city blocks instantly. Smoke and ash billowed into the night sky, drowning even the massive light pillars on the far side of Krenz. Screams of the dying rang out above the sound of incoming rescue sirens. Initial reports suggested a ruptured gas main, but it quickly became apparent that more was involved. Rumormongers flooded the communication networks with wild speculation of terrorist attacks on the capital. Panic soon gripped the city.

Alain Nye read the morning reports with unusual interest. He looked up as Mobus Kale was shown in.

"Ah, Mobus. The campaign has begun successfully?"

Mobus nodded crisply. Menace glared through his eyes. "More than nine hundred dead and rising."

Nye found the casualness with which Mobus answered disturbing but kept it to himself. Much sacrifice would be required from a great many in the coming days if his plan was to succeed.

"The Cardinal Seniorus will be forced to act," he said instead.

Mobus disagreed. "No, she will dither with the Forum, asking questions that none can answer. A formal inquiry will be drawn out, and the result will be the same. Nothing will happen."

"You should be more optimistic. Good things happen with a positive mindset," Nye scolded.

"Good things happen to people who make them happen."

"Indeed, but to succeed, we must remain positive. Phos will no doubt seek the counsel of her Forum, but as you so succinctly put, she knows they will dither. Phos is no fool."

"All the more reason to eliminate her now," Mobus argued.

Nye shook his head ruefully. "That is perhaps the dumbest thing I've heard you say. Suspicion would immediately fall on this office — suspicion that I don't need, not until I am firmly set in position to assume control of the universe. We are not ready to act."

"Then we have no choice but to step up our attacks. The Conclave must be made to learn that they are fallible. I want them on their knees begging for salvation before this is finished."

Nye sighed. "And that will happen eventually."

"Eventually? It must happen now. This entire little plan of yours will fall to ruin unless we begin immediately."

Mobus's face flushed crimson with rage. His fist clenched and released repeatedly. The current inability to act infuriated him, and, worse, doubt suddenly arose, gnawing at his conscience. The first inkling of betrayal by the Inquisitor General entered his mind. He knew the story behind Ursal Prowl and was determined not to fall into that same trap.

"Calm yourself, Colonel. You are still an officer in the Prekhauten Guard and will remain so as long as you continue to provide outstanding service." Nye leaned back in his high back chair. The old leather was worn and more comfortable than his bed. "The collapse of the Conclave will leave a power vacuum that the remaining Guard loyalists will be forced to secure. Men like you, Mobus, will help determine the course of the future. Don't mess this up."

"Inquisitor General, I have remained loyal from the moment of the oath I took upon enlisting. Do not question that again," Mobus warned casually.

Nye smiled falsely. "Now that we have that issue behind us, we need to discuss our next move."

Mobus edged closer to the front of his chair, eager for the chance to stretch his imagination.

"One attack will not plunge our tidy little world in chaos. More is required before we can convince Phos to move against the cult of Rengu."

"I thought the cultists were on our side," Mobus commented.

"They are, but they are the most expendable players. Cultists are dangerous without universal recognition. The fools believe their death god will return and consume us all in a wave of hatred, thus liberating untold trillions of people from tyranny. Rubbish. The gods are gone and not coming back." If only the cultists knew how false that statement actually was.

"The gods are the least of my concerns. What do you want me to do?"

Impatience only serves my purpose. "I need to be able to lock Krenz down under martial law before we can move against the Conclave. How long do you think it will take for panic to consume the population?"

Mobus shrugged. "That depends on how many civilians I can kill. The attacks must be at a level that inspires fear at unprecedented levels."

Nye paused. There were too many moving parts, and Mobus was becoming a liability. His lust for carnage threatened the stability of Nye's plans. The man would eliminate all Vau Prime's population before sating his appetite for bloodshed. Nye's thoughts turned, briefly, to Vicente Blackheart and his damnable pirate clans. Prowl's imprisonment proved a major setback. If the pirates pulled out now or showed any sign of reluctance to act, the rebellion was doomed while still in the womb. Unfortunately, the campaign was already started. He settled his predatory gaze back on Mobus.

"Continue your terror campaign but maintain operational security. If even a hint of suspicion gets back to me, it will all be ruined. I, personally, do not want to live out my days in a Conclave prison."

Mobus grinned. "My cells are prepared to act now. All I need is for you to give the word. I'll have Krenz locked behind closed doors in a matter of days. This city will grind to a halt."

"Good. I want Phos begging me to enact martial law as quickly as possible. Do try to keep the civilian body count as low as possible," Nye urged. He truly did want to keep as many civilians alive as possible. The only deaths he wanted were those dressed in Conclave robes.

He looked up and patiently waited for Mobus to exit. The man was clearly going to present a problem, sooner rather than later. Nye idly scratched his jaw. The time was coming when loose ends would need to be clipped. Mobus Kale had just made himself into a very inconvenient loose end.

Pirate haven of Drespai, orbit of planet Spindle.

Vicente Blackheart marched down the empty deck of the *Shrike*, hands clasped patiently behind his back. His jaw was clenched in consternation. Anger and ignorance clashed. Not for the first time, he almost felt lost. He'd never imagined dealing with the Inquisitor General would prove so difficult. Not to mention his failed efforts at turning Geres Auk. The bigger man was a born killer with unquestionable loyalty. He'd be a great asset to Blackheart's plans. The pirate clans had been leaderless for too long. Blackheart hoped to change that, placing himself on the throne.

Realizing it would be no easy task; Blackheart struggled to find the necessary edge to get ahead of any competition. He was a callous man, cold and calculating, but his kind was notorious for stubborn attitudes, which was the reasoning behind their inability to form a cohesive unit. If Blackheart had his way, the clans would become as solidified and organized as the Prekhauten fleets. Or, rather, what was about to be left of them when his current assignment from the Inquisitor General was completed.

The thought of devastating the main battle fleet of the vaunted Prekhauten Guard left him giddy with excitement. Interstellar commerce would collapse, leaving a void for smugglers and pirates to fill. The protection of shipping lanes would fall on his united clans — for a fee, of course. The idea of breaking the Conclave for good put a smile on his face. All it would take was a push.

"Why so glum?"

Blackheart answered without stopping. "We have much yet to do, Therill, and time is dwindling."

Therill fell in step beside him. "You want the big man to betray his oaths too badly. He is a proud man."

"I don't give a damn about his pride. I want his guns. His damned cunning."

"He's only one man."

"One man that can make a difference," Blackheart countered. "There's a war coming, Therill, and we're not strong enough to come out on top, not yet."

Therill bristled at the implied insult. "You underestimate what we've already accomplished. Twenty captains have already pledged to your banner."

"Twenty out of hundreds. It's not enough!" Blackheart stopped suddenly, rounding on his First Mate. "The only way to succeed is to show the other captains that I have an unbreakable power. Men respect power, Therill, nothing else."

"I beg to differ. Men are filled with exploitable weakness. We should turn the other captains against each other."

"And ruin any chance of becoming strong enough to control the shipping and commerce lanes? No."

He kept the building conspiracy within the Inquisition to himself. Therill was a good man, but Blackheart couldn't shake the suspicion he was plotting against him. Too many plans rested on a delicate edge, a blade so thin it was almost transparent. He didn't care for the situation, knowing that his plans could go either way. Control was almost beyond his grasp despite everything he was doing to change that.

He'd already made his demands to Prowl's masters on Vau Prime, and, for the moment, they'd agreed to play along. Blackheart was no fool, though. He couldn't afford to place any measure of trust in the Inquisition or their Prekhauten lapdogs. Blackheart knew Ursal Prowl was an important piece to the coming war, but for him to be so casually abandoned by Alain Nye was more disturbing than helpful. It left Blackheart feeling uneasy.

He needed reassurances before committing the bulk of the clans to the coming campaign. It could just as easily be a trap as anything else. Blackheart understood the backstabbing nature of this business, but it left him immobile at the worst moment. The other clan leaders would turn on him if he didn't act quickly.

He turned to Therill. "I need to see Auk."

"Are you sure that's a wise idea?"

"What harm can possibly come from it? I need him to join us."

Therill shook his head. "He's too dangerous, Captain. Who's to say that, even if he gives his word, he won't go back to his previous employers?"

"Because I'm going to vent his previous employer if he does." Blackheart's voice hardened. "Why are you opposing this so vehemently?"

Therill paused. "I have the security of the crew to think of. We've never undertaken an operation this large. There are too many variables. I don't like it."

"When have the odds ever been in our favor? There is still time. We need to wait until as much of the plan as possible is in place and ready before we act."

"The clans will not sit still for long," Therill cautioned.

"Nor do I expect them to. Two things need to happen first. The Guard fleet needs to be deployed to Hawker's Gate, and I need to formalize my arrangement with the Inquisitor General. He's the key player in all of this."

Therill struggled to contain his surprise. One of the three most powerful people in the universe was at the head of a multifaceted conspiracy? The implications staggered him, forcing him to abandon some of his personal plans. Therill suddenly felt very small. He worried that Blackheart was all too willing to abandon him when matters grew too dire.

"Go and prepare Prowl to be transferred over to the brig on Drespai. I'll have Auk sent over when I'm done," Blackheart ordered.

"Yes, Captain. Anything else?"

He paused. "The crew needs some downtime, especially before we go back into the fight. I want the Shrike refitted and ready to sail by the end of the week. Hopefully, the other clan leaders will give in so we can proceed."

Therill nodded his compliance and went about his task. Thoughts of plunging a small blade through Blackheart's back almost demanded action. Almost.

Blackheart gave a quick jerk of his head to the guard on duty, who immediately unlocked the door to the cell holding Geres Auk. Pale light from the hallway washed into the cell. Geres threw an arm up to cover his eyes as Blackheart walked in and sat on the small stool a few meters away.

"I have nothing to say to you," Geres said dully.

Blackheart shrugged. "What do you owe that man? He's a disgraced Inquisitor, a traitor. You have more honor than to waste on him."

"Honor is subjective, pirate."

"Indeed, but, unless I am greatly mistaken, it is at your core. You understand the principles behind right and wrong and don't give your word freely or without reservation. Am I correct?" Blackheart asked.

Geres's eyes narrowed dangerously. "Be careful. You've only given me one reason to kill you thus far. I do not want another."

Blackheart grinned sheepishly. A breakthrough. "So you are a man of reason. Good. I can't talk with unreasonable men."

The bigger Geres remained silent. His eyes studied the pirate, searching for weakness. A chance to escape.

"What do you really want?"

The question threw him. Geres was unused to being asked his opinion, much less any wants or desires. He fought, he plotted, and he killed, all at the discretion of his employers. It had been so long since he'd acted of his own accord he was afraid he had forgotten how to do so.

"Does it matter?" he asked, stalling.

Another shrug. "Not to the Inquisitor, I assure you. I've already told you how much of an asset you could be to me. I need men capable of thinking on their own, with little direction or guidance. Men who understand what it is I need done and can rationalize and improvise when necessary. Are you such a man, Geres Auk?"

"I am many types of man. Do not make the mistake of confining me."

Blackheart barked a laugh. "I like that, Geres. I do. You have character. More reason why I don't want to vent you into space, like I am considering doing to your counterpart."

"He's not my concern."

Not even a flinch. Interesting. "What exactly is your concern?"

Geres flashed a toothy grin. "Living, at the moment."

"There's not much life to be had inside this cage."

"It's not the first time. A cage is only as strong as the man who holds the key. Who's to say I can't convince one of your men to come to my side?"

Blackheart barely managed to keep from glancing back at the guard. "My men are unquestionable. I have their complete obedience."

"Truly?"

The pirate captain cursed himself for allowing Geres to turn the tone of the conversation in his favor. Mistrust was a dangerous weapon, one he couldn't afford to have used against him. Prudence cautioned against trying to turn Geres. Common sense begged him to vent both Geres and Prowl. They were unnecessary complications in an already dangerous game. One tiny slip up, and it could all come crashing down.

Blackheart offered a wide smile. "Cute, but you're wasting your time."

"I can say the same of you, pirate." Geres grinned back.

Revelations suddenly hit him. Blackheart looked deep into Geres's eyes and asked, "Who are you really working for? It's not Prowl. You've shown him about as much love as a jilted dock whore. Who, then?"

Geres tilted his head back defiantly, jaw set and eyes hard.

Blackheart had seen the act before. A display of bravado designed to throw off the interrogator. Being no fool, Geres had to know how Blackheart was going to respond. The bigger man folded his thick arms across his chest and waited.

"I don't want to kill you, but you're not giving me much choice," Blackheart said after allowing a few moments of uncomfortable silence settle between them.

Geres leaned forward slightly, just enough to show his intent clearly. "He's going to betray you at the first opportunity."

"Who?"

It was Geres's turn to laugh. "You know."

Blackheart reached behind and banged on the door three times. It groaned open. "We're about to dock, where your fate will be decided. Don't wait too long to change your mind. It would be a shame to waste such potential."

Vicente Blackheart stalked off more troubled than before. There was little doubt about who Geres was talking about.

The *Shrike* docked a short while later. Drespai was a myth that romantics and fools fell in love with, a magical harbor where lawlessness and mayhem dominated. It was a lie the pirate clans allowed to perpetuate. The fewer who knew the truth, the better. Those less cautious suddenly disappeared. The fact that a physical place existed was almost anathema to conventional theory. Throw in how the platform was able to move around the universe at random and, more importantly, undetected, and the myth took on a cult following.

Blackheart stared out at the orbiting platform. It was an ugly thing, a discard from some failed Conclave design. Rumor had it the builders ran out of funding and left the hulk to rot in space. It certainly made sense, given how quickly the pirate clans had claimed it as salvage and turned it into their secretive meeting spot. The outer hull was battered from thousands of asteroids and minor engagements between arguing captains. The dull grey platform was three thousand meters long and five hundred at the widest. Roughly cylindrical, it boasted enough modified gun ports and docking bays to give it an odd radar signature.

Drespai should have fallen apart decades ago, breaking away and burning up in reentry a thousand times over. Any reputable contractor would be ashamed to have the hulking monstrosity credited to their name. Blackheart found the cold metal oddly comforting despite the ramshackle appearance. The void of rules offered freedom at a level that was incomparable anywhere he'd ever been. Even that wasn't enough.

Blackheart wanted the one thing he couldn't have. He wanted the glory and the power having a permanent seat on Vau Prime offered. He wanted what the Inquisitor General enjoyed daily. The indignity mocked him silently from unseen distances. He came from privileged beginnings but had quickly discovered that life wasn't earned. It was irritating having his every need and desire executed by someone else. There was no freedom, no self-indulgent liberty. Life was hollow. He left home young, hardly past his coming-of-age celebration.

A few years spent begging and scrapping for survival had taught him lessons his parents were never able to. He'd learned how to live. Looking back, Blackheart was positive destiny wanted him for greatness, but it had to be on his terms. He discovered Drespai and signed on with a pirate crew. Once he'd gained enough experience and a healthy following of cutthroats and murderers, Vicente had killed his captain and taken his ship. He'd added "Blackheart" to his name and gone on a five-year rampage across the universe. It wasn't long before death penalties and wanted posters were spread over a hundred different planets. He had finally made a name for himself.

He stared out at the familiar platform without really seeing it. His mind replayed the last part of his conversation with Geres. Of course the man was talking about Therill. Truthfully, Blackheart would be disappointed in his First Mate if he didn't at least try to lead the crew in mutiny. That being said, he was disappointed in Therill's obvious behavior. He briefly contemplated removing Therill now, before matters grew complicated, but explaining it to the crew would not be easy. He blew out a deep breath from his pursed lips. There were simply too many variables keeping him from relaxing.

"Captain, we have been given clearance to dock."

He didn't bother looking at the helmsman. "Take us in."

Therill rose and said, "Several of the captains have already arrived. I counted thirteen ships confirmed to be docked."

"Good. The sooner we can have this meeting, the sooner we can be on our way. I don't want to —"

"Captain Blackheart, you have a coded message incoming from Vau Prime," the communications officer interrupted.

Blackheart dropped the hand propping up his head. His eyes widened. *This is unexpected.* "Are you certain of the point of origin?"

"Confirmed. It is encoded and for your eyes only."

Therill passed him a nervous look.

Good, be nervous, Therill. It might help you live longer. "Put it through to my quarters. I don't want to be disturbed."

"Aye, Captain."

The walk back to his private quarters was more troubling than the final few hours in deep-space transit and much longer than the thirty meters suggested. His door hissed closed behind, and he locked it before spooling up his data screen. Alain Nye's distorted image flickered on.

"Captain Blackheart, we have much to discuss," the Inquisitor General opened.

Blackheart laughed off his surprise. "I didn't think you were much interested in dealing with a lowly pirate."

"Matters change more often than we would like. The time that I required Ursal Prowl for has come."

"You mean the time that you wanted the pirate clans to waste their strength against a Prekhauten fleet has come," Blackheart countered suavely.

Nye's image hardened slightly. "One in your position lacks the ability to choose his battles. You wanted Prowl's task. It is time to perform. Unless, of course, you find a lack of support or willingness among your peers?"

"That's my concern."

"Not when it affects my designs, pirate," Nye scolded.

The smug bastard thinks he has the upper hand. Blackheart leaned back and offered his best smile, hoping to throw Nye off. "Considering you still haven't taken me into your confidence, I can't promise any support."

Nye paused, deliberating how much to tell. He steepled his hands in front of his face and began. "Inquisitor Prowl was sent to coordinate your clans for an attack on the main Prekhauten Fleet."

"You're not asking much," Blackheart balked. He didn't mind taking on an occasional cruiser or frigate, but the entire fleet was suicide.

"I'm not asking anything. This is your task."

Blackheart opened and then closed his mouth quickly, snapping off his thought. He frowned. "My clans will be decimated, even should we succeed. You're not giving me any incentive to cooperate."

A malicious smile leered back at him. "Your incentive will be full pardons for any man who survives to serve me."

"Again, there's no guarantee. A man of your quality should be expected to offer better terms."

"I have no doubt that I can, but those would be irrelevant to my needs. You pirates are filth, a stain upon the universe. What difference is it to me whether you live or die? Don't mistake my willingness to deal with you as acceptance." Nye glanced over his shoulder, as if an unseen someone was speaking to him.

Blackheart knew he was being set up, knew and could do nothing about it. Still, he had one final card to play. "Inquisitor General, I grow weary of this cat and mouse game. Transmit the details for your proposed attack, and I will reply shortly."

"Unacceptable. Perhaps I can give incentive," Nye said with a grin. "There is a Prekhauten fleet already dispatched to your current location. And, before you waste our time blustering or denying, we know you are currently orbiting planet Spindle. Your ships will be blown to pieces long before they have the chance to escape."

"You'd risk losing our support?"

"What support, exactly? I still haven't heard you commit," Nye replied. "Time is against you, Captain Blackheart."

You son of a bitch. Playing me all along. Blackheart decided to make his move. "Did Ursal mention how I got my start as a pirate? Oh, I was quite young. The ship I was on came across a great prize, a lone Inquisition frigate in deep space. I believe the name was the *LodSpear.*"

Nye visibly froze.

Blackheart blew off the look and continued. "We came in and caught them unawares. There were no survivors, naturally. We're pirates, after all. Oh, it wasn't anything spectacular. Just another raid, or so I thought at the time. Then I noticed the captain was acting off. We'd recovered a long box. It was made of a material I had never encountered."

"That box was property of the Inquisition," was all Nye managed.

"Was it? That's not the impression I got. In fact, we waited for your landing party to return from one of the larger asteroids in the Mefgelin Belt. If the box belonged to your Inquisition, it wasn't for very long. We brought it back to Drespai and added it to our accounts. It was quite some time before I saw it again, but I could never shake the image from my mind. Curiosity got the best of me.

"I decided to mutiny. I convinced most of the crew to join me, and then I personally murdered the captain. It was the only way to gain access to the accounts, and the box." He paused, giving Alain time to digest this revelation. "You don't know what's in the box, do you?"

"As you said, it was only in our possession for a brief moment."

"Of course. There was no way I could have prepared myself for what greeted me when I finally summoned the courage to open the box. It was…remarkable."

Nye shifted uncomfortably. "Is there a point to all of this?"

"My point is that I have, in my possession, a weapon capable of reducing your precious fleet to burned-out hulls drifting through space."

Alain broke out in light laughter.

"I don't recall saying anything humorous," Blackheart snapped.

"If you had such a weapon, you would have used it by now," Nye countered. "Now who plays games? The fleet will be there in two days. That gives you more than enough time to deploy your battle groups into prearranged coordinates around Hawker's Gate where they will wait for the main Prekhauten fleet to arrive. Time is your enemy, Blackheart, just as much as I am. Do this for me, and I will pardon you all."

Try as he did, Blackheart failed to find any other viable option. There was no way he'd be able to fight off a fully armed battle fleet. The casualties would be too high, even amongst men who'd rather butcher each other than combine forces. The clans would never recover. Truthfully, he had no choice.

"Very well. Send me the details. You'll have your war, Inquisitor General," he relented. "But I want Prowl."

Nye feigned giving the idea consideration. "Agreed. It would be best if you had him killed, of course. He is a dangerous man to have underfoot."

"I don't need your approval on who I can kill."

"Now you do," Nye replied smoothly. "All pertinent data will be streamed to a secure location. Do not attempt to contact me until after you have completed your task. Oh, and Vicente, please ensure Ursal Prowl suffers before he dies."

The image dissolved, leaving a very confused and angered Blackheart alone in the dark.

TWENTY-TWO

3212 A.G. (After Gods), the Wells, planet An'kuruku.

Elisa awoke clutching her stomach. Her muscles ached. Her bones felt like they were grating on each other. Breathing was difficult. The beating Tanzeil's men had administered left her sore, immobile. Self-preservation instincts cried for her to give up, to abandon the notion of fighting for her freedom. She couldn't. Ah'muf depended on her. He was still weak from the scorpion attack, and she suspected Tanzeil was keeping him that way to keep Elisa in line. So far, it was working.

She hadn't seen Ah'muf since being herded onto the skiffs the night before. She didn't even know if he was still alive. The uncertainty ate at her. There'd been plenty of times when she'd found herself helpless, most memorably when she was a prisoner of the Ugri. But even then, there had been the slightest chance of escape. Elisa couldn't find hope in any aspect of her current situation.

She forced herself into a sitting position and scanned her immediate surroundings. Tanzeil was keeping her in a large cage, probably used for large animals, at the far edge of the camp. A few of the more curious had come by to see the redhead personally. Even fewer had ever seen a woman with fire-colored hair. The absurdity of it was insulting. She was being treated like a zoo animal, a beast imprisoned for the amusement and enjoyment of the masses. Fresh anger blossomed in her heart. She vowed, for the thousandth time, to kill Tanzeil before leaving An'kuruku.

She made an aborted attempt at stretching before the lances of pain sped through her torso. Lost in the haze of her own agony, Elisa barely recognized the screams and cries of battle coming from the opposite side of the camp. The Wells were under attack. She judged this was the way things were, basing her opinions off the way Tanzeil and his tribe had brutalized their path into the camp. Conflict seemed to be a large part of life in the deep deserts. Elisa opened her eyes and focused on the unmistakable clash of steel on flesh.

The night had grown cold, but she was too engrossed in discovering the source of the conflict to shiver. New hope sprung to life. Her chance at escaping had risen sharply. If only she wasn't all but crippled with pain. Elisa scowled. Gritting her teeth, she half-dragged herself across the cage to the lock. The bars were far enough apart that she could slip through, but, as she'd painfully learned earlier, they were also electrified by some strange, blue power. The fingertips on her left hand were blackened as proof.

The screams were getting closer. Elisa looked up, hope twinkling in her eyes. A tent collapsed. Flames burst up from another. A trio of armed guards fled past her cage. Fear dominated their faces. One dropped his sword, too far away to be of any use to her.

Elisa thought she caught a flicker of movement. A shadow stalking through the darkness. She finally shivered. Had death come to claim what was long overdue? The weakness struggling to maintain control over her soul begged for it. She was tired, physically and emotionally. Life had been unkind through most of her experiences. Sweet release offered to relieve her of the endless cycle of torment hounding her.

A loud crash, like thunder booming across the camp, made her jump. The broken remains of one of Tanzeil's men flopped through the sky before crashing into the bars of her cage. Sparks exploded, singeing her face and hair. She shrieked and rolled back. The guard gave a strangled gasp before the blue power disintegrated the flesh from his bones. What remained of his skeleton clattered down in a random heap. Elisa stared, suddenly very afraid.

A large shadow detached from the surroundings. Elisa looked up at a figure twice as tall as she was. *No!* That old horror awakened, terrifying her. The godling had come back to finish what had begun five decades ago. Dressed in black, the figure was nearly indistinguishable from the night. Elisa sat helpless as the figure stopped on the opposite side of the bars.

"I have seen you before."

It took a moment before Elisa realized the voice belonged to a woman. *A woman? That's not possible. I've seen the Three, and they are all men. Who or what is this?* "What do you want with me?"

"They were going to kill you."

That crippling fear subsided briefly. She was more terrified of the concept that a person could be so large and not be trying to kill her. "People do that, from time to time. Who are you?"

Paradise Tear knelt, respectfully. "It is true. Your hair is the color of flames. I did not think to find one like you in the desert."

"You're one of them, aren't you?" Elisa asked suddenly. The desire to know agonized her.

Paradise cocked her head. "One of whom?"

"The gods." Elisa's voice fell off to a whisper.

"I am not a god. Can you walk?"

Elisa reeled from shock. *Not a god? How many other giants that we don't know about roam the universe?* She found the thought appalling. "Show me your face."

"Is that important?"

"I'm not going anywhere with you until I see your face," Elisa said defiantly.

Paradise Tear slowly removed the thin fabric veiling her face. The realization that the human woman crouching before her had seen others of her kind ignited a spark of fear. The thought that Amongeratix might already be looking for her was frightening beyond words. How many lifetimes had it been since she'd first gone on the run? She'd lost track. All she knew was that he mustn't find her. The alternative would destroy the universe.

Elisa gasped as she looked on the most beautiful woman she'd ever seen. The classic beauty was etched upon a million statues, sung by bards, and written in the prose of countless poets. Strong jaw lines ran up to high cheekbones. The eyes, an immaculate blue, were soft and perfectly rounded. There wasn't a blemish on her perfect skin. The slope of her nose accented the fullness of her lips. Elisa hadn't thought such a being could actually exist.

"Satisfied?" Paradise asked.

A nod. "Why do you want me?"

"I don't know. All I know is that you must not die. I need you to come with me. We must leave now if you want to live."

Elisa shook her head. "I'm not leaving without Ah'muf."

Paradise paused before remembering the rest of her vision. "You are referring to the local man who traveled with you?"

"Yes. Ah'muf is my closest friend, only I don't know where he is being kept."

A crisp sigh followed a furtive glance in each direction, but Paradise rose stiffly. "I will find him, but you must be ready to move."

"The cage is energized," Elisa offered.

Paradise brandished her short sword and hacked through the locking mechanism on the door. "I shall return shortly."

She dashed off, leaving Elisa more confused than before.

She had no way of knowing just how much time had passed before the tall blonde stranger returned carrying a sedated Ah'muf. Elisa almost cried out in joy. Still weak, she found it nearly impossible to stand.

"We must leave," Paradise restated.

Elisa nodded. "I can barely walk. They beat me badly."

Paradise Tear entered the cage and gently lifted her off the ground. She winced at the sharpness digging into her side but kept her pain silent. One body over each shoulder, Paradise moved through the camp surrounding the Wells like a giant scorpion. Elisa wasn't sure, but she could have sworn she looked down on Tanzeil's broken and bloodied corpse before passing out.

The sharp light hurt her eyes, forcing her to bury her head beneath the down-filled pillows. Elisa tried going back to sleep but found the act pointless, despite the luxuriousness of the bed. The sheets were smooth as silk, finer than anything she had ever slept on. The pillows were almost too soft, and the blankets left her feeling soothed, relaxed, and like a queen. She yawned and stretched, surprised that the pain was gone. Her eyes narrowed to slits. The last time she was shown kindness had turned out to be less than expected. Suspicious, Elisa sat up and looked for any sort of weapon.

The double doors opened, and a pair of women dressed in pure white robes glided in with welcoming smiles. Both had dark hair and golden bronze skin, the product of growing up in the deep desert. One had a porcelain basket full of fruit and nuts. The other carried a crystal pitcher of water. They set the gifts down and patiently folded their hands across their waists.

"Do you require anything else?" the taller one asked.

"Where am I?" Elisa asked after they finished.

"You are safe. This is the abbey of the Wells."

Recognition flashed. "The violence…"

"Was regrettable, but it has passed. You must be very special for *her* to come for you personally."

"Who is she?"

The woman lowered her eyes meekly. "It would be best if she were to tell you."

Elisa frowned. She felt confused. These women weren't afraid of the mysterious woman but weren't willing to talk openly about her. Her mind was still too clouded — from painkillers, she concluded — to grasp the implications.

"Will I be seeing her soon?" Elisa asked, the need to know compelling her.

"Yes, mistress. She shall arrive shortly."

The women bowed again and excused themselves, leaving Elisa alone and more confused than she had been. Never one for games, Elisa preferred to tackle matters head on without guile or subterfuge. She still felt imprisoned, despite the simple opulence of her surroundings. Fearing she'd traded one jail for another, Elisa looked for a way out.

A new pain speared through her stomach. She didn't remember the last time she'd eaten. The fruit was fresh, grown and picked from the abbey's gardens. Elisa slid from the sheets and padded across the marble floor. *What sort of monk lives in such splendor? There are thousands mired in poverty, terrorized by nomadic clans of men barely more advanced than barbarians, and these monks live like gods.* She paused. Gods. Of course. The tall woman must be one of them. But how? The gods were asleep, trapped in suspended animation, all but forgotten relics. *So why is this one here, and awake?*

Elisa ate slowly, lest she make herself sick. The nuts were already shelled and had a sweet taste unlike anything she'd eaten before. She made fast work of the small container of dates despite never having acquired a taste for them. Hunger forced her hands. The random assortment of exotic fruits was much like those found in every street market and bazaar in Tenemenah. The water was surprisingly cool, despite having been sitting out for close to an hour. The desert heat was already beating down on the abbey, promising to get worse before dusk.

She'd finished eating before it dawned on her that she was naked. The hanging wall mirror was not kind. Elisa stared at her painfully thin body with regret. The lower half of her ribcage protruded sickly into her skin. She was still too pale, her shoulders covered with freckles. Blue veins made her self-conscious. Her hair was stringy, dried out. It had been years since she had allowed herself to be pampered. She turned from the mirror with a heavy sigh and slid into the thin robe hanging off the back of the nearest chair. The doors opened a moment later.

Her natural reaction was to draw back and ready for an attack. The giant woman flowed into the room with natural grace that left Elisa feeling jealous. She was everything a proper lady was supposed to be, not the wastrel Elisa had allowed herself to become.

"Good, you've eaten," the blond said with a genuine smile.

Elisa merely nodded, still too stunned to think clearly.

"Where are you from?"

"Very far away, from the planet Crimeat," she replied.

The blond thought for a moment. "I am not familiar with it. You might have guessed that I am not from here, either. Funny, isn't it? How life moves in seemingly random directions without our concern. Faith is required if we are to find any positive meaning in life."

"You still haven't answered my question," Elisa said boldly.

The warmth in the smile spread through Elisa unexpectedly. "Which question? I was distracted last night."

"Who are you?"

The blond nodded crisply. "Ah, yes, that. Truthfully, I wouldn't know where to begin. Much of what I knew, the core of who I am, has been lost."

"You could start with a name."

"My name is Paradise."

Elisa's eyes flew open. It couldn't be. Nervously, she asked, "Paradise Tear?"

Paradise smiled again. "Yes, that's right. How did you know?"

Exhaling sharply, Elisa sat down to calm her shaking knees and began the long, confusing explanation.

Paradise paced the length of the room, weaving around the rows of marble columns stretching the full height of the ceiling. Ten feet tall, she still had room to spare without ducking or worrying about hitting her head. Elisa's story had been devastating to hear. Much of what she'd once believed had unraveled. The Three, as humanity named them, were neither the monsters nor the saviors mankind believed. Paradise knew the truth, that the brothers were victims of their own greed. It wasn't the first time people had grown corrupted. She blamed it on their status as sons of the king. Not enough people were willing to tell them no.

"It's been centuries since I last saw any of them. That time seems so distant, almost a negligible memory. The war changed things," Paradise said suddenly.

"It changed more than just your world. I grew up without a family because of one of your kind," Elisa accused. She wanted to hate Paradise but found she couldn't. Years of pent-up rage, misunderstanding and hatred suddenly dissipated in the presence of the stunning woman sitting opposite her.

Paradise wiped a tear away. "I cannot take responsibility for his actions, but I will promise my cooperation and support to you until the coming confluence is past. The man you came here with, not Ah'muf but the other, the haggard one, he is not far."

"Mollock Bolle?"

"Yes. He has grown into an important figure, or so I gather from people passing through. They say he stands on the shores of the Bo and preaches against your gods. My father has gone to learn the truth in this. My heart tells me he is part of something larger than any here comprehend."

"Father? I thought all of your kind were gone," Elisa asked.

She offered a sad smile in return. "He is the closest thing I have to a father. People in the Deeves used to seek his wisdom and advice. Now they have abandoned him for the depredations of Mollock Bolle and his cult. War is much closer than any of them think."

"Can we stop it?"

"I don't know."

Elisa shook her head, hoping to clear her thoughts. The cycle of events begun on Crimeat were restarting here. She tried to think why the Bloody Man had insisted on sending her to An'kuruku. There had to be more than just finding Paradise Tear. One being didn't have the ability to shape or change the future. For the last two years, she'd believed she was searching for a jewel or a weapon to use against the Three. There was no way she'd ever be prepared to accept she was searching for a woman.

Instead of answers, Elisa had found twice as many questions. Nothing made sense. The Three weren't here and, more than likely, were not coming. So why send her on a hunt to find Paradise? Worse, what was Mollock Bolle doing? He'd been named the Prophet, in the same manner as she had been named the Paladin. Clearly, the Bloody Man had intended her to be a protector, but from what she'd witnessed last night, Paradise needed no protecting. If anything, it was the other way around.

Prophet. Mollock was certainly living up to the name if what she'd just been told was true. Elisa was at a loss. She'd distanced herself from him purposefully, though for her own reasons. She was still fighting the idea of being a servant of the Three, much less the proposed champion Sorrow claimed. The direction of her life had been altered irredeemably because of the monsters. There was no way she would willing serve their cause.

"Did you hear me?" Paradise asked.

Elisa looked up slowly, her eyes slightly glazed. "I'm sorry. I drifted off."

"I understand." And she truly did. Learning the universe was not what you had made it out to be was daunting, frightening. Paradise found herself in a mirrored position. The only difference was that she was being hunted for an old sin. "I said that it would be best if I were to take you to the Bone Father. He will be able to help you in your quest."

Elisa wasn't sure how anyone with "bone" in his title could possibly be a positive influence, but she was running out of options. A nagging feeling in the back of her mind told her to go to the Bo to confront Mollock and his cult. The answers to everything tormenting her for the past two years were there, nestling in the ruins of an age gone by and dripping the manipulations of words only Mollock understood. Elisa sighed. She hated having the ability to choose for herself stripped away.

"There is more you should know," Paradise added quietly. "An army has been raised and is preparing to march against the peasants gathered to hear the Prophet."

"An army? What army? There isn't that much military strength on An'kuruku," Elisa replied, confused.

"They are called the Prefects."

"Prefects?" Elisa was shocked. The very reason she had dragged Ah'muf out of his safe tavern and to the edge of death. Every decision she'd made since leaving Crimeat had turned out to be wrong. Now, the man she had genuine feelings for, the one man she had ever come close to being in love with, was about to die in the very war she'd struggled to avoid. Paladin indeed. She was a poor excuse for a champion, and she knew it.

Paradise cocked her head, studying the look in Elisa's eyes. She instantly grew concerned. "Don't lose yourself in doubts, Elisa. You have a great destiny before you. All it takes is for you to rise above yourself and become the woman you were meant to be. A great many lives depend on your next decision."

No pressure there. How'd she like it if I dropped a bomb on her dreams? Elisa struggled to swallow the rising anger, a bitter taste worse than bile. "I want to see Ah'muf first."

"He will not be able to travel with us. Moving him would likely kill him, though." Paradise took a tentative seat at the end of the bed and watched, helplessly, at the hurt etched on Elisa's face. "I'm sorry, Elisa."

"I want to see him."

Paradise rose. "Very well. I will await you in the hallway."

She left Elisa with too much to think about while she dressed. The need to see her friend was overwhelming, and Elisa hurried into her clothes and out the door.

"*Farisi*, I did not think to see you again," Ah'muf said as he struggled to sit up.

The pair of monks at his bedside gently forced him back down, one shaking her head in admonishment.

Elisa smiled grimly and sat beside him. "I found her, Ah'muf. I found Paradise Tear." Tears clogged the corners of her eyes, threatening to stream down her face.

Ah'muf, his ribs heavily bandaged, struggled to smile. "That is wondrous news! Where is it?" he asked.

She noticed half of his moustache had been removed, whether from his imprisonment by Tanzeil's men or the abbey's surgeon, she didn't know. "It is a she, not an it. She is waiting in the hallway. In fact, she's the one who rescued us. Without her, we'd already be sold as slaves." *Or worse.*

"What of Tanzeil?"

Finally, news she could deliver happily. "Dead, along with all of his tribe. They were not nice people."

Ah'muf nodded, painfully. "Such is the way of the desert. The sands give, and the sands take away. They got what they deserved."

He gasped suddenly and shifted his weight. The pain killers were wearing off, leaving him in nearly unbearable agony. Poison continued to course through him despite the best efforts of the surgeons. Ordinary scorpion venom was treatable, but Tanzeil had concocted a particularly dangerous poison.

Elisa sniffed back a sob. "Ah'muf, I need to leave for a while. There is a task I must do, but I will be back. I promise."

"Let me get my things, and I shall travel with you," he wheezed between strained breathes. Fresh waves of pain twisted his face.

"No, I need you to rest here. Get your strength back. When I return, I will take you away, perhaps back to my world," she smiled.

His eyes twinkled, slightly. "I would like that. I've never been off An'kuruku."

She leaned forward and kissed his lips. The impulse of it shocked them both, her the most. Elisa closed her eyes and enjoyed the feeling of her lips meshing into his. The feeling was delicious. Warmth spread through her. She felt lightheaded, like her breath was being taken away.

Her spirit lifted, leaving her with an intense sensation of euphoria. It was unlike anything she'd ever felt. And it ended much too quickly.

"I promise I'll be back for you," she whispered.

He smiled before closing his eyes. Elisa left quickly, lest temptation kept her at the Wells. Paradise Tear already had a skiff waiting. It was similar to the massive barge-like ones Tanzeil had used but much smaller and with slightly better accommodations. A pair of cushioned seats filled the small cabin. The back deck stretched out twenty feet or so, plenty of room to hold supplies and equipment. Paradise had the foresight to load enough supplies and weapons to keep the pair in the field for a few weeks. Elisa rushed past her and took the empty seat. Obvious questions went unasked. Sometimes it was best not to know.

The skiff raced west. The uneven desert terrain gradually gave way to scrub brush and more solid ground. Golden peaks of sand transformed into dirt. The unfamiliar aroma of the ocean met them, and Paradise grew giddy. Elisa leaned her head back and smelled deeply. She'd never seen the ocean before. The promise of the Bo, the mystical body of life-giving water the people of the Deeves had flocked to for countless centuries, offered her redemption. She felt the weight slip from her shoulders.

Her thoughts turned more serious. Mollock Bolle awaited what promised to be a less than pleasant reunion. Elisa hadn't anticipated crossing a growing cult and an army of zealous Prefects. Life continued to deal from the bottom of the deck, leaving her with doubts about her true purpose. Even the hardest-pressed champions from all the stories had those rare shining moments where the stars aligned to help them succeed against impossible odds. Elisa wondered when it was going to be her turn.

The fetid smell of downtrodden humanity soon drowned out the freshness of the Bo. Unwelcome noise broke the spell of the ocean, leaving her with a sour feeling. They'd traveled through the night to arrive at the shore of the Bo and the filth that had taken over. It never failed to amaze Elisa how poorly her kind took care of themselves when thrown together in large numbers with little wealth or supplies. Thousands had to be assembled, most of the population of the Deeves. Great sadness welled inside her. No one deserved to live like this.

"How?" she asked, more to herself than Paradise.

Paradise Tear shook her head sadly. "They have forgotten what it means to be free. So twisted are Mollock Bolle's words that he has stolen from them the one thing that makes humanity special."

"What's that?"

She looked Elisa deeply in the eyes. "Free will."

Elisa had no reply. Again, more questions came to life. What misery had befallen Paradise to dim her view of life?

Paradise slowed the skiff as they eased into more densely populated areas. Heads turned their way. Strangers were welcome, but only if they had come to praise the Prophet. Elisa subconsciously reached for her sidearm.

"We won't need that, not yet," Paradise told her. "I'm going to pull off to the side once we get past the main village and go look for the Bone Father."

"Leaving me to guard the skiff?" Elisa asked.

"Yes. These are genuinely not bad people; they have simply fallen under the sway of manipulative words delivered by a gifted speaker. We must take great care not to harm them."

Elisa grimaced with doubt. "Unless they don't give me a choice."

Paradise smiled, shaking her head slightly. "You will be fine, Elisa. I'll return as soon as I find him."

Elisa left the obvious reply unspoken. She pulled the skiff to a stop and settled in for what she assumed was going to be a long wait. After all, nothing went smoothly when the promise of violence loomed on the horizon.

Althas Pey watched with grim satisfaction as the army of the Prefecture marched out of Tenemenah. Most of them would not return. They lacked proper training and even the most basic military equipment. Not that they'd be a great loss. Althas saw this campaign as a cleansing. The wastes and unwanted, on both sides of the conflict, were about to be purged, opening the way for the more eager and deserving to rise through the ranks. He had no issues with sacrificing the great majority so long as he accomplished the tasks set to him by Lezorsu.

Momentary thoughts of returning triumphantly and removing the head Prefect by force danced through his head. Althas Pey was a hungry man, always searching for the next position, the next challenge. Removing Lezorsu would be troublesome, but he'd have more than enough support from the Prefects he was taking to the Deeves. The idea was tempting, but now was not the right time. Soon, he promised himself. Soon.

Lezorsu stalked out of the command building, his face a mirror of intensity. His eyes were so focused they nearly eclipsed the rest of his face. He stopped beside Althas. "It is time."

"The last units are boarding the sky skiffs now. We should be at the shores of the Bo in less than a week," Althas told him.

Lezorsu looked up at the taller man. "Break them, Althas. Bring me back an ocean of blood. This rebellion should never have happened."

"We've had this discussion, Lezorsu. My men are prepared to act accordingly. I will send word back when we make contact."

Lezorsu, named Doomspell by the masses, gave a wicked leer. "No need. I will be deploying with the forward command element. I want to witness their final moments for myself. This will be a moment long remembered."

Althas Pey clicked his tongue gently. This was most unexpected and unorthodox. He shifted his stance uncomfortably and waited for the senior Prefect to continue.

"Bring glory back to the Prefecture, Althas. Succeed, and I will have statues erected in your honor."

Althas Pey saluted crisply, without feeling, and watched his superior stalk off. Matters had just gotten more complicated.

TWENTY-THREE

3212 A.G. (After Gods), Hawker's Gate, deep space.

"Get the gods-damned Inquisitor back on the radio!" Fies snarled as another ion round sizzled into the wall behind him. He popped up and fired off a trio of rounds in reply, rewarded by the cut-off cry of someone dying.

Annalilly tied off a strip of cloth on the burn wound striping her right bicep. She was cursing more than Fies had ever heard. The attack had come without warning, and if it hadn't been for his combat reflexes, she would have taken the round to the chest rather than merely grazing her arm.

"I'm trying to, but the signal is jammed," she snapped back angrily.

Fuck! Fies fired again. Aiming was a waste of time. The main marketplace on Hawker's Gate was filled with armed militants eager to test their skills against the under-armed Prekhauten Guards. The change was sudden and unexpected. One moment, he and Annalilly were going through the motions of scouting out the station, preparing to answer Breed's summons, and the next, they were surrounded by near impossible odds.

Using an overturned cloth vender cart, he and Annalilly cursed the Inquisitor's decision to have them go in undercover. "Can you see a lane out?"

"No, they've got the whole damned plaza sealed off. I'm fine, by the way," she shouted.

He winced. Emotions had no place in combat, and his feelings for her were only going to muddle his decision-making capabilities as the firefight went on. Unless, of course, the enemy killed them first.

"Can you raise any of the others? Beve, Jers?"

She shot him a withering glare that said *what part of the signal is jammed don't you understand?* He frowned and swung around to the opposite side of the cart. Sporadic rounds scorched the air around his head. Fies took satisfaction from his enemy not actually aiming. Clearly amateurs, they were content with volume over accuracy. Three of their number had already paid the price for their complacency. He drew a bead on a long-bearded man with eyes too large for his square face and fired.

The ion round struck him just below the throat, a spray of blood and steam puffing up from the wound as the body dropped back.

"Do you see an exit, or are we just going to sit here and wait for them to kill us?" Annalilly asked. She spit a mouthful of blood from the cut on her tongue she'd received diving under the initial barrage.

"I can't tell. Looks like we might be able to squeeze out down that corridor if we had a distraction."

Annalilly smiled and removed the thermal grenade from her jacket pocket. "You mean like this?"

"What are you doing with that? I said no heavy weapons on station," Fies said angrily. He tried to feel genuine anger but knew the grenade was potentially going to save their lives.

"You didn't think I was going to leave everything to chance?"

He nodded. "We'll deal with that later. Throw it about twenty meters to the right when I give you the signal, and then stay on my ass when it detonates."

"Try keeping up with me." She pressed the activation button, holding down the pressure plate.

Fies gave a quick look, identifying the largest group of enemy. "Twenty-five meters on your one o'clock," he told Annalilly.

She nodded and cocked her arm back.

Fies fired three rounds at three targets, forcing the enemy to duck. "Now!"

Annalilly threw the grenade as hard as she could, and accurately. It detonated less than a second after hitting the deck in the middle of a group of close to ten combatants. Flame and shrapnel eviscerated everything in a fifteen-meter radius. Bodies were reduced to a dull pink mist. The sonic detonation pounded Annalilly's eardrums, nearly knocking her unconscious. Fies snatched her by the collar and ran.

No return fire came back at them. Whatever was left of the enemy was too disoriented to react. Fies grinned fiercely. Civilians should know better than to play at being soldiers. He shot a wounded woman in the chest before she could drag herself up to aim the aged long rifle in her hands.

Both Guards were clear moments later and dashing down the empty corridor. Aside from the combatants, there was no other foot traffic. The population clearly knew what was happening and supported it. He'd worry about that later. Now he needed to figure out how to get in contact with the rest of his platoon and regroup while the enemy was still moderately disorganized.

They kept running without encountering anyone until reaching what remained of the customs station. Bodies lay draped over consoles and desks where they'd been gunned down mercilessly. Fies ducked inside while Annalilly covered from a few meters away. He quickly surveyed the rooms, coming back disappointed.

"Anything useful?" she asked.

"Nothing. They trashed the communications panels. We couldn't reach anyone if we wanted to."

Annalilly looked back down the long corridor. Burn marks from dozens of ion rounds lined the walls. At least the customs agents didn't die without a fight. "What's our next move?"

He looked around, hope quickly dwindling. Common sense said to get back on the *Indomitable* and get their weapons and armor. That would be great for him and Annalilly, but without the rest of the platoon, he'd only be wasting time and jeopardizing the lives of his Guards. He needed combat power, and that meant finding his Guards, if any were still alive.

Fies grabbed a beat-up ion rifle the combatants must have overlooked and checked the charge. "Let's go hunting."

She knew, as well as he did, that there wasn't an exfiltration plan in place. Annalilly was opposed to random searching but realized the docking sleeves were more than likely under guard and the *Indomitable* unaware of the current situation, leaving little choice. She followed Fies back down the corridor and into the hell Hawker's Gate had become.

Jers cried out when Beve slammed him to the ground, combat knife in hand. The smaller Guard was about to let lose a string of curses when an unarmed man leapt at them. Beve plunged his blade to the hilt in the man's chest and twisted to let momentum pull the body free, then dropped into a hand-to-hand fighting stance.

Jers, still confused and now sore, looked up at the heavy weapons specialist. "You almost dislocated my shoulder, you son of a bitch. What was that?"

"We're under attack," Beve said in his usual monotone voice.

Jers looked down at the twisted corpse by his feet. A growing pool of blood was spreading from the wound. "I can see that, but by whom?"

"Doesn't matter. We need to leave."

Drawing his sidearm, Jers rolled up to his knees and then scanned their immediate surroundings. Most of the crowd in the food court was hurrying towards the exits. He cursed again. This was not good.

"Can you see anyone else?" he asked.

Beve shook his head.

"I say we try to link up with some of the others and find out what is going on," Jers suggested. He could have given an order by virtue of rank but didn't see the need. As of now, it was just the two of them. Rank had no place even though Beve would be expecting him to come up with a solid plan. Jers wasn't the type who wanted to be in charge, but he had no problem reacting to a bad situation.

"Which way?" Beve asked. He now had both hands full, one with a knife, the other a pistol.

Jers wasn't entirely sure, but the look on Beve's face warned the big man was barely containing his rage. *Gods help us all if Beve gets pissed off enough to unleash.* "Back to the central market area."

"I've got three armed men moving in from the east."

Beve left the second part unsaid. They were obviously being hunted. Whoever was in charge knew who they were looking for and where to find them.

The pair headed out, moving slowly. Jers hoped he'd guessed correctly. Otherwise, it was going to be a very long day.

Haggle put down the portable data device and rummaged through illegal copies of favorite movies and holodramas. He was already bored with the assignment and growing increasingly agitated with Kedric and his unending string of questions. Haggle wondered if he had annoyed his team leader when he'd first been assigned a regular unit and babysitting the new guy was some sort of twisted karma.

"How about this one?" Kedric asked from the back rack of disks.

Haggle rolled his eyes without looking. "Guardsman Kedric, we're not here to go shopping. This is a recon mission. At least pretend to be looking out for potential threats."

Kedric lowered his eyes, some of the fire going out of them after the scolding. He wasn't much younger than Haggle, each Guard having to go through an average of seven years of waiting just to begin training, but he lacked experience. This was his first real-time mission.

"Sorry, Kedric," Haggle relented. "I know it's not easy being the new guy. We've all been there at some point. This mission has my nerves on edge. I don't like fighting in enclosed areas. Don't mind me."

"No, I know I've been asking too many questions," Kedric said.

Haggle offered a thin smile. *Maybe the kid has potential after all.* "Come on. We need to hurry up and get back to Sergeant Fies."

Neither knew where deck P 12 was, or even the transit tubes, for that matter. Haggle tried to comm Fies, jerking his head wildly at the loud burst of static flooding his earpiece.

"Everything ok?" Kedric asked, nervousness creeping into his voice as he started to notice the massive amounts of people clearing away.

"I don't know. I can't raise anyone on the net."

"Look at everyone leaving," Kedric said.

Haggle did and felt that familiar feeling he didn't like. Something bad was about to happen.

"You need to leave now," whispered a young woman half-hiding behind a stack of different colored bolts of cloth. Fear bleached her face, and her shoulders had a slight tremble.

"What's going on here?" Haggled asked just as quietly.

She looked around furtively, as if expecting a knife in the back any moment. "The word has gone out. They are hunting you."

"Hunting us?"

Her eyes widened, their softness filled with tears. "Go now before it's too late!"

"Over there!"

Haggle cried in pain before the sound of the shot registered. Blood fountained from a thigh wound, dropping him to the deck. Kedric drew his weapon and dropped into a good kneeling position. It took too long to identify the shooter, but by then it didn't matter. Dozens of men and women, all armed, were marching down the corridor at them. He fired into the crowd, felling several before jerking Haggle up and dragging him away.

The vertical tube hissed shut and began going up to deck P 12. Tolde stood with a stiff back, hands patiently folded across his waist while Luma tried to get as much information out of Bethis as she could.

"How many guards does Von have?"

Bethis cocked his head thoughtfully. "That depends. She's a very secretive woman. At times, she is surrounded by guards; other times, she goes alone. One man never leaves her side, August the eunuch. He is her go-to man."

Luma frowned. "Why haven't we heard this before? If he's half the man you suggest, he's a dangerous target."

"Not to mention a very valuable one," Tolde interjected. "We could use him to turn the tide here."

Bethis flicked his gaze from Luma to Tolde. A nervous tick jerked the right corner of his mouth repeatedly. His breathing turned shallow. His muscles felt tight. "I'm afraid you won't."

Tolde reacted without thought. His right hand hacked Bethis across the throat while drawing his sidearm with his left. Bethis gagged, eyes bulging from the force of the blow. Spittle and phlegm sprayed from his mouth.

"What in…" Luma started to ask as she automatically slid back a step and armed herself.

Tolde ignored her, striking Bethis twice more in the head and throat. Luma knew better than to second-guess an Inquisitor's instinct and hit the stop button. The tube slid to a stop at the next level, the pneumatic door hissing open. Bethis struggled to get away, a hand snaking towards his outer jacket pocket. Tolde kicked down hard on Bethis's right knee, snapping it at an awkward angle.

"Keep his hands away from that pocket," he ordered crisply.

She stepped on Bethis's hand, applying enough pressure to keep him immobile. "What's going on, Tolde?"

"He was about to detonate."

"What?"

"Remove his jacket. He's got an explosive device in that pocket."

Luma roughly stripped Bethis of the flat brown jacket, pulling clumps of hair out as she jerked it over his head. She noticed Tolde step back and then looked down. Her jaw dropped. Bethis was rigged with enough explosives to destroy a battle cruiser.

"A suicide bomber?" she asked.

Tolde nodded. "It appears so."

Bethis gasped through the pain, taking advantage of their momentary confusion to reach for the secondary detonator switch attached to the front of his vest. The ion round burned into his forehead, punching out the back of his head even as he heard Tolde shout, "Secondary detonator!"

Gore and brain matter speckled Luma's boots.

"Tolde, what's going on?"

He knelt, examining the suicide vest. "This is not homemade. He had help."

"Presha Von," she seethed.

"Most likely. I think we're too late to catch Von."

"We need to move quickly. There's no telling who else is in her pockets," Luma said. Her red hair shimmered brightly in the luminescent corridor lighting. "Do you think Felp betrayed us?"

"No. He was much too nervous. I fear the same is already marching towards him. We need to regroup the Guards and request backup."

"The fleet is due to arrive soon," she offered.

"Not soon enough to help. We're going to have to do this on our own for now, unless there are any security elements still loyal," Tolde replied darkly. "Sergeant Fies and his Guards should be en route to P 12. We meet them there and strike out for the operations center."

Inquisitor Luma Kai followed Tolde, silently questioning what she had gotten in to. Nothing in her limited experience as an Inquisitor had prepared her for an insurrection on this level. She subconsciously checked the charge level in her sidearm and exhaled a long breath.

The series of concussion grenades knocked Matthias to the floor. Dust and small bits of construction debris filtered down from the ceiling. The deck continued to tremble long after the concussions ceased. The Jhedge relaxed his grip on the small counter he'd anchored himself to. Horror reflected from his shimmering eyes. Clearly this wasn't supposed to happen so soon.

"What was that?" he asked.

"It has begun. We must move quickly if this station is to remain in the Conclave," Gedrick Silk said quickly. His skin flashed from dark black to a shade of purple Matthias had never seen.

Matthias pulled himself up, ignoring the myriad aches and pains shooting through his body. He hated getting old. "What's happening? Speak plainly, Jhedge."

Gedrick shook his head. "Rengu is making their move. The Gate is no longer safe. You and your kind are going to be hunted."

"My kind? What is that supposed to mean?"

"Those loyal to the Conclave. The enemy is finally making their move to liberate Hawker's Gate and claim it as their own. War has come at last."

Still confused, Matthias began checking his weapons. He wasn't expecting to come marching into a fully developed combat situation but had served long enough in the Guard to be prepared for almost any eventuality. That didn't mean he appreciated being caught in the middle of another insurrection, though. "I need to get in touch with the Inquisitors that just docked. They have a contingent of Guards and enough firepower to hold off the insurgents."

Gedrick offered a sad look. "You do not understand the severity of the situation. There are very few here still loyal to the Conclave. No one recognizes the rule of the priests. That's why you don't see many walking the corridors. We are alone out here, and it is very far from Vau Prime. The cult of Rengu leaders know this and have been secretly building strength since your first visit with Tolde Breed all of those many years ago." He smirked at Matthias's shock. "Oh, yes. They know exactly who you are and that you are here now."

"Impossible," Matthias protested. "No one knows about me. I've been reprimanded and officially discharged."

"As I said, you are not safe here. Rengu is more powerful and connected than even your General Strannan has surmised. You are alone and outgunned."

That's never stopped me before. "I need to get to Tolde and the other Guards. Can you help me or not?"

The shape shifter paused, as if contemplating walking away with his life and abandoning his contract with Strannan. "My word is all I have. I will see you to the security office. Hopefully, someone will still be alive."

Those few security forces still wholly loyal to the Conclave were overwhelmed by the rush of twenty armed combatants bursting through the front doors of the main office. Small arms fire ricocheted off the walls, bouncing back to strike a handful of the attackers. Most of the guards went down quickly. Blood splattered the walls. The iron smell of death tainted the air. Three managed to hide under the bodies of their friends, men and women with whom they'd shared countless hours of patrols and potentially dangerous situations. None had been prepared for the high level of violence executed upon them.

Matthias stared down at what was left with a grimace. No one deserved to die like this, not even his worst enemy. He and Gedrick had killed a handful of insurgents along the mostly deserted route to the nearest security office. They'd also hidden from several others, making the trip longer than should have been necessary.

A quick look around the wreckage told the aging veteran all he needed to know. "The communication console is smashed, and the weapons locker has been raided. If my people came here, they didn't stay long."

"What do you wish to do?" Gedrick asked as he shifted into a child with pale skin and light blond hair.

Matthias looked down at him with concern but said nothing. "If I know these Guards, they'll be out on the station causing as much havoc as possible. Let's go hunting. Hopefully, we can hamper this Rengu's plans enough to get attention from Vau Prime."

Gedrick knew they were going to die.

"It is done," Okolo Mung said without emotion. His eyes drifted quickly across Presha's private office. Surprisingly, nothing seemed out of place. He'd assumed the office would be in total panic by now. That it wasn't was almost wrong. Much of what he'd seen on his return from the administratum suggested that any sane person should be running for the emergency exits by now — a thought not very far from his own mind.

Presha scarcely acknowledged him. She pored over schematics, analyzing possible avenues of approach and attack angles for the Prekhauten Guards Tolde Breed had brought to the Gate. She was infuriated with the man, although they'd never actually met. Her hatred and aggression stemmed from his bumbling through her carefully wrought plans back on Crimeat. That unsuspecting world should have been the glorious birth of the Rengu. Instead, it was a shallow reminder that she hadn't thought of everything. She was determined not to make the same mistake here.

"Felp was more annoying than harmful," she said dismissively.

Okolo ran his tongue over the tops of his upper teeth. He believed her ability to rationalize true threats was diminished. She'd sent him to kill Roule Felp, adamant that the overweight administrator would prove problematic when open rebellion was declared. Okolo had no qualms about killing the man. He'd killed hundreds over his career and expected to double that number before someone got him.

Okolo asked quietly, "Why kill a man if he's not a threat?"

Her head snapped up, and she fixed him with a vile glare. "Are you questioning me?"

His hands went up defensively. It would be a shame to have to kill her so early in the game. "I question what doesn't make sense to me."

"I'm not paying you to understand my motives, Mung. You are my hired killer. You go and kill whatever targets I give you. Nothing more. Don't make the mistake of overstepping your bounds." Presha lowered her gaze back to the blueprints stretched out across the aged cherry table. Thin grey streaks ran through her hair. Wrinkles and lines creased her once flawless face. She'd aged too much over the last two years. The temptations of power were draining her.

"Very well," he said nonchalantly. "Who do I eliminate next?"

Pressure finally getting the better of her, Presha sank down into the leather chair and ran a hand over her aching temples. Her breath grew shallower. Her skin had a pale gleam to it, almost unhealthy. "I don't know. I wasn't expecting a fully armed detachment of Guards arriving before we acted."

"A trivial thing at best. The Guards were bound to arrive, and in force. Defeat the unit here, and the pirate fleet will secure space around the Gate, preventing further assault units from arriving."

She dropped her hand and stared across the room at Mung. "Why do you do it?"

He shrugged, knowing immediately what she meant. "I am a creature of my surroundings. Killing makes sense to me, and, if I might indulge, I am quite good at it. Call it a natural gift from being a Mastieq. Why do you do what you do?"

Presha had no reply. It was the one question she was afraid to try and answer. "Find the Inquisitors. They will foil our plans at every turn, given the chance. They are relentless. Only by hunting them down will we be able to move ahead with focus." She failed to mention that she hadn't heard back from Bethis, suggesting the weaker aide was more than likely dead by now.

Okolo Mung nodded curtly. "I need to see current images and know something more about them. The Gate is a large place. They could be anywhere by now, if not already dead."

"No," she said slowly. "They aren't dead. I'd have their heads on display in the main docking bay if they were. See August. He can provide with all the information you require."

She leaned back slightly after he left and tried to relax. Despite the sudden rise of her nerves, all was going according to plan. The most recent communiqué from Vau Prime suggested the first of the pirate clan battle groups were already en route and scheduled to arrive shortly. Everything was going smoothly. So why couldn't she shake the gripping sickness twisting her stomach?

"Captain, we have multiple incoming warships!"

Falchi looked up almost nonchalantly at his helmsman. He'd been expecting as much. "The fleet is early."

"No, sir. None of the ships have Prekhauten transponders."

Falchi rose stiffly. "What?"

"They are hostiles."

"Sound general quarters. All hands to battle stations!" Falchi dropped his mug of half-drunk coffee. The ceramic shattered across the deck plating. "How long until weapons are online?"

The pause before the answer was entirely too long for his comfort. "Twenty minutes, sir. We were almost completely powered down."

Shit. He'd been caught unprepared for the second time in as many weeks. Falchi knew there wouldn't be a third time. Instincts subsumed the urge to panic. He was the captain of a Prekhauten Guard ship of war, not a weekend yacht pilot. Training for this type of situation had been ingrained in him for decades.

"Get me positive identification ASAP. We need to report back to Vau Prime," he barked as he slid into body armor held out by one of the ensigns. "Inform Inquisitor Breed that we need to disembark. He might not be able to make it back to the *Indomitable* in time."

"We're being jammed, sir!" the communications officer all but shouted.

Falchi's worst fears were confirmed. Any jammed communications suggested this was a coordinated attack, not mere coincidence. He stared intently at the view screen, desperate for visual recognition of the incoming fleet. The ragtag armada edged into view at a casual pace. No two were the same model. Falchi cursed. Pirates.

"I want a security detail deployed to the Gate with all of the weapons the undercover unit left behind. We can't afford to stay here. Full power to engines. Find us the nearest moon, and put it between us and the enemy fleet."

Heads turned to him, some questioning, others in disbelief. They'd never retreated before. Many found the idea insulting, a wound to their pride. Falchi knew there was no real choice. They could stay and maybe cripple one of the pirate ships, but the *Indomitable* would be shredded in the process. There were advantages to running, though not many. His only hope was the faint chance that he might get out of blocking range and raise the fleet before it walked into a trap.

TWENTY-FOUR

3212 A.G. (After Gods), the Deeves, planet An'kuruku.

"You were foolish to come here. They will kill you if you are discovered!" the Bone Father admonished.

Paradise knelt and hugged the old man regardless. Her smile was warm and genuine, not at all like his disturbed demeanor. After a time, he hugged her back.

"This place is changing you, father," she chided, trying to belay her legitimate concern.

His head drooped. "I do not like what is happening. The people of the Deeves are being deceived but are too blind to see it."

"People with free will are often the most dangerous animal," she reminded him, the words coming from an old conversation. "You can't control what any man thinks."

"It's not about control. I've never wanted to control anyone in my life, but I expect each of us to have the ability to reason and make educated decisions. Instead, they follow this prophet as blindly as a newborn babe. I fear for our future."

She leaned back, careful to duck low enough to avoid scraping her head against the roof of the human-sized tent. It pained her to see the man who had guarded and protected her for decades in such turmoil. He was lost. The blank look deep in his eyes suggested worse. Paradise sighed and hugged him again.

The Bone Father closed his eyes and leaned into her shoulder, lost in the solace her presence offered. He knew she was more than human but less than a god. She was the closest thing he could imagine to an actual daughter. Her will replaced his waning resolve, offered him hope, however slim, that all was not already lost.

He looked up into her soft eyes, the sight making him smile. "Paradise, not everyone has the benefit of your wisdom. It may already be too late to avoid bloodshed."

"Perhaps it's not," she offered, lowering her voice. "I've brought one who is connected to Mollock Bolle. She, too, has been cursed by my kind."

He gave her an odd look, thoughts lingering on her use of the phrase my kind. "Where is he? I would like to learn more of our prophet."

"*She* is waiting on the edge of camp. It wasn't wise to bring her into this nest of vipers," Paradise replied.

The Bone Father thought, much of his mind focused on what might happen rather than what could be prevented. His desire to eliminate Mollock continued to rise. His disgust with the cultists and their leaders sickened him to the point where he found it difficult to concentrate. He hadn't been expecting Paradise to come or to bring any help with her. This gift was too precious to pass up.

"Take me to her. The sooner I can discover what she knows, the faster we can end this madness and try to return our lives to normalcy."

She smiled again. "Father, there is nothing normal about our lives. We live in unprecedented times. It is a bane and a blessing to see our days march by."

"I have done my best to keep you safe, Paradise. Ever since the day I saw you crash into the waters of the Bo, I've given you my heart and devotion. You are a special woman, despite not being human. This gift of yours has bolstered my confidence, seen me through dark days when I feared the sun would never rise. I am a better man because of you, but I do not agree that there is blessing to be found in what we are being forced to endure here. The Deeves are polluted with this cult of Rengu."

Her eyes hardened. It had been a long time since she had last heard the name Rengu. "Come, Father. I will take you to her, but we must move quickly."

The Bone Father didn't comment on her newfound sense of urgency, though her suddenly brash behavior caused much concern. He waited as she poked her head through the heavy tent flap before gesturing him out. They slunk through rows of tents and sleeping wastrels huddled against rusted pieces of tin and aged bags. No one stirred, surprising considering how much crime and violence was spreading through the camp. Women were being raped daily, people being robbed and left for dead. There was no higher authority to report to, no semblance of law. Those who couldn't fend for themselves were left to the predations of the merciless.

Paradise pushed through the filth of the camp, thankful for her height, though the stench rose to meet her. Soon enough, she and the Bone Father were at the partially concealed skiff. She sighed with relief upon seeing Elisa.

"I was starting to grow worried," Elisa said defensively upon seeing the old man at Paradise's side.

Noting the look, Paradise said, "This is the Bone Father of the Deeves, a wise and venerable mystic who has protected the lands for countless generations."

"Well, not only me," he interjected modestly. "I am merely the latest in a very long line of men who have dedicated their lives to the betterment of others."

"He is also my adopted father. I trust him implicitly," Paradise finished.

Elisa gave him a second glance before nodding. "Good enough for me. If she trusts you, then so do I. What is going on here? I don't recall a village being here on the maps."

"That's because it's not. This camp is a travesty of humanity, a collection of suddenly lost souls bending knee to the lies of Mollock Bolle," the Bone Father said with obvious disdain. "Paradise tells me you know this man."

"We're not exactly friends," she answered quickly and went on to explain her twisted relationship with Mollock. It felt good explaining everything that had happened to her since being hired to hunt Mollock down, especially with a relative of the Bloody Man's. She left out how her life had begun. That was a tale for daylight, not the oppressive darkness clinging to them.

The Bone Father stared in wonder, finding it difficult to imagine a life as hard as what she'd already endured. "He has changed since you first arrived on An'kuruku. This cult has made him into a prominent figure. He spews lies, corrupting otherwise good people. The Deeves are falling under his influence, and I am powerless to stop it from spreading. I have failed in my task."

"No one has failed anything yet," Elisa said defiantly. "Mollock was a step away from being a basket case. He's not the leader here. Whatever he lived through on Crimeat only helped steal him further away from reality. He is broken."

"But it is his words that steal my people. I will see him dead," he replied, just as defiant. "The people of the Deeves are under my protection. I will not surrender them so easily as this cult wishes."

Elisa folded her thin arms across her chest. "What can you tell me about the cult? I haven't encountered them yet."

"Rengu is a very old evil," Paradise interjected. "He is a devil from my time and a very dangerous idea."

"Idea?" Elisa asked.

"There are very few of us walking amongst the stars, Elisa. Rengu was one of the first to fall during the war that all but destroyed my race. His hatred helped propagate the war after the Three were expelled. Somehow, he has found a way to manifest his will among your people and begin his war anew."

"How can the dead influence us? I'd have thought most people were evolved beyond simple superstitions."

"We are not so strong as you would have us," the Bone Father cut in. "Elisa, you have a deep heart, but until you come to accept what is, you will find yourself falling short of your expectations. This cult is very real and every bit the threat Paradise claims it to be. We must excise this tumor before the rot grows too strong to stop."

Elisa sat down on a small pile of wooden supply crates. She hadn't come here expecting to fight her way through thousands of fanatics cheering Mollock Bolle. It was partly her fault, or so she believed, since she was the one who had willingly brought him to the once peaceful desert planet. Forget that the Bloody Man had all but forced them here on some fantastical quest. She briefly looked back on her life with regret before shaking it from her head. Looking back was pointless. Mistakes were made, paths taken that shouldn't have been. All of her hardships and regrets helped forge her into the woman she was today.

Asking how the cult of Rengu had grown so rapidly and become so prevalent here in the fringes of civilization was equally pointless. The facts were more important than the "what ifs". "How can I get to Mollock?"

Both Paradise and the Bone Father stared back at her, surprised at the boldness of her request. It was the Bone Father who answered. "He is guarded night and day by soldiers, mercenaries most likely. I have tried to gain an audience with him but have been rebuked at every turn. There is one, however, that may be our only way into the castle."

Her eyes drifted up to the broken ruins in the near distance. She wouldn't have chosen the term "castle" for what she was looking at. "Go on."

"Her name is Kaline. I believe she is the true power here, but she remains behind the scenes, ever out of sight."

"Is she a local?" Elisa asked.

"No. She is another offworlder. She came to me last night and told me to leave while I was still able."

"You've made yourself a target," Elisa said softly.

Paradise felt her eyes water. "Father, you mustn't take such chances."

He held out his hands. "I will do what I must to ensure the safety and security of the people of the Deeves. They are all I am."

"So it's a fair bet her goons will come looking for you tomorrow," Elisa said. "We can use that to our advantage."

"I don't see how. There are a lot of angry people here, people all too willing to visit violence on their fellow man," he replied. Pangs of guilt over his own base desire to kill Mollock Bolle mocked his sense of morality.

"Too many people means she won't be able to track who's working for her and who's not. I say we wait for her people to come."

"And you take one of their places," Paradise concluded.

Elisa nodded.

"I will not kill, not like this," the Bone Father protested.

"I'm not asking you to. I'll do the dirty work. Besides, I owe someone."

Paradise forced a thin smile. She'd taken no pleasure from the slaughter at the Wells and certainly had been looking for a better solution. Tanzeil hadn't give her a choice. Paradise had merely finished the nasty affair as quickly as possible. No stranger to violence, she preferred a subtler approach to problem solving.

"There is the possibility you will be killed before getting anywhere near Kaline," the Bone Father said.

Elisa grinned, idly counting the number of times when there had been the possibility of getting killed. Her life seemed a mockery of odds, and, thus far, she'd managed to come out on top. She hoped that luck continued through the next few days. She needed to get Mollock out of the Deeves and off An'kuruku before he singlehandedly started a war.

Thoughts of the Bloody Man suddenly sprang forth, much to her confusion. She hadn't seen or heard from him since the battle of the Plateau when he'd named her and Mollock as the future champions of humanity. She didn't feel like a champion, but Mollock was living up to his title. Prophet. His firebrand rhetoric was inciting dormant rage in thousands, all under the direction of the cult of Rengu and Kaline. Elisa very much wanted to punch a blade through that woman's throat and be done with the whole sordid affair. Had the Bloody Man known this was going to happen all along? If so, why didn't he try to stop it or at least change the course of events? Nothing made sense, frustrating her to no end.

"If death is the only thing standing in my way, I think I'll be fine," she finally said with what little light humor she could muster. Then, it dawned on her she had no idea what Kaline looked like. Elisa shook her head. It didn't matter. There couldn't be very many women with authority in the ruins.

The Bone Father strode forward to take a seat beside her. His face bore more concern for her than for himself. Placing a fatherly face on her right knee, he asked, "What can we do in the meantime?"

"My friend is very sick. I'd like it if he didn't die before I returned to the Wells," she said.

"You have my word," he swore. *What that I can give.*

His mind was already drifting to the dawn. All their fragile plans hinged on them surviving the morning.

Smoke billowed up from the burning wreckage of wagons and the carcasses of freshly slaughtered draft animals. Bodies littered the dunes at twisted angles, rivulets of blood staining the golden sand. Prefects stalked the bodies, ensuring each was dead as the barely trained militia did the only thing they knew, create chaos on the battlefield. Screams from the wounded mingled with cries from women being taken and abused by men without morals.

Althas Pey watched the scene from the cupola of his armored air car, hovering a foot off the sand. His face was twisted in disgust at the inelegance of it all. War was certainly the most brutal human act, but this slaughter was much beneath his station, despite his oaths and promises to kill every man, woman and child in the Deeves. Oh, he'd meant that, but just not in the way being played out.

Rape and murder showed a lack of vision. If he had been able to control the militia just a little better, he'd have had the survivors lined up and beheaded one at a time. The message would reverberate through the countless villages and nomad clans across An'kuruku. His name would go down as the greatest slaughterer of mankind, a title he was more than willing to wear like a crown of gold.

"Prefect, we have secured the site. No one escaped."

Althas looked down at the captain reporting. "Very well, Captain. I want a thorough check of vehicles and weapons within the next fifteen minutes. Load everyone onto the skiffs. I want to be underway before the sun goes down."

The Captain nodded crisply, not letting his disgust for the slaughter show. "What of our wounded?"

Althas swept his glare over the battlefield once more. "Leave them."

"Sir?"

"I said leave them. They are dead weight, and I can't afford to slow this army down to treat them."

The captain couldn't believe what he was hearing. His orders were tantamount to murder, murder of his own people. Still, he was a Prefect and expected to follow orders. "Very well, sir. I'll have the Quartermaster arrange food and water for them."

"Was there a part of my orders you didn't understand?" Althas snapped. "I said leave them. Dump the bodies and get us underway."

"But they are our people!"

"Expendable people! Don't make the mistake of thinking for a moment that I care what happens to any of the militia during this campaign. They are just as much filth as the rabble we march to fight. So be it if they die. That means less for me to worry about betraying us. My one concern is the lives of my Prefects. Now go about your orders, Lieutenant, or I'll find someone who will."

Rebuked and demoted, the Prefect saluted and did as he was told. As if on cue, the communications node in Althas's helmet chimed. He cleared his throat and spat before answering. "Prefect Lezorsu."

"What is your status, Althas? Why has the army slowed?" Lezorsu asked.

Althas sighed angrily. He despised having anyone looking over his shoulder. "We paused to eliminate a column of refugees headed for the Bo."

Silence drifted between them, making Althas slightly nervous.

"How many killed?"

Althas relaxed, "Several hundred I believe. They were poorly armed. We caught them unawares. Success was complete."

He knew Lezorsu understood the need not only to eradicate pockets of potential enemy fighters whenever possible but also to hone the fighting skills of their largely untested army. Althas wasn't under the delusions that there was even the remotest chance of failure, but he anticipated the loss of many, perhaps even half, of his militia in the coming battle. Their losses meant nothing but losing too many would only serve to make maintaining the Prefects rule on Tenemenah more difficult when the general population learned of the massacres.

"Very good, Commander Pey. Keep the army moving. I want them entrenched in the Deeves before dawn," Lezorsu's voice crackled over the headset. "We are on the verge of a great victory. Keep up the pressure. Break these miscreants now before they can poison the rest of the planet."

Althas turned his helmet off. He'd heard enough. Lezorsu's empty rhetoric was better wasted on the young, those still unwise to the true ways of the world. His dark eyes fell back to the scene of carnage. A hunger had awakened, one born of the senseless slaughter played out before him. He wanted more. Needed more. The day of battle was fast approaching, and Althas Pey intended to bathe in a river of blood.

He staggered out of the desert, thirsty and burned. Skin peeled and flaked off even as new layers burned. The desert sun was merciless, hammering him down until he could stand. He'd run out of food and water sometime late in the night, a regret he feared he wouldn't need hounding him much longer. Death was riding his shoulders, driving him down. He'd already stopped sweating. His tongue felt too large for his mouth. His eyes ached from the strain of fighting the heat. Every fiber in his body wanted him to just lie down and surrender. It was the will of the desert.

Jut slowed, finally stopping. Eyes focused on the near horizon, the endless sea of brown distorted. Darkness was introduced. He watched the shape emerge from the sheen of rising haze and started laughing deliriously. Falling to his knees Jut pounded a fist on the sand. His lungs hurt from laughing so hard. Tears formed in the corners of his eyes, refusing to fall. The salt stung his abused flesh. He didn't understand how poorly he'd handled his trip across the desert, and it was about to cost him his life.

The Prefecture had escorted him from the luxury of Tenemenah, roughly and with as much zeal as Lezorsu ordered. More than a few bruises peppered his body from the casual beating his former colleagues had administered. They had given him a camel and enough food and water to last a week. It wasn't enough. The only reason Jut was still alive was through the kindness of strangers and passing trader caravans guiding him to the nearest oasis or way station.

Not that any of it mattered anymore. His water skin was cracked, as dry as his flesh. His empty food bag was just more weight to carry, but he couldn't bring himself to drop it. The camel was the most disheartening. It had died a day ago, and Jut suspected it had been poisoned back in Tenemenah. Lezorsu had much to answer for. Unfortunately, he wouldn't be the one exacting revenge. Jut had no illusions about his skeleton being picked clean by vultures or worse and his bones left to bleach and rot under the punishing sun. He laughed so hard he blacked out.

Jut awoke, much to his surprise. It took a few moments for his eyes to adjust to the relative gloom of his surroundings. It was so unlike the open sky of the desert, he felt like he was in a cave. Hushed voices echoed around him. Ghosts? Was this the entrance to the afterworld? He blinked rapidly, biting back the torrent of sorrow flooding him. He'd never truly wanted to die, despite the bravado of his position in the Prefecture.

"Is he awake?"

Shuffling moving closer. "I believe so. Remarkable, considering. He shouldn't even be alive."

"Who says he's going to live much longer anyway?" the first voice asked.

Jut squinted as a bright light was shined in his face. "What do you want with me?" he asked groggily. The words were slurred, distorted.

"I told you he was alive."

A snort. "What's your name?"

Jut shook his head. Tried to move. He was strapped down. Why? "Who are you? Why am I strapped down?"

"This will go smoother if you answer my questions," the first voice snapped. "Your name?"

"Jut."

"Tell me, Jut, why are you so deep in our desert and wearing a Prefect uniform?"

He frowned, having forgotten his uniform, the uniform that clearly marked him as an enemy of the desert tribes. *Damnation. Not only do I need to worry about surviving the desert, but now I have a host of people wanting my head.* "I'm not a Prefect anymore."

"So you were?"

He frowned at the ignorance of the question. Were they trying to irritate him? "My reasons for leaving are my own."

The questioner leaned in close, his hot breath caressing Jut's cheek. "For your sake, I hope they are very good reasons. They might be the only thing that keeps you from getting skinned and left for dead."

"Who are you people?" Jut demanded, tired of the games. "If you're going to kill me, kill me already."

"Oh, I would if it were up to me," the voice answered sharply, and with a trace of annoyance. "But there are higher powers at work here. They want you alive, but not unharmed."

They? Who is "they"? Jut wished he'd been left to die, thinking it the better of the choices being offered. He'd been given water, but his stomach still cramped from the lethal combination of hunger and dehydration. Death wasn't out of the picture yet. Jut decided to press his luck. "Where are you taking me?"

There was a long pause, as if the speaker was having trouble deciding what to divulge. When he finally answered, it only made Jut more confused. "To the Deeves. We are taking you to the Prophet."

Jut nearly broke out in laughter. *The Prophet. These fools are taking me right where I need to go.* He blacked out again, not sure if he heard laughter in the background.

Time lost meaning. Day and night blurred into one long period of captivity and incoherence. Meals were brought along with just enough water to keep his body from going into shock. Jut never realized how good life in Tenemenah had been, but that was no justification for the slaughter of untold thousands at the hands of the overzealous Lezorsu. There were some lines even the most hardened Prefect shouldn't cross.

The only thing Jut knew for certain was that he was traveling by the fabled sky skiffs of the desert tribes. Naturally, such vehicles were considered outdated and misplaced, a mockery of modernization, by the citizens of the northern cities. Jut had only read about them when he was in school, never actually thinking to see one, much less ride on one. The deserts were full of many surprises.

Eventually, they arrived at the ruined castle on the shores of the Bo. No one bothered speaking to him. His initial interrogators never returned. Jut presumed they'd gotten whatever information they needed and were content with letting him wallow in self-doubt and apprehension. The argument between them was enough to tell Jut what he needed to know. They weren't professionals. Pilgrims, more than likely; disaffected souls with little aspirations in life other than raising children and struggling through their miserable days.

Two men entered the makeshift storage tent that had become his prison and roughly placed his head in a burlap sack while zip-tying his hands behind his back. A few angry kicks and punches tagged his ribs and stomach for good measure, much to their amusement. They dragged Jut out into the burning sunlight. The heat immediately overwhelmed him. His breath came in short gasps. His skin prickled as sweat beaded. As if the first time wasn't convincing enough, Jut thought again that he hated the desert.

The Deeves were a seemingly unending sea of broken dunes and scraggly bushes. Dry stalks of grass tickled his knees as they half-dragged, half-carried him through the sorry excuse for a village. Abhorrent smells assaulted Jut, the filth and decay of a generation soiling the ground. Bile rose in his throat.

"Behold! A mighty Prefect!" a voice cried.

Jut tensed, knowing what was to come. He'd seen it before, though from the other end. The first stone hit him between the shoulder blades, eliciting a sharp groan as the edge dug into his already tortured flesh. Jeers and curses broke out amongst the gathered crowd. Something warm and soft hit the side of his head. He sniffed. *These savages are throwing their own shit at me.*

"Kill him!"

"String him up."

On and on the variety of shouts pelted his consciousness. At first, he was angered. How could these people justify being so foul towards him when he had come to warn them of what was coming? Anger quickly dissolved into sorrow. Jut realized they were just as lost as he had become, eager to find an outlet for their confusion. More rocks hit. He stumbled and was shoved.

"Enough!" The strong feminine voice sang across the mass, and silence fell.

Jut could feel the crowds dispersing, as if in fear or awe. He'd never heard a voice so wondrous inflicted with venom before. The thought was both provoking and dangerous. Whatever power controlled these people here in the Deeves was more wicked than anything his imagination could conjure.

Lithe footsteps glided over the worn stone stairs until they stopped just in front of Jut. The hands gripping him let go. He heard them back off. Jut waited patiently while the woman studied him. He'd taken a grave chance by wearing his uniform all the way from Tenemenah, but he hoped it would prove his point. Prefects simply didn't turn on each other.

"I would like to apologize for the rough treatment, but my men have no love for the people of the Prefecture. I am Kaline," she announced. Her voice was light, confident.

The sack was jerked from his head, and he winced at the light.

"What have I done that warrants being treated like an animal?" he found the courage to ask.

She flashed a charming smile that sent chills down his spine. "There is a war coming, Prefect. Anyone in that uniform is our enemy. The better question is what are you doing so far from home? All alone in enemy territory?"

He returned the smile, if with less grace and poise. "I have news that you could use. You say a war is coming. I've come to warn that the war is already here."

TWENTY-FIVE

3212 A.G. (After Gods), the Ice Caves, planet Antil IV.

Howling winds swirled across the frozen plains. Snows kicked up in the wake drifted on the wind with hurricane force. The purple sky was constantly obscured from view by any foolish enough to venture into the storms. The ground was broken, an undulating scar of rock and ice. It was unlike any world under Conclave jurisdiction, and it was the only place Amongeratix felt comfortable.

The universe had changed so much since his people had reigned. They were nothing more than fragmented memories, lost hopes that humanity desperately clung to in search of find some mythical sense of purpose. The giant sneered at the level of weakness. His kind was beyond godhood. They had ruled the stars with iron fists. Humanity was like the afterbirth of the fall of a grand society. They needed to have something higher than themselves to believe in. Faith for their own kind was anathema. It was a belief system he didn't understand, nor did he want to.

Mortals were utterly weak, a mockery of what his kind had stood for. And they had the audacity to bend knees and pretend to rule the universe in the image of the gods. Statues were erected on hundreds of worlds to appease them. They based an entire society around a lie, a forfeiture of potential. The Conclave arose from the ashes of his fallen race. It offered a place for people to forget their sorrows, to find a better place in the great scheme of life. In truth, it gave only false hope. The legacy of the Conclave was a lie, and he intended to expose them for the charlatans they were.

Amongeratix sat on a throne made of black ice overlooking the frozen rock sea. He almost laughed at the foolishness of it. His throne. His rule was nothing but a barren world forgotten by any wise enough. Life was abundant but meant nothing without opposable thumbs or the ability to reason. He was a king of animals and Neanderthal humans incapable of speech.

"My lord, we have it," said a timid voice behind him.

Amongeratix swiveled his throne around to the cave's interior. An entire wall was filled with computers and sensor banks. Viewing screens almost as large as he was tall stretched up to the ceiling. The floor was corrugated, broken up only by several stations occupied by blind and mute humans, genetically altered to serve his purposes. He alone of all his brothers found solace in such a place. It comforted him in dark hours and offered the opportunity to think clearly.

Amongeratix looked down at his equerry. The man was old and should have been dead a lifetime ago. His skin was parched, drawn taut across his frame. The eyes were cybernetic augments, along with most organs and his right leg. Plugs and wires ran across the back of his bald scalp. The equerry was able to plug into the main computer drives directly, thus avoiding the need for third-party interactions. He was the product of Amongeratix's advance intellect.

"Have what?" Amongeratix asked. The edge never left his voice.

The equerry failed to notice the consternation in his master's voice. "I believe we have discovered the location of Paradise Tear."

The giant practically leapt to his feet. His twelve-foot frame barely had room to stand without ducking. Excitement surged through his veins, an electric thrill akin to ecstasy. *At last! I knew you couldn't hide from me forever, you little bitch. Soon, you will be mine, and I will finally be able to fulfill my purpose. The death knell for humanity has sounded.*

"Where?" was all he asked.

"Planet An'kuruku. It is a desert planet on the far side of the universe, close to one hundred thirty-seven parsecs from Antil IV. Initial surveillance suggests there is a small civil war fomenting in the deep desert region, my lord."

Amongeratix smirked. Another civil war. He found it astounding that the humans had managed to come so far. Their very nature seemed bent on destroying one another. His thoughts briefly touched on the battle with his brothers on Crimeat. He was convinced he was winning until Sorrow unleashed his sorcery and banished them all to different parts of the universe. It had taken half a year for Amongeratix to return to Antil IV and another year and a half recovering from his injuries.

The wasted time was but a pinprick in the skein of his life, but that did little to ease the rising anger consuming his thoughts. His dreams centered on ripping his brothers limb from limb and grinding their corpses to bloody pulps. There was savage thrill in such vain imaginings. The secrets of violence were a delicacy learned during the long, dark nights after the rebellion. His only regret stemmed from not being able to kill the Oracle. Her death would have been the spark needed to unlock the true powers of the cosmos. His life had been an endless quest to discover another source capable of elevating him above his peers.

His recent finding of the Oracle on the Acumensiis Comet had been heartening. Unfortunately, the protective wards had kept him from stealing her away. The defeat was only temporary. He knew events were progressing as he desired. Snatching the Oracle wouldn't prove difficult at all. That left Paradise Tear; a failed remnant of a weaker time.

"Ready my shuttle. I want to be on that planet as soon as possible," he ordered.

The equerry bowed, knowing his task was nearly impossible. Voicing any concerns, though, would be instant death. "As you command, my lord."

Amongeratix ground his teeth and spun back to face the frozen plains. *Soon, brothers, soon. I'm coming for you.*

Hawker's Gate, deep space.

Explosions rocked the spine of the great, forgotten space station. Bodies littered the corridors, helpless civilians caught in the crossfire between loyalist and cultist forces vying for control. Fires burned unchecked in a dozen vital areas. All communications with the rest of the universe had been cut off. The Gate was truly alone now.

Sergeant Fies lead a group of ten survivors deeper into the station. Only three were his Guards. The others were still scattered across the station. He hoped they managed to avoid the initial salvos that had already claimed the lives of so many. The older sergeant was thankful he and Annalilly had picked up the changes before they had happened. Otherwise, they'd both be cooling corpses right now. Trophies to a minor victory, for surely the Guard would retaliate in force and crush the cultists without mercy.

"How much further?" he asked. His breath came in ragged gasps. They'd been running for what felt like hours.

Annalilly checked the handheld data processor she'd taken from a dead security guard, cursing again their lack of armor and proper weapons. "Twenty meters and then left. We're almost there."

A huge chunk of wall exploded over her right shoulder. She dropped and spun, already raising her weapon to return fire. What she saw was disheartening. A dozen men and women were storming down the corridor. All of them brandished long rifles and had murder in their eyes. She spat and kept running. There was no point in wasting a round.

"Move faster!" she shouted.

Fies didn't bother looking back. He knew her enough to know when the situation had gone from bad to worse. His legs felt heavy. His lungs burned. More rounds slammed into the walls and ground. Shrapnel dug into his calves. Every combat instinct begged for him to stop and meet the threat head on. Running away was the next thing to cowardice, not in a proper Guard's vocabulary or moral composure.

Reality, however, was a far different thing. Outnumbered and outgunned, Fies knew they didn't stand much of a chance at all. Not even the most rookie soldier was foolish enough to close with a handful of Prekhauten Guards. Some chances just weren't taken. Fies regretted their reputation, knowing it served to damn them here. Suppressing the urge to stand and fight, he gained the turn and hurried the others around it.

"Come in, Sergeant Fies."

The sudden communication froze him, and he nearly lost his head for it. Two ion bolts struck a few inches from his head. Plaster and metal shavings raked into his flesh. He cursed. Death stalked him, hungry for his blood. He feared his time had come at last.

"Who is this?" he demanded.

"Captain Falchi. What is your current location?"

Fies fought back the smile struggling to break free. "Closing on deck P 12. We are trying to rendezvous with the Inquisitor. Are you still on station, Captain?"

"Negative. The *Indomitable* was forced to retreat. Massive enemy space threat is securing the system around the Gate."

More bad news. Fies was starting to get used to it. Without the *Indomitable,* they were effectively cut off and had no way of getting their armor or weapons. Death might have her day after all.

"Roger that, Captain. What are your orders?" he asked reluctantly. Not that any order meant much given their current situation.

"I have a detachment of Guards en route to your position with your arms and armor. The entire station is under assault. We fear control is no longer feasible. Hawker's Gate is likely in enemy hands."

Fies refrained from giving the obvious "no shit" reply. Regardless of the current peril, he was still expected to maintain military discipline. In fact, he counted on it to see them through. The battle needed to be taken back to the enemy on his terms, not theirs. His heart lightened at the good news. All he needed was a proper twin barrel ion rifle and a few concussion grenades.

He keyed the borrowed security guard headset. "Copy. We'll be expecting the package. Inform detachment to expect heavy enemy resistance, mostly small arms. They are unorganized but lethal."

"Roger. Keep your heads down, Sergeant. Help is coming. Falchi out."

Fies clicked offline and fired a handful of shots into the oncoming enemy. He was rewarded with a strangled groan and the smell of burnt flesh.

"What was that?" Annalilly asked after he caught up.

He flashed a tight grin, debating whether to tell her or not. "We're getting reinforced. Get to Breed and set up a defensive perimeter until our weapons arrive."

Deck P 12 was a nightmare. Fires raged on the far walls. Craters pockmarked the floor and ceiling. The fighting had been furious here. Scores of bodies lay where they'd been murdered. Intermixed with civilians and cultists all bearing the red inverted cross were the abused bodies of a handful of Prekhauten Guards. The Gate's garrison was small by any standard and clearly underprepared for the outbreak of violence. They were decimated but appeared to have given as good as they got. At least the fallen were given the dignity of falling in battle.

"Spread out! I want all exits and entrances secured with a clear field of fire. Snipers take the obvious approaches."

Annalilly shot him a questioning look. He'd instantly fallen back into the platoon sergeant role, forgetting they didn't have any of the kit they normally used and there weren't any snipers, except, of course, on the enemy side. Shaking her head, she ducked into the bombed out remains of what looked like a coffee shop and started building a barricade with what was left of the furniture.

"Don't just stand there, give me a hand!" she barked at the local security.

Dumbfounded that anyone could still have the will to fight, the guards slowly joined in. Gunfire echoed from down the corridor, steadily edging closer. It wouldn't be long. Annalilly couldn't figure out why she had a dumb grin plastered across her face as she threw the last chair on top of the wreckage. The prospect of fighting an unknown force with only handguns and a pocketful of looted nitric grenades was less than promising, despite her unhealthy desire to prove herself in a manner befitting the heartiest Guard.

"I need you to stay frosty on this one," Fies warned after coming up from behind. "Don't do anything stupid."

"Or what?" she asked in reply, already worried that their developing relationship was going to interfere with military discipline.

He ruefully shook his head. "Or I kick your ass."

She shrugged. "If you think you can."

"Here they come!"

All banter ceased as the experienced veterans took cover and started searching for enemy contact. A pair of men eased down the corridor, weapons at the ready. Both wore security uniforms. Fies frowned. Either these men had taken the uniforms off a pair of dead men or they were traitors. Neither prospect sat well with him. The pair stalked into the open area, eyes swiveling for signs. These men were clearly professionals, confirming Fies's suspicions. *Don't things ever go easy?*

He was about to order his men to fire when one of the locals jumped up and shouted, "Over here!"

The pair of guards instantly dropped and started firing, killing the man who'd cried out. Fies kicked the body aside, scowling. At least the traitors had spared him the trouble of doing it himself. Ion rounds cracked and sizzled past his head. He cursed and returned fire.

"Try hitting one," Annalilly joked but held her own fire.

"These bastards are pros. We need to conserve ammo."

A hail of rounds shredded the outer wall of furniture. Wood chips and paint flew up in hundreds of tiny shards. Several ripped across his left cheek. Drops of warm blood trickled down his face, reminding him of their near-death situation.

"I thought comms were down," Annalilly said suddenly.

Fies looked up, wiping the blood away. "What?"

"How was the *Indomitable* able to contact you if comms are down?" she asked.

Enemy fire picked up. Fresh fires erupted from the back wall, showering them with sparks and small bits of flame. His mind stretched to find relevance for her comment. Cut off and outgunned, he failed to see her point.

She fumed and snatched the radio from him. "Give me that! Inquisitor Breed, come in."

Static was the only reply.

"I got one!" a security shouted jubilantly.

She barely looked up to see the cultist drop. *Gods damned idiots. They're going to get us all killed.* "Inquisitor Kai, come in. This is Sergeant Annalilly."

"Go ahead, sergeant."

Annalilly almost relaxed upon hearing Luma Kai's voice. "What is your current pos? We are pinned down in a ruined coffee shop on deck P 12. Awaiting further orders, over."

"We are approximately twenty meters from your location. Stand by. I have eight people with me."

"Come quick. We're taking heavy fire. Do not expect to last long as is. Out."

She tossed the radio down. Nothing else needed saying. Annalilly dug into her pocket and pulled out the small sphere of nitric grenade. The liquid nitrogen made one of the best explosives in an urban environment, though she had her reservations about using one too close to the bulkhead. The last thing they needed was to tear a hole in the hull of the station and vent everyone into space. Pushing the thoughts aside, she pressed the detonation switch and heaved it towards the second group of cultists who had emerged from the opposite side of the corridor.

Mere chance kept it from being struck by the hail of ion fire. The grenade landed amid the group and exploded. A combination of chemicals and gases mushroomed through the cultists. Flesh froze, bleached white as it iced through to the bone. Horrified screams died in their throats as they tried to outrun the impossible. A dozen men became living statues, but for a moment only. Cracks spread, and the men crumbled into chunks of icy flesh.

That was enough to force the initial assailants to back off and rethink their strategy. They were clearly unprepared for the carnage even a thin handful of Prekhautens were capable of. Fies took advantage and burned through the remaining charge in his weapon's energy pack.

He turned and stared down Annalilly with a menacing glare. "What the hells was that? You could have killed us all!"

"I was saving our asses."

He left the next part unsaid. They both knew what a nitric grenade could do. It was a reckless move, no matter how successful. Fortunately, recklessness occasionally saved lives. Fies knew he didn't have much ground to stand on for issuing a reprimand. "How many more of those damned things do you have?"

"Three. It won't be enough unless the Inquisitors get here soon," she said.

Fies grunted and reloaded his handgun. There was no point in worry about things beyond his control.

Jers watched in muted horror as Beve drove two quick thrusts into the neck of a cultist. Arterial blood fountained from the wounds, thick ropes of the dark fluid trailing after the combat knife. The man died with a gurgled sound and fell limply.

"Watch out!" Jers shouted as three more cultists leapt up at the bigger Guard.

Beve went down beneath them. Fists struck. A bone snapped. Jers jumped in, taking a cultist in the ribs to the hilt. The man barked a sharp cry and tried to roll over to confront his attacker. Jers didn't wait. He slashed his knife across the man's throat before drawing his handgun and putting two rounds between the second man's eyes. The head snapped back violently. Bits of bone and brain matter exploded against the wall. Beve emerged from the pile strangling the last man.

He shot Jers a foul glare and pointed at the gore covering his face. "I don't like this, Jers."

"Hey, you could be dead."

The big man frowned and stalked after another target. Jers exhaled sharply and tried to keep up. He hadn't seen Beve go on a rampage since the spice runner revolt on the moons of Uon nearly a year past. Images of that day continued to haunt him. Pushing the thoughts aside, he followed Beve deeper into Hawker's Gate. They remained cut off but without the nagging sense of despair. Jers was known by the rest of the squad as a complainer, at least until ion rounds started flying. Then he transformed into a stone-faced killer. Beve. He looked up at the big man's back as they ran. What else needed to be said about Beve?

"Any idea how much further?" he asked through strained breaths.

Beve kept running. "Dunno. I'm not looking for the Inquisitor."

Jers shivered at Beve's tone. Bad things were happening across the station, but one worse was about to happen here. He feared Beve was about to go berserk. If that happened, when it happened, the only safe place was far away. Jers slowly started making plans for separating from his friend. Gunfire echoed in front of them. *Great. We're headed into a fight, and I've got a loose cannon in front of me. I should've retired.*

"Come on," Beve urged. "There's a battle ahead."

Jers rolled his eyes. His every instinct was to turn and run. His mind begged for it. His body wanted to rebel, to turn and flee. Pride and training refused them all. Jers charged headlong into the firefight.

Besides, being next to Beve was probably the safest place on the entire station.

Tolde calmly took aim and squeezed the trigger. The blue-white ion round sizzled across the twenty meters and struck the cultist just under her heart. Crumbling in a waste of flesh, reflexes made her squeeze her own trigger. Rounds struck the walls and ceiling in a random spray.

"Come quick. We're taking heavy fire. Do not expect to last long as is. Out."

Tolde glanced back over his shoulder. "Which element is that?"

Luma shoved the handheld radio back into the pouch on her belt. "Fies and Annalilly. They're pinned down not far from here along with a handful of Guards and local security."

Tolde snarled but kept his thoughts to himself. He'd grossly underestimated the situation, again, and it was going to cost them several lives. The idea that he was missing a key element to this entire affair hounded him more than he wanted to admit. Conspiracy theorists amongst the Inquisition whispered a thousand different scenarios, but none of them seemed plausible to Tolde. He was practical, if nothing else. Yet he continued to stay a few steps behind whatever was directing events.

He stepped over the dead woman, noting her clothes and professional appearance. She'd put up a good fight, marking her as more than just a local with a gun. They'd arrived at Presha Von's establishment but found it deserted and locked up. Only this woman had been waiting. More disturbing was the proclamation issued over the Gate's loudspeaker array. The Conclave was usurped, replaced by the Cult of Rengu. Presha Von had declared martial law and decreed everyone still loyal to the Conclave was to be captured or killed.

Tolde and Luma narrowly escaped the failed suicide bombing of Administrator Felp's assistant. They could only assume that Felp was also dead. The situation reminded Tolde of his experiences hunting Amongeratix on the derelict freighter headed towards Occanum. It had been harrowing, and he'd barely escaped with his life. Only a handful of Guards, Matthias included, had returned to Vau Prime alive. Tolde feared his lack of understanding now was going to lead to similar results.

"We've been taken," he said.

Luma cocked her head in confusion. "Taken how? There was no way to anticipate matters had devolved this badly."

"I should have seen it coming. We've been skirting the signs for months."

"Stop blaming yourself. We are only Inquisitors, not gods," she protested.

"That doesn't make our ignorance acceptable."

The finality of his tone worried her. She'd struggled to fit in as his partner, even though she'd been ordered to recruit him. Luma bore a deep suspicion that she was meant more to keep an eye on him than to be a productive partner. The complexities of Inquisition command frustrated her to no end.

Any stray thoughts disappeared when the radio squelched on.

"Inquisitor, where in the hells are you? We're getting cut to pieces!"

Luma looked to Tolde. "We need to get moving. This is the largest asset we have on the Gate, and they won't last much longer."

Tolde frowned. His thoughts continued to revolve around the overarching theme of disappointment in his actions. *What am I missing?* No answers were there. He was adrift, fighting a losing war. Making matters worse, the Guards he had fought beside and specifically requested were in dire straits because of him.

"Tolde, did you hear me?" Luma asked.

His eyes refocused, and he nodded. "Let's go."

The pair of Inquisitors stalked down the corridor, abandoning their quest to engage and detain Presha Von. Deck P 12 had been a trap all along, and most of their forces were steadily being gunned down. They needed help, even if that help was no more than a pair of Inquisitors. Ion rounds struck the walls just ahead in a blinding display of misguided fire. Tolde and Luma edged into an opening, careful to avoid any potential field of fire.

"Fies, we're coming in," he called out.

Sergeant Fies helped rush them into their perimeter before enemy fire could strike. The sight of two Inquisitors bolstered confidence, especially amongst the local security.

"We figured you two were already dead," Annalilly admitted. "Haven't heard from anybody else since the fighting began."

Luma shook her head, long red hair flowing about her shoulders. "What is the current situation, Sergeant?"

A glimmer of darkness shimmered behind Annalilly's eyes and was gone quickly. "We have eight combat-capable people and almost no weapons."

Luma stole her gaze to the frozen chunks of body parts strewn across the plaza. "And that?"

The Guard shrugged innocently. "I have a few toys just in case."

Luma ignored the comment, unwilling to start an argument. Guards were notoriously hardheaded on their best days. Instead, she asked, "Have you gotten any word from the rest of the detachment? What about remnants of local security?"

Annalilly gestured at the four shaken men to her right. "There's your remnants, and we've only heard from the *Indomitable* once since the communications blackout."

The *Indomitable*? Luma found it curious Captain Falchi hadn't tried contacting the Inquisitors. Besides, she'd gotten the feeling that Falchi was anything but comfortable with two members of the Office of Heretical Persecution on his decks. A small, shoulder-fired missile streaked past her head, exploding in the back of the coffee shop.

"Where the fuck did they get rockets?" Fies cried out.

Tolde stepped forward. "Everybody down! Did anyone see where that came from?"

"Five o'clock at twelve meters," one of the Prekhautens said. Part of his scalp hung down over face.

"Fies, what do we have to counter?" Tolde asked sharply.

Fies shook his head. *Not a damned thing.*

"Inquisitor, allow me."

Annalilly slipped through the huddled Guards and crouched beside Tolde. "Where is the shooter?"

"To the right of those stacked tables. He's hiding, probably waiting for one of us to expose ourselves."

She nodded, digging back into her pocket for her last nitric grenade. Pressing the detonator switch, she raised the weapon and kissed it softly. "Give me a warning shot."

Tolde leaned forward and fired a pair of shots in the shooter's general direction. Annalilly waited long enough for the man to poke his head around the corner and sight in with his rocket launcher before heaving her last grenade. The tiny sphere bounced and rolled beneath the tables. She barely managed to close her eyes before the explosion vaporized that part of the plaza. The shooter died horribly as did the reloader squatting behind him. Even with these successes, the Guards were fighting a losing battle. Twenty more cultists swarmed into the plaza, firing at anything that moved.

Forming a ragged fire order line, the cultists advanced on the beleaguered Guards, firing as fast as they could squeeze the trigger. Tolde watched the scene with mechanical analysis. Whoever was in charge had a military background. He briefly considered ordering his survivors to prepare for battle but abandoned it. There was nowhere to hide, and surrender wasn't an option. They were going to die. He rechecked the charge of his handgun and let out a slow breath.

The plaza erupted with deafening noise. Thunder echoed across the empty shops and stores. Haze from hundreds of ion rounds choked the air. Tolde risked a glance and was surprised to see most advancing cultists were in shattered lumps of flesh on the deck. A few were on their knees in a vain attempt at surrendering before being cut down with their brethren. Behind them, a troop of fully armored and heavily armed Prekhauten Guard Marines from the *Indomitable* stood abreast. Smoke oozed from their weapons.

"Clear!"

"Roger that. All clear, Lieutenant," a second Guard said before lowering his weapon, slightly.

The Lieutenant saluted Tolde. "Inquisitor, with Captain Falchi's compliments."

"Lieutenant, it is very good to see you," Tolde replied with a genuine grin.

Fies pulled himself from a pile of rubble that had collapsed on him.

The Lieutenant offered a curt nod. "Sergeant, my men have been hauling your kit all over this gods damned station. If you would be so kind as to take it back?"

"With pleasure, sir. All right, you bastards, get armored up! We've got an insurrection to squash."

Any relief Fies might have felt was subsumed by the fact that he was still missing most of his people. Without them, the fight to take back Hawker's Gate was almost moot.

"What are your orders, Inquisitor?" the Lieutenant asked crisply.

Tolde passed a sidelong glance to Luma, who nodded. "Secure the perimeter. Our priority is to find the remainder of Sergeant Fies's Guards. After that, we take this station back."

It was enough for the Guards, but Tolde still wasn't sure how they were going to succeed, not with a quarter of a million people against them.

TWENTY-SIX

3212 A.G. (After Gods), pirate haven of Drespai, orbit of planet Spindle.

First Mate Therill stared out the viewport, studying the stars. His mind raced with too many possibilities. Foremost was the suspicion that Blackheart was leading them down a foul path. The pirate clans had shrugged off the imposed mantle of authority in favor of a better way of life, freedoms that were oppressed on virtually every world ruled by the Conclave. Now, they were faced with being forced back into that failing political system. Therill suspected Blackheart had hidden motivations.

He absently scratched the back of his right hand. Spindle rotated below, the hues of brown and orange somehow out of place amidst the cold blackness of space. Therill had always felt more comfortable in space than on a planet. He was about to go back to the command deck when a hail of twinkling lights burst like birthing stars on the horizon. Alarm rippled through him. Quickly counting more than twenty, Therill immediately understood what was happening. He turned and ran.

The corridors of Drespai were mostly empty. Much of the combined pirate strength had already deployed to Hawker's Gate under the promise of annihilating the mighty Prekhauten fleet. That left only one possibility. They'd been betrayed. His first thought was to confront Blackheart and have done with it. Too long had he been forced to sit back and accept the pirate captain's will. Therill chafed at the continued insult. The privileged didn't deserve such loyalty. He briefly considered running a blade across Blackheart's throat. The thought left a wry grin on his face as he stormed through the deserted space station.

As he walked, he decided against going to his captain at all. The man would spew lies, smothering the truth under a web of deceits. No. Vicente Blackheart wasn't the man to go to now. Therill needed someone with enough understanding of their situation to possibly change the impending outcome. Someone who wasn't going to turn his colors at the first opportunity and save his own hide.

"Therill, you're not expected down here," the Drespai jailor said with a sneer. He'd already been warned that the First Mate was too eager to murder the prisoners.

Latent anger rising, Therill snapped back, "Blackheart sent me. Get out of my way, Bavil."

The larger guard rose slowly. His back snapped and creaked as he stretched to his full six and a half foot height. "I don't believe you."

Therill frowned but kept his composure. "I don't care. Orders are orders." He briefly debated telling the dimwit that a Prekhauten fleet had just entered the system but decided against it. The others on Drespai were going to find out all too soon. "Move, Bavil."

"Or what?"

Therill lashed out quickly. His hands found soft areas in the sternum and throat, dropping Bavil to his knees with a strangled groan. Therill drove a knee up into the bigger man's groin and dropped a sharp elbow across the bridge of his nose. Bavil fell, eyes bulging from the sudden lack of oxygen.

The First Mate of the *Shrike* knelt, no emotion in his eyes. "You should have moved." Drawing the short dagger from his hip, he plunged the blade through Bavil's left eye, killing the man instantly.

He wiped the blood on the dead man's shirt and lifted the keys to the cell bank. Therill knew from eavesdropping on Blackheart which cell he was looking for, so it only took a moment to make his way down the row of cells. Stopping, he peered into the gloom. His face twisted from the overpowering stench of human waste and rotted food. The shape hunched in the back of the cell didn't move.

"Get up. It's time you and I came to an understanding," he called with as much authority as he could muster.

Geres Auk slowly lifted his head, studying the pirate the way a jungle predator looks down on its prey. "What is to understand? You wish to kill me, and I want you to try. Only these bars stand between us, pirate scum."

Therill clenched his fists. "That's not why I am here. We've all been betrayed."

Geres cocked his head, wary of deceit. "By whom this time?"

"You by your precious Inquisition and me by my own captain. The Conclave has sent the Guard here even as we race to ambush them halfway across the universe."

Geres shrugged. "I don't see how that's my problem."

"The Guard will kill everyone on this station," Therill fumed.

"They'll kill everyone not in a cell. I'm a prisoner, for whatever reason. The Guard operates on an inflated sense of honor. Everyone in these cells will be spared, taken back to the ships and Vau Prime. I am in no danger. You, on the other hand, are about to meet your end here in this shithole of a space station."

Geres sat back, the smug look carved into his face all but unseen in the gloom of his cell. Both men knew the truth in what he'd said. The Prekhauten Guard was many things, but a band of murderers wasn't one of them. Therill and the rest of the pirates on Drespai were as good as dead, removing any semblance of power he might have tried to exert over the prisoner. Therill absently bit at the inside of his cheek.

"It would be a shame if someone accidentally left these cells open. In the heat of battle it would be too easy for a soldier to overlook the fact that these might be prisoners. After all, who wouldn't try to hide in a cell to protect his own life? I don't have time for games, Auk. Your Inquisition masters have abandoned you and Prowl. You're just as much of a liability as I am. They can't afford to let either of you live. What makes you think they aren't coming to vent your bodies into space and wash their hands of it?"

"I never had much use for what if. They can kill me, or you can. It doesn't matter. Neither of you will find it a pleasant chore."

"Damn it, man, I'm offering you a way out," Therill barked louder than intended. "Stop being so stubborn and take it."

Geres grinned savagely. The muscles under his powerful frame rippled. "Now we can speak. What do you have in mind?"

Ursal Prowl threw a hand up to block the sudden glare of light entering his cell. A pair of blurry shapes slowly focused, leaving the former Inquisitor in mute shock. Geres Auk seemed to take a measure of amusement from this.

"It is time to leave," was all he said.

Ursal's gaze fell on the imposing figure of Therill standing behind Geres. "What did it take to make you abandon me?"

Dark anger flashed in Geres's eyes. "I am not a traitor."

"No, that would be only you and I," Therill said suddenly. "One of your fleets in en route to reduce this station to slag, and I'd rather not be aboard when that happens. Geres and I have come to an understanding, but he won't abandon you to the fate you deserve. That puts me in a strange position, but I'm no fool. This is the only chance I am going to afford you to escape with your life."

Ursal rose, clasping his hands behind his back. "You've wanted both of us dead from the moment we first boarded the Shrike. I find it difficult to accept the sudden change of heart."

Therill briefly reconsidered his plan, imagining Ursal's brains splattered across the wall in the back of the cell. The momentary satisfaction would prove unfulfilling at best and leave him in the same predicament. He decided to change tactics and lay everything out for Ursal.

"Blackheart knows you've been abandoned by the Inquisition. The Inquisitor General didn't blink an eye when Blackheart informed him of the change. That makes you a loose end in a time when a great change is about to sweep through the stars."

Geres shifted in the background, arms folded across his massive chest.

"Nye doesn't need you anymore. He's made his peace with that and is dealing solely with Blackheart."

"And you believe your dear captain has sold you out as well," Ursal concluded.

Therill nodded curtly. "Blackheart is using the artifact we recovered from the wreckage of an Inquisition frigate as a bargaining chip. He's overlooked one significant detail, though. I know where he's keeping it."

Genuine excitement flushed through Ursal. The sole reason for being assignment to the pirate clans was to find and recover the stolen artifact of the gods. He hadn't been told what the artifact did. Nye wasn't so foolish as to trust anyone with that knowledge. But Ursal was no fool. Any artifact so desperately sought after must contain unimaginable power or unlock secrets. Delusions came easily with such power so close to his fingers. He struggled to remain grounded, focused on what needed to happen, not what could.

Ursal pointed down to the far corner where a large, dark shape was casually gnawing on an old soup bone. "Can you explain how a space station has rats?"

"Are you in, or do I leave you here for your precious Inquisition?" Therill asked angrily. He was already fed up with Prowl and giving serious consideration towards killing the man.

"I'm in so long as I get to be the one that kills Blackheart."

Therill shrugged. He didn't care. Treachery was a staple amongst the pirate clans. Crews were always mutinying, and captains had to watch their backs. One more death would mean little in the grand scheme of things to come. He stepped back so Geres could unlock the cell door, noting for the first time the abhorrent amount of filth and slime covering the walls and floor. Most of the paint had peeled away from the bars long ago, leaving a speckled pattern reminiscent of a sickened animal. Therill found it odd that he'd never noticed any of this before. The door swung open with more than a little force, and the trio hurried back to the guard chamber at the end of the dimly lit hall.

"What happened to him?" Ursal asked as they filed past Bavil's cooling body.

Therill ignored him. He knew a little about Prekhauten procedures, and it wasn't going to take long before the incoming fleet had the system quarantined and made ready their assault. Judging from the sheer amount of engine flares he'd witnessed, there would be no demands for surrender. The Guard had come to blow them out of space. Prisoners were a secondary consideration. Self-preservation took over, forcing Therill to move more quickly than he liked. Mistakes were born from carelessness.

"Blackheart keeps the artifact on the *Shrike* in his private quarters. He moved it there after we docked."

"Which means he's expecting the Inquisitor General to come after him," Ursal finished the thought. "We have less time than you led me to believe."

Therill nodded sharply. "It will be guarded."

"Are you prepared to kill your own people?" the ex-Inquisitor asked, his tone suddenly serious.

The First Mate paused, if only briefly. He hadn't considered that possibility until now. Killing Bavil had been one thing; he'd barely known the man and didn't care for what he did know. The men aboard the *Shrike* were a different story. They'd been his family, for good or bad, for the better part of the last ten years. None of them deserved the death he was bringing. He also realized none of them would be turned from Blackheart's side. The captain prized loyalty above all else. Any suspected of less than honorable action, for a pirate, was vented into space. Therill knew he was about to murder men he called friends in the cause of saving his own neck. The thought bothered him slightly, but in the end it was a matter of life or death. For that, he was willing to drown the corridors of the *Shrike* in blood.

His face hardened in a stony expression. "I will do what I must."

Ursal stopped and faced the pirate. "Why now?"

"What?"

"Why turn your back on the one man who has your back now? I can't believe it's only because of an enemy fleet about to engage this station. So why now? What changed between the two of you?"

Therill clicked his tongue on the roof of his mouth. Ursal was sharper than he'd given him credit for. "Loyalty is a dying concept among the clans. It is time for us to separate."

Nothing else needed saying. Ursal understood all too well the implications behind Therill's words. They'd both felt the bitter sting of betrayal and abandonment, Ursal perhaps worst of all. He'd done most of the dirty work, paving the way for Nye to begin his insurrection. The only saving grace Ursal had was his relationship with Kaline and Presha Von. The trio had been working in concert for nearly a decade before Nye took control of the Inquisition. The thought might have brought a grin to his face, but the current situation was much too dire to dither on anything else.

Alarm klaxons blared to life, drowning out conversations. The deep hum vibrated through the fabricated decks. Men and women scrambled, dropping what they were doing in the pointless effort to discover what was happening. It didn't matter. The first Guard missile struck one of the boarding decks and exploded in a violent storm of flame and melted metal. Reinforced doors slammed down, preventing too much oxygen from venting into space.

Ursal cast a firm glance to Geres, who merely nodded. Time was almost up, and getting through Blackheart's crew was going to be difficult at best. He turned to Therill. "We need to hurry. The Guard will not waste much time dismantling Drespai."

A handful of pirates stumbled down an adjoining corridor, stark terror etched in their faces. Therill pushed through them and hurried towards the Shrike. He casually drew his sidearm and rounded the last corner to the docking sleeve. A pair of startled guards jumped up at his arrival.

"Sir, what's going on?" one asked before the other shot him a silencing glare.

The second man stepped forward aggressively. "We been warned about you, Therill. Turn around now, and we ain't seen nothing."

"I can't do that," Therill replied calmly and fired.

Ion rounds sizzled across the space between them before striking the guards in the heads and chests. The wounds cauterized instantly, sealing the superheated energy inside the bodies. Acrid smoke filtered through their nostrils and slack mouths before they collapsed in heaps of expired flesh. Ursal was impressed, if only slightly. His mind raced ahead to the possibility of getting Therill to sign on. Having another cold-blooded killer on hand would prove beneficial in the long run. If they survived.

Geres was obviously impressed with the callousness of the deed. "How many more will Blackheart have waiting?"

"Most of the crew, if my guess is correct. We're running out of time."

Pressing a series of keys, Therill waited for the access hatch to slide open. He kept his sidearm pointed down the hatch, anticipating an ambush. Half-dark empty halls greeted them instead. His guard raised, Therill gestured with his head for the others to follow. Alarmingly, the *Shrike* was empty. They encountered no one as Therill led them into the very heart of the ship. His mind screamed silent warnings. None of it was right. There should be plenty of crew aboard getting the ship ready to depart. Instead, they were met with darkened corridors echoing their every footstep.

"We should leave," Geres whispered. Both he and Ursal were easy targets, considering neither had a weapon. He wasn't worried about himself; too many times he'd been forced to fight his way out of degenerating situations outgunned or outmanned. But Presha Von had insisted he protect Ursal Prowl for as long as possible.

Ursal concurred. "Why is the ship empty? You said Blackheart was anticipating the attack."

"I said I believe he knew about it, not that he was expecting it so soon," Therill defended. He slowed as he came to the junction between the corridors leading to the bridge and the captain's cabin. A faint thump echoed down the tight passage, so light he wasn't sure he'd heard anything. Old ships had unique sounds, and the *Shrike* was no different. It was part of the character of the ship. This noise wasn't natural, more like a hurried mistake someone tried to cover up.

Therill stalked forward. His ears desperately searched for the source of the noise while imagining acts of betrayal being played out behind him. His distrust of Ursal and Geres was well founded, making it difficult to ally with his former enemies. Any direction he turned held a knife waiting for his back. Therill damned necessity and moved forward.

Clink-clink-clink. He froze. The metallic clinking rolled to a short stop a few meters away. Therill's eyes flew open. "Take cover!"

Geres pushed Ursal to the ground and dove behind a stack of shipping crates a moment before the explosion rippled through the decks. Hot flame washed over his back, blistering and burning the flesh raw. Geres bit back a cry and winced as thick, black smoke choked the air.

Shrapnel punctured the walls. Angry shouts came from the now open bridge doors. Therill came up firing. The white-blue rounds spat back at their attackers, forcing them to take cover.

Blood trickling from his ears, Ursal shouted, "Damn it, Therill, we don't have time for that!"

Another, bigger, explosion rocked Drespai. The Prekhauten assault was intensifying. Ursal managed to sneak a glimpse of space through the bridge viewports and winced. Long torpedoes streaked towards the space station with paltry few anti-missile defense rounds going back. The pirates had clearly been caught off guard, but whether on purpose or not remained to be discovered.

Therill paused, reluctant to abandon exacting his fury. His left bicep was shredded, blood and strips of ragged flesh hanging from the muscles. He shook his shoulder, as if testing the pain, before backing away. Ursal was right, though he didn't like admitting it. The sooner they found the artifact, the sooner they could escape. Hopefully, some of the escape pods were still present. Otherwise....

"Come on, you traitorous bastard! I've been wanting to stick a blade in you for a while now," a deep voice challenged.

Therill bristled. "Piss off, Sedge. If you want to try me so badly, meet me face to face. I'll skin you from head to toe."

More rounds sizzled past him. Blackheart had known he was going to try and take the artifact all along, leading Therill into a false sense of security. Now that arrogance might have gotten them all killed. He briefly glanced back at the pair of men huddled behind him. Realistically, they were only in his way, more liability than asset. The temptation to kill them was getting increasingly harder to resist.

"Captain said you'd be coming. You're gonna die today."

Therill looked Ursal in the eye. "Get in the cabin and find the artifact. He keeps it in a long, rectangular box with a power lifter attached. Get it and head to the escape pods. I'll handle this."

"Come," Geres urged, a giant hand on Ursal's shoulder.

The rest went unsaid. Plenty of ships were anchored on Spindle, and the Guard hadn't sent enough ships to efficiently blockade the planet. Therill was unnecessary for either of them to survive. Once they found the artifact, it was a quick trip to one of the escape pods and a ride planet side. Only Blackheart and a few dozen Prekhauten warships barred the way.

Ursal relented and followed Geres down the short corridor to the captain's cabin. The sound of gunfire chased after them. The cabin was empty, much to his relief. He'd relish the opportunity to kill Vicente Blackheart later. Escape was his only priority. Revenge would come later.

The cabin was small, much smaller than he remembered during their long journey across space. He and Geres split up and started to ransack the cabinets and chests. Clothes and books were strewn recklessly around the cabin. Another explosion dropped them to their knees. A loud, metallic tearing sound was entirely too close for Ursal's liking. Still, he risked a glance out the viewport. What was left of another vessel tore free of Drespai and plunged towards Spindle's surface. Flames chased bodies out of the wounds in her hull.

"We need to hurry," he said.

Geres ignored him, intent on finding the artifact and leaving. He'd had enough of pirates and political intrigue. Gripping the small bookcase, Geres ripped it from the bulkhead. Books and collected knick-knacks spilled across the deck. He kicked a pile of books away and paused. Carved into the recess of the *Shrike's* frame was a long, black box that could only be the artifact.

"Here."

Ursal let the painted glass vase he was holding crash to the deck and peered into the recess. He fought back the grin forming. "Open it, Geres. We need to make sure."

The big man did as instructed. He strained at the dead weight, using his full strength to move the box into the open. He studied the smooth surface, impressed with the absence of markings or damage. The box was ancient, having survived millennia before humanity first understood the concept of what was within. Sheer impossibility had kept the box and the artifact undamaged even as men struggled to gain dominance over it. Geres was suddenly reluctant to interfere.

Ursal noticed his reluctance and reached for the box. His fingers barely touched the smooth edge when it sizzled and hissed open. Pale brown light drifted up from the box. Both men edged back and stared. Tears filled Geres's eyes while Ursal felt his knees go weak. Here, in their grasp, was an artifact capable of bringing the universe and every living soul within it to its knees. The raw power emanating from the box was almost overwhelming. Ursal fought the sudden urge to vomit.

He waved at Geres. "Close it, quickly!"

Geres did, but not without a warning. "We should not have this. No man should ever possess such a thing."

"It doesn't matter. That box is the only thing that's going to keep us alive, Geres. Find the power lifter so we can get the hells out of here."

He noticed the sounds of battle from the corridor were eerily missing, meaning one of two things. Either Therill was dead or he had succeeded in turning the ambush. Ursal was disinclined to find out. Let the pirates kill each other. He needed to escape and find a way back to Vau Prime.

The lifter was under Blackheart's bunk. Geres daftly triggered the gravity drive and pushed it under the edge of the recess. It took both men to position the box on the lifter. Finished, they turned and were met by another leering pirate with an ion rifle pointed at their chests.

"Fucking thieves," was all he said before brain matter and bone exploded from his forehead, splattering both men. His eyes rolled back into his head as smoke poured from his mouth and nostrils.

The body collapsed in an undignified heap, revealing a very wounded Therill leaning against the wall.

"We need to go," he said, coughing blood.

Ursal took in the abused state of the man. It wouldn't be long before the First Mate found his way into the ground. His flesh had already paled from loss of blood, thick blue veins pushed up tightly against the skin. Ursal had seen the look before and knew that certain death was stalking close behind.

Therill noticed the look he was being given and attempted to smile. "I've had worse."

I doubt that. "We have the artifact. Is the way to the escape pods clear?"

Another fit of debilitating coughs. "Yes. There is no one else aboard."

Geres stepped into the corridor, scanning each direction. Bodies were piled close to the bridge. Explosions continued in space, their blossoms and quickly dying fires burning into the viewports. The Prekhauten fleet was systematically dismantling Drespai's defenses in what he assumed was preparation for boarding action. He enjoyed the thought of tackling Guard Marines. It had been far too long since the last time he'd found anyone worthy of fighting.

"You fought well," he finally said, shaking off the adrenalin empowering him.

"There were six. All men I'd known for years. Killing them was not easy."

Ursal empathized. Killing those one thought to be friends was never easy, despite the necessity of it. The *Shrike* trembled again but hadn't taken any hits yet. Ursal found that curious. Could it be the Inquisitor General was leaving the ship intact for other reasons? As interesting as the question was, they didn't have time to explore the potential avenues. Drespai was literally disintegrating around them.

"Can you make it?" His real meaning was clear: do I need to leave you here to die?

Therill nodded again. Fresh pain twisted his face. "Yes. No need to worry about me."

Fresh blood trickled from the corners of his mouth. His breathing was shallow. Death was closer than any of them was ready to admit. Ursal gave a curt nod and started pushing the power lifter down the now empty corridor. Thanks to Therill's actions, the *Shrike* was deserted, more tomb than ship. The smell of burnt flesh was strong, making him gag.

They made the short trip relatively quickly. Therill punched in his code, and the hatch hissed open. Ursal looked within, half-expecting Blackheart to be sitting in wait. Instead, he found only empty impact seats and the long path to freedom. He gave the artifact a final shove inside before ducking in. Natural and unnatural suspicions collided, forcing him to accept that the other two could just as easily leave him to die aboard the *Shrike* as follow him planet-side. Thankfully, no one protested, following him inside wordlessly. The odd trio strapped in as Therill closed and sealed the hatch and ejected the pod. Ursal didn't sit back until the pod was well below the engagement area.

His pulse slowed as the danger shrank, allowing him to take in the action going on around them. Most of the docking sleeves were either gone or shredded metal. Burned out hulks of numerous pirates ships caught attempting to flee crashed into each other as they took up orbit around the ruined station. Bodies floated everywhere, and still the Guard continued the attack. He counted at least twenty-five ships pounding the mythical pirate haven. Nye and Strannan weren't taking chances.

The pod's engines stalled as Spindle's gravity took hold of the small craft, drawing it down to the surface and away from the brutal assault on Drespai. Ursal leaned back in the soft cushions of the specially designed impact seats and closed his eyes. His mind was already racing ahead to what to do with the artifact and his betrayal by the Inquisitor General.

"You said we were secure! That our base of operations would remain outside of Prekhauten jurisdictions!" Blackheart bellowed at the image of Alain Nye.

Nye offered a menacing grin. "You were, until you decided to exceed your authority. You've become a liability I can't afford to have hanging around my neck."

The pirate captain fumed as more torpedoes tore gaping holes in Drespai. The world he'd carefully constructed was being dismantled around him. All his grand plans and illusions of the future were becoming dust, ashes slipping through his grasp.

"Don't be so ignorant as to misunderstand the situation, Vicente. You've outlived your usefulness to me. Your clans are about to engage my fleet like we agreed. You, however, stand in my way. You never should have threatened me with the artifact. I will admit that I hadn't known where it was until you couldn't keep your lips together. Thank you for that. Once my ships destroy your pathetic base, salvage teams will come in and take the artifact, preferably from beside your frozen corpse."

The pirate felt oddly deflated. It had been too long since the last time he'd been humbled, rendered immobile. Cold realization started to set in. Drespai wasn't going to last much longer. The Prekhauten fleet was pounding away with everything it had, killing any craft that tried to flee. Most if not all the defense platforms had been blasted from orbit, leaving the aged space station open to attack. There was nothing in the pirate's arsenal capable of disabling a Prekhauten warship, and both sides knew it.

Nye had been playing him all along. That was the only reasonable explanation for the speed with which the Prekhauten fleet had arrived. Virtually every available pirate ship had deployed to Hawker's Gate to ambush and defeat the main Prekhauten fleet, leaving Drespai with a skeleton crew at best. Most of what remained was down on Spindle drinking and whoring their way through what monies they had left. Of the remaining ships, only the *Shrike* was combat ready, and she had less than half of her crew on Drespai. Blackheart had been caught flat.

"Good-bye, Captain," Nye said and cut the transmission.

Vicente Blackheart sank back into his chair, deflated and struggling with the reality of defeat. His embarrassment was going to be short-lived, at least, and with few to witness such cataclysmic failure. He idly wondered what impact the memory of his name would have on future generations if any at all. Surely Nye would expunge all records of the pirate captain in his efforts to consolidate power and control after the insurrection was finished. Blackheart was a dead man about to be wiped from history.

"Captain Blackheart! It's Therill. He's betrayed us!" Sedge came running in, out of breath and bleeding from a pair of wounds.

Blackheart winced before swiveling his command chair around. It had only been a matter of time before his First Mate abandoned him. Of course it would be at the most inopportune moment. "Explain yourself."

"He came aboard the *Shrike* with them two Inquisitors, just like you said he would. But they was stronger than us. Killed half a dozen crewers before breaking into your cabin."

The news continued to worsen. First Nye's abandonment and now Therill's. He'd known it was coming. It was as inevitable as the sun chasing the moons. But for Therill to sell him out to the Inquisition was almost unthinkable. Wars were won or lost by less, forcing him to reconsider his position. If he couldn't trust his First Mate to have his back, then who was left? The thought of being alone was disturbingly stark and left him with a hollow feeling in the pits of his soul.

Lethargy threatening to settle in, Blackheart lurched from his chair and reached for the belt and pair of sidearms. "Where is he now?"

Sedge lowered his gaze. "Away to the escape pods. Only one is missing, Captain."

Unfelt hatred flared to life in Blackheart's dark eyes. "Did he take anything with him? Answer me, damn it!"

"They had a box. Dunno what it was, but it was long and looked heavy. I think we got Therill good, though. He was bleeding all over and barely on his feet."

Blackheart had stopped listening after Sedge confirmed Therill and Prowl had stolen the artifact. He cursed himself for being foolish enough to think it was secure onboard the *Shrike*. Complacency and arrogance plied together to open the path to his downfall. All his carefully laid plans were tattered shreds of what might have been.

None of that mattered now. His life was reduced to a pair of thoughts. Alain Nye needed to be dealt with, but that was going to take time and a lot of effort. Ursal Prowl, however, was a closer target. If he moved quickly enough, Prowl and his cohorts would be bits of flash-frozen skin and bones drifting towards the nearest sun.

"Send the word to evacuate the station," he ordered. "The Inquisition has betrayed us. All forces are to rendezvous at point alpha.

Do not engage the enemy. I want all crewers onboard the *Shrike* immediately."

"Orders, Captain?"

Blackheart leered. "We're going to kill Therill."

TWENTY-SEVEN

3212 A.G. (After Gods), the Deeves, planet An'kuruku.

The sprawling pilgrim camp hadn't had a moments rest since the beleaguered Jut had arrived with news of the approaching Prefect army. Many had already fled in panic, fearful that the Prophet wouldn't be able to protect them. Small fights and riots were breaking out, and Mollock Bolle was yet to be seen. The cultists had managed little in pacifying the growing sense of fear tearing the camp apart.

Sunset was particularly brilliant. Orange and golden light ripped through the storm-blackened sky as the sun dipped below the horizon. The air smelled fresh, cleansed by a million drops of rain washing the dirt and filth away.

Mollock stood on the rocky shore, head titled back. He was drenched but unwilling to leave this personal sanctum. Eyes closed, he enjoyed the feel of the wind tickling his long, unkempt beard. His hair, now down past his shoulders and nearly all silver, dripped remnants of the storm. The sound of gulls feeding was as music to his tormented soul.

Mollock wanted a way out, needed to return to obscurity and forget the madness of the cult of Rengu and especially Kaline. The lies came easily enough. A façade to hide behind while he struggled to understand his position. He wasn't sure if he believed what he told the crowds. Lies were faster. A more elaborate conclusion to the whispered prayers of the bereft. Each time he spoke from the rocks his honor diminished.

His life was a tragedy played out again and again when he looked into the eyes of those foolish enough to find faith in his words. He was a charlatan, a fraud with no convictions or moral boundaries. The lies left his lips too easily. They poisoned everyone, including himself. Mollock tried to remember a time when his life had been simple, when he had been a mere fugitive with unlawful knowledge. Those days were vague memories now, faded and blurred beyond recognition. Circumstance had changed him into a powerful figure with no real influence. Try as he did to change or ignore it, he was a puppet in a dangerous game. Puppets never survived to the end of the tale.

"Don't you ever grow weary of standing on these abominable stones?"

He frowned, the purity of the moment shattered among the rocks. "Kaline. I only grow weary of being disturbed when I most wish to be alone."

She ignored the rebuke. "I didn't come out here to bandy ill-spoken words, Mollock."

"Those seem to be the only type of words we know how to exchange," he replied.

"Regardless, there is trouble looming. You've heard the army of the Prefecture is en route?"

He sighed, lowering his head and turning to face her. "It was inevitable. You've spurred a rebellion. The powers that be have no choice but to retaliate. This is not the first time I've witnessed such. Our troubles on Crimeat seem to have been just the beginning. Has the Conclave gotten involved yet?"

"No. They are strangely absent, as if their masters on Vau Prime gave implicit instructions to remain neutral. I don't care for the current situation."

He wanted to laugh. "A situation you clearly intended to create. Look at the masses you vehemently claim have gathered to hear me rant against the Conclave and the very gods themselves! The audacity of it is staggering. Did you really think you could outwit the most powerful organization in the history of humanity? Or get away with insulting the deity structure that we've relied on for thousands of years without suspicion or jealousy? You've played a dangerous game, Kaline, and put us all in jeopardy. I never should have come here."

"You didn't have a choice. The Prefecture was already closing in on you when my agents rescued you from the streets of Tenemenah. Don't try to convince me of false innocence. You're as guilty of leading these people and keeping them here as I. We both serve different tyrants, Mollock Bolle. Your hands are about to be stained in blood the same as mine."

He couldn't help his eyes bulging, the whites straining against the violent backdrop. "Blood? I'll atone for my crimes after I die, but not for the thousands of people you've led to their doom in this godless wasteland. Don't you dare lump me in with your villainy."

"Villainy?" She laughed, light and melodious. "What have I done to spark this newfound suspicion? I have done nothing but be your friend and ally since getting you away from the Prefecture."

"Perhaps a prison cell would have been a better fate than this," he gestured towards the panicked camp.

"You never would have made it that far. I know Lezorsu. He'd have taken you down a back alley and executed you without question. This, which you have already abandoned as a doomed cause, is the birth of a new freedom these people would never have known without hearing the confidence of your words. All their lives were being wasted under the oppression of alleged leadership with the good of everyone in mind. When has the Conclave ever been your friend? When have you ever felt comfortable enough to go to the local Inquisition office with concerns for your spiritual wellbeing?

"I already know your answer. It's the same as mine. Never. The Conclave and Inquisition have strayed far from their founding principles. They no longer serve the people, instead keeping us ignorant to the truth. The truth that you discovered for yourself beneath the black mountains of the Plateau fifty years ago. A truth they've tried to have you silenced over, time and again.

"How much more can anyone take before the breaking point is crossed? How many lines need to be shattered by false justice and empty rhetoric before the people rise up and take back what rightfully belongs to them? That is what they have come here for. Not because you have a golden tongue. You, me, any other random person. It doesn't matter who stands before them and speaks the words their hearts yearn so badly to hear. Will you deny them that?"

She fell silent, her chest rising and falling much faster now. Her face was flushed. The impassioned plea had come from the heart, unrehearsed and raw. Kaline hoped it would be enough to keep him in check, at least for a while longer.

Mollock might have been moved if not for the decades of constantly looking over his shoulder, checking every shadow. He'd learned not to trust, and that skill set had kept him alive for all that time. What little of his core remained was shelled and callous. Friendship had become anathema, an unnecessary tie to humanity that would only serve to hasten his demise. The closest thing he had to a friend was Elisa.

Thinking of her brought a thin smile to his concealed lips. She'd come to him in the Ugri lands with murderous intent, clearly making her more enemy than friend. Still, she was able to understand his position, whether from her own personal experiences with the gods and their bastard sons or from keeping a level head throughout their ordeal. Reluctantly, he was forced to admit that her involvement was all his fault. Without his little survival ploy in the Ugri prison cell, she never would have gone to Reven — never would have seen the truth for herself.

His twisting of the truth, just enough to intrigue Elisa to the point where she couldn't resist going to see for herself what nightmares had spawned the Bloody Man and the other Three, was all it had taken to eventually lead them here to planet An'kuruku and the budding insurrection of the Deeves. Immense sorrow filled his heart. Mollock lacked the conviction to continue. It was an old crisis of faith holding him back, keeping him from achieving his full potential. He suddenly found himself hating his life.

There was darkness crowding in on him. What little control he had over himself was fading into obscurity, gripping his soul tighter with each passing day. He desperately needed a way out, a final solution absolving him of his sins and crimes. Mollock believed only his death would achieve that inglorious goal. More than once, he gave serious thought to ending his life here on the ancient rocks where he felt most secure. The temptation quickly turned into a compulsion.

It wouldn't take much, a whispered prayer and a quick jump to the waiting rocks below. Perhaps they would accept him where the rest of humanity found it so casual to abandon him, to use him as a puppet rather than a friend. His thankless life was sadly friendless, and it made his soul weep for better days. All it would take was just one final jump.

"When have I ever been given a choice? Life has conspired against me, forcing me into deepening wells of confusion and emptiness. There is nothing you can say to convince me otherwise, Kaline. I have finally reached the bottom."

She saw the raw desperation in his face, the choking sorrow in his words, and realized any chance of maintaining the presumption of his salvation was quickly disappearing. Kaline reached out to him, a warm hand caressing his forearm. "You're not alone, Mollock. There's no reason for despair. Every great hero must overcome challenges specific to his nature. This will —"

"Hero?" It was his turn to laugh. "I am many things; hero is not among them. Look around you, Kaline. My life is a fragment of what might have been."

"Stop feeling sorry for yourself. It's unbecoming for a grown man, especially one who has lived through the things you have. A war is coming, not of our choosing. Crying over it won't change the fact that very soon we will be forced to defend ourselves."

"Against a trained and zealous army? The Prefects will wipe this merry encampment out to the last child, and you'll be left with a sea of bones for as far as the eye can see."

She stiffened. "One of their own trains able-bodied volunteers as we speak. We are not as defenseless as you would make us out."

Mollock cocked his head, studying her. There was something odd he couldn't quite place — and then it hit him. "You're not staying."

"No. The work I have begun here is larger than just the people of the Deeves. I have sparked a hundred fires on a hundred worlds. Soon, the revolution will come. An'kuruku is just the beginning, a testing ground, if you will," she admitted blandly.

His mouth dropped open. "All of these people duped into a lie. Murderer."

"I give them hope where they had none before! This is the shape of the future, Mollock Bolle. Or should I call you by the name these cattle use? The madman on the rocks. You saw what becomes of insurrections on your homeworld. Why should this be any different?"

"You were there? On Lethendweil during the war?"

She nodded. "Briefly. Ideations like that don't just happen. The spark must come from somewhere deep inside that men can find personal faith in. I merely assisted."

Mollock dropped his head in shame. "Leave me. If we are to die, I wish it to be in peace. I don't want my last sight to be your gods damned face."

Biting her lip, Kaline turned and stormed off. She briefly wondered if this was the last time she was going to see him alive.

For most of the camp, sunset was nothing but the clock slowly ticking away what little time remained before the hammer of the Prefecture struck. Fewer fires burned in the whispered hopes of being unnoticed. The old thought it all foolish. Death and hatred knew no mortal bounds. They warned the Prefects would come in like the grim angels of retribution, scything souls down like so much wheat. The young and brave scoffed and waved their elders off. What did the old and infirm know? They already had a foot in the grave and were jealous of the young.

Bodies were discovered almost hourly, but with no formal law enforced, there was little concern. Most were trampled underfoot. Elisa sat in the Bone Father's tent with her head cradled in her hands. No stranger to violence, she'd regretfully been forced to kill a pair of would-be brigands trying to get rich off the ancient man. Enough people had witnessed the act to prevent others from attempting the same. Not everyone in the camp was without teeth.

"This is madness," the Bone Father lamented. "How could we have fallen so far?"

"People will do anything when they think the end has finally come. Don't hold them so tightly in your judgment."

Paradise Tear stirred behind them. Her immense size was barely contained within the tent. "I have seen this too many times before. First comes inescapable panic. Many will perish without a shot ever being fired. After that comes betrayal. Men will turn on each other in the hopes that they will be spared. It won't matter. The coming storm will engulf them all and leaving nothing alive. Humanity learned nothing from our mistakes."

The sorrow in her voice tore at Elisa. How many more souls needed to be ruined in the name of an empty cause? Hardships were to be expected in life, even embraced, but no one deserved to live under the iron blanket of fear and hatred. Whatever violence Elisa had seen over the course of her life was infinitesimal compared to the forced genocide of Paradise's race. Now the remnants of a once proud and powerful race had returned to bring humanity to its knees. Elisa was beginning to believe she was witnessing the end of humanity. It seemed an injustice for Paradise to have to go through the same event a second time.

"What can we do?" she asked suddenly, staring at a small blood stain on the tent flap. "These people are scared, and they have every reason to be. The Prefects will not be gentle — not if the man I think is leading their army."

The Bone Father got up and began to pace. "I feel responsible."

"Nonsense. You can't control this situation any more than you can another's life," Elisa admonished. "These aren't your people anymore, Bone Father. Let me take you and Paradise away from here."

"We can't leave," they both answered in unison.

Elisa lifted her head. She'd expected his protests, but not hers. "You, I understand, but what do you mean, Paradise?"

The giant smiled sadly. "You were told to seek me out, but not why. It is time you learned that truth. I am more than just a survivor of my species. I am the hope for rebirth. Tannus hid me from everyone else, especially Amongeratix, when he realized the war was going badly. He was the one who took our people and placed them in sleeping chambers on every world in the known universe. His brother knew this and tried to stop it. He was too late. Tannus had already saved as many of us as he could before imbibing my essence with the ability to awaken our people."

"Is it possible that all of this is to get at you?" Elisa asked.

Paradise shook her head. "No. Apart from the Bone Father, no one knows of my true nature. He found me floating in my stasis tube when I crashed on this world. There is something more sinister at work in the Deeves."

Elisa turned and looked the Bone Father in the eyes. "I need to get you out of here. The Prefect army is coming with one purpose: to kill everyone. She and I can take care of ourselves, but I am worried about you."

"Don't make the mistake of thinking me feeble just because I am old," he snapped back, putting her in her place. "My task is not yet accomplished. Mollock Bolle has much to answer for. I will see him pay for the perversions he encouraged in my charges."

"You'll never get through all of the cult's security. They keep him locked away for reasons just like that. Your best bet is to get into space and blow him away from orbit."

"Space? I've never left the Deeves, and you expect me to travel into the heavens? No. This is my home, and if I die defending, it so be it. I have made peace with that decision."

Elisa wanted to throw up her hands in frustration but knew it would have no effect. He was just as stubborn as she. Options severely reduced, she decided to throw in with him and see what they could accomplish. "How do we get into those ruins? You could have picked an easier target. Kaline won't let him out once the Prefects attack."

"A fact I'm counting on. When the attack does come, there will be absolute chaos here. No one will be paying much attention to anyone but themselves, making it easy for an old man to slip through the defenses and do what needs to be done."

Elisa had to admit it was a simple and probable plan. Her only issue was in whether they'd have time to find Mollock. Any hope she'd once reserved of finding him alive and getting him to safety had died the first time she'd listened to his rant against the Conclave and the gods. Heresy was punishable by death under the codes of the Inquisition, but what he spoke was akin to open rebellion. The venom lacing his words showed her he had crossed the line, and there was no returning. The Mollock Bolle she had known and spent two years with was dead, replaced by the twisted image standing before these people inciting rebellion and promising the ultimate freedom. She didn't want to believe Mollock was the monster whispered about, but until she confronted him directly…

Killing Mollock wouldn't solve the problems plaguing the Deeves. If anything, he was already a relic. Whatever incendiary fervor Kaline had given birth to, it was destined to be consumed by an even greater mechanism. Lezorsu and his army was coming to purge the desert with their own brand of holy fire. The righteous, if ever there was a thing, were about to do battle. But over what? Elisa couldn't figure that out. There was nothing here but sand and wind.

"Who is going to do it?" she asked slowly, as if afraid of the answer.

The Bone Father sighed and spoke his words clearly so that there would be no misunderstanding. "I must atone for my laxity. I will do it. No one else need stain their hands, or souls, by the filth of the deed."

Part of her felt instant relief. She hadn't been able to bring herself to kill Mollock before and had even turned against the man who had hired her. Not that they'd ever been friends, but Mollock didn't pose any threat to her. Now. She shook her head. Now, it just didn't make sense how any one man could get so caught up in false prose that he lost sight of his original intent.

"Doesn't that violate some stricture of faith?"

He offered a smile. "I'm no clergyman, young lady. Don't worry about me. I can do what needs doing."

Elisa fell silent. There wasn't anything left to be said. The three of them had just conspired to commit murder, which was ridiculous given their current circumstance. Death was almost a given, regardless of the means. Murder had become another empty word that held no meaning. Only the smallest part of her conscience protested. Some part of her still sought a way to escape this with Mollock alive.

As if reading her mind, the Bone Father placed a calloused, wrinkled hand on her knee. "Just because I know what needs to be done doesn't mean I am at peace with the decision. No man should be killed, even though we all die, but that doesn't change the fact that a great evil has been delivered to the people of the Deeves. It falls upon what good remains to search for redemption and, possibly, salvation before all is lost and the light dims to black."

Something within her stirred. Emotions that had been repressed for too long surged against their restraints, desperately trying to break through and be known. She nearly succumbed, so strong was the raw power. Her eyes watered, and it was all she could do to keep from letting those tears pour out in a river of unchecked feelings.

The Bone Father smiled, as did Paradise. Both knew all too well how hard times had become. It was no easy thing admitting to oneself that it was all right to cry, to feel joy or sorrow, to stand under the morning sun and be at peace. Elisa hadn't given in to her emotions since the night the Bloody Man had slaughtered her village.

"It's alright, you know," he confided in her. "Crying does more than just make our eyes sore. We should all have an emotional outlet. You, especially."

Paradise smiled. "I don't profess to know the future, but I can promise to do my best to protect you in so far as I'm able."

It was enough; it had to be. Too much depended on Elisa surviving for anything less. Above all, she had to get to Occanum. The pressure was almost too much, and she decided to step outside and get what little fresh air dared hover over the filth of the ever-growing encampment. The time was fast approaching when the endgame would be played out. She doubted if she'd make it to Occanum.

Jut watched the hundreds of peasants drill on the open field with passive disgust. They lacked precision, skill and, most importantly, basic ability. Most, if not all, would prove no match for the disciplined Prefect army. Wars were won through will as much as sheer brutality. Jut shook his head. These people had no idea what they were getting into. And he was going to be standing beside them when the worst happened.

"You disapprove?" Kaline's soft voice asked.

He turned, watching her stroll up beside him. She might have been beautiful at another time. He smirked and shook his head again, shamed at the thought. "They don't stand a chance."

"You might be surprised. They know life and death are in the balance. We are capable of extraordinary feats when backed into a corner."

"Nothing you or I do is going to change the fact that a lot of blood is going to be spilled here," he replied blankly.

Kaline shrugged. "Perhaps because it is supposed to be shed. Who among us can claim to know the will of the gods?"

"I place no faith in the gods. They've abandoned me at every turn. Best they keep to themselves and leave me alone."

She regarded him softy, her deep eyes studying the former Prefect. He was an invaluable resource, provided he maintained his composure. Kaline knew all too well that most of the people here were going to die. It was all part of the plan — a plan she couldn't disclose to anyone until she was positive they were entirely on her side. The war here on An'kuruku was just the beginning. Her last communication with Vau Prime suggested all was going according to schedule. Soon, the entire universe would know the truth of what she was destined to accomplish. All would kneel in praise of a new master.

"I've found that we place too much value on the wants and desires of beings no one has been able to prove still exist," she confided. "It's past time mankind learned to stand on its own two feet."

"If only we could. The Conclave and Inquisition drive everything. We don't think but what we are told to." Jut looked back to the masses. Instead of proper lines and standard formations, he saw only a rabble clumped together. Prefecture energy weapons would make short work of large groups. He had much to do and nearly no time left in which to do it.

"There is a change coming, Jut. Can't you feel it?" she pressed, eager to discover if his heart followed his mind.

He snorted. "Change is seldom the kind we wish for. If we're done, these people need to learn more before they're all killed."

He stormed down the gentle slope, bellowing orders and shouting at the sweat- and grime-covered masses. Kaline watched him intently. Mollock Bolle had served his purpose and was now obsolete. She began to see Jut as the man to replace him in the coming struggle. Now, all she needed to do was ensure he survived long enough.

Prefect Lezorsu stood beside his command vehicle and slowly poured his canteen over his head. The cool water sizzled as it struck the heated flesh of his face. Days were becoming much too long for his liking. The casual comforts of Tenemenah were lost during the hot marches and short nights. Insects and arachnids assailed them constantly. Too many to bother counting had already been lost to a number of hazards. More than a hundred had died to heat exhaustion alone. The army was starting to grow demoralized, forcing him to send Prefects through the ranks to eliminate dissenters and firebrands. Lezorsu felt control of his army slowly slipping and wasn't sure how to respond.

"Prefect Lezorsu, are you there?"

Lezorsu growled at the interruption before clicking on his transmitter. "What, Pey? I'm in no mood for your comments."

The momentary silence told him all he needed to know. "Our scouts report they have arrived within visual range of the heretic camp. How do you wish me to proceed?"

At last! A genuine grin, the first he'd had since leaving Tenemenah. "Continue your report."

"The heretic camp is large, much larger than we previously believed. I put their numbers somewhere between seven and ten thousand. It looks like a large body is conducting some sort of combat drill in one of the nearby fields. Not much to worry about, judging from what I see. An abandoned castle sits directly behind it, against the shores of the Bo. Their command structure should be situated within. The perimeter lacks any formal defenses, at least as far as I can tell. We shouldn't have too much trouble hitting them head-on."

Lezorsu forced himself not to give the command to attack. His enemy was commonly judged simple and backwoods by most of the more civilized, but he knew better than to underestimate his opponents. The hammer blow needed to fall in concert with his overall plan, and, sadly, he wasn't in the position to engage yet. Still, it wouldn't hurt to let the heretics know he was breathing down their necks.

"What size force do you have that is combat ready?" he asked, the idea already forming before the answer came.

"Five hundred," Althas paused. "Not enough to take on a force of this size."

Lezorsu instantly regretted placing Althas in charge of the advance. A truly brutal tactician wouldn't have hesitated, especially knowing how his commander wanted to drown the Deeves in blood to produce a lasting memory to prevent further uprisings. "Deploy your vanguard accordingly, Prefect Pey. I want you to begin a terror campaign immediately. Eliminate as many high-ranking officials as possible. Throw their camp into complete chaos."

"You wish me to engage with only five hundred men?"

"I wish you to obey my commands. We have a chance to break them now before the bulk of the main army arrives. Engage at your discretion. Once the artillery is in place, I will show them the true path to the underworld."

Lezorsu clicked off his transmitter and threw it down in the sand. He turned to his adjutant with a menacing glare. "Get this fucking army moving faster. We've a war to fight, and I won't be denied the glory due me."

TWENTY-EIGHT

3212 A.G. (After Gods), Krenz, planet Vau Prime.

Lorenu Phos, Cardinal Seniorus of the Conclave and the single most powerful woman of over seven hundred colonized worlds, sat helpless in her private chambers nestled in the heart of Conclave headquarters. Her world was crumbling around her, and she was lost. Smoke from a hundred fires across the capital drifted up into the light pillars shining into space. Sirens and gunfire echoed through the streets. Redemption Boulevard, once the triumphant symbol of freedom and peace, was blackened from homemade firebombs and vacant.

She couldn't help but feel it was all her fault. She'd been blinded by political maneuvering and personal agendas, forcing her into this unenviable position. It was with a heavy heart that she'd directed Alain Nye to enact marshal law. Hundreds had been rounded up and locked away. The Inquisition was strained. Rebellions on too many worlds to keep track of stretched their ranks thin, forcing Nye to incorporate more and more of the local law enforcement.

The pirate engagements by the Prekhauten fleets left Vau Prime virtually undefended, an issue that would only bear fruit if the capital planet was attacked or invaded. That was the least of her worries. Lorenu didn't know where to turn to find the answers she desperately needed. Nor did she know whom to trust. Suspicions were running rampant, through the commoners as well as the clergy. Priests and low-level clerics were being attacked by mobs. One had already died, and there was no telling how far this wave of violence was going to extend before Nye managed to get matters back under control.

Chaos had come to rule over order and justice.

Lorenu fought back what had turned into a steady fit of tears and went to her balcony. She hadn't been to the gardens in so long, she'd forgotten the solitude that had so often soothed her during her tenure as Cardinal Seniorus. Now she wished she'd never run for the position, heeding the warnings of family and friends. All power came with enemies. Only now was she beginning to realize just how dark those enemies were, but not who.

"Are there any answers?" she asked no one. The night mocked her with its silence. She almost summoned Aliz, if only to see a friendly face and feel the warmth of unconditional love. Lorenu also knew that she wouldn't be able to live with herself if anything happened to Aliz because she exposed her to unnecessary risk.

As if in answer to her prayers, a dynamic blue flare blossomed in orbit. Lorenu instantly recognized it for what it was. The Acumensiis Comet had steadily been approaching for more than a month, the elongated plume growing larger and brighter nightly. The Conclave had already received requests for a delegation to arrive, and, curiously, only Lorenu knew that Grand Mistress Ruma Zzein was secretly communicating with her alone as the false delegation met with the Forum and Inquisition officials. Webs within webs. Seeing the legendary home of the Order of Blood Witches entering Vau Prime's orbit gave her hope for the future.

The one hundred Cardinals of the Forum, the inner circle of elected clergy that created legislation and policy for most of the known universe, noisily filed into the meeting chamber. Arguments and angered comments were traded. Very few of the illustrious group appreciated or accepted the arrival of the Blood Witches. Word had passed quickly through the compounds and sanctums as the Forum, along with most of Krenz, was informed that the entire comet abbey had come.

The event was unprecedented. Never had such an eccentric group come to treat with the rulers of the universe. The cardinals were largely unimpressed by the gesture. Outcasts one and all, the witches were the product of a failed program aimed at redeeming those society had no place for. To find three of the witches standing in the center of the Forum chambers sent many cardinals into fits.

"I thought the purpose of their order was to remove the undesirables from our ranks? Now they have the nerve to come here and issue demands. How low have we fallen," Cardinal Tinus Har sniped.

Cardinal Arbalas waved him off, her twin chins jiggling across the top of her collar. "Perhaps you can mention your ideas for a euthanasia program to Lorenu again the next time you have a meeting."

"I'll never be able to get her out of her offices. Our vaunted Cardinal Seniorus has become a shadow ruler."

Ott Gorman leaned down from the row behind. "We are on the verge of war and you abandon our leadership?"

"I am abandoning nothing, Cardinal Gorman." Har's eyes darkened. "When is the last time any of us saw her in public? When is the last time she officiated over anything? We're the ones being abandoned."

Gorman's liver spots flared. "That's convenient considering your own planet was unable to prevent the destruction of the Prekhauten station in orbit."

"Shut up, Gorman. You and I both know I had nothing to do with what happened there, just like you don't know what's happening on your own world. We've moved on to bigger matters."

"You are failing to recognize one crucial factor in your decision-making process, Gorman," the elder Cardinal Thent added quietly.

Gorman regarded the man critically. They'd never gotten along, and he was positive whatever came out of Thent's mouth next would be pure nonsense. "Don't waste my time, old man."

"Time is many things but doesn't belong to any one of us," Thent retorted. "What I was going to say was you fail to consider that we are a broken body of legislature. Nothing we do or try has worked well over the past two years, not since Amongeratix escaped our prison on Crimeat. Lorenu Phos is ineffective as Cardinal Seniorus. She is the root of our problems."

Gorman's eyes narrowed critically. "What are you saying?"

"The time has come for Lorenu Phos to step aside or be removed if she is unwilling to relinquish her power."

Feeling his heart pound up into his throat, Gorman struggled to find the right words but knew he was only going to create a stir amongst the cardinals. His mind reeled under the implications of what he'd just heard. The audacity! The Conclave was bordering on open war against the rising number of cults, not to mention the military actions that already begun against the pirate clans that had been, in Gorman's opinion, ignored for far too long, and here was one of the senior-most Cardinals of the Forum openly declaring that the Cardinal Seniorus should step down.

"I think one of them is about to speak," Arbalas said, eager to break the rising tension before the two elder Cardinals came to blows.

An uneasy silence settled over the assembly. Most of them had never heard a Blood Witch talk, much less seen a living one in person. They sat riveted to the three slender figures hovering inches above the freshly polished marble floor. Floating! All had heard the rumors, but few bothered believing in such childish fairy tales. People couldn't float, and that was it. Standing there before them, more than a few cardinals were forced to rethink their theories and beliefs. The burning question of what else they might have miscalculated weighing heavily on their minds.

"The Grand Mistress of the Order of Blood Witches thanks your Cardinal Seniorus for this audience," Deius Mlth, Mistress of Arms, addressed the assembly. Her voice, normally lithe and wispy, echoed throughout the chamber with authority. The gossamer folds of her gown rippled softly. "Our two great factions have long been allies, if somewhat strained by politics. We are here now to reaffirm our commitment to the Conclave and to deliver a dire warning."

She waited for the murmur to fade before continuing. "The beings you know as the Three have resurfaced with the intent of awakening their brethren to regain dominance over the known universe. They are aided by a growing faction of humanity that has become disillusioned with your strictures and societal constraints."

"This is preposterous! How dare you come before us and insult us with base threats?" Tinus Har stood and roared. "We've ruled the universe for three thousand years without your help. Naturally there have been bumps along the way, but this body has remained the sole, true power. Our rule is unquestionable."

"We did not come to trade insults or harsh words, merely to speak the truth," Algiss Her, Mistress of Novices, interjected. "You face a war of unprecedented size. Nothing you have experienced in your *brief* history has prepared you for what is coming."

"You expect us to think you have clairvoyant powers? A roving band of psychics and charlatans that deign to grace us with their infinite wisdoms moments before the old gods return from oblivion! Go back to that rock in space you call home. We will handle this crisis as we've handled all others that came before."

The Blood Witches remained still. Much of the reaction of the cardinals was expected. Algiss briefly turned her head to Deius with the unspoken knowledge that no one in this room truly understood the beings they worshipped and revered as gods were not dead at all. Ruma had warned them before entering Vau Prime's orbit, but not even her most ardent supporters were willing to accept that nearly all of humanity was being kept in the dark, purposefully. Deius gently shook her head and returned her gaze back to the enraged Forum.

"It is no secret that the women of the Order are...gifted in ways the majority of humanity is not, but we don't carry ourselves with empty titles. Your anger is misplaced, Cardinal. We come as allies, not enemies."

Ott Gorman rose and beckoned for silence. "Disputing the reasons for your sudden and, admittedly, unexpected arrival is a pointless endeavor, Mistress. You must realize that contact between our factions, as you put it, has been so severely constrained that it would be most unusual for any of us to accept your words on face value. Scripture tells us that the gods were all destroyed at the final battle of Occanum. The Three are the sad remnants of their race and, while infinitely dangerous, pose no real threat to the continuity of the Conclave."

"You are mistaken about a great many truths, Cardinal Ott Gorman," Deius countered softly. "Unfortunately, it is not my place to enlighten you."

"Enlighten us to what? Lies spun in the dark holds of your isolation? The Acumensiis Comet may float across the heavens, but it is not the know-all, be-all source in the universe. How many times have we needed your Order only to be met by silence or worse? There is a truth to be had among the stars, but I highly doubt it can be found on that rock you call home."

If the Blood Witches were incensed, they refused to show it, further infuriating many of the Forum. Deius continued, "Perhaps you have forgotten that our Order began long before the rest of humanity climbed out of its caves and learned that fire was not to be feared? None of the past matters, at least not the parts with which you are familiar. War is coming, ladies and gentleman, a war that you cannot hope to stall or stave off. Our message is delivered. We will go now."

The trio of Blood Witches began to fade, blurring into the light marble floor in a brilliant light. Blinded, the Cardinals were forced to shield their eyes. When their vision finally cleared, they looked down in a strange combination of wonder and suspicion. The Blood Witches were gone.

"Do you truly believe this is the end?" Lorenu Phos asked reluctantly.

Ruma Zzein waited a moment and nodded. "I have seen it. Amongeratix is much stronger than he was when he escaped his prison on Keltoo. For him to breach my shielding and ward spells in the abbey suggests he is nearly ready to begin his quest to finish his long war. The key has been discovered, the artifact in play, and Amongeratix will stop at nothing to get them."

"The Inquisitor General has assured me that the Inquisition is doing everything it can to retrieve the artifact."

Lorenu trembled at the thought of Amongeratix getting his hands on the artifact. He would be unstoppable, despite anything Nye or she could muster to throw at him. The power of the Three was rising at last. It was inevitable. The closest the Inquisition had come to recovering the artifact was seven years ago when the *LodSpear* had been destroyed in the Mefgelin Asteroid Belt by what was now known to be a coordinated pirate attack. Unanswered questions had plagued her at the time; questions that shouldn't have been asked. Very few people had knowledge of the expedition, forcing her to reluctantly accept that one or more of her closest confidants was a traitor.

If Amongeratix got both totems, he could awaken, or destroy, his entire race. Even facing only a few hundred, the Conclave would be hard pressed to stop them from reclaiming the thrones of the universe. The Three had proven elusive and nearly too powerful already. Cold dread ran down her spine at the thought of hundreds more causing havoc across the stars.

An incredible sense of failure settled on her frail shoulders. Guilt gnawed at her, breathing new life into doubt and regret. Lorenu had accepted the position of Cardinal Seniorus to protect humanity, not lead it down into the throes of chaos. No matter which direction she looked, only uncertainty stared back.

The Cardinal Seniorus bowed her head, choking back her sorrow rising like bile in her throat. "I had hoped it would never come to this. What did I do wrong?"

"A pointless question, Lorenu. The past cannot be changed. Amongeratix has made the opening move in the war and has the support of millions of your people, including men and women in all three of the ruling organizations. Treason is about to become a meaningless word."

The Grand Mistress of the Blood Witches fell silent, allowing Lorenu time to understand what she'd been told. That same level of enlightenment was being delivered to the Forum now but with severely opposite results. Ruma suddenly came to realize the sad truth that had helped fuel much of the troubles now facing the Conclave.

"How many know the truth?" she asked.

Lorenu glanced up. "What truth?"

"That the gods are not dead."

The straightforwardness of it produced a chuckle. "Perhaps twenty-five. It has been as closely guarded as anything in our history. We fabricate the lie to keep panic and fear from seeping into the hearts of the people. Those that came before me thought it wise to keep this secret. Now, I don't know."

Ruma nodded, keeping a darker, more damning secret private. "It is the same secret that will undo all who have sat in your office have striven to accomplish."

"What hope do I have? Is there anything I can do?" the desperation in her voice made her tremble.

Ruma reached out and gently took Lorenu's hand in her own. She fixed a soft gaze on the aging woman, that same sorrow reflected in her own eyes. "The pieces are in place. Amongeratix is already moving. You will be betrayed by those in your closest confidence. There is but one act you can commit that will see the war end with at least some vestige of humanity still alive. Lorenu Phos, you have to die."

Mobus Kale folded his arms across his chest and watched as the file of prisoners was lined up against the blackened wall. His robotic right arm pressed tightly against his uniform, creasing the dark fabric. The glare in his eyes bordered on maniacal. He truly enjoyed what he was doing. For too long he'd languished under the moral constraints of the Prekhauten Guard, denying his true nature. Mobus had always known he was a violent man, prone to fits of rage and capable of extreme levels of barbarism. That inner beast was finally freed thanks to Alain Nye.

The six men and women huddled together in the vain hopes of finding escape. Blindfolded and tied, they were being executed for the crime of loyalty to the Conclave. All were lower-level priests. Fabricated charges of heresy were issued, and they were rounded up in the middle of the night. Hundreds more had already been eliminated since the Inquisition had declared martial law, all under the auspice of protecting the Conclave. Mobus nodded as the sergeant of the guard gave him an expectant look. Ion rifles cracked and sizzled, and the prisoners fell dead with agonizing screams.

"Sergeant, leave the bodies," Mobus ordered.

"Sir, our orders say —"

"I give the orders! And I say leave these heretics where they are. I want everyone to see the bodies."

The sergeant opened and closed his mouth, finding discretion the better of his choices. Unlike many of his peers who readily followed Kale's orders, committing one atrocity after another, he found his duty at odds with his sense of morality. Dark times were on the horizon, and a keen sense of self-preservation kept him from overstepping his authority. He carried out his orders, all the while suffering in his soul.

A runner came up and saluted Mobus. "Colonel, the Inquisitor General wishes to speak with you."

"Kindly tell him that I am occupied but will make contact once I'm finished," Mobus said, his eyes never leaving the cooling pile of bodies.

"Perhaps you would care to tell me yourself."

Mobus turned sharply. He looked upon the poorly camouflaged image of the Inquisitor General and frowned. Not in the same chain of command, Mobus could get away with considerably more than an average Inquisitor, but even he recognized his limits. Nye was unpredictable at best, vindictive at his very worst. The insurrection was still too young for Mobus to risk provoking the most powerful man in the universe.

"Inquisitor General, I was finishing up this operation," he announced, hoping to deflect some of Nye's ire.

Nye glanced at the row of abused bodies. An eyebrow peaked but he refrained from commenting. "The Blood Witch delegation has arrived and is addressing the Forum as we speak. I want all loyalist forces ready to act once the witches return to their floating abbey."

"Is that wise? We have too many units dispersed across the planet. We're not ready to move on the Conclave. Phos will have her entire security detail out in force, expecting anything to go wrong. It would be wiser to wait until tomorrow. Strike hard and fast right before dawn when most of the city is asleep."

Nye disagreed. "Curfew will be ending. There will be too many witnesses."

"What difference does that make? Once Phos is removed and the power of the Conclave broken, the people will fall in line. I doubt many truly care who rules them," Mobus countered.

"A modicum of patience is required, Colonel. The Forum will be distracted by the Blood Witches. Security will be lax, curious to see if all they have heard and been led to believe is true. Time is as much an enemy as an ally here." Nye clasped his hands behind his back. The platoon of Inquisitorial Guards behind him stood motionless.

Mobus stared into their reflective facemasks and wondered how far they were willing to go to protect their commander if he made a move. Where they as fanatical as Nye appeared? Or would they stand by and allow him to stick a blade in Nye's belly? The Guardsman was half-tempted to find out.

"We stand to lose more lives than anticipated," he said instead.

Nye shrugged. "What are lives but reproducible resources? Sometimes it is good for people to die. It lets the survivors know what their leaders are capable of. This matter is not up for debate, Colonel. I expect a status report the moment your men are in place."

Mobus was forced to admit a measure of respect for Nye. Leading soldiers to their deaths was no easy feat, though one he had gotten used to over the course of his career. Their deaths fueled his rage and, at least in his opinion, made him a better commander than many of his peers. Conventional wisdom and current doctrine viewed lives as the Guard's most valuable asset. Mobus debated that with any willing to hear it. His enemy/friendly kill ratio was the highest across all deployable battalions, save the campaign on Crimeat. General Strannan had officially reprimanded him for carelessness, but that only pushed him harder. For the Inquisitor General to voice a matching view was encouraging.

"How much time will I have?" he asked.

"A few hours at the most. There's no telling what those bitches want or how long they plan on staying. Begin moving your forces into position. I will be in touch shortly."

Mobus watched him stalk away. "What dark purpose brings you out this night?"

Only the stale wind answered.

TWENTY-NINE

3212 A.G. (After Gods), Hawkers Gate, deep space.

Explosions echoed down the abandoned corridors, remnants of firefights. Bodies lay where they had been gunned down. An acrid tang fouled the manufactured air. The weary band of Prekhauten Guards struggled through Hawker's Gate, desperate to gather the remainder of their forces. Many were wounded; one was dead. The Inquisitors ordered an operational halt so the Guards could catch their breaths and drink water. The pace of action had been furious, and many were already at the breaking point.

"We're running low on ammo," Annalilly told Sergeant Fies. Grime and sweat streaked across her face. The twin lightning bolt tattoos had an angry glow.

Fies grunted. He'd known that for a while. They'd been engaged in one long firefight. "Spread the word to start policing ammo packs from the dead. We can't afford to get caught short."

He didn't mention the obvious question. So far, every heretic they'd killed had been found with standard issue Prekhauten ion rifles. New ones, too. It was damned peculiar and left Fies with a troubled feeling. The heretics had better weaponry than his own Guards did. What they lacked was combat experience.

"What the fuck is happening, Fies? We shouldn't be caught up like this," she asked. Anger skewed her tone.

"I don't have answers, and it doesn't matter. We've got a fight to win. Worry about the little shit after." His rough words didn't change the fact that they were going to run out of ammunition long before they managed to kill enough heretics to force a surrender or stalemate. Fies wanted to laugh. *Who am I kidding? We're not going to make it out of here alive. Our best chance is to beat these bastards into submission before they kill enough of us to make us surrender.*

"We need to take out their leadership. These people don't have a fight in them. They're being driven by that Von woman. We kill her, and the rest will give up," she suggested before swallowing a mouthful of water.

"We need to worry about finding all of our people first," Fies countered. That so many were still missing and, he feared, dead bothered him. Flashbacks from Crimeat were starting to haunt him. Thus far, only Haggle and Kedric, the new guy, had managed to link back up with them.

A sudden commotion at the end of the corridor on the right drew his attention, his weapon raised even before his head snapped around. Tolde Breed and Luma Kai were the first to arrive, confronting the pair of scouts from the *Indomitable*. After a brief, and animated, conversation, the Inquisitors returned to Fies.

"Bad news?" Fies asked.

"It could be better. The scouts report both side corridors are rigged with magnetic mines. There's no way we can push through," Tolde said.

Fies lowered his rifle and wiped his face with a small rag. "Meaning the only way forward is certain to be a trap."

"I'm afraid so."

"Can we go back? Loop around and hit them from the rear?"

Luma cut in. "No. The passage behind us has already been blocked."

"So it's forward or let them come to us," Fies ground out. "What are we waiting for? Best to get it over with. I never liked waiting anyway."

"There may be another way," Tolde offered. "The digital schematics show us an access tunnel running parallel to this one. It's large enough for single file and has multiple exit points well beyond the ambush area."

"I got it," Annalilly jumped in. "Give me five Guards and twenty minutes."

"No. It's too risky. I'll lead," Fies said too quickly, producing a confusion of reactions from her. He instantly regretted it, knowing that he had just allowed his personal feelings to get in the way of proper military discipline.

Tolde glanced at both but said nothing. He wished he felt the same about someone. Love was alien to him — his one true regret.

Annalilly grinned savagely after she calmed down. "What's the matter? Scared that a girl can't do it? I proved you wrong during training on Vau Prime."

"That was an exercise," he protested.

"So is this. Time is running out, Fies. We don't have a choice."

"Sergeant, this is not the time for indecision," Luma said. "You are the ranking NCO. We need you with us to coordinate movements."

His eyes narrowed, but he couldn't dispute the truth. The idea that he was a valuable asset was hard to admit. "Fine, take Haggle and Kedric. Be careful. I need as many of you alive as possible."

Annalilly flashed a grin that sent chills through him. It was a look he knew too well. He almost feared for whatever enemy ran upon her before that rage expired. "Give me twenty minutes and begin your advance."

The access hatch flung open with a heavy kick. Annalilly emerged firing. The steady stream of ion rounds superheated the air, burning great gouts in the walls and a pair of heretics caught unawares. She ducked under the return fire, allowing the rest of her half squad into the corridor. The Guards quickly spread out, firing from the shoulder. Ion rounds sizzled back and forth. Bodies fell, smoke rising from the cauterized wounds.

She looked down, noticing the small sphere rolling towards them. "Grenade!"

Guards dove for cover moments before razor sharp shrapnel whistled through the air. The concussion tore into eardrums. Kedric screamed. Annalilly struggled to her knees and resumed firing. *Bastards are ready to blow out the hull. Not good.* She spotted the grenadier, a long hair man in a tattered green shirt and pants, and grinned. The grenade had done as much damage to the heretics as to her Guards. Fear twisted his face, and rightfully so. Not yet a man, the youth fumbled with pulling another grenade from the ammunition pocket stitched into his vest. Annalilly put two rounds between his eyes.

"Clear!" Haggle shouted.

"Anybody hit?"

When no one answered, Annalilly rose, quickly looking for herself. A dozen bodies lay at twisted angles against a hastily erected barricade of broken furniture and crates. The idea was good but wouldn't hold up long against a well-armed squad of professional soldiers. She pushed into the center of the carnage, weapon still in the ready position.

"Check the bodies. I don't want anyone popping up on us," she ordered. "Keep Fies up on the net and tell him to advance."

Haggle nodded and gestured with his head, "Kedric, start on that side. Anyone moves, put a round in their head."

The rest of the Guards spread out and began tapping the bodies with their boots.

"Haggle. Give me an updated weapons status. We keep moving forward. The others will be here in a moment."

Kedric nudged the next body, got no response, and moved on to the next. His back was turned when the heretic slowly produced a small handgun from under his stomach and fired. The rounds struck Kedric above the waist, just beneath his plate armor, and punched up into his lungs. The rookie Guardsman cried out before one of the rounds penetrated his heart, killing him instantly.

Haggle reacted first, driving his right boot into the prone heretic's face before firing three ion rounds at point blank range. The head all but disintegrated in a pale, pink mist. The portly Guard slung his rifle behind his back and knelt beside Kedric. He frowned and closed the sightless eyes. Haggle looked up at Annalilly and shook his head. Dead.

Annalilly fumed. She'd had enough. Enough of watching her people get gunned down by incompetent civilians. Enough of struggling to find a way to get out of the current situation. Enough of not being able to fight the way she wanted. "Gods damn it! From now on, I want everyone to plug the enemy *before* checking! No one else gets killed. Am I clear? And tear down this barricade."

Haggle directed a pair of Guards to begin dismantling the barricade and went up to his sergeant. "What about Kedric?" he asked softly.

She looked down at the body, fresh anger blossoming. "We have to leave it. Get his tags and strip him of any ammo."

"But…"

Her finger tapped him in the chest. "He's dead, and I can't afford to spare any guns in carrying the body. Get your head straight, Haggle. This isn't the first Guard we've lost. Death is a part of what we do. We grieve later. Use that anger and take it out on these fuckers."

The bigger man nodded reluctantly and set about securing the ammo and ID tags from Kedric. He couldn't help but feel like he'd failed the rookie. Guilt took hold, choking him up. He'd seen enough comrades fall over the course of his still young career, but never one he felt directly responsible for. Every time he closed his eyes, he knew he was going to see Kedric's face haunting him.

"I'm sorry," he whispered.

"This is Administrator Presha Von. As of now, Hawker's Gate declares independence from the tyranny of the Conclave. All agents of the Conclave, Inquisition and the Prekhauten Guard are considered enemies. I urge all citizens to rise up and stamp out our foes in the name of freedom and justice. As I speak, the mighty Prekhauten fleet is being destroyed by forces loyal to you. The new day has dawned, and with it comes the fires of insurrection. Rise up and achieve your destinies!"

Annalilly stopped and looked at the speaker embedded in the ceiling. As if they didn't have enough problems already, Von was inciting a general rebellion. The small detachment of Guards was going to have to fight their way through the quarter of a million inhabitants of the Gate if they had any hope of escape. Forget victory; any success would be measured when— if — they got away alive. "We're fucked."

Matthias tore his combat blade from the back of his attacker's neck and kicked the body away. His body responded through decades of conditioning and training. A small group of heretics had ambushed him and Gedrick shortly after the mismatched pair had entered the main corridor leading from the docking bays to the command and control center. Four lay dead at his feet, and only one had gotten away. Matthias knew that one was going to bring more, especially now that Presha Von had openly declared against the Conclave.

His steel grey eyes took in the shape shifter. *How far can I trust you, I wonder?* "Here's your chance to leave. I doubt you'll get a second one."

Gedrick shrugged almost too casually. "General Strannan secured my services…and loyalty. If I am to die here, so be it. We should all be so fortunate as to choose the time and place of our death."

Matthias didn't bother commenting. If the Jhedge had a death wish, that was on him and had nothing to do with Matthias. The sudden thumping of heavy feet running down the corridor pushed those thoughts from his mind. He quickly scavenged the dead for any useful weapons and rechecked his handgun's power pack.

"They are coming, and we truly have nowhere safe to go," Gedrick reminded, unnecessarily. "If your other forces are still operating, they will most likely head for the operations center, which, unfortunately, will be the true test. Lady Von will most assuredly have her trained fighters waiting. It will not be like these poor civilians taken in by a cunning deceit."

"I wouldn't expect anything less," Matthias answered. "We need to try and link up with any surviving Guard elements. The Inquisitors would be nice, but if I were leading this rebellion, they'd be the first targets I moved against. One is bad enough, but there are two and both from the Office of Heretical Persecution. Their heads will make a powerful statement when this thing goes universal, if it hasn't already."

"What direction do you wish to proceed?"

Good question. The sheer size of this station makes finding Tolde and the others damned near impossible. Where to start, indeed? "Head for the operations center but try to find a path less likely to be heavily defended. Hopefully, we can pick up a few stragglers along the way."

Gedrick tilted his head back and closed his eyes. His body blurred; skin blistering and what looked like small fists pushing his insides in different directions. Matthias stepped back reflexively and brought his weapon up, slightly. Facial features melted before his eyes as the Jhedge transformed from a middle aged, dark-skinned man to a twenty-something woman dressed like a soldier.

"I am ready," Gedrick said, the last bubble on his shoulder settling into place.

Matthias nodded and headed out. They pushed down the corridor that had been the Gate's central hub for commerce and foot traffic, now deserted save the litter of corpses and wreckage. It took time for his thoughts to calm enough to where he was comfortable asking, "Does it hurt?"

"Only the first couple hundred times," Gedrick joked. "Down this passage. We should be able to bypass the majority of Von's guards."

They continued, moving faster. An unspoken air of urgency drove them on, Matthias more than the paid Gedrick. The Prekhauten fleet should be arriving in system soon, and that worried him. If Presha Von had gone through so thorough a planning process, it was evident she would have plans in place for dealing with an incoming fleet. Based on what he knew of the massing pirate clans and their growing propensity to attack bigger and more prominent targets, it wasn't a stretch for him to look out the nearest viewport and find hundreds of pirate ships attacking the Guard. The results would prove disastrous on too many levels. Any defeat here would open the way for a strike at Vau Prime and the Conclave. Civil war would grip the universe. And it all started here.

They'd made it another twenty minutes, distance meaning very little in this instance, when they came upon two of Sergeant Fies's Guards. Jers and the heavy weapons specialist Beve were creeping along the same general direction with little to no weaponry. Both were bleeding and had torn clothes. Most men might have already gotten to the point where they were ready to give up but Matthias could feel the ire pulsing from them. That was a good sign. These two were still in the fight.

Jers took point, using an ancient standard gunpowder rifle looted from one of the dead. He was down to a handful of rounds but had made as many of them count as he could. Jers was known by the rest of his squad as the complainer. All his dissatisfaction was immediately set aside when bullets started flying. He became the ultimate Guard, a true leader on the battlefield. Matthias knew his reputation and was relieved to have found the man. Beve, on the other hand, scared him. Matthias had witnessed his capacity for sheer violence on Crimeat and felt bad for his enemies when the big man let his inner berserker loose.

"Gedrick, how much further?" Matthias hissed.

The closer they got to the operations center, the more Matthias was forced to tighten down on noise discipline. The logical part of him thought it foolish considering how much combat action was going on across the station. Chaos had settled on the Gate, and it was entirely possible to slip through any lines with minimum effort. The professional Guard part, though, demanded adherence to protocol. Lives often depended on whether a Guard obeyed his training.

Sporadic gunfire echoed from the corridor behind them, forcing Matthias to turn and address the potential threat. He had Gedrick continue forward another twenty meters to secure the nearest junction and turned the others back on the firefight.

"Sergeant Major, how did they get away with it for so long?" Jers asked quietly.

Matthias grinned despite the severity of their situation. Old habits die hard, and he would always be a sergeant major to the men and women with whom he'd served. That pride drove his need to ensure they all left Hawker's Gate alive. They deserved that much and more.

"Beats me, Jers. And it doesn't matter. We're in the middle of the shit here and now. Focus on the task at hand, and we'll see this through. Besides, you and I have both been in a lot tougher spots than this."

At least I don't have to worry about all of the Three engaging us, I hope. The gunfire died off and faded completely. Matthias could just make out a shape moving down the suddenly darkened corridor. A stray round took out the power. Sparks drifted down like a waterfall, casting much of the nearby area in broken shadows. He squinted, violent colored spots dancing in his vision. The figure grew larger the closer it got and left Matthias with a foul suspicion in the pit of his stomach.

"No," he whispered as Tannus emerged from the shadows, weapon in hand and angry intent blazing in his eyes.

Fies threw everything he had at the heavy defensive barrier protecting the operations center. Heretics fell by the score but were replaced before their bodies started to cool. Presha Von had planned almost too carefully. More than two hundred heretics barred the way. All were willing to give their lives in what they believed to be the true path to paradise. Fies was willing to help them along the way. Thanks to the resupply from the *Indomitable's* contingent, he was able to place a heavy weapons squad in the center of his own line and watch as they wrecked havoc on the enemy.

"This is taking too long!" Tolde shouted to him.

Fies agreed but saw little other option. "They're dug in well, and we're under strength, Inquisitor. Even if we breech that wall, I don't have enough Guards to secure the compound."

"Punch a hole in that wall, Sergeant."

Fies understood the unspoken order as well. They had no choice and if they all died in the attempt at least it was for the right reasons. He swallowed and reached for the shoulder fired energy rocket by his feet. The weapon was designed for indoors fighting and was little danger to penetrating the hull. It would, however, cause enough damage to send all but the most foolish running for their lives. The ones that survived.

"Annalilly! Give me covering fire."

She glanced back and saw him extend the tube, lock it in place and heft the heavy weapon to his right shoulder. "Shift fire right! Aim for the center of their lines."

"Fire in the hole!" Fies shouted.

The rocket erupted with gouts of flame and sped towards the enemy line. Heretics dove for cover. The Guards activated the lens dimmers in their helmets just before the rocket exploded. Flames and debris burst outward in a tremendous pattern of destruction.

Tolde seized the advantage. "Now! Advance!"

"Forward, you sons of bitches!" Annalilly roared as she leapt up and led the charge.

The Prekhauten Guards assaulted with reckless fury. Fire intensified the closer they got to the breach. A handful of heretics regained their senses and tried to put up a defense. They were gunned down and run over. Annalilly and Haggle were the first into the breach. They secured the gap, laying down withering cover fire. The air became superheated. Smoke and acidic residue settled over the firefight. A Guard to her right took a projectile round to his throat, killing him slowly. He rolled on the ground, desperately trying to keep his precious blood from leaking away.

Annalilly stepped over him, knowing there was nothing she could do even if they had a medic. He was already dead. She fired into the small knot of heretics trying to reestablish a defense. Two dropped, forcing the rest to duck.

"Frag out!" she shouted and tossed the grenade into their midst. The explosion sent gore and body parts in random directions. "Haggle, take two men and secure that position! Cover fire from twelve to four o'clock!"

The rest of the Guards poured into the breach, taking up a crude semi-circle defense even as a fresh wave of heretics, over a hundred strong, emerged from one of the side corridors behind them. The Prekhautens were surrounded and running dangerously low on ammunition. Fies looked around, taking in the desperation of their position. He spared a moment to look towards the Inquisitors, but they were already involved in their own battles.

"Fix bayonets! Prepare for hand to hand!" he shouted and slid the cold steel blade down onto his ion rifle. Realistically, the weapon was useless once he ran out of rounds but was heavy enough to be a decent club. When it came to that, not even his extensive training was going to be enough to keep him alive.

A few of the younger Guards turned to look at him, fright reflected in their eyes. Even Tolde paused. Asking warriors to die for a cause was nothing new, but the realization that their time was quickly coming to an end finally dawned. They fought harder, meaner. Every stab was meant to kill or maim. Every round aimed to inflict horrible agony. The men and women of the Prekhauten Guards and local security fought for their lives, knowing they were already forfeit.

Fies wished he had some inspirational speech ready, but he had none. He wasn't a hero. He was merely a leader doing his damnedest to ensure at least a few of his Guards lived long enough to escape. One fell to his right with a cut off cry. Another pitched back with an old-fashioned spear sticking out of his helmet visor. At this moment, Fies felt like a complete failure. He'd led them to this place of remorseless carnage and was rewarded with watching them die.

A trio of heretics rushed him, and he gunned them down with the last of his ion rounds. The weapon cycled to an abrupt stop. He was out of ammo. Fies gritted his teeth and crouched into an offensive fighting stance. Another heretic leapt over the growing pile of bodies. Fies slapped the woman's arms aside and stabbed hard into her abdomen. Her green eyes rolled back into her head as her mouth twisted in a grimace. She tried feebly to wrap her hands around his neck, but the strength was already gone. She died on his bayonet and was cast aside to make room for the next.

The next heretic was more fortunate. He managed to duck under Fies's weapon and drive his full mass into the Guard's middle. Both men went down. Fies lost his weapon in the fall, and they traded blows with fists and knees, anything to keep the other down. Fies landed a blow to the man's right temple and nearly rolled free before three others piled on. His breath was crushed from his lungs. Fists hammered into his face. A tooth was knocked out. His nose broke. Darkness crept in on the corners of his vision.

An inhuman roar rippled through the battleground with the force of seismic concussions. Those with weak minds dropped to their knees and screamed. Others simply fell dead. Most of the combatants immediately stopped fighting and turned to see the giant come storming down the corridor. Fies blacked out a moment after recognizing the necessary evil leaping into the middle of the fight.

Tannus tore through the pitiful human defenses with reckless abandon. Heretics tried to flee but were gunned down by the suddenly free Prekhauten Guards. The twelve-foot-tall giant easily stepped over debris and wreckage, kicking heretics away and snatching them by their necks as they tried to flee. Tannus was merciless in his attack. Every blow was calculated to inflict the most damage. Every round struck true. He became a killing machine, intent on ripping those unfortunate souls from the very fabric of the universe. Arms flew. Heads rolled from shoulders. A thin coat of blood spread across the metal deck.

The battle was over in moments. Those who were able fled as far as their legs would take them. Those less fortunate were killed before they fully understood what had happened. Tolde helped Luma to her feet, her nursing the right side of her ribs. Bruises were already coloring her face. She was going to be fine, having suffered far worse over the course of her career, so he turned his attention to the giant breathing heavily amid so much carnage.

Any doubts he might have had were dispelled as he found himself looking, again, on one of the Three. Thankfully, it was not Amongeratix, though after the amount of ferocity Tannus had unleashed, it seemed there was no real difference between them. Tolde eased forward on shaky knees. Tannus regarded him, his eyes hard, angry. The pair stood frozen for a moment as the surviving Guards, now less than twenty, picked themselves up and checked for wounds.

"You should not be here," Tolde finally found the courage to say.

Tannus's expression softened. "I should not be many things, Tolde Breed of the Inquisition. Much has happened since you and I last met. My brother is moving at last. War is coming to humanity, and you are poorly prepared to fight it."

"He knows you?" Luma asked, amazed.

Tolde shifted his gaze to her. "There is a great deal about my career you haven't been told. When this is finished, I will explain." He looked back up at Tannus. "This battle isn't finished. Our enemy has taken control of the station and is inside the main operations center. We don't have the manpower or the firepower to reclaim the station. Can you help?"

"I thought you knew better than to get involved with one of the Three," a familiar voice asked from just down the corridor.

Tolde smiled when he saw Matthias and a pair of Guards joining the group. The strange female standing beside the retired sergeant major drew his attention for reasons he couldn't quite grasp. He chose to focus on his old friend instead. Too many questions plagued him, but the answers had to wait. "And you took your time in getting here."

"It looks pretty bad," Matthias said after taking in the massive amount of dead. "The whole station is in rebellion. He's left a trail of bodies. We need to get out of here, Tolde."

"Not yet. Presha Von and her command element are inside there. We have to break them, Matthias. The injustice of today cannot be allowed to spread. Anarchy will grip the Conclave. She needs to be taken into custody and brought to trial."

"Or shot in the head," he suggested with all seriousness. "Any idea how many people she has with her?"

"No, but she will not have been taken off guard."

Tannus stepped closer. "The time for talk has ended. This space station no longer belongs to the Conclave. Indeed, if what my brother has set in motion comes to fruition, the Conclave itself may be in jeopardy. You cannot hope to gain anything from confronting the person in command here. Enemy fleets are waiting for your own to arrive. Your ships will be destroyed, leaving you stranded. The time has come to escape."

"I can't. The woman in there has gone too far for me to stop. She is one of those responsible for what happened on Crimeat and a key player in this growing rebellion. If we can get her, it will cripple a large part of their organization. We must try, Tannus. These dead deserve the effort."

"I will never understand humanity," Tannus said slowly, "but I admire your passions. I'll break open the doors. You do the rest. Tolde, time is now your enemy. You must be swift."

"Sergeant Fies, are your Guards prepared?" Tolde asked, purposefully bypassing the senior ranked Matthias. Fies had led them this far and, officially, Matthias was dropped from the rolls, retired.

"As soon as Beve gets his lazy ass over here and gets his machine guns, Inquisitor. What are your orders?"

"Kill everyone except Presha Von. I want her alive."

Luma asked, "What if they surrender?"

Tolde remained silent, eliciting a tender wince from Tannus. The dishonored son of the gods nodded and strode to the operation center reinforced doors. Designed to prevent the very thing Tolde was attempting, the doors were the strongest part of the entire station. The pitiful amount of Guards remaining would never have been able to succeed on their own. Fortunately, they weren't alone.

Tannus struck the outer set of doors with the force of an artillery round. Metal fractured and groaned. Repeated blows drove a man-sized hole in the center, but it wasn't enough. Another set of doors barred the way. Tannus stopped long enough to tear a thick metal conduit from the wall and started using it like a hammer. The continued assault gradually wore away the structural integrity, each blow forcing the doors to buckle in on themselves.

"Get ready," Fies told him Guards. "Beve, hit first. Blow a hole through their defenses while they're still in shock. Everyone else, sweep and clear the room just like you've been trained. Don't stop until the last one is dead."

Annalilly double checked her rifle. "My guys on me. We go in as soon as Beve lights them up. That means you too, Jers. About time you got your sore ass back here. Vacation's over."

A final blow, and the door collapsed back into the command center. Stunned men and women could only stare as the giant figure stormed through the smoke and sparks of torn wiring. None noticed Beve charge forward and begin firing from Tannus's right. Dozens of heretics died almost instantly. Switching his weapon to a short-range grenade launcher, Beve began lobbing concussion grenades into his enemy. The explosions were deafening.

"Now!" Annalilly shouted and led the attack.

Her ravaged squad poured into the cavernous room, shooting at anything that moved. Heretics continued to fall. The Guards managed to establish a foothold in moments, allowing Fies and the rest to reinforce them to continue the assault. Corners were cleared with violent precision. A Guard went down, dark arterial blood flooding down his trouser leg. Fies and Annalilly pushed their troops harder.

Tolde and Luma entered last, being the least armed or armored. Neither Inquisitor had come to Hawker's Gate with the expectations of getting into heavy combat. Tolde was still in shock at the massive levels of hatred and destruction he had seen since the insurrection began only a few short hours ago. Even so, he had trouble adjusting to the violence his Guards had unleashed in the command center.

Beve's fire was indiscriminant and murderous. Bodies hung draped over ruined consoles. Panels and wiring hung from the ceiling. Flames sputtered inside broken computer equipment. A cloud of black smoke clung to the ceiling. A handful of survivors huddled in one of the far corners. The fight had been beaten out of them. Too much death and destruction reminded them of their former lives. They weren't soldiers. Tannus and Beve helped remember that.

Presha Von stood against the main view screen. Her hair was disheveled, ash and blood smeared across her skin. Her clothes were torn, and there was a wild look in her once serene eyes. She swept her gaze over the semi-circle of Prekhauten Guards facing her, unimpressed. Then her eyes fell on Tannus, and her heart quivered. The arrival of any of the Three was unexpected and had been the deciding factor in the battle. His fury had casually undone all her plans and left her broken.

"Surrender, Presha Von. Your insurrection is over." Tolde moved closer, his pistol aimed at her heart.

She smirked. "Surrender to what? The Inquisition's justice? You are a fool, Tolde Breed. Even now, events are in motion that will tear your universe apart. You may have defeated me here, but there is darkness coming. Darkness that will drown the famous lights of Vau Prime."

"Enough talk. Step into the open, or I'll have my Guards fire," Annalilly snapped, momentarily forgetting her place.

The senior leadership briefly glared at her but did nothing to correct the outburst of insubordination. They'd all been through too much to expect everyone to adhere to strict military discipline. Every man and woman with a rifle was more than ready to shred Presha with ion rounds.

Tolde wanted her alive. Needed her alive. She was the one person with answers that had eluded him for more than two years. "Lady Von, look around. Your fighters are dead or fleeing. A Prekhauten fleet is approaching to reclaim the Gate, and you are left with two choices: surrender or die."

Presha broke into open laughter. "You truly don't know, do you?"

Tolde shifted his gaze quickly to Luma, who shook her head with the briefest movement. "Know what? No more games. I'd rather you live to answer for your crimes, but your death satisfies other desires."

"My dear Inquisitor, the time for games has indeed ended."

She moved much quicker than even Tannus expected. Her hand dipped into the folds of her elegant forest green dress and came up with a snub nosed pistol. Malevolence gleaming in her eyes, she fired two rounds before Tannus slapped her to the ground.

"Clear!" Fies shouted as his Guards eagerly searched for more targets. "What the fuck! Is anyone hit?"

Annalilly looked at each of her survivors. "I don't think so. She must have…"

Her voice trailed off as she noticed the slumped figure of Tolde Breed desperately clutching his chest. Twin trails of blood ran down his jacket, staining the oppressive black fabric. His eyes fluttered. Luma and Matthias raced to his side, exchanging helpless looks.

"Medic up!" Matthias ordered. Panic laced his voice.

The lone surviving medic collected his kit and hurried to the fallen Inquisitor, knowing the man was probably going to die. Then things really got bad.

THIRTY

3212 A.G. (After Gods), orbit of Hawker's Gate space station.

"Approaching Hawker's Gate, sir," the ensign announced, and both Admiral Fhi and Captain Tygg ceased their conversation to look up.

The Admiral caught himself about to start issuing orders. He was senior man on this expedition, but the *Righteous Fury* belonged to Alten Tygg. The pair had served together for nearly a decade, and Fhi had no reservations about Tygg's ability to complete the mission.

The smaller Captain smirked, hoping the Admiral wouldn't notice, and stepped forward. "Drop to real speed and sound general quarters. I want weapons batteries ready in one minute. Inform the *Spirit* and *Pride of Krenz* to place fighter and bombers wings on standby."

"Aye, Captain."

The bridge went from quiet murmurs to a relative explosion of action. Men and women relayed messages and tracked the progress of the work and gun crews manning the *Fury*. As flagship, Tygg found it necessary to be the first into the engagement area. He'd long believed that the best way to inspire subordinates was to lead by example. He could think of no better example than to be the first into a potential combat zone.

Truthfully, the Guard had had no official communication from Hawker's Gate since that unexpected proclamation of independence a few hours ago. The fleet, more than one hundred of the universe's finest built ships of the line, was speeding through space blind. That didn't sit well with Fhi or Tygg.

"Real speed in five...four...three...two...one," the *Fury's* helmsman announced and the ship slowed and stretched as its massive engines all but cut power.

Fhi braced himself, rocking only slightly as the entire kilometer-long command ship lurched beneath his feet.

"All stations reporting in. The ship is at general quarters, Captain."

"Very well. Helm, guide us on a straight line to the Gate." Tygg turned back to Fhi, "Admiral, with your permission, I'll deploy the fleet."

"Do so. I believe it's time we let our insurrectionists know who exactly they are facing," Fhi said, idly scratching at his graying goatee. He didn't care for their current situation but had enough experience to rely on his captains. The Guard prided itself on discipline and a developed structure that allowed men and women to work their way through the ranks. Every captain in this command had been handpicked by Fhi and General Strannan. The last thing any of them needed was for him to get in *their* way.

He slowly clasped his hands behind his back and watched as Tygg ordered the fleet into combat formation. Squadrons of cruisers and frigates, sleek ships designed like grey darts, bulky square-like battleships bristling with almost too many guns, Prielth built destroyers oblong and slow, surrounded the massive wedge-shaped carriers designed and built in the Vau Prime shipyards. The fleet was a combination of shapes and sizes that didn't make sense to the casual observer. It had a combined firepower the equivalent of ten ground divisions.

"All squadrons are reporting in, Captain," the young female Intel officer said. "*Predator* is assuming the lead."

Tygg nodded, going over the ship's specifics. *Predator* was an Astris class dreadnaught with six heavy cannons, twelve close-range sonic cannons and a crew of forty-eight. Faster than most of the other models, *Predator* was designed as a scout-picket ship. Tygg watched the deadly vessel pull away from the rest of the fleet. The elongated superstructure of Hawker's Gate came into visual range, if barely.

"Are we expecting any armed resistance, Admiral?" Tygg asked to pass the time.

Fhi wished he had a better answer. "Official sources say no, but you and I both have enough years in these white uniforms to know better. It never hurts to prepare for the worst."

The brilliant flash of light and exploding gases forced many on the bridge to shield their eyes. Mouths dropped open. Even Fhi found himself surprised.

"Helm, what was that?" Tygg asked, recovering quickly.

The helmsman paused, stuttering his answer. "The *Predator*, sir. She's gone."

"How?" he demanded.

"Multiple contacts! Unidentified vessels approaching from the far side of the Gate."

"Show me." Tygg tensed. He hadn't been sure what to expect, but a full-scale naval battle wasn't it. His gaze narrowed on the main view screen as a fleet of ragged ships appeared on the near side of the station.

"Weapons, plot me a firing solution. Full spread. Send orders to the fleet, weapons free. Engage at will."

"Aye, sir!"

"Captain, incoming!"

Tygg's head snapped up. "Defensive fire! Deploy counter measures. I don't want anything getting through."

"Too late, brace for impact!"

The *Righteous Fury* rocked as a pair of Hunter-class anti-ship missiles crashed into her spine. Oxygen and chunks of metal floated off, taking those unfortunate souls caught in the blast with them before damage control managed to seal the decks where the breach had occurred.

"Admiral, what are your orders?" Tygg asked as he pulled himself off the deck. Blood trickled down the corner of his lip.

Fhi watched as more and more enemy ships arrived. His heart sank. "A trap," he whispered. "This was all a trap."

Tygg frowned at Fhi's uncharacteristic behavior. "Admiral, we have an unknown number of hostiles approaching. What are your orders?"

Flares from more explosions rippled across the cold darkness of space as the battle got underway. Prekhauten frigates and dreadnaughts were racing ahead of the larger battleships and carriers in an attempt at screening enemy fire and reducing the number of targets before the heavy guns could be brought to bear. Fighters and bombers from the *Pride of Krenz* were already deploying, Captain Vel Iss was not waiting for orders.

Fhi stared helplessly at the scene. Nothing in the intelligence briefings had suggested such a massive enemy presence. He'd been caught unprepared, and now his people were dying for it. Anger sparked to life, snapping him from his temporary daze. Straightening his white jacket, his face hardened.

"Captain Tygg, order all fighter and bomber wings to deploy immediately. Take out their larger ships. Cruisers to set a defensive shield until we can bring our big guns to bear. I want this space cleared as quickly as possible."

Tygg clenched his fist behind his back. "Aye, Admiral." Turning to his bridge crew, he began barking orders, "You heard the Admiral. Send these bastards into the void."

"Captain, scanners are picking up two massive fleets in orbit around the Gate."

Captain Falchi rubbed his eyes. They were sore and felt heavy from a decided lack of sleep. The stubble irritating his chin was the result of a minor lapse in discipline as he worried more about keeping the *Indomitable* from being destroyed than the proper appearance of a professional naval officer. So far, he'd managed to keep his ship hidden from the roving squadrons of pirates. But so many enemy contacts made getting out of the system intact, or rescuing Tolde and the others, damned near impossible. He'd kept the Indomitable hidden on the far side of the third moon for almost a week, but supplies were running low. Staying much longer wasn't much of an option.

"Another pirate fleet?" he asked. His voice was haggard, weary. Worst of all, he couldn't find a single plausible strategy.

"No, sir; the second set of signals is Prekhauten."

Falchi stood abruptly. "Guards? Don't they know what's waiting for them?"

The First Officer shook his head. "Doubtful. They show no signs of expecting an attack. I think they're coming in blind."

Damnation. If Strannan had any notion of what was awaiting them at Hawker's Gate, he'd have deployed the fleet with orders to engage upon real space entry. Falchi was suddenly torn between his obligations to the men and women he'd been forced to leave on the Gate and warning the unsuspecting fleet. His own survival never entered his mind as he began war gaming his immediate future.

"General quarters! Plot firing solutions on the nearest pirate ships and raise me a channel with the incoming fleet. We can't let them walk into a trap," he ordered.

"Aye, sir. Weapons officer, get our guns up and ready."

The bridge crew came alive with new energy. They were just as exhausted as their captain and more than ready to dole out their measure of payback to the pirates that had forced them into hiding. Flak vests and helmets were issued, weapons handed out in the event the *Indomitable* was boarded. Hope and urgency moved the ship.

Falchi wasn't nearly as optimistic as most of the crew. Any sized fleet Strannan deployed would be seriously under strength to deal with the current threat. Chances were the *Indomitable* would be blasted to scrap metal in short order, but the thought of striking back was too powerful to ignore. For now.

"Weapons impact! One Prekhauten frigate has been destroyed!" the Intel officer announced frantically.

"Show me," Falchi ordered, even as the main engines powered up beneath his feet. The situation might already be beyond his sphere of control. His eyes scanned the wreckage of the Astris class dreadnaught as the flames sputtered and extinguished. Tears formed as he watched the charcoal-blackened bodies, frozen in their death screams, drift helplessly into space.

"First Officer, I want an accurate count of enemy targets," he barked suddenly.

"One hundred and ninety-seven ships. Our navigational computers are having trouble tracking enemy fighters but estimates their number over three hundred, Captain."

"That's less than half of what we ran from," Falchi said. "Have we identified our command ship?"

"Yes, Captain, it's the *Righteous Fury*. Captain Tygg commanding."

"Break radio silence. Inform the Fury that this isn't the only pirate fleet," Falchi stared hard, trying to pick out the massive capital ship amongst the largest naval engagement he'd ever imagined. "Weapons, I want to know the instant you've targeted those pirate ships."

"What do you have in mind, Captain?" his First Officer asked.

Falchi rubbed the irritating stubble again, suddenly wishing for a razor. "We need to shake things up before the fleet gets too heavily engaged. Otherwise, it will be a slaughter."

"What about the men on the Gate? Are we going to leave them?"

The captain opened and closed his mouth, his previous thought dying on the tip of his tongue. He refused to wholly abandon Tolde and the rest, but his priority was to minimize the damage to the Prekhauten fleet. Half of the pirate force was about to come down behind friendly lines. The butcher's bill promised to be horrific.

"The Inquisitors are going to have to deal with their own problems for the moment, Commander. We've got bigger issues. Patch a message through to any friendly elements on Hawker's Gate. Inform them we are engaging the pirate fleets and may not be able for recovery for a while." He avoided stating the obvious, lest it ruin the already fragile confidence spreading among his crew.

"Aye, sir."

"This is not the engagement we wanted, nor the way we wanted it, but this is what has been dealt. I expect every one of you to perform your tasks as only soldiers of the Prekhauten Guard can. It's time the *Indomitable* lived up to its name. May the gods ward over your souls, and if not, gods damn them all. Action stations, Master Crown."

"Aye, Captain. Action stations! Prepare for combat."

Alert sirens droned throughout the ship as the *Indomitable* powered up and roared towards the engagement area.

"...is Captain Falchi of the *Indomitable*. Come in, *Righteous Fury*."

Tygg perked up. The last thing he'd been expecting was another friendly voice. He knew Falchi from their Academy days, but as much as it eased some of the stress of the situation, it made him worry even more. Why was the *Indomitable* here? Did Strannan know more than he was telling? Tygg and Fhi both knew there was a substantial pirate threat gathering around the Hawker's Gate subsystem. Guard headquarters could only speculate if that threat was ready for action.

"Falchi, this is Tygg. It's good to hear your voice. What are you doing out here?"

"Doesn't matter. You're moving into a trap. There is another fleet lurking somewhere, bigger than this one."

The hustle on the bridge momentarily stopped as Falchi's dire warning sank in. One ship was already destroyed, three others crippled enough to withdraw to safety. Multiple pirate ships had been obliterated, including dozens of fighters and two-man craft. The Prekhauten fleet was struggling against the current odds, affected heavily by the disadvantage of being ambushed, but Tygg had little doubts as to the outcome. The pirate fleet was large but not used to working together. It was also severely outgunned. It was only a matter of time before his ships busted a hole in their line big enough to force the others to turn and run. At least, he thought it was.

Tygg swallowed, his mind racing through possibilities. "Are you certain? We've picked up no additional signals."

"I've been hiding on the dark side of the nearest moon for almost a week, Alten. Trust me," Falchi advised.

Passing a glance back at Admiral Fhi to gauge his reaction to the news, Tygg had already made up his mind. "First Officer! Redeploy the fleet. Give me a three-sixty perimeter and prepare for another group of fighters."

Tygg paused to watch his massive ships, sleek grey objects highlighted by the nearest sun against a pitch-black backdrop turn to confront a nonexistent threat. His captains operated to his highest expectations, recovering quickly from their initial shock. A squadron of light missile frigates in tight formation pushed towards the pirate lines. Exhaust plumes connected the frigates to their fired missiles. Flak exploded around them, puffs of flame quickly turned to black smoke. A midsized enemy cruiser, Tygg guessed an early model of the Astris class, took two hits to the stern. Bodies and debris vented into space as what remained of the ship began to tumble away.

Two flights of fighters swooped in to engage a squadron of enemy bombers, desperately trying to break through the screen and strike the *Spirit*. The huge capital ships were easily the most powerful and dangerous ships in the engagement, for more reasons than the obvious. Each was powered by nucleonic reactors that, if detonated, could rival the effects of a small sun. The devastation would be unrecoverable. Tygg caught a pair of dreadnaughts using the bombers as a screen.

"Weapons, target those dreadnaughts running on *Spirit*," he ordered calmly. A fighter exploded close enough to the bridge he felt the shockwaves ripple through the gunmetal grey decking beneath his feet.

The battle intensified at a rapid pace. Whole flights of pirate fighters threw themselves at the Prekhautens. Many exploded from the withering anti-ship fire pouring from the battleships. A pirate heavy cruiser stitched streams of heavy ion cannon fire into the midsection of a light cruiser. The ship exploded almost instantly. All hands were lost. Escape pods from a dozen ships pumped from the bellies of dying ships; some were picked off by zealous pirate fighters looking for a cheap kill. Others plummeted away from the battle.

Oddly, the defensive patterns from the Gate were silent. Tygg suppressed the false hope that their forces had reclaimed the space station so quickly.

Fhi laid an aged hand on Tygg's right shoulder. "Captain, instruct all bombers and dreadnaughts to attack that pirate battleship in the center."

Tygg looked closer. The ship Fhi pointed out was the largest in the pirate fleet, clearly a command ship based on the massive amount of escorts surrounding it. Both fleet officers understood that many of the pilots weren't going to survive. It was a calculated risk that needed to be taken. Destroying the enemy command and control would prevent any serious attempt at an organized counterattack, leaving the surviving pirate ships easy targets for the well-trained, well-disciplined Prekhauten gunners.

"Helm, bring us about. We're going to provide cover for the Admiral's plan," Tygg ordered. The urge to get his hands dirty was almost too strong. He wanted to enact his own brand of justice on the cowards that had already taken the lives of so many Guards.

"Aye, Captain. Bringing us on assault trajectory."

"Contact! Bearing one-one-three-seven," the First Officer shouted suddenly.

Tygg quickly processed the bearing and felt his veins chill. That was directly behind them! Falchi had been right. Hundreds of new signatures instantly appeared on the radar screens. Tygg's fleet was outnumbered nearly five to one. Near impossible odds for almost anyone. Almost.

"We need to pull back and regroup," Fhi cautioned. His heart raced. His palms sweat. The urge to break and run was growing stronger, that initial panic setting back in. Life or death depended on how fast he could get the order through the fleet. He watched helplessly as three of the smaller cruisers were crippled beyond repair. Fighters were being blown apart under the second wave's onslaught. A dreadnaught's engines exploded in a dazzling ball of flame, inertia sending the ship end over end until it caught a Prekhauten battleship in the middle. The explosion tilted the *Righteous Fury* off cant.

"Admiral, our position is untenable," Tygg said with uncertainty. He'd never expected to face any trial this daunting in career. Hundreds of lives had already been lost with who knew how many more wounded. "What are your orders?"

Fhi could only stare as the battle quickly turned into a slaughter.

Tygg swore under his breath and wrote the Admiral off. *He's only giving in to what we're all feeling. Can't say that I blame him, given the circumstances. But I'll be gods damned if I let my crew see me break down.* "Patch me through to the fleet."

A score of smaller strikes tore into the *Fury*, throwing Tygg to his knees. The comm officer, pulling herself back into her chair, threw him a thumbs up. "Channel open, Captain."

"All Guard vessels, full defensive and offensive spreads. I'm ordering a full withdrawal." He was careful not to mention retreat, though every captain was surely thinking the same thing. Merely uttering that word would plunge a dagger in the hearts of too many of his people. It would also open the way for a full rout, leaving his ships vulnerable. The death toll would be catastrophic. "Disengage the enemy and pull back. I want all squadrons and wings to regroup at rally point one."

Another cruiser exploded. Tygg listened as his captains acknowledged, his mind already wandering to the steadily shrinking number of friendly signatures on the radar. He hoped there would be enough of a fleet left to regroup.

"Send a message back to Guard headquarters. Fleet ambushed. Heavy losses sustained. Disengaging and regrouping." Tygg brushed the stray hair from his face. "Weapons, once all friendly ships are clear, I want as many seismic torpedoes as we have fired into the heart of the enemy fleet. They're not going to get away from this unscathed."

"Aye, Captain," the weapons officer said with grim satisfaction.

Admiral Fhi shook from his stupor. His mouth open from shock at the command just issued, he felt his control slipping. "Captain, we have no clearance to use those weapons. The damage could tear apart Hawker's Gate and us in the process!"

Tygg rounded on the Admiral, all respect lost for his long-time mentor and friend. "Admiral, this is my vessel, and I fully intend on doing whatever needs to be done to keep my people alive. General Strannan can court-martial me later." *If I survive.*

The majority of the Prekhauten fleet was far enough away from the pirates that the blast range of the seismic torpedoes wouldn't affect them much, or so he hoped. Tygg didn't relish the idea of those men and women trapped by the destructive forces that were about to shred the pirate fleet. Such was not an honorable death, but he found little other choice. Sheer numbers were stacked against him, and not even the superior design and armament of the Prekhautens was going to prevail for much longer. Tygg had no intentions of becoming a smear on the history of his order.

"Seismic torpedoes activated, Captain," the weapons officer barked.

Tygg nodded. His heart froze for a moment only. The decision had been made, and he prepared to issue the command to fire.

"Captain Tygg! I am relieving you of command! Your actions betray your incompetence," Fhi snarled from behind. The thought of having standard protocols subsumed by one man infuriated him.

Tygg rounded on the Admiral, anger clouding his eyes. "Admiral, you've done nothing but whimper like a child with a broken toy since this engagement began. Thank you for your advice, but I will handle this in the manner I see fit. Security! Remove the Admiral from *my* bridge and see him escorted to his wardroom."

"How dare you!"

"I dare! Lives are being lost out there, Admiral, and I'll be gods damned if I let you or anyone else talk me into losing more. Now get off my bridge."

Tygg didn't bother waiting for a response. He spun back and took in the sights of the battle. More explosions. More ships spiraling out of control, gravity gone. Debris floated in massive sheets. Bodies hung in grotesque shapes, faces frozen. He needed the upper hand. It was the only way to salvage this battle.

"Fire."

"Seismic torpedoes launched from the *Fury*, Captain!"

Falchi's eyes widened in horror. "Say again."

"She's launched seismic torpedoes into the pirate fleet," the weapons officer said shakily.

"Are we in the blast radius?"

"Affirmative," helm replied.

Damn. We've taken enough of a beating that the force of the blast will rip us apart. "Full impulse. Get us clear now!"

"Course, Captain?"

"Just move the fucking ship!" *We can figure the rest out later. If there is a later.*

The *Indomitable* slowly started to distance itself from the battle, desperately trying to pull free. Hands gripped consoles and chairs. Hearts fluttered with nervous anticipation. Death opened its mouth wide to engulf them all.

Fires raged unchecked through the infrastructure. Thick black smoke forced many of the crew, those still alive, to the floor in search of any scrap of clean air. Alten Tygg clawed his way up to his knees. His hair was plastered across his face with blood. His uniform was burned and ripped. Most of the bridge crew was dead, their limp forms draped over consoles or worse. Tygg's gaze fell on Admiral Fhi. The shorter man had been impaled when a broken beam slashed down from the ceiling. His only solace came from instant death. Both of the security guards attempting to remove him from the bridge were crushed beneath the weight of the collapsed ceiling plates. The Captain almost envied them.

Tygg struggled to piece together what had happened. They'd just fired off a heavy salvo of seismic torpedoes, and his first thought was that one had detonated prematurely. But no. The entire ship would have been obliterated. *So what happened?*

"Helm, what was that?" he barely managed to croak.

The helmsman, pressing a bloody rag to his right temple, swiveled his chair around to face Tygg. "The *Pride of Krenz*. She's gone, Captain."

Tygg's face fell. The nucleonic reactors powering the carrier must have detonated and taken out a large chunk of the surrounding battle, damaging the *Righteous Fury* in the process. He looked at the partially broken view screens and his heart sank. Kilometers of space were cleared of everything in all directions. It was as if nothing had ever happened. Slowly, he looked deeper, towards Hawker's Gate. The scene was anything but peaceful. Scores of ships had been reduced to scrap metal by the seismic attack. Thousands of lives lost. The torpedoes didn't discriminate between friend or foe. Any ship not fast enough to win free had been mercilessly destroyed. Less than a quarter of ships that had started the battle remained, and most of them were crippled.

Recognizing the battle was all but over and that the Guard couldn't claim victory, Tygg did the only thing he could. "Sound the withdrawal to any survivors. This battle is over."

"What about escape pods?"

Tygg nodded. He'd taken more of a thump to his head than he thought. The idea of saving anyone trapped in an escape pod hadn't even occurred to him. "Order as many picked up as possible. The pirates have taken a beating, but they're not out of the fight yet. I don't want them regrouping on us."

Truthfully, the pirate fleet had been rendered combat ineffective. The majority of ships had been destroyed, leaving a skeleton force from what they started with. Unfortunately, the same had happened to Tygg's fleet. That left Tygg with one choice. Return to the shipyards at Vau Prime, refit, and strike out to hunt the remaining pirate threat. He hoped Rear Admiral Khe-Zhehan found more luck at Spindle.

"Tygg, this is Falchi. What in the hells just happened?"

"Incoming!"

What? How? "Evasive moves! All hands brace for impact!"

Tygg caught the flare from multiple engine drives. Enemy fighters and bombers were screaming towards the crippled *Fury*. Without fire control and almost no protective screen, the capital ship was defenseless. Dozens of missiles and rockets streaked away from the pirate ships. Alten Tygg knew he was dead.

"What in the hells was that?" Falchi asked as he shielded his eyes from the sudden blinding glare.

The bridge crew scrambled to make sense of the tragic chain of events that had changed everything in the battle for the Gate. So much had happened at once that Falchi was struggling to make sense of it. The seismic torpedo barrage had literally decimated the engagement area. *Indomitable* had barely cleared the blast range when a second, larger explosion had rippled across the heavens. There was only one possibility: a nucleonic detonation. He moved quickly to the radar station, searching the ship identifiers. Two carriers and the massive command ship were in the fleet. One carrier remained: *Spirit*.

Falchi blinked. *It can't be*. Nothing in the pirate arsenal was powerful enough to destroy a Prekhauten carrier. "Get me the *Righteous Fury*."

"Channel open, Captain."

"Tygg, this is Falchi. What in the hells just happened?"

The second detonation was much brighter than the first. In a burst of sunlight and unmitigated destruction, the command ship was gone. The last-ditch effort by the all but crippled pirate fleet had gutted the Prekhauten command structure and effectively ended the battle around Hawker's Gate. Falchi's heart fell. He knew what needed doing but was loath to give in. Command fell to the captain of *Spirit*, which was already revving the engines for a jump back to the rally point. Technically, *Indomitable* didn't fall within the fleet's command structure, leaving Falchi with more options than the other captains. His thoughts turned back to the Inquisitors and his security detachment trapped on the Gate. He was about to issue orders when a broken call came in.

"…is Matthias. We need immediate…Inquisitor…has gunshot wound to the…"

"Clear that up," Falchi ordered. "Say again, Matthias. This is Captain Falchi. Who is shot?"

"…Breed. Not sure…die."

Eyes fell on Falchi, silently judging him in anticipation of a decision that was already made. He licked his lips, his mouth suddenly dry. "Matthias, I can't risk coming in to get you. Matters have devolved. The *Indomitable* is no longer safe. We are falling back with the remnants of the fleet. I'm sorry, my friend. We'll try another attempt once we refit and rearm. Can you hold?"

The channel went dead, and the quiver in Falchi's stomach intensified. It had been a long time since he'd last felt so much disappointment. It didn't sit well. Worse, a friend and colleague was going to die, and there was nothing he could do about it. He reluctantly turned to his helmsman. "Get us out of here."

THIRTY-ONE

3212 A.G. (After Gods), the Deeves, planet An'kuruku.

Chaos engulfed the camp. Men and women ran screaming as flames spread through the scrub grass and tinder surrounding the tents and hastily made shelters. Old-style lead bullets cut through the air, gunning down those unfortunate enough to be caught in the open. Bodies already covered the ground in a grizzly carpet. War had come to the Deeves, and it was unlike anything the people had expected. The darkest horrors were unleashed, and it was all many could do not to break.

Armies of the Prefecture wasted little time with preparations. Lezorsu ordered a full-blown assault the moment his lead battalions had the decrepit camp in sight. Weeks of being punished by the grueling desert sun and an incredible pace many did not survive left the militias ready for battle. Killing the heretics was the first step towards their own salvation.

Cannon fire tore into the camp, specifically targeting the old, women and children. Men lost the stomach to fight when they saw their families being slaughtered like stock animals. Who could blame them? Those brave, or foolish, enough to stand the line watched in muted horror as the rank and file of the Prefect militia formed up and prepared to advance.

The battle began shortly after dawn when the vanguard broke the plain of the horizon and charged. Jut's defenders held their own, narrowly avoiding being swept from the field. Althas Pey sent all ranks forward. The more he was credited with killing, the greater his glory and the more prominent his position in the new Prefecture once the campaign was finished. He greatly desired to eclipse Lezorsu and claim the Doomspell reputation for himself, even if he had to kill the man to get it.

The first ranks dashed towards the defenders, suffering heavy casualties. Jut had prepared his people as well as could be expected, given the lack of preparation time. It wasn't enough. The Prefect vanguard had specific orders. Casualties were not a limitation for victory. Fueled by the fervor of Lezorsu's rhetoric, the militia flung themselves at the heretics. Men died by the score. Most were militia. Fervor was no match for desperation. The defenders held their ground until the vanguard was chewed up enough to become combat ineffective. Althas reluctantly called for a withdrawal, berating his subordinate commanders for their ignorance. Still, he had successfully gauged his opposition, and the main body was extremely close. It was only a matter of time before the slaughter played out. He could wait.

The other side of the battle was far less serene. Too many had died during those frantic first few hours. They held, but it was tenuous. Jut knew that it would only take one serious push and his hastily crafted defenses would crumble. He briefly wondered how many would die in the ensuing chaos. All of the lucky, he hoped. Lezorsu wasn't a man to treat prisoners well. Thousands had already been tortured for the madman's amusement since he'd claimed the title of High Prefect. Thousands more waited to be damned — unless Jut managed to pull victory from certain defeat.

Jut stood atop the low rise overlooking the seemingly endless plain of sand and scrub brushes. He wasn't entirely disappointed with his defenses. The knowledge of what was enveloping them was well known to him, and the heretics had virtually no chance. Lezorsu was a man possessed, intent on crushing the rebellion from their hearts and watching them all die at his pleasure.

"We can't survive another assault," a broken farmer said, leaning heavily on a dull spear smeared in dried blood and gore.

Jut looked down on the man, carefully considered how to respond. There was no fault in his sentiments. The farmer's only mistake was voicing what everyone must have felt. Death was coming, devouring any foolish enough to stand in the way. The heretics weren't prepared for the level of hatred opposing them. It was only a matter of time.

"There are other things to worry about than that, my friend," he finally replied.

The farmer shot him a queer look, uncomprehending. Jut bit off a whimsical laugh. "This battle was never about us. There's a man over there who would very much like to kill or dominate every living soul on An'kuruku. If there's even a chance of stopping him here, we'll have changed the course of history."

"Words too fancy for my liking, General," the farmer said shaking his head. "But I'll die a content man if we can kill that bastard over there."

"Well said. Well said. All we need is a little hope and a few strong arms. We may yet win the day."

Jut moved off, continuing his tour of the line. Haggard faces looked back to him, all desperate for answers that just weren't there. He wished there was more, but his own reserves were quickly draining.

Facing his former friends was much different from commanding them. All bonds of fellowship were broken, lost amidst the hyped bloodlust and need to prove their worth with Lezorsu.

The main body arrived during the first few hours of combat. Thousands upon thousands of blood-hungry militia, antagonized by the rhetoric of hundreds of Prefects, marched across the scrub grass and sand of the Deeves in sloppy ranks. Those in the front ranks took in the horrors of the battle raging ahead of them. For many, it was all they could do to keep marching, to stride into the grinder with the knowledge they wouldn't live to see the sunset. Those more fortunate couldn't see the battle and continued to march. Their combined weight pushed the front lines ever onward, all but deciding their fate for them.

Lezorsu came onto the scene from the cupola of his vehicle. He watched with glee as men and women stomped over a sea of corpses to reach their enemy. Black smoke choked the air, obscuring the heavens. Decades had passed since the last time the Deeves, all An'kuruku even, had suffered such inane bloodshed. None of it would have been possible if not for a random stroke of chance. Lezorsu hadn't been in command long before receiving that fateful communication from Kaline. Her words had sparked a thought. That thought had gradually turned into violent reality. Doomspell reveled in it, fully living up to the gruesome nickname.

He swept the field with enhanced visual sensors, finally settling on his former right hand. Hatred twisted his features. Jut looked haggard, worn down, a man straddling the fractious line between life and death. All he needed was a little push. Perhaps the gods did still exist. Lezorsu growled in pent-up rage as, by some miracle of fate, Jut appeared to look him directly in the eyes and smiled. The defiance! Doomspell ordered all forces into the assault. He wanted the defenders crushed to dust before sundown.

Whether or not Jut spied Lezorsu leering down on him from atop his vehicle was a moot point. It was all he could do to keep his people with some semblance of morale. The sudden influx of the main Prefect army disheartened him on levels far deeper than he'd expected. He'd helped train most of them, turned them from raw recruits into a manageable militia with enough skill to win a battle. For his sins, he now had to face the army of his creation. It was a bitter test of wills that never should have happened.

The people of the Deeves were guiltless of the crimes Lezorsu accused them of. That didn't make up for their willingness to abandon the principles of the long line of Bone Fathers or their wholesale decision to support the cult of Rengu. Jut didn't fight for them. He fought for the old, the women and children incapable of defending themselves. He fought for the ideation of a greater power and the continuation of liberty, even at the expense of his own life. More men had died for less. If death wanted him, who was he to turn his back now? The legacy of a man is often judged by his final deeds.

"Here they come again!" a voice cried.

Men wearily rose and prepared to meet the charge. Most of the energy weapons were depleted or broken. His shattered lines lacked the strength to stave off another hard assault. Morale was nonexistent. Sadly, there was nothing for it. Mother battle seldom asked men whether they wanted to survive or not. Blade and bullet fell where fate decided. Nothing Jut did would make a damned difference at the end of the day. Chance was an evil thing, soulless and cruel. Jut drew his curved saber and knew he wasn't going to live much longer.

"Look! In the skies!" came a faceless voice.

All eyes paused to look up and were frozen with amazement. Weapons dropped slightly. Mouths fell agape. Very few brought themselves to believe what they were seeing. Hundreds of bird-like shapes dropped down through the thin clouds, gruesome and dark and. Perched upon the back of each was a single rider swathed in pure white. They were the defenders of the Wells, priests of old. Secret warriors. Jut watched in awe and dread as the desert dragons tucked their wings and dove towards the army of the Prefecture.

Great balls of flame spat from hungry mouths. Huge sheets of fire burned hotly, straining up into the skies. Men and women screamed. Others shouted in triumph; salvation had come upon the wings of avenging angels. The pilots, such as they were, started dropping large pottery jars filled with a liquid explosive. Each blast created wanton destruction.

Jut grabbed the nearest adjutant by the collar. "Spread the word to all commands. Hold the lines! No one advances until these creatures leave."

Althas Pey saw victory and urged his forces forward. His bloodlust rose with each passing moment. Bodies continued to pile up unceremoniously. Pools of blood turned to puddles and more. He sensed victory, could feel it in his veins. Soon, the thought of turning on Lezorsu reentered his mind. The triumphant commander of the Prefecture army would take his surviving militias and wipe Doomspell from the Deeves just as easily these pathetic scrubland villagers.

His initial assault met staunch resistance and still nearly broke the lines. He continued the assault, feverishly throwing fresh resources into the mayhem. Yet still the enemy held their ground. The army of the Prefect had come into the Deeves expecting to trample their opponents without pause. Instead, they found a ready force waiting for them. Althas begrudgingly offered Jut a salute. The man was good, one of the best he'd seen during his time in a Prefect uniform. Killing him was going to be a rare personal pleasure.

Getting to him was another problem altogether. His presence bolstered the enemy, straightened their sagging backbones and drew forth a deep well of strength and pride. They suddenly remembered they fought for their homes, their families. They fought for their very lives, and no man could easily lay down their arms and let death walk over them in such odds. Althas ordered the cannon batteries to continue firing, even at the expense of his own forces. The artillery commander's protests fell on deaf ears. Wars were won through will, and Althas had what was necessary.

Every man and women in his vanguard was committed to the attack. Lezorsu and the main body were close, expecting to be engaged in a matter of moments. Althas needed to strike now if the glory was to be heaped upon his shoulders. He decided to attack. Marching alongside his forces, Althas Pey strode into battle with a light heart and murder on his mind. As a result, he failed to see the dragon-like creatures swooping down upon them from the skies. His world exploded in walls of flame and death.

Explosions rocked the ruins. The force of the concussions knocked Kaline down. Dust and chunks of rock pelted her head and shoulders, coating her long hair. Bruises, dark and ugly, blossomed across her body. She had a wild look in her eyes. Clearly, this was not the end she'd anticipated. An'kuruku was aflame with war, and soon it would spread beyond the borders of the Deeves. There was grim satisfaction in that, but her life was more important than waiting to see the fruits of her labors mature.

"Mistress! We must abandon the keep. Our position is untenable."

Kaline scowled angrily at her second in command as he helped her up. "You overstep your bounds. I will decide when it is time to leave."

He snapped his mouth shut and stepped back. The ground trembled, threatening to rip apart under the constant bombardment. Escape craft were prepared and waiting in the small cavern beneath the ruins. Kaline didn't care about the hundreds of men and women being slaughtered on the battlefield. They were a means to an end, not the solution. Her only concern was keeping Mollock alive long enough to move on to another world where she could begin again.

"They've broken into the keep!" a frightened woman shouted as she ran down the hallway. The look in her eyes was wild panic.

Kaline glared accusingly at her second. "You were in charge of ensuring no one broke through. Fix this now!" Kaline rounded back on the woman and slapped her to her knees. "Calm yourself. We have been through much worse. Now, who is in the keep?"

The woman, fresh red marks staining her cheek, looked up through tear-choked eyes. "A giant."

Giant? Her skin flushed so sudden she nearly fainted. There were no giants, only the Three. And if one of them was here… She had to move quickly before all was lost. "Inform General Jut to commit all strength to the defenses. I want him to turn the battle on our enemies. And have as many security guards as are available report to me in the command chamber immediately! Even giants can die."

She wrapped her forest green gown around a fist to keep it from slowing her down and glided off in search of any weapon capable of killing one of *them*.

Elisa fired a pair of shots and was rewarded with watching both targets drop in undignified heaps. Storming past, Paradise Tear swung a heavy iron bar she'd found at the forced entrance to the keep. The aged wooden barricade smashed apart, clearing the path for them to push inward. With the battle raging outside, no one was expecting to face a threat from within. Elisa used that to her full advantage. It was the only chance she was going to have at getting to Mollock and ending the madness consuming the people of An'kuruku.

"Come on!' she hissed back at the Bone Father.

Old and borderline feeble, she doubted his ability to keep up. That made him a liability, one she couldn't afford. She cursed herself for being talked into letting him come along. The entire notion was foolish.

Elisa was sure the desert air must be getting to her, affecting the way she thought. There was no circumstance in which she could imagine ever agreeing to his demands otherwise.

The tip of his capped staff echoed through the stone corridors. She winced. Each sound had the potential to give away their position, complicating her responsibility. She knew, as did he, that the core of the fanatics would be situated within the keep. The coming fight was going to be difficult under the best circumstances. Having the old man around compounded things, perhaps gravely.

"Where would Mollock be?" he asked with a strained voice. His free hand clenched the rusted dagger he intended to thrust into Mollock's heart. Or back. When Elisa had asked why he carried a rusty piece of steel, he merely shrugged and said, "So he won't forget me in those last few moments before he dies."

"The most secure part of the keep," she replied tersely. Killing Mollock wasn't her first option, and the thought sat ill with her. She didn't know why but knew that he still had a part to play in things before they ran their course. Unfortunately, time and the will of too many were against her. The only way to stop the Bone Father from committing murder was to either kill Mollock herself or kill the old man. Neither was a choice she was prepared to make.

Paradise looked down the hallway, searching the shadows for signs of lurking enemies. "Unless they are planning to escape, and if that's the case, he will be en route to a transport out of here."

Please let that be the case and save us all the trouble. Elisa's thoughts darkened suddenly at the mention of escape. None of her conspiracy had involved an escape route of their own, and now she feared it was too late. The Prefect army had arrived much sooner than anticipated and was slicing their way through the feeble defenses at will. It wouldn't be long before the keep was exposed. *No thanks to that damned mortar and artillery fire they've been hammering us with since dawn.*

"We need to move. They're not going to be distracted for long," she growled, torn by the unpleasant decision awaiting her.

The misfit band continued deeper into the ruins. Most of it was abandoned. All able bodies had been sent to the lines for the battle. Those that did remain were either too preoccupied with saving their own hides or huddled in a corner praying for salvation that would never come. Dust and broken stone rained down from the ceilings, eliciting a curse and snarl from Elisa. Again, she wished for her simple life as a bounty hunter on Crimeat in what seemed a lifetime ago. Nothing in her past had prepared her for the tough decisions necessary in the future — or present. She felt alone. Adrift.

A pair of lightly armored guards slid from behind a dust-covered pillar. Broken and cracked like an eggshell, the pillar concealed both men perfectly. Elisa slid to a halt, eyeing the blasters aimed at her. She knew her skills in battle but wasn't good enough to best both before one managed to get her. Her small hands slowly began to rise. Paradise didn't hesitate. She leapt forward, smashing the guard on the right into mangled heaps of flesh and crushed bone before leaving the iron bar at the visibly shaken survivor. A dark stain ran down his trouser leg, and his face blanched.

"Please. Please don't kill me. I'm only following orders," he whimpered and fell to his knees wracked with sobs.

Elisa knelt in front of him and pointed the heated end of her blaster at his mouth. "I'll think about it if you tell me where we can find Mollock Bolle. You only get one chance."

His eyes flew wide. They were wild, uncomprehending. He clearly never imagined a moment like this might come to pass. "I don't…I don't know."

Elisa's face hardened, and she squeezed the trigger. "Wrong."

Brain matter and bits of skull plastered the dull brown pillar. The Bone Father bent over and wretched his stomach up. Only then did Elisa realize the severity of what she'd just done. Killing in battle was one matter, killing a broken shell of a man something else entirely. In most systems, the act would have constituted a war crime. And she'd killed him without pause. Her own stomach threatened revolt. She dared a glance at Paradise Tear, instantly regretting the decision. The giant stared down with a strange combination of apathy and regret.

"We must all endure difficult decisions during times of grave stress," she soothed. "Do not lose heart in yourself, Elisa. War makes monsters of us all."

"I could have made him talk," Elisa protested, more for personal vindication than anything else. She needed to believe her humanity remained deep down inside. Otherwise, what was she? A bitter husk of what might have been a promising life. A waste of flesh better left for dead in a long-forgotten shadow.

Paradise laid a gentle hand on her shoulder. "Perhaps. Perhaps not."

"I'm not the one you people seem to think I am. What kind of paladin have I turned out to be?" she struggled to say.

"True champions seldom choose to be. Foul deeds and dark times are thrust upon them. The cold fires of death and loss harden them into beings of myth and legend. One day, men will look back upon your deeds and see the righteousness in your heart. Now come, we have a task to complete before time expires."

Hope burning in her heart, Elisa found new strength in Paradise's words. Even the Bone Father, feeble and hunched with grief and sorrow, seemed taller, prouder. The trio pushed on. The interior of the ruins was completely void of life. They passed store rooms half-emptied with overturned boxes and broken items scattered across the floor. An elderly man lay curled up alongside the wall where he'd been stabbed to death, presumably by his own people. Madness gripped the Deeves, and it went deep if men were so willing to murder their own.

The smell of brine and salt started to choke the corridors. A strange pale light crept into the ruins, slowly slashing the shadows apart like shreds of tissue paper. Elisa frowned. They were already heading out the backside of the ruins, completely missing Mollock.

"We need to turn around," she whispered. A pair of cannon rounds exploded against the outer wall, and the sounds of a chamber collapsing quickened her heart.

Paradise shook her head adamantly. "No. He is near. Your task on An'kuruku is nearly complete, Elisa. See this through."

Unsure what the giant meant, Elisa tightened her grip on her blaster and gave a curt nod. She spared the Bone Father a glance to ensure he was still capable of keeping up and gestured with her head for Paradise to lead on. A fresh wave of explosions, with what had to be the entire artillery contingent of the Prefect army, slammed into the defense. The entire eastern part of the ruins crashed down, killing any unfortunate enough to be trapped inside.

Elisa felt sudden urgency. She picked up the pace. Sensing desperation, Paradise felt the slender balance between focus and fanaticism starting to slip and dropped back to help the Bone Father. He offered a grateful smile and clutched his dagger tighter. Unexpected hatred simmered in his eyes. Paradise Tear felt like crying. She'd allowed this world to denigrate into madness that could only be broken with the murder of yet another wasted life.

The passage leading to the back of the ruins ran straight, allowing Elisa to scan for lurking enemies with relative ease. She felt tired, strained. Her arms were heavy. Her chest ached from continued exertion. Captivity and malnutrition contributed to her lack of strength. More than anything, she wanted to stop, to abandon this foolhardy quest and go back to Ah'muf.

Such thoughts were certain to end badly for all parties. She shook her head and charged forward. Blinding light poured into the gloom. The sound of waves crashing upon the rocks challenged the battle on the opposite side of the ruins. Sea spray blasted the entryway, slapping them in the face. She frowned. The ocean held no lure for her, so intent was she on completing her task and leaving this gods forsaken planet. Elisa felt it now. An end to so many nightmares and convoluted dreams.

She slowed just inside the edge of the door and gave her eyes time to adjust to the sudden light. A small, silver shuttle craft idled on the edge of the crudely made landing platform. Two guards patrolled the base. Their movements were stiff, their looks nervous, shaken. Clearly neither wanted to remain any longer. Elisa almost felt pity for them. Sympathy was a useless emotion, however. She gunned them down with second thought, knowing neither was intended to depart anyway.

"That was unnecessary," a smooth woman's voice lamented to Elisa's right.

She turned slowly and found herself staring down the barrels of half a dozen soldiers in tan uniforms. The woman in their midst immediately drew Elisa's attention. The very air around her commanded respect. Elisa swallowed hard and lowered her weapon.

"Don't expect me to believe you were going to take them with you," Elisa ground out. "These men are nothing but puppets to you."

Kaline laughed. "Don't be naïve. Every man under my command is willing to lay down his life for the cause. All it takes is the simple snap of my fingers. But that's not why you've come, is it?"

"Where is Mollock Bolle?"

Pursing her lips with mock thought, Kaline slipped through the ranks to confront Elisa directly. "What business is it of yours? He is safe."

"He's a danger. To himself and to the people of the Deeves."

"Indeed?"

Elisa took a step forward. The thought of strangling the arrogance out of the woman was suddenly appealing. "Crimes have been committed. I know him. I can help him in ways no other might."

Kaline laughed in her face. "You expect me to believe that? What are you? A useless waif, dried up and used beyond your expiration date.

Go back to your home and beg for the end before regret consumes you. There is no place for your kind in the new universe, Elisa."

"How do you know my name?" she stammered.

"Don't be so foolish as to think my intelligence gathering is simple. The people of the Deeves are fodder for the Prefecture cannons, but I am not a simple person. Very little escapes me."

"You have robbed the Deeves of dignity! Usurper! Betrayer!"

Weapons were raised. The guards tensed. Kaline's mirth faded to consternation, forcing Elisa to turn to the sound of the new voice. The Bone Father stormed from the ruins with an accusing finger pointed at Kaline. His tattered robes billowed in the breeze. Long, stringy hair was quickly pasted to his face, concealing the deep lines. It was his eyes that commanded attention, though. They were clear, focused and intent, the opposite of his abused body and delicate psyche.

Kaline recovered first. "Ah, Bone Father. Another relic of a wasted age. I've usurped nothing. The people of the Deeves were ready for change. Centuries of being mired in the wastelands of An'kuruku left them hungry. They wanted more. To be important again. What has your meddling done? Nothing."

The old man fumed, trembling with barely contained rage. "I am the guardian of the Deeves. Ever has it fallen to those in my line to protect these people. I gave them hope. A life! Now you squander those lives against a superior army. You're a soulless witch."

"Your insecure devotion to an obsolete religion kept your followers from achieving true greatness. Destiny cares little for wants or needs. I've opened their eyes, relic. Given them the opportunity to rise above the deeds of all their fathers. Do not think to lecture me on your uses, for they are few."

Elisa felt the moment slipping away and decided to take control before it was too late. "Where is Mollock? I don't care if you stay or go, but I want Mollock."

"You can't have him. He belongs to me now," Kaline said, folding her arms across her chest. The dark green of her dress gave her a severe look.

Paradise emerged suddenly, instantly shifting the dynamic of the confrontation. The anger in her was unmistakable. She'd come to avenge the innocents so casually slaughtered for the whims of a madwoman. Paradise immediately caught the taint of Amongeratix polluting Kaline's mind. She suddenly realized An'kuruku was unimportant in the scheme of the ever-changing cosmos. The fires raging here were meant as a distraction at most. Something more sinister lurked behind her actions, making stopping Mollock even more important.

"She is corrupting Mollock Bolle," Paradise announced. "Her words are corrosive and dominating."

The look in Kaline's eyes registered shock and sudden nervousness. Rumors of one of the gods roaming the Deeves had reached her, but until now they had been nothing more than shadows, whispers men lamented over in the dark places of the night. Only once had she met one of the Three, and that meeting had left her mind broken. The woman she once was, once aspired to be, had died that day. What was left exuded hatred and the unbending desire to bring all life to ruin. Paradise threatened her.

Paradise felt almost forgotten tightness in her stomach. The woman standing before her was more dangerous than any other human. She felt Amongeratix, heard his irrational rhetoric in Kaline's speech. The great war the oracle had predicted upon her exile appeared to be rushing towards them now, and Paradise Tear was woefully underprepared.

"Kill her!" Kaline shrieked.

Energy weapons fired rapidly, sending beams of orange and blue light streaming towards the giant. Paradise threw an arm up to protect her face, knowing no weapon created by man was capable of harming her. Elisa tackled the Bone Father the instant before enemy fire slashed through the space where he'd been standing. Daring to pick her head up, Elisa spied Kaline rushing towards the shuttle. Flashbacks from her own flight from the Plateau on Crimeat haunted her unexpectedly.

Then she noticed Mollock Bolle. He sat cowering in the shuttle, head hung and shoulders wracked with sobs. At that moment, she felt sorrow for him. Mollock had never been intended for greatness. His one mistake lay in discovering the god buried deep in the mountains. Decades of being hunted and tormented by the truth of that single moment of chance tore him down, remaking him into the callous shell he now was. Elisa regretted coming to An'kuruku. Regretted listening to the Bloody Man. Regretted becoming the Paladin to Mollock's Prophet. If only she'd stayed, perhaps Mollock wouldn't be the mess she gazed upon now. If only.

Lost in momentary lament, she failed to notice the Bone Father slide from beneath her protective embrace. He charged through the hail of fire miraculously unscathed. Sunlight glimmered from the raised dagger. The end of so much trial strode with him, echoing his footsteps with undisguised hunger. Conflicting emotions struggled for supremacy. He suddenly felt his age, and he was old, worn out like clothes frayed and abused through overuse.

The Bone Father needed to kill Mollock if only for the salvation of his own soul. So much damage had brought the Deeves to ruin, and there seemed little other choice. The people cried for redemption, all those dying now and the ones left behind in their villages and hamlets. He found difficulty in fathoming how such hatred, such sheer malevolence could be allowed to exist in the hearts of men. Were the gods truly gone? The Bone Father felt abandoned.

But there was also the gripping sense of sorrow, regret. Great and terrible pain pierced his heart with each injustice. He looked into Mollock's eyes and suddenly realized the man was as much victim as antagonist. He'd been duped into perpetrating these crimes, a willing fool led by the hand by those who wanted to see the social order of the universe drown in flames. Victim or prophet, Mollock Bolle surely deserved the title of the madman on the rocks. And he deserved to die.

Mollock slowly raised his head and watched the old man stalking towards him. Instead of an assassin, he saw only salvation. There was undeniable liberation in the old man's intent. Mollock's eyes fell on the dagger, and he smiled. The end was finally near. His eyes drifted towards Kaline, noticing the fear and rage twisting her features into a frightful grimace. Regrets formed. He knew he never should have followed her people all those months ago in Tenemenah. He should have allowed the Prefecture to arrest him and been done with it. Should have was a useless sentiment. What was done was done. Nothing he did could change the fact.

Briefly considering killing Kaline, he understood that wouldn't make his own crimes right. Mollock was no fool. His indignant rhetoric fueled an entire generation into panic and unrestricted fury against the Conclave and the gods. Flames were already spreading in what was sure to become an unquenchable inferno. No, Kaline was merely the catalyst, not the solution. He looked deep down inside his soul and found only disgusting blackness.

Mollock crawled from the back of the shuttle and stretched his arms wide.

"Get back in the shuttle!" Kaline screamed.

The normally wild look in his eyes had been replaced by unexpected calm. Her nerves fluttered, knowing he stood on the brink of doing an act utterly foolish. She was too far away to stop him.

Mollock strode purposefully towards the Bone Father. His heart rate remained normal. His mind was at peace. This was the end he was destined for. The quick flash before eternal night. His life had turned out to be a waste from the moment he'd stumbled upon the sleeping god in the caverns beneath Reven. Decades of being hunted and haunted had driven him ever closer to insanity's grasp. Soon, very soon, he would be free. *Do it. Take my life and end this torment. I'm sorry. So very sorry.*

The blade struck deep and true. He gasped only a moment as the bitter steel pierced his heart. Sounds sharpened. Wind caressed his face. Sea birds called him home. His fingers tingled. The corners of his sight closed in with darkness. *Fifty years I have lived in torment and struggle. If only I had known death was so peaceful. Elisa.* He felt the blade twist savagely and dropped to the ground dead. Cooling, lifeless eyes fell upon her in silent judgment.

"No!" Kaline screamed and ran to the corpse.

Stunned by what he'd done, the Bone Father left the dagger in Mollock's heart and stumbled back. He stared down at his shaking hands and felt his knees go weak. Elisa, still on the ground, closed her eyes in a vain attempt to keep the tears from falling free.

Kaline lifted Mollock into her arms, desperate to find a flicker of life, anything she might be able to save him by. Mollock Bolle was dead and at peace. Wreathed with hatred, she pushed the corpse aside, realizing all too well the setback to her plans. She took in the battle raging around her. Most of her guards were dead or maimed. Broken corpses littered the landing pad. Only two guards remained, struggling to find a way to survive. Paradise, however, wasn't in the mood to grant clemency. She slashed and smashed with centuries of pent-up fury. The lies of previous generations threatened to subsume her. She had become death.

None of it mattered to Kaline. Her task was specific enough not to allow leeway. Right now, the only thing that mattered was getting off planet and onto the next. She knew she was no match for the barbarism of the giant woman. The similarities between Amongeratix and the female were striking, almost familiar. But where this woman was intent only on helping her friends, Amongeratix would show no reservations against ripping Kaline's head from her shoulders and sending her corpse to the cold eternity of space. Escape was paramount if she stood any chance of finding salvation.

Tucking her robes tightly against her thin frame, Kaline turned and dashed into the shuttle. She paused briefly to give the Bone Father a withering stare and disappeared into the belly of the ship. The doors hissed closed immediately, and the engines fired up. White hot flames spit from the mass propulsion engines. The concussion blew stray bushes and stone wildly. With a tremendous lurch, the shuttle lifted off the ground and darted across the eastern sky. It took only moments before the sleek, egg-shaped craft was a mere blip fading into the clouds and was gone.

Elisa watched the scene unfold but didn't move. She'd had a chance to kill Kaline, but doing so meant nothing. They'd finished what they'd come to the shores of the Bo to accomplish. Mollock Bolle was dead. The rebellion had ended. All that remained was pain and the suffering of collecting the dead and wounded. Many lives would never be the same. She'd seen it before. War is the most wicked of man's creations. Slowly, she pulled herself up and went to the Bone Father.

The old man, sunk to his knees, trembled uncontrollably. He looked up with his tear-streaked face, void of emotion. "I am a murderer."

Elisa knew nothing she said would make a difference. Not now. Perhaps that would change with time, but the horrors of discovering how foul the human spirit can truly be was devastating. He was forced to live with his grief. She wrapped a consoling arm around his shoulder and was silent.

THIRTY-TWO

3212 A.G. (After Gods), Krenz, planet Vau Prime.

The halls of Inquisition Headquarters were surprisingly void of life. Minor wars raged on a dozen different worlds, all under the guise of the cult of Rengu. Inquisitors, Guardsmen and Conclave priests were being dispatched at rates unseen in generations. Never had the offices of the Cardinal Seniorus and Inquisitor General been forced to deal with so many brush wars. Worse, the sudden coordination and cooperation of the pirate clans had turned the ruling orders on end.

Lorenu Phos and her closest advisors locked themselves away while intensely debating the best, most appropriate way to deal with the pirates. She cursed and, reluctantly, accepted the combined strategies of General Strannan and Alain Nye, sending secret fleets to deal with the pirates. One reported back complete success. The operation over Drespai had met little to no resistance and destroyed the fabled pirate lair. She knew it was much too soon to celebrate victory. There'd been no word from Admiral Fhi and the main assault fleet dispatched to reclaim the Hawker's Gate space station in the name of the Conclave. She grew increasingly troubled.

"You need to relax, Lorenu," Aliz tried to console her. Strands of graying hair dangled over her right eye, lending her a deceptively cunning look.

They'd been together for three decades, and she'd never once held a moment of regret. Theirs was true love capable of standing the tests of time. But she found herself growing increasingly worried. Lorenu hardly slept these days. Her meals, when she did eat, consisted of a light soup and little else. She was wasting away, and there was nothing Aliz could do. That helpless feeling burrowed deep into her soul, leaving her emotions gutted. She desperately wished for an end to all of this. The wars. The incessant bickering between religious orders and the nonstop demands of the Inquisition for more power, more control.

Lorenu's eyes twinkled briefly before the now-familiar gloom returned. "How can I relax when everything I've worked for during my long life is now crumbling around me? Did you ever think the day would come when we'd be forced to endure terrorist attacks right here in the capital city of the Conclave? Aliz, we are losing this war, and I don't know what to do."

Aliz struggled to contain her sigh. Letting Lorenu see her frustrations and sorrows now, when she needed strength to keep her going, was counterproductive. "No, but the universe changes without our consent."

"When did you become my sage council?"

A soft laugh, sweet and melodious. "Haven't I always been? Perhaps it's time you considered Nye's proposal."

Lorenu stiffened. "Let the Inquisition unleash their wolves? Nye has always been a zealous man. I know that. Give him a little power, and he'd reshape our lives. Don't make the mistake of trusting him. There is some nefarious purpose in his deeds, only I don't know what."

"He's got the military power necessary to end these wars quickly."

"A directionless power," Lorenu countered. "We're facing an unprecedented number of wars, but all of them are small, localized. If we give Nye complete control, he's just as capable of turning the universe into one giant battle within the year. That's a risk I can't afford to take."

"It may be the only chance we have of stopping this cult."

Taking a sip of her rapidly cooling tea, Lorenu felt her face tighten at the mention of the cultists. They were a nuisance, yes, but not one requiring expansive military actions. A few Inquisitors and priests should be more than enough to put those fires out without causing too much collateral damage. Still, there was a measure of merit in Aliz's advice. Each conflagration revolved around the cult of Rengu.

They had sprung up unexpectedly and in so many different locations it was almost too hard to imagine the coordination efforts from a central command structure. That didn't negate the fact that thousands already converted to the death god. Images of flames and blood sprouted everywhere, even here in the capital city. Crews worked around the clock to remove the filth, but to no avail. As soon as a section of the city was cleaned, the miscreants returned with more propaganda. It was a never-ending headache and cause for much concern in the inner circles of power.

Insurrectionist attacks diminished slightly thanks, in part, to the energy the Inquisition placed on stopping them. Colonel Mobus Kale, already well decorated for various campaigns, executed his tasks with ruthless efficiency. She briefly recalled reading that he was scheduled to receive another commendation for his efforts today. *No doubt those preening fools expect me to show myself in some ridiculous display of solidarity between our orders to reassure the people we are still in command.* Only she didn't feel she was in command. Too much had changed too rapidly. The universe casually slid over the precipice of total chaos.

The only premeditated insurrection, at least in Lorenu's opinion, seemed to be Hawker's Gate. Loyalty to the Conclave had never seemed overly important to the station dwellers. She wondered if it came down to mere coincidence that Presha Von, wanted felon and deviant from the Crimeat campaign over two years ago, had found her way across the stars to the solitary station. Initial reports, those few that managed to make it out before the station fell, spoke of reprehensible bloodshed and the willful destruction of all things loyal to Vau Prime.

"I feel lost, Aliz. Like the universe is awakening to discover its distaste for us. I fear my time is running out," she admitted quietly.

"How can you say that? You are the most powerful figure in the universe. Times are troubling, but we will endure. We have always endured. That's what makes humanity special. Don't make the mistake of allowing doubt into your heart."

Lorenu forced a false smile. "Doubt is the cornerstone of leadership. Are you certain humanity is special? Are we blessed by any secret knowledge or given command of immense faculty to come to terms with how small we truly are amongst so many stars? No, Aliz, we aren't special. We're just the current custodians. The old gods once thought themselves special as well, I presume. Look where that left them. All gone but a handful of relics and three very dangerous men locked in a brutal struggle we don't comprehend. I fear our time is drawing nigh. We will fade like the old gods and be remembered one day. Or perhaps not. Perhaps this is the end of all things."

The words had a chilling effect on Aliz. She'd always been Lorenu's greatest support mechanism, her staunchest supporter when times grew terse. Her shoulder to lean on when the weight became unbearable. Now, her soul felt cold, frigid as the pale winter morning. She looked at her lover with unveiled eyes and didn't like what she saw. Lorenu looked much older than just a year ago. Her shoulders were slumped, back bowed. She walked on shaky legs as if her body refused to continue. Much of the intensity had faded from her once stern eyes.

She opened her mouth to speak when sounds of confrontation interrupted them. A struggle ensued just beyond the outer doors of the Cardinal Seniorus's offices. A gunshot echoed, muffled slightly by the aged oak doors half a foot thick. Lorenu stiffened. Aliz felt her heart quicken. The unthinkable had happened. Infinite possibilities, all dark, cycled through her thoughts. Aliz reluctantly found herself lending credence to Lorenu's apprehensions. The office of the most powerful figure in the universe was under armed attack.

"We need to get you out of here!" she said hastily and began collecting the small stack of important documents on the desk.

Lorenu closed her eyes, head drooped. "No."

Aliz froze. "What? They are coming to kill you!"

"I know, but I will not be cowed by murderers or assassins. I am the Cardinal Seniorus of the Conclave! This office is the highest representation of humanity. I won't let cowards diminish that. No matter the cost."

"You're willing to throw your life away over what, exactly?" Aliz scolded. "The same people you swore to protect are abandoning you by the thousands! Flee while there's still time. I will hold them off."

The words stung bitterly. Lorenu had grown accustomed to being alone. The mantle of leadership proved much heavier than she had anticipated. She casually reached into the desk drawer and withdrew the Osari Stone, the amulet of office. The lightweight material settled easily over her shoulders, dangling down between her breasts. When she opened her eyes, it was with that old glint. Fear and desperation shrugged away, replaced by the fire and determination of a much younger Lorenu Phos.

"It must be this way, Aliz. They are coming for me, and I have a duty to uphold. The Conclave has stood for three thousand years. I won't be the one to be remembered in shame or embarrassment."

"I can't convince you, can I?" Aliz asked, her heart breaking slowly.

Lorenu slid around the desk and hugged her. "I love you dearly, Aliz. I always shall, but this a task I must do alone. Go now, before it's too late. Take the passage behind the bookcase to my personal quarters and get out of Krenz. No doubt they'll come after you as well."

Aliz shook her head weakly. "But I…"

Lorenu kissed her softly, passionately on the lips. "It must be this way. Go. Avenge me when you can. I love you, my darling Aliz."

"Please don't leave me. Not now." Her voice was barely a whisper.

"Go, for me. For us."

Immeasurable sorrow shone in the tears welling behind her eyes, but Lorenu remained strong. She had to, if only for what little dignity remained in her. One of them needed to survive if there was any hope for the future. She didn't dare to dream. Reluctantly, Aliz slid from their embrace, gave one final kiss and hurried to the secret passage. She didn't look back for fear of breaking Lorenu's heart.

Alone, the Cardinal Seniorus straightened her back, patiently folded her hands across her waist and waited. She didn't have to wait long. The doors burst open, followed closely by a dozen men in Prekhauten Guard full battle dress. She sneered. The insurrection reached deeper than she'd wanted to believe.

"How dare you violate this office?" she bellowed.

The Guards halted at the unexpected defiance. They'd come expecting to find her meek and timid in the face of overwhelming military superiority. Instead, the Cardinal Seniorus stood tall, proud. Her steel gaze withered their resolve.

"You have violated it enough yourself, Cardinal," a menacing voice seethed from the back ranks.

She searched the faces. "Who are you? Show yourself at once."

"Ever have you desired to rise above all your predecessors to become what? A goddess? A saint, perhaps? The universe is not as naïve as you would make it. You are a dinosaur, a relic best archived and left forgotten."

Mobus Kale emerged through the Guards. Hatred twisted his face, contempt for everything weak she represented. The bionic arm attachment made his side bulkier, more war-like. Instead of the neatly pressed dress uniform Guards were expected to wear daily, he came dressed in combat greys and well-worn boots. She instantly knew her fears were realized. He had come to kill her.

"Colonel Kale, I must admit I was expecting someone of a higher station to come for me," she chided, hoping to goad him into pulling the trigger himself, thus martyring her. Only then did her memory stand a chance at sparking the necessary uproar. Otherwise…

Refusing to rise to her baiting, Mobus unlatched his holster and rested his one real hand on the comforting pistol grip. "Indeed. I've been looking forward to meeting you, though not in the manner you supposed."

"They were going to make you a hero this afternoon," she said.

"I am making myself one right now. Your medals are a sign of vanity, of the decay this office stands for. Time has come for change in the order of the universe."

She shook her head, suddenly sad. "You're delusional. The change you seek is not what's coming. I have seen the future. Shall I tell you?"

"Keep it. Your future ends today. Cardinal Seniorus Lorenu Phos, you are being arrested on charges of sedition, attempt to commit heresy, and the willful negligence of the defense of the people of the universe."

The accusations, while false, stabbed deep. Much of her strength fled under the condemnation. She barely managed a croak when she replied. "On whose authority do you make these claims?"

Kale smiled cruelly. "Inquisitor General Nye."

Her world shattered. Alliances that should have been solid were naught but strangled lies, twisted and warped. Her own vanity had propelled her down this irreversible course, ruining countless lives in the process. Lorenu had sought to do good, to keep the universe from spiraling out of control under the manipulations of the Three. She had thought she wasn't alone. Only now, at the end when truth came to light, did she begin to realize she'd been pushed in this direction all along.

Nye! That worm has been plotting against the Conclave from the moment he took command. Chances are the rumors of his involvement in the previous Inquisitor General's death were true, leaving her more the fool. She'd ignored her instincts for too long, damning her. Any trial would be manipulated to the point of ridiculousness. Nye would have the jury panel and judges rigged. The farce would be broadcast across the universe for all the people to see how corrupt and devious she had been. Lorenu decided the best course of action lay in avoiding the charade and thwarting Nye's plans.

"I will not be arrested by a disfigured criminal and traitor to the Conclave," she ground out, knowing it pronounced her death. "I am the Cardinal Seniorus, the most powerful woman in the universe. What are you? Nothing but a madman's lackey. Leave my offices, *Colonel*. I have no time for you."

Infuriated, Kale turned his back on her and dropped his hand in a sharp gesture. Gunfire thundered through the office.

"It is done," Mobus Kale finished his report, and his image disappeared.

Alain Nye leaned in the soft leather of his high-backed chair and steepled his hands in front of his face. He didn't know whether to laugh or brood. At last, after decades of groveling under the decrepit old Farius

Graeme, former Inquisitor General, and then even more shackled under the constraints of Lorenu Phos, he finally stood free. The path to his ultimate goal lay unobstructed.

Still, he felt disappointed with her defiance. The thought of plunging a dagger into her heart personally had warmed him on cold winter nights. She represented everything he despised about humanity. Her weakness, her willingness to accede to the lesser masses. True rulers should wield immeasurable strength. Fear kept populations in line — fear and the willingness to use military force when matters grew out of control. None of the wars or battles breaking out across the seven hundred worlds would be happening if Phos had bothered to see clearly.

Now it didn't matter. Her corpse cooled in pools of her own blood, a fitting tribute to the foolishness of the old ways. A new power had risen, given life in the dark corners where men seldom dared to look. The old alliances were void. Humanity no longer needed to languish under the divided rule of three great orders. Nye planned to move quickly to secure power. If the Conclave managed to reorganize, he'd be exiled and hunted down like a rabid dog.

Too many cardinals remained loyal to the ideals the Conclave represented. He'd managed to subvert a good number, but not enough to secure the transition of leadership on his own. A purge was in order. Nye knew the only way to ensure complete success was through thinning the ranks of all three orders, culling those who refused to submit to the new order. The bloodshed promised to be intense, perhaps the worst in modern human history.

"I will do what must be done."

Swiveling around, Nye stared out the curved bay window. The massive pillars of light blazed into the fading night sky, immense beacons announcing the promise of tomorrow to the entire universe. Perhaps it was time for those lights to dim a little. He smirked as he took in the drooping willow branches dancing on the breeze. Redemption Boulevard was already filled with traffic. Days started early in Krenz. His gaze finally settled on the sprawling complex of the Conclave.

The very shape of the sprawling buildings was an affront to his core beliefs. He stood at odds with everything the priests and cardinals preached. Society was inherently weak and in need of stern control measures. Only through expanding dominating amounts of power were those populations kept in check. Too many wars were fought over inconsequential matters. Not under the new order. He intended to rip away the binding fabrics of current social order and rebuild the universe from the ground up, his way.

Entire divisions of Prekhauten Guards had already converted to his cause. Hundreds of cardinals and thousands of priests had done likewise. They stood ready to serve once the purge concluded. Only the senior leadership remained defiant. Very few were willing to switch allegiances, thus condemning them to death or worse. It began with Lorenu Phos. Her death, now tiredly martyred thanks, in part, to the slow reactions of Colonel Kale, should send the proper message through the ranks of her followers. There was no room in the new order for dissenters.

Killing Lorenu was but the first step in a long, winding path. Others either needed to convert to his way of thinking or follow her into death's warm embrace. Alain keyed the small console built into his desk. "Prestus, inform all elements to begin their parts of the operation. I am going to pay the Prekhauten Headquarters a visit."

He neglected to mention why. Foul deeds were best done anonymously.

"Are you fucking kidding me? Impossible!" General Davith Strannan fumed as he reread the hastily scratched report. "Where did this information come from?"

The newly promoted Major shifted his weight to the other foot and looked down. He didn't want to believe the message any more than the General did, making it all the worse for having delivered it. "From the Conclave emergency operations cell."

"And you're positive the assassins wore our uniforms?"

The very thought rocked his belief system. Until now, treason belonged among the ranks of Inquisitors and priests. His Guards went through the most complex and intensive screening system, ensuring their loyalty and unending commitment to furthering the cause of justice and order. That any of his men should turn against the founding beliefs sent tremors through his perceived notions.

"Yes, General. Several witnesses say they watched Colonel Kale lead a detachment into the Cardinal Seniorus's offices and murder her."

Murder. The word produced bile. To think the most guarded figure in all three orders was assassinated in her own offices just as the sun rose. It was blasphemy on the basest level. Strannan struggled with the information, unsure which direction to move in despite knowing the action needed to be reciprocated. The guilty needed to be punished, if for nothing else than the sheer audacity of their crimes.

He shook his head sorrowfully. "Has there been any word from Nye?"

He already knew the answer, knew that Nye was the only man capable of turning one of the most well recognized Guards with little effort. To be fair, Strannan knew Kale had a quick temper and faster trigger. His distaste for society bled through the ferocious nature of his deeds. The man was dangerous.

"No, General. We have been unable to get through to Inquisition headquarters."

Strannan began to pace. His movements were quickened, almost frantic. The darkest hour had finally descended on the Conclave, and it threatened to consume them all before most knew what hit them. *What in the hell was Colonel Kale thinking? He's supposed to get an award today.* Shaking his head, the Prekhauten Guard commander suddenly felt left out. Plots were hatching, having brewed for countless years. They'd been so entirely focused on finding the Three after the final battle on Crimeat a full-scale rebellion had formed.

How could we have been so blind? Is this what our efforts have come to? The downfall of society and the rise of anarchy, hatred and violence? He forced himself to stop thinking about the potential depths of treason until further proof came to light. The old Strannan would have already had units deploying to combat unknown terrors on a hundred worlds. Sadly, that was part of the problem. His ranks were stretched too thin to combat the uprisings spread across the universe, leaving him a skeletal reserve force barely capable of conducting a major offensive.

Slamming his fist into the nearest wall, Strannan pointed an angry finger and said, "I don't care who you have to kill. Get me through to the Inquisitor General. I can't act until I have positive information on the assassins."

The major clasped his fist to his heart in salute and hurried about his task, leaving a brooding general alone in the office of half-shadows and diminishing hope. He waited until the pneumatic door hissed shut before returning to his desk to pore over old intelligence reports and troop displacements. Hours later, and no end in sight, he arrived at the conclusion that none of it made sense.

A war, albeit undercover, raged across the stars with little fanfare. He scratched his head in confusion. Pirate attacks were up five hundred percent over the previous year. Cult uprisings, the damned cult of Rengu the death god, spread from planet to planet like an avenging fire come to cleanse. Traitor Guards and Inquisitors, dating back two years to the insurrection of Ursal Prowl, riddled the honor of the great orders. Doubt and latent fear rose amongst the general population. Folks weren't willing to place their trust in the very powers sworn to protect them anymore. The most important detail, the one linking these episodes together, remained out of his grasp, infuriating him to no end.

He felt the answer was so close, but not in his offices. He needed to go to the operations center to discover the truth. The sprawling rooms that comprised the hub of intelligence were the very brains of Prekhauten activities. Strannan knew the only way to solve the mystery and twine the clues together rested within. Besides, he needed to get updates on the pirate action on both Drespai and Hawker's Gate. Most of the fleets were deployed in support of Inquisition operations to quell the pirate threat. It didn't sit well with him to be so far from the action. He was a leader of combat forces. Sitting behind a desk, while a great honor to command, was an affront to the very core of his being.

Brooding, he passed through multiple layers of security and entered the brains of the Prekhauten Guard. The operations center never fell silent. Dozens of clerks and operatives manned rows of computer stations and massive viewing screens lining the walls. Every single action involving any of the three major orders was tracked to the smallest detail. *Making it more intriguing how we've been compromised so thoroughly.* Strannan eyed as many of the administrative personnel as he could, stewing over what he knew of each. Certainly, many of them could be turned based on certain personal problems or family issues on their home worlds. His thoughts turned from epic space battles and violent rebellions to the traitorous stench lurking behind every console. He couldn't keep the sneer from tainting his face.

"General, we weren't expecting you," Lieutenant Colonel Albright Severs saluted.

Strannan returned the gesture. "Colonel, I don't make a habit of broadcasting my movements, especially during times of distress."

"General, I assure you the war is far from Vau Prime. We can handle the influx of reports and data enough that you don't need to be present."

"Don't presume to tell me what I may and may not do." He waved the comment off. "Forgive me, but I am not myself lately. Too much on my mind and all. What is the status of the battle at Drespai?"

Severs brightened slightly, though his face remained mired in gloom. "Most of the pirate vessels are destroyed. The space station itself is crippled beyond repair, breaking up in orbit as it burns down into the atmosphere. Rear Admiral Khe-Zhehan reports only one Prekhauten frigate sustained enough damage to make it non-combat ready."

"Casualties?"

"Minimal, sir. Two dead and thirty-seven wounded."

Strannan nodded. He would have preferred less, but those were the sort of numbers any commander liked to receive. "And the battle for Hawker's Gate? Any news yet?"

"Nothing," Severs replied, shaking his head. "All communications have been jammed for a dozen sectors surround the Gate. Whoever is coordinating enemy movements is good. They know our frequencies, primary and emergency. We haven't heard word from Admiral Fhi since the fleet prepared to revert to normal space and begin the offensive."

Dire news for dire times. Fhi's fleet was the largest the Guard had assembled in a lifetime. He bore few doubts as to the admiral's abilities to deal with the enemy threat, no matter how significant it was, but being virtually blacked out infuriated him. Worse, Strannan knew there wasn't a thing all the Guard's advanced technology could do about it. Vau Prime was effectively blind.

"Keep at it. We need to know exactly what's happening. Hells, the whole fleet could be destroyed, and we'd never find out until it was far too late," Strannan said.

Severs balked. "Sir, are you suggesting Admiral Fhi walked into a trap? He has our finest ships of the line. The war fleet can handle itself in a fight, and he is one of our very best."

"It's not him that worries me, Severs." His eyes flicked around the room again, careful to pick out anyone suspiciously trying to eavesdrop. "Follow me."

Severs obeyed unquestioningly, following the Guard commander into one of the private meeting rooms attached to the side of the main room. Soundproof and encrypted with the most up-to-date anti-listening protections, anything they had to say would remain between them. The younger colonel clasped his hands behind his back and patiently waited for his commanding officer to speak.

Strannan sat back on the edge of the cherry wood table, embossed with the Guard emblem and polished to a high sheen. He suddenly felt old, more tired than ever before. The stress of not knowing the future or the present tore holes in his carefully conceived notions of the righteousness of his actions. His next words came uneasily.

"Severs, I have grave concerns."

The colonel stiffened as if insulted. "Sir, I can assure you that…"

"That you have no idea about the level of my fears." He paused. "Yes, fears. Too much is happening to be coincidence. We are coming upon a great conflagration. A crisis, if you will. The universe is changing, and it's going to bring the ruin of us all."

"General, I can understand your concerns given the current situation, but the Guard has ever been the forbearer of combat. The task falls upon us to stop the seeds of heresy from taking root and spreading," Severs replied carefully.

Strannan smiled and lowered his hand to his sidearm. "What have you done with Albright?"

"I'm sorry?" Severs asked.

In one fluid motion, Strannan had his weapon out and pointed at the junior officer. His thumb clicked the safety off. "Drop the pretense. The real Colonel Severs would have played up to my fears, licking my boots after every comment. A good man, not one to deserve the fate you gave him, but ever an ass kisser aimed at moving up through the chain of command. Now, you only get one chance. Who are you?"

Severs finally exhaled the breath he'd had pent up since Strannan arrived. At last, the ruse was over. Now he could execute his mission.

"I am the faceless."

Blood froze like ice. Strannan stepped back, knowing it wouldn't do him much good should the imposter act. "Assassin."

"We have infiltrated every level of the Conclave, Inquisition and your precious Prekhauten Guard. Albright Severs was a vain man. His vanity proved his undoing." The assassin mirrored Strannan's move.

"Tell me why."

The Vaumagian assassin pulled a facsimile of the faceless gold mask each assassin had surgical implanted from the inside of his jacket, easily slipping it into place face in a rehearsed move. No Acceptant was permitted to operate without a mask, furthering their legend and myth of unity, of ambiguous shadows striking terror into the hearts of the weak. They were one. For the man confronting Strannan to don the facemask of a dead man and move so freely around Prekhauten headquarters spoke volumes for the daringness of the order.

The gold-faced killer tilted his head almost curiously. "Does it matter? No answer will affect the outcome of what happens next. You should know you are a dead man."

Strannan fired twice. The assassin leapt out of the path of the ion rounds a moment before. Superheated energy burned through part of his sleeve. Stunned by the assassin's quickness, Strannan began firing wildly in the desperate hope of hitting something. Even a minor flesh wound would be enough to give him the chance to turn and flee. More rounds burned through the wooden chairs. Into the shock-absorbent padding lining the walls. Careened off the polished table. Scorched the blue and gold marble floor tiles. The assassin ducked every single one.

The side arms cycled through and died with a soft whiz. Strannan tossed the now useless weapon down and reflexively crouched in a traditional hand-to-hand combat stance. The assassin merely shook his head and opened his uniform to reveal enough explosives to rip out half of the interior of the Guard headquarters. Eyes wide with fear, Strannan turned and managed to get the door halfway open before the explosion sent waves of flames and debris at him. The world disappeared under sheer chaos.

Surgical strikes began shortly after dawn. Krenz spiraled down into panic. Neighbor turned on neighbor, friend against friend. Fear became the new standard of living. Social graces fled in the wake of such obscene violence. Two hundred cardinals were assassinated in what would come to be known as the great Purge, in the span of an afternoon. Vaumagian coffers filled instantly, propelling the shadowy order to untold wealth while bringing them more closely under the scrutiny of those with the power to act against them.

Alain Nye watched the reports scroll across the massive holo-screens dominating the shops just off Redemption Boulevard. Only the brave and foolish remained to finish their meals, drinks and casual shopping. Nye took in their stunned faces as each struggled to comprehend just what the information meant. For them, the universe had permanently changed. Freedom started to die, marching blindly down the path of ultimate destruction. He wanted to laugh, to shout to the highest towers that it was all thanks to his foresight and planning. Only reluctantly did he give credit to the unusual alliance.

Alone, the Inquisitor General took a seat at a rustic café with black iron chairs and tables in an outdoor bistro setting and ordered a black coffee. Despite the intensity of years of plotting finally coming to fruition, he couldn't help but focus on what needed to happen next to bring the Conclave's rule to an end, or at least turned to a new direction. He dearly wanted to see the entire priesthood removed from society. That made confronting what remained of the Forum his top priority. The thought of unleashing his silent partner to end the debate for good wasn't strong enough for Nye to make the call. The war, if it could be classified as such, was still in its infancy, and any good tactician understood that no plan survives first contact with the enemy.

Alain Nye sipped his coffee and tried to enjoy what remained of the day. Law enforcement air cars sped by, followed closely by emergency vehicles. Echoes of explosions continued throughout Krenz, announced by plumes of black smoke, cruel and wicked. He smiled and tried to enjoy the remainder of his day.

THIRTY-THREE

3212 A.G. (After Gods), Hawker's Gate, deep space.

War is a fickle entity, never moving in the direction one expects no matter how long and thoughtful the planning process prior to execution. The unexpected lurks behind the first vehicle in the convoy, the point man on patrol. Heroes seldom lived, quite the opposite of fiction spread across the stars by those lost in fantasy. Real life was hard and cruel. Good men died just as easily as bad. There was but one certainty in war: nothing planned happened.

Matthias looked to what remained of his Guards. A score and a few were still mission capable. More bodies decorated the floor where they fell. Presha Von lay bundled in a corner. Her mouth was gagged, hands and feet bound behind her back. There wasn't much chance of her escaping, so he didn't waste any manpower guarding her. Besides, he'd already resolved to shoot her himself should she try anything foolish. He had much greater concerns.

Tolde lay in a pool of his own blood, unconscious and barely breathing. The round had struck in the center of his chest, narrowly missing the important organs. Their lone surviving medic had performed a quick battlefield scan of vital signs. Neither lung was punctured, a good sign he reassured them while packing the kit. Matthias never fully trusted battlefield medics, not after a misdiagnosis that nearly cost him a leg on the jungle world of Fedril.

"We need to get him out of here if he's going to live," the medic said direly.

Matthias winced. The last thing the survivors needed was the death of their leader looming over their actions. Morale teetered on a very fragile edge. Any bad news carried the possibility of breaking their backs, leaving them open to ambush and worse. They'd taken the operations center but nothing else. The rest of the Gate belonged to the cultists who far outnumbered what few loyalist troops remained. The veteran Guard found himself with virtually no choice.

He looked up to the hulking Tannus, loathe to speak to one of the Three yet knowing he must. "Can you get us out of here?"

Tannus blinked before answering. "Some, certainly not all. We're going to need a bigger ship to escape with all hands."

"I'm afraid that might be harder than you think," Matthias replied. Most of the Guard fleet drifted as wreckage in the cold black. Tens of thousands of lives lost in the blink of an eye. Enemy losses were equally destructive, but the damage done to the image of the Prekhauten Guard went beyond recoverable. Matthias knew, as did everyone else, that the old ways were gone. "Fies, see if you can raise the *Indomitable*. We need a backup plan."

"Roger that, Sergeant Major. Annalilly, open up a channel."

Sweat and no small amount of blood covered the lightning bolt tattoos streaking over her head, but she didn't seem to notice.

Jers shook his head sorrowfully. "Even if they were still in orbit, Captain Falchi wouldn't dare risk the ship and crew to come for us. We're trapped here."

"Jers, shut the fuck up now! If you don't have anything to contribute to the discussion, keep your lips together," Fies lashed out because he had to. They all knew standard operating procedure stated any vessel compromised in battle was ordered to turn and fight an immediate withdrawal. Speaking such truths could only be detrimental.

Matthias intervened before a full-blown argument developed. Military discipline tended to be at its weakest in the most distress. He needed to figure out the fastest route out of the Gate with minimal enemy contact. His fighter held three, and that pushed the manufacture specs past the limits. Who knew how large Tannus's vessel was?

"He's got a point, Tannus. Falchi won't risk the ship if he's following protocol. Can we make it to the landing docks?"

"Mostly likely not. There are a lot of very angry people on this space station that want you all dead."

Matthias stiffened. "What about you? You're the biggest target."

Tannus smiled, as if expressing sorrow. "They cannot harm me, Matthias. I am beyond your mortal weapons."

"Good, you take point. I want everyone ready to move in five. Time's running out, people. This is our only shot," he announced, instantly falling back into his former Guard role. "I need station schematics. Plot me the quickest route out of here."

"I'm on it," Jers said, forgetting the futility of their situation for a moment.

"Most of the docking bays will be sealed and defended against such a maneuver. I would prefer not to kill my way through half of this station's compliment," Tannus said solemnly.

"Fair enough, I suppose."

Gedrick slipped through the battle-damaged room in the guise of a female Guard, leaving Matthias extremely shocked. "Perhaps I can help."

"I thought you left," Matthias said.

The Jhedge smiled savagely and shrugged. "I can't get paid if everyone's dead. You'll never make it out of the main concourse. Von's people have this station fairly locked up, at least the main thoroughfares. There are ways, though. The big guy might not fit."

Tannus looked down on the shape shifter in mild amusement. "I will manage."

"I got it!" Jers shouted out. Matthias and Fies ran to his position and tried deciphering the troubling maze of one-dimensional blue lines representing the confusing interior of Hawker's Gate.

Fies shook his head. "I can't make sense of any of this."

"Me either, but, then again, we don't really need to with Gedrick here," Matthias replied. "Can you get us out of here?"

The shape shifter nodded without bothering to look at the plans. "I know this station's interiors like I made them. If there's a way to the landing bays, I will find it."

"Which leaves us with another problem," Fies added. "Where do we go?"

Matthias looked up, concerned. "What do you mean?"

Reluctant to speak the dark thoughts forming, Fies decided it was best for them all. "The main fleet is destroyed, for the most part. The Gate has been taken by the same organization that worked against us on Crimeat. Anyone with that much power will certainly be making a move for something bigger."

Matthias' face darkened. "Get to the point, Sergeant."

"I believe these people are trying to overthrow the Conclave, making us an endangered species."

Fies had never felt so nervous. The words were nearly too painful to speak, and his chest hammered with an exaggerated heartbeat. He'd never thought the day might come when the Conclave stood in danger of failing. The Inquisition and Prekhauten Guard stood on its flanks to prevent such a thing. Recent events were changing his mind. He grew increasingly more concerned that something unspeakably bad loomed.

Tannus interrupted the suddenly enraged Matthias. "I am afraid he is right. There is much going on you don't understand. War is approaching, and mankind has been blinded by subversive agents. You are not prepared. The storm will sweep across the seven hundred worlds in sheets of cleansing flames. What remains will not be recognizable. The Blood Witches refer to it as Forever Night, the long, slow dark from which there is no return."

"How do you know this?" Beve asked, surprising everyone.

The giant's face filled with sorrow. "Because my brother started it. His hatred of our father nearly destroyed the universe once. I failed to stop him, and now he is trying again. It began two years ago after he escaped one of your prisons."

"But we stopped all that," Haggled added.

"No, you only halted its natural progression. My brother has ever been cunning. He subverted your Inquisitor General, infiltrated the priests of the Conclave and influenced millions to worship Rengu, the death god. What you witnessed on Crimeat was but the prelude to a far worse nightmare. As we speak, his armies wage war on a desert planet, and that war threatens to spread to distant worlds."

He debated telling them the entire truth, that Amongeratix needed to find Paradise Tear and kill her. That she was the only being capable of ultimately preventing him from destroying their entire race. All he needed to do was get his hands on her, and the universe would fall. The debate lasted a mere fraction of a second. No, best not burden them with more than was necessary.

"So the Conclave is collapsing?" Beve asked.

"And will continue to do so until my brother is stopped. Will you help me? For all my might and insights, I can't beat him alone," Tannus offered. Many centuries had passed since the last time he had placed faith in humanity and used them to wage his war. He was loathe to do so again but didn't see an alternative. Great sacrifice was needed if there was to be a future.

Matthias gestured down to the prone Tolde. "We'll help if he lives. Otherwise, you're on your own."

"Fair enough. Gedrick, please lead us out of here," Tannus ordered.

Matthias said, "You still haven't said where we're going."

"To an old home. The librarian world of Wexanos."

The giant knelt and gently cradled the severely wounded Tolde Breed, staining his tunic with blood. Guardsmen collected weapons, gear and ammo from the bodies. Two were sent to collect Presha Von, still unconscious but weighing barely one hundred pounds. At this point, she became more of a burden than valuable prize.

"...is Captain Falchi. Come in Hawker's Gate."

Fies gave Annalilly a surprised look she shrugged off smugly. "What did you expect? I ain't a rookie."

"Captain, this Matthias. What's your status?"

"The *Indomitable* took a lot of damage, but we're still mission capable. I can't say the same for the rest of the fleet. Most of the capital ships are gone, the flagship included. We got hit hard, Matthias."

He didn't say what they were all thinking. The entire affair had been a trap from the moment the *Indomitable* was dispatched. Morale sunk lower. The hope of rescue faded as quickly as seconds spun from the clock. Stranded, trapped behind enemy-controlled lines, the beleaguered knot of survivors struggled to understand their situation. Only Tannus remained unaffected. He'd witnessed this too many times since humanity had risen as the dominant species in the universe. Untold millions of lives had been wasted in his vain efforts to stop Amongeratix and bring peace. Once again, he stood on the edge of disappointment and defeat, helpless to keep from peering into the abyss.

"Can you get us out of here?" Matthias asked, careful not to divulge too much sensitive information, lest their enemy gain more of an upper hand.

The delayed pause told him enough. "Not without exposing ourselves, and we don't have the firepower necessary to break through the enemy fleet."

"Roger, *Indomitable*. We will exfil on our own and find a way to link up."

The link went dead, leaving them feeling like the air had just been stolen. Doubt, fear and the unknown plagued them. Matthias knew the feeling well enough, especially after his personal failures on Crimeat, perceived or otherwise. They'd won that battle without even knowing it had sparked a war.

"Ruck up," he ordered. "We've got a long way to go. Anyone we encounter is to be considered hostile. Shoot if necessary. If we can go around, we will. Understood?"

"Yes, Sergeant Major," a chorus of voices echoed.

He nodded in reply and turned to Gedrick and Tannus. "Our lives are in your hands."

A tremor rippled across the giant's face, but he said nothing. After all, when death became a near certainty, what really needed saying?

The Deeves, planet An'kuruku.

Thick clouds of smoke clung to the battlefield long after the action ended. Vultures and other various carrion eaters crowded in to feast on the thousands of corpses littering the sand and scrub grass. The unmistakable stench of rot polluted the air for leagues in every direction. Not even the sea managed to beat back the horror of so much blood and mangled flesh. Fires raged lazily, pock marking the grounds. Those that survived understood what hell truly was, and none wished to see it again.

What remained of the Prefect army had withdrawn far enough to find clean water and unspoiled land to bivouac. Most neglected their duties, as well as themselves. Staying so close to so much death was unnatural. Haunted looks etched their faces. Soldiers around campfires sat silent, occasionally passing troubled looks back to the fields of corpses. There was no banter, no celebration of victory. So many dead in such a short period of time. Sorrow became the sole inhabitant of the Deeves.

Lezorsu stood atop the small ridge, hands on his hips, surveying the product of his desires. He felt giddy. War invigorated him, aroused him. The sight of such much-controlled mayhem filled his heart with warmth. His hatred for life grew stronger as days went by, culminating with the near genocide of the peoples of the Deeves.

"Sir, I have the updated casualty figures," Umbrun Hal said, coming up behind.

Lezorsu frowned at the disturbance. He didn't particularly care how many lived or died. Numbers were inconsequential. What mattered was death. Nothing more. Umbrun Hal had become a necessary nuisance since Althas Pey's untimely demise when the dragon beasts had attacked. The move, while entirely unexpected, didn't lack results. Much of the Prefecture's army had been caught in the blasts. He'd never seen so many burning men and women running wildly about. Their screams echoed in his mind in a delicious symphony every time he closed his eyes.

"Continue," he replied.

"Two thousand seven hundred and thirty-three dead, another thousand wounded. Half of those are not expected to see the dawn."

The numbers meant nothing in the grand scheme of things. Sacrificing the faceless became easier for him. Lezorsu had always felt something sinister whispering to him from the corners of his mind. Until now, he hadn't realized what it was. Now, staring down on the mindless carnage, he finally understood. He was born for greatness. Humanity had become a scourge, a blight upon the stars in need of extermination. His sole purpose for living, he saw now, was to hasten the end.

"Prepare the army to move. We march on the Wells," he ordered.

Umbrun stood in shock. "But sir, the army is exhausted. You've won a great victory here, but at cost. How much more do you expect them to have left?"

Snatching his new adjutant by the throat, Lezorsu pulled him closer and snarled, "We are marching on the Wells. I want this planet pacified and will not stop until I've ground every last soul to bones. Do you understand?"

"Y…yes sir."

Thunder rumbled across the heavens. Fires spread violently across the storm-darkened skies, turning the blue and black into red and orange. Those still capable of feeling shock glanced upward and watched the sleek, battered grey hull slip down through the clouds. Some broke down and wept at the sight. Others scrambled for cover. Men and women screamed suddenly, blood flowing from their eyes. Only Lezorsu stood unaffected. He watched the ship, tall and long, touch down beside the ruins on the shores of the Bo. A strange feeling tugged at him, drawing him closer. He didn't resist.

The Prefect marched towards the ship without pause. He took in the massive amounts of weapons jutting from the hull, the way the paint was missing on half of it. This ship had seen better days. Unlike most Guard vessels, this had no viewports. No way to see the outside world as it hurtled through space. The ramp hissed open and lowered slowly even as a massive figure marched out without waiting for it to finish. His knees gave out. All courage fled, bleeding his flesh pale. Lezorsu stared up at the giant, angry and filled with hate, and knew his true god had arrived. He dropped to his knees and wept tears of joy.

Amongeratix frowned on the diminutive man kneeling before him before snatching him by the throat and lifting him eye level. "Where is my cousin?"

Face turning purple from asphyxiation, Lezorsu struggled to pry a finger from his throat.

Amongeratix leaned closer. "Where is she?"

Frustrated, he threw Lezorsu to the ground and stormed off. Suffering from broken collar bones and a partially crushed windpipe, Lezorsu used every ounce of strength to pull himself to his knees and stand. "My lord, there was one here that matched you in size. A woman, yes. But she fled with three others. They are long gone by now and could be anywhere in the desert."

Amongeratix halted and turned. The intensity blaring from his eyes wilted Lezorsu's composure. The Prefect whimpered at the sensation of warm urine running down his leg. Resisting the urge to crush him under heel, the giant instead asked, "Who are you? What is this rabble in the field?"

A momentary flicker of composure returned. "I...am Doomspell."

Half amused, Amongeratix shifted his gaze to the battlefield and the overpowering stench of decay and blood. He made his decision quickly, knowing there was little time to lose. "You will come with me. I have need for an army. This rabble will suffice for now."

"My lord, where are we to go?" Doomspell asked.

Amongeratix fixed him with a deadly stare. "To bring war across the stars."

EPILOGUE

3212 A.G. (After Gods), Order of the Blood Witches Abbey, Acumensiis Comet.

The universe was changing. Thousands of years of fragile peace and the rise of a new dynasty of lesser beings stood on the brink of destruction. Humanity suddenly found itself alone, friendless in the cold void of space. Subversive agents ranged across hundreds of worlds bringing chaos where order had once reigned. Those on the side of justice, righteousness, were trampled under the unexpected onslaught suddenly unleashed. Many abandoned their principles in those dark moments, throwing in with the foul powers rising. Others ended their lives lest their souls be claimed. Despair became the new currency, and nothing the Conclave — what remained of it — did could stop it from spreading.

Ruma Zzein cast the bones. Her heart fluttered. Portents of death stared back at her, mocking her very existence. Old, she was a relic of best forgotten times. Her kind had all but died during what humanity termed the war of the gods. If only they knew the truth. None of this would be happening. Yet some truths needed to remain cloaked in shadow, for they were much too powerful to be allowed loose.

The Grand Mistress of the Blood Witches abandoned her bones and walked to the tower in which she had once found so much comfort. Space raced by. Stars blurred into lines of impossible colors. The sights held nothing for her anymore. Lost were the dreams of salvation, of creating a better life where the vivid memories of what once was faded into obscurity. Now the stars were nothing more than mere light.

Thoughts of war burdened her mightily. Her greatest ally in the coming struggle lay dead, murdered at the hands of those once thought to be loyal. The Conclave was already fracturing along lines of crossed beliefs. Much of the Inquisition and fully half of the Prekhauten Guard divisions had broken away from the light. Amongeratix collected all armies of darkness to him for his final war against his kin, and nothing Tannus or anyone else could do was going to slow him. After so long, he was finally getting what he wanted.

Yet he didn't count on the hope of many. Tolde Breed's life hung in the balance and could easily go either way. Ruma knew instinctively that the Inquisitor was vital if the light stood any chance of victory.

Tannus had collected a small band of heroes, but they wouldn't be enough. Much more needed to be done if any hope remained.

She briefly considered abandoning humanity and taking her comet to distant places unreachable by anyone else. The easy way offered much, for she'd done it once before. Then, it had been a matter of saving her life. So much more weighed on her shoulders. In the end, Ruma Zzein knew she couldn't leave.

War was coming. Humanity needed her witches if it was to see a new dawn. She sighed, clasped her hands behind her back, and tried to forget the moment, if only for a while.

END

The Saga is just beginning. Forgotten Gods continues in

Anguish Once Possessed

ANGUISH
ONCE POSSESSED
A FORGOTTEN GODS TALE
CHRISTIAN WARREN FREED

17,592 D.G. (During Gods) farm world of Uwenil.

Billowing columns of black smoke, acrid and noxious, poured into the sky. Fumes drifted on the fringe, killing bird and insect without remorse. Vultures dropped like fleshy stones, their black feathers bursting upon impact. Whole forests were gone, naught but charred husks remaining. Lakes and rivers evaporated, the steam turning the atmosphere almost putrid with humidity. Uwenil had been a paradise before this. An agricultural world, its citizens were among the hardest working in the universe. Numerous civilizations had relied on the produce, but no more. Uwenil was dead.

The giant walked through the wasteland, thoughtful eyes remembering what had once been. Sadness burdened his heart. He felt lethargic. Incompetent. He'd stood and watched as a hundred thousand lives were lost in the span of mere heartbeats. *How could anyone accept this as reality? This casual disregard for life. Is this the legacy we threaten to leave behind? The constriction of what I am binds me into oblivion. Where is the sun?*

He paused, looking down at the bone pile blocking his path. Empty eye sockets gazed back as if questioning the validity of their deaths. He longed for answers to give them, to quell their unrest as the souls passed into the next world. But he couldn't. He was just as much to blame as his brothers. Their petty jealousies had allowed this travesty to occur—allowed a jewel amongst the stars to take the agonizing crawl into nightmare. Bile filled his throat.

Fresh decay rode the winds across his face. He winced. Some memories shouldn't be relived. Far from innocent in most things, he began to understand what it meant to have such vast amounts of power in his control—began to see the horrors he'd encouraged, even participated in. Looking back, he realized he had become a mere shadow of his former self. Change was in order.

Ruminations disturbed by the sudden arrival of the only other living being on Uwenil, he abandoned the bones and looked up. They were similar in stature and appearance. Each wore a ruined uniform and now-useless armor. Unkempt hair ran flat down their backs. Weeks of grime concealed their features, transforming them into monsters—or worse.

"You are well. It does my heart good to see so," the newcomer said, his voice deep, inspiring.

"What have we done, brother?"

Tannus, soot staining his face and hands, lowered his eyes. "What had to be done. These are troubled times."

"Troubled times? We have destroyed this world."

He threw his hands out in frustration. "What else would you have had me do? Our brother's army was intent on utilizing this world for their war efforts."

It was a tired story. The bloodlines had been devouring each other for almost two centuries. With no end in sight, world after world became enmeshed in what had devolved into pointless struggle without direction or purpose. The innocent continued to suffer in countless masses.

"This war has gone on far longer than it ever should have. I was there, Tannus, with you and Amongeratix when our father passed his decree. You and I both know he was wrong."

Tannus's eyes narrowed. He held up a finger. "Father…rules with unquestionable authority. Who are we to debate his will?"

"Father has grown lethargic. He no longer recognizes the way the universe is developing. Tannus, we were meant to be the custodians of justice for all races." He swept an arm across the battlefield. "Not this. Never this. Instead of preserving life, we have turned to taking it at every corner. How far are you willing to push this issue? Until there is no one left to protect?"

The eldest son of the god king couldn't bring himself to look at his brother. For him the hurt of what had just occurred was still to near to emerge from his despondency.

"As far as I must."

He watched Tannus for any sign of remorse, only slightly disappointed to find him lacking. His brother had grown cold these last few centuries, as if a forgotten piece of his soul had been blackened by rot. Tannus had always been the best of the three. Righteous, proud, he defended the weak, championing those without voice even at the risk of inducing his father's wrath. *Oh, brother, what has truly happened to make us into these pathetic creatures? Do we deserve to protect the universe? Perhaps it is time we stepped away from this moral obligation gone horribly wrong and let life advance as it will. We no longer contain the morality that once guided us. These are sad days.*

He reached out to place a palm on Tannus's shoulder. "There is such a thing as too far. You begin to sound like Amongeratix."

"You dare compare me to…him?"

A simple nod.

"He is the slayer of worlds. Have you any notion how many hundreds of thousands of souls he's butchered in the name of his unholy crusade? You never did have the stomach for the hard work, brother. I am all that stands between our brother and the death of everything."

"You are failing. Amongeratix should have never been allowed to make planetfall. What's to stop your armies from battling in deep space, where no innocent lives may be lost? No one will miss those unfortunates enlisted in either of your armies."

Tannus tilted his head back to laugh. "That is where you err."

"How so?"

"There is no innocence in the universe. No victims. We are all to blame."

"I don't believe that. How were these farmers responsible for the atrocities committed upon them? The children who were cut down by random weapon fire? The wives and mothers trying to prepare meals for those in the fields even as our armies dropped from the clouds to kill and destroy? Tell me, Tannus: what did they do to provoke our ire?"

Tannus shrugged his brother's hand away and turned. He'd avoided staring at the dead. They accused him, and rightfully so. He was no better than his brother, and that was what pained him the most. "You miss my point, brother."

"Explain. Raise me above the ignorance I wallow in so that I may comprehend the mastery of your thesis."

Tannus grinned at that. His brother had always been the wordy one, the first to question when matters failed to make sense. The last to go to arms when it could be avoided at all costs. His brother, without knowing it, was the best of them. It was both blessing and curse, for Tannus would never be able to explain satisfactorily that he was the one who looked up to his brother, not the other way around.

"I wish I had the clarity to view everything in shades of black and white," Tannus replied finally. "Unfortunately, my reality is not so simple. I can't explain why these people should have been prepared. Or why they shouldn't have died like this." He paused, carefully considering his next words. "Father should never have left us free to follow our instincts."

"Debating the quality of past decisions is often moot, Tannus. What's done is done. There can be no going back. Not even the oracle is so mighty. All we can do is try to fix the future before it becomes irreparable."

Tannus turned back around to meet his brother's gaze. "I wish it were that easy. Amongeratix already assembles a new host. This war will continue."

"Have you any idea how many died on this world?"

"Too many."

The younger brother shook his head. "Over two million. Million. Sooner or later, we will run out of lives to abuse, Tannus."

"I would end this war myself if I thought killing Amongeratix was the point. Too many have fallen under his sway. He raises cults of fanatics none of our blood kin have managed. The rot permeates all life, brother, a cancer only war can excise."

"When does it end?"

"I don't have an answer for you. It is time to leave, brother. Will you return to my flagship and help me rebuild? We cannot allow Amongeratix to gain the upper hand again," Tannus asked. He'd come to rely on his brother's counsel, valuing the opinions in contrast to his own.

"I cannot."

Tannus froze, the words coming unexpectedly. "What? You have ever been at my side during this long war. I wouldn't know what to do without your sage advice. Come, we can discuss this over a hot meal and mead."

"No, Tannus. I am done with this war. My heart aches from the obscene loss of life that neither of you seems to notice. Go and fight Amongeratix like you always have. Ever since we were children there has been rivalry, but my part in this sad tale ends here. Today. I can no longer fight for what I don't believe in. Goodbye, Tannus."

Tannus realized there was no point in arguing with his brother. They were preordained to rule the universe. Either he would return or he wouldn't. Such matters were well beyond Tannus' control. He offered a final nod and strode back towards his waiting shuttle.

Alone again, he watched the bright engine lights burst through the clouds and disappear. Great sadness claimed him then. His mind raved against the atrocity. Madness took him, and he wandered down broken paths of bereft dreams. Tears clogging his eyes, he looked around for a weapon, settling on a jagged, broken sword. Grinning, he rose to his full height and proceeded to flay his own skin.

He tossed the ruined blade into the muck and raised both arms skyward in the acidic rain. The blood refused to wash off. Laughing madly, he cursed his brothers for fools. "I renounce my name, father! From this day forth, I shall only be known for what I have become. My name…is Sorrow."

BIO

Christian W. Freed was born in Buffalo, N.Y. more years ago than he would like to remember. After spending more than 20 years in the active-duty US Army he has turned his talents to writing. Since retiring, he has gone on to publish over 30 military fantasy and science fiction novels, as well as his memoirs from his time in Iraq and Afghanistan, a children's book, and a pair of how to books focused on indie authors and the decision-making process for writing a book and what happens after it is published.

His first published book (Hammers in the Wind) has been the #1 free book on Kindle 4 times and he holds a fancy certificate from the L Ron Hubbard Writers of the Future Contest. Ok, so it was for 4th place in one quarter, but it's still recognition from the largest fiction writing contest in the world. And no, he's not a scientologist.

Passionate about history, he combines his knowledge of the past with modern military tactics to create an engaging, quasi-realistic world for the readers. He graduated from Campbell University with a degree in history and a Masters of Arts degree in Digital Communications from the University of North Carolina at Chapel Hill.

He currently lives outside of Raleigh, N.C. and devotes his time to writing, his family, and their two Bernese Mountain Dogs. If you drive by you might just find him on the porch with a cigar in one hand and a pen in the other.